Twelve years ago, the  Wood, introduced the world duo of Dane Maddock and 'B Navy SEALs on a quest to treasures of the ancient world. than twenty novels, you've live ___, from the beginning of their career a ___c commandos, to their battle against the worldwide conspiracy known as the Dominion.

Now, the time has come to tell the story of Dane and Bones' final, shocking mission as Navy SEALs.

THERE WILL BE BLOOD....

While still mourning a great personal loss, Maddock and Bones are sent undercover to Moscow to assist an old acquaintance, Navy Intelligence officer Zara Leopov. Leopov is orchestrating the defection of a Russian archivist who has discovered a crucial clue concerning the fate of a high-ranking Nazi official who went missing at the end of World War II, a man who may have carried with him the most sacred relic of the Third Reich.

The search to discover the truth, will take Dane and Bones around the world, and throw back the curtain on a conspiracy born in the early hours of the Cold War—a shadow government that is manipulating the global powers, driving them headlong into the storm.

Praise for David Wood and Sean Ellis!

"*Bloodstorm* takes us back to the beginning, weaving treasure-hunting SEALS Dane and Bones into a globe-spanning clash with Russian mobsters and the lost supernatural power of the Third Reich. If you like ancient artifacts, Nazi gold, and empire-ending conspiracies delivered like a punch to the teeth, you'll love Wood and Ellis' latest addition to the Dane Maddock universe."—Taylor Zajonc, award winning author of *The Maw*

"Dane and Bones. Together they're unstoppable. Rip roaring action from start to finish. Wit and humor throughout. Just one question - how soon until the next one? Because I can't wait."-Graham Brown, author of Shadows of the Midnight Sun

"What an adventure! A great read that provides lots of action, and thoughtful insight as well, into strange realms that are sometimes best left unexplored." -Paul Kemprecos, author of *Cool Blue Tomb* and the *NUMA Files*

"Ellis and Wood are a partnership forged in the fires of Hell. Books don't burn hotter than this!" -Steven Savile, author of the *Ogmios* thrillers

BLOODSTORM

A DANE AND BONES ORIGIN STORY

DAVID WOOD
SEAN ELLIS

Bloodstorm- ©2019 by David Wood

The Dane Maddock Adventures™

All rights reserved

Published by Adrenaline Press
www.adrenaline.press

Adrenaline Press is an imprint of Gryphonwood
Press
www.gryphonwoodpress.com

Edited by Melissa Bowersock

This is a work of fiction. All characters are products of the authors' imaginations or are used fictitiously.

ISBN: 9781093550047

BOOKS and SERIES by DAVID WOOD

Devil's Face
Herald
Brainwash
The Tomb
Destination Rio
Destination Luxor

Jade Ihara Adventures (with Sean Ellis)
Oracle
Changeling
Exile

Bones Bonebrake Adventures
Primitive
The Book of Bones
Skin and Bones
Venom (forthcoming)

Jake Crowley Adventures (with Alan Baxter)
Blood Codex
Anubis Key
Revenant (forthcoming)

Brock Stone Adventures
Arena of Souls
Track of the Beast (forthcoming)

Myrmidon Files (with Sean Ellis)
Destiny
Mystic

Sam Aston Investigations (with Alan Baxter)
Primordial

Overlord

Into the Woods (with David S. Wood)
Callsign: Queen (with Jeremy Robinson)
Dark Rite (with Alan Baxter)

David Wood writing as David Debord

The Absent Gods Trilogy
The Silver Serpent
Keeper of the Mists
The Gates of Iron

The Impostor Prince (with Ryan A. Span)
Neptune's Key
The Zombie-Driven Life
You Suck

BOOKS and SERIES by SEAN ELLIS

The Nick Kismet Adventures
The Shroud of Heaven
Into the Black
The Devil You Know (Novella)
Fortune Favors

The Adventures of Dodge Dalton
In the Shadow of Falcon's Wings
At the Outpost of Fate
On the High Road to Oblivion
Against the Fall of Eternal Night

PROLOGUE

May, 1945 Flensburg, Germany

Most of them wore civilian clothes, as if they already knew how this night would end, but the man who had called for the meeting was attired in his customary dress uniform, replete with the distinctive and unique wreathed oak-leaf insignia on the gorget patches at his collar, the badge that marked him as the senior commander of the Schutzstaffel. In fact, he no longer held that office. For the crime of trying to save Germany from utter annihilation, he had been branded a traitor and stripped of his rank. Moreover, the SS itself was no more. The men assembled in the room with him—all that remained of the senior leadership of the organization—were now the most wanted men in Germany. Tomorrow, they would disperse, assume new identities, attempt to lose themselves amidst the rank and file of the defeated army. He would become "*Unterfeldwebel* Heinrich Hitzinger, formerly of the Special Armored Company attached to the Secret Field Police" demobilized and released from duty a week earlier—but tonight, for one last time, he would stand before them as *Reichsführer* Heinrich Himmler.

When the last of them had filed into the small office, he rose and greeted them with a defiant salute. The gesture seemed to catch them off guard. One and all, they returned the salute, almost reflexively, only to lower their arms quickly, guiltily. He allowed them their moment of shame.

"My brothers," he said by way of preamble. "This is a difficult time. Grand Admiral Dönitz has made his plans, and they do not include us. So be it. We will write our own destiny."

He knew how empty the words must sound to the men; he could scarcely draw up the courage to speak them. But he knew something they did not. He knew—he believed with every fiber of his being—that they could succeed.

He circled around to the front of the desk and bent over the glass-topped presentation case. He opened it, took out the carefully folded piece of red cloth within, and then slowly, reverently, unfolded it and spread it out across the front of the desk, careful not to let it touch the floor. Even before he was finished, he heard a gasp of recognition from behind him; they all knew what it was.

When he had finished, he turned to them again. "You have heard that our Führer is dead by his own hand. I swear to you, this is a lie, spread by our enemies, to weaken our resolve and break our spirit."

He let the declaration hang in the air, watching their reactions to this revelation. There was doubt, but there was also hope. He seized on that. "The seeds of our return have already been sown. For a time, we will rest. Lick our wounds. Gather our army together again. The tide will turn, my brothers. The Americans already know that Stalin is a far greater threat to their dominance, and soon they will come to us and beg us to join a new alliance.

"Until such time, however, we must go into hiding. Do not attempt to contact your loved ones; the hunters will be watching them closely. Dönitz has supplied us with forged identity papers." He gestured to a stack of paybooks on the desktop. "Burn your uniforms. Sink yourselves in the Wehrmacht."

He paused a beat, sensing that the spell of his initial pronouncement was already beginning to fade. These men were survivors, driven more by self-interest than fealty to the Führer. "But never forget," he went on. "You have sworn an undying oath."

He snapped to attention, the click of his heels striking together sounding like a gavel in the quiet room, and then pivoted to face the draped flag with its distinctive emblem—a black swastika imposed upon a circle of white. He reached out with his left hand, gripping the fabric, and snapped his right arm out again in an impassioned salute, and then repeated the words he had spoken for the first time so many years ago, before this very flag: "I vow to you, Adolf Hitler, as Führer and chancellor of the German Reich, loyalty and bravery."

As the first few syllables were uttered, other voices joined him. They all remembered the words—the loyalty oath taken by every officer of the Schutzstaffel. Soon, everybody in the room was speaking as with one voice. "I vow to you and to the leaders that you set for me, absolute allegiance until death. So help me God."

Himmler then added a final, "Sieg, Heil!" before dropping his arm. When he turned to face the men again, he saw that some were openly weeping.

The moment reminded him of the last time he had presided over a ceremony like this, just seven months earlier—the induction of the Volkssturm militia—the army of old men and boys raised up to defend Berlin against the advancing Russian and American forces. Many had wept then, too, caught up in the moment.

Most of them were dead now.

"The Führer lives, my brothers," he went on. "And while he lives, your oath remains. We will never stop fighting for Germany. Now, go. This very night. Begin your new lives, while you secretly begin building the army of resistance, until our Führer chooses to reveal himself. I promise, you will not have long to wait. The Ancient One will protect us, and will not let us perish."

That final blessing was a delicate matter; he knew that few of the men present here shared his unique belief system. But if his desperate plan was to work, it would take more than just a momentary burst of zeal. He would need to possess them, heart and soul, and for that, he would need more than just the power of his former office.

He struck his heels together once more, and then allowed his posture to relax. He let go of the flag, circled around to the other side of the desk, and sank into the chair, saying nothing as the men filed by, collecting their new identity papers before leaving the room. After a minute or two, all were gone, save for his aides, Werner Grothmann and Heinz Macher. He sighed wearily—the ceremony had taken its toll on him in ways the two men couldn't imagine—but then he managed a smile and stood up again.

"A rousing speech, Heinrich."

The voice belonged to neither of his aides, but it was a familiar one. Himmler looked up quickly and found the man standing in the doorway through which the others had just exited. The man, who wore a black trench coat over a charcoal gray suit, was small but exuded a gravity that made him seem much larger. His name was also Heinrich—Heinrich Müller—and until just a few days ago, he had been the head of the Secret State Police—the *Geheime Staatspolizei*, or as it was commonly abbreviated, Gestapo. Grothmann and Macher had both whirled to face the newcomer but froze as soon as they recognized him.

Müller regarded Himmler with eyes that were the color of steel, and just us hard, but it was the Luger Parabellum pistol held casually in his right hand, that gave him command of the room. The gun was not aimed at anyone in particular, but the mere fact of its presence was ominous.

Himmler took a deep breath and leaned over his desk, supporting himself on outstretched arms. The top edge of the flag was just inches away from his fingertips, and he was acutely aware of its proximity, even as he met the other man's stare. "I did not realize that you had escaped Berlin."

Müller raised his left hand, palm facing upward in a gesture that seemed to say—*Well, here I am*—and then shot a sidelong glance at Grothmann.

Himmler immediately grasped the unspoken request. "Werner, Heinz. Wait for me outside."

Though their concern was evident, the two men snapped to attention and briskly exited the room.

"What do you want, Heinrich?" Himmler asked, doing his best to project authority.

"What do I want? The same as any man, I think. To live. To survive."

"And so you come to me, asking for protection?"

Müller spat out a harsh laugh. "You? You are no one, Heinrich. You are worse than no one. A traitor and a coward. That worm Fegelein told me how you tried to sue for peace against the Führer's explicit orders."

Himmler's lips twitched into a smile. "We both know of your skill in getting a man to tell you whatever it is you want to hear."

"No skill was required. He was drunk. He vomited on the floor. It was disgusting."

Himmler inclined his head. "So, I have been convicted on the testimony of a drunkard?"

Müller waggled the gun back and forth. "You did what you did. Perhaps it was even the right thing to do, but you were deluding yourself to think that they would have made peace with you. Men like you and I are beyond forgiveness."

"We shall see. When the turmoil of the moment subsides, the Americans will realize that their true enemy was always Stalin, and I think they will forgive a great many things." He leaned forward a little more, adjusting the position of his hands so that they were in contact with the flag. "So, if I am less than nothing, why are you here?"

"It's simple really," Müller replied. The gun was now pointing forward, pointing at Himmler. "The Americans and Russians are hunting us. Me, you, Gebhardt, Olendorf, and all the other members of your little army of resistance. But I think they will want you most of all. So I intend to give you to them. You will be my ticket to a new life."

Himmler curled his fingers into claws, pulling the scarlet cloth into his grip. "Who is the coward, now? You call me a traitor, but I name you a deserter. An oathbreaker."

Müller laughed. "My oath died in the Führerbunker."

"The Führer lives," hissed Himmler.

"I doubt that very much," Müller countered. "I was there."

"Did you see his body?" asked Himmler, knowing full well what the answer would be.

Müller frowned. "I saw what was left after they were burned."

"All part of the Führer's plan."

Müller waved his hand, dismissively. "Even if what you say is true, I have no intention of dying for a lost cause, nor will I ever let the Russians get their hands on me."

Himmler stared at the man accusingly. Despite his well-earned reputation for ruthlessness and an unflinching dedication to following orders, Müller had never been a true believer, refusing to join the Nazi Party until forced to do so as a matter of survival. He had once even disparaged Hitler himself, calling him "an immigrant unemployed house painter" and "an Austrian draft-dodger."

Yet somehow, it had been Müller, not Himmler, standing beside the Führer at the end.

Himmler tightened his grip on the flag, as if he might somehow squeeze his will into it. "Heinrich, listen to me. This is not the end. It is only a temporary setback. We need only survive the next few weeks, perhaps only days."

"I intend to. By any means necessary."

"What if I offered you something more than just survival?"

Müller chuckled. "I would say that you have no power to offer anything of the sort."

"We planned for this, Heinrich. You know we did. A fortune in gold was hidden away. I can tell you where to find it. And we have friends. Allies all over the world who will give us sanctuary. There is an *Unterseeboote* convoy assembling in Norway. In two days, it will depart for Argentina, where our friends have promised refuge."

"If that were true, why do you and the others slink away in the night to hide among the Wehrmacht?"

"You know my intention. I mean to be a part of the New Germany. But you... If I am not mistaken, you have no such ambition."

The gun remained motionless, its barrel a black maw waiting to devour the former Reichsführer. For a moment, Himmler believed he had failed, but then Müller prompted, "Tell me more about this secret convoy."

Himmler hesitated. Did he dare trust this man? Was he offering Müller an even fatter prize—information about the convoy, which he might trade to the Allies, in exchange for amnesty? "I will tell you everything, but first, I would ask something of you."

Müller frowned. "Your life is not payment enough?"

"I would only ask that you reaffirm your allegiance. Swear the oath again. Is that such a difficult thing?"

Müller held his gaze a moment, then his eyes flicked down to the flag. "I was wondering what became of that. How did you convince Jakob to part with it?"

Sturmbannführer Jakob Grimminger was the standard bearer of the SS, entrusted with guardianship of the Nazi Party's most revered relic.

"His permission was not required."

Müller's stare returned to him after a moment. "No," he said, with a tone of finality. "I have already fulfilled my oath. I am finished with your crusade." He waved the gun as if to indicate that he would hear no more talk of oaths. "This convoy—where is it?"

Himmler frowned, though the response was not completely unexpected. "The boats are hiding off the shore of Holsenöy. It is an island near Bergen. They surface at night to take on supplies and refugees."

A gleam of avarice appeared in Müller's eyes, but then he lowered the pistol, concealing it in the folds of his trench coat, and inclined his head. "Very good.

Now, you will take me there."

"I am not ready to leave Germany."

"I don't care," snapped Müller. "For all I know, you're trying to send me off on a wild goose hunt."

"The convoy is real."

"For your sake, I hope so."

Himmler pursed his lips together, but then nodded in compliance. "Very well."

He circled around the desk and began gathering in the flag, patiently folding it until the swastika was hidden beneath scarlet that was stained splotches of darker crimson. He placed it inside the presentation case, and then put the wooden box in a larger satchel.

"You should bury that somewhere," Müller said in a flat voice. "If we are caught with it, I do not think they will believe that you are just a soldier from the ranks."

"I will not leave it behind," Himmler replied, resolutely. "This is our future."

"You are a fool." Müller stepped forward and took the satchel with a brusque sweep of his hand. "But if it is so important to you, I will look after it until we reach the convoy. But know that I will not die for a piece of cloth, any more than I will die for what it represents. I will throw it into a privy rather than be caught with it."

Though the thought was absolutely shocking, Himmler hid his dismay. It pained him to be separated from the flag, even if it was still within arm's reach, but for the present, he would have to accept the former Gestapo leader's terms. If anyone could evade the Allied soldiers roaming the countryside and keep them all safe, it was Heinrich Müller.

Besides, with the flag in his possession, maybe the man would have a change of heart.

ONE

Bosnia and Herzegovina—1999

The man was so tall that he had to bend himself almost in half to pass through the flap of the olive-drab tent. Nearly naked, his only concession to modesty was a breechclout that looked like it might be buckskin, but was in fact made from pieces of chamois cloth crudely stitched together. More of the soft leather fabric had been fashioned into moccasin-like overshoes which almost completely covered his size-fifteen Nikes. His attire, or rather the lack thereof, would have been shocking enough to anyone who might have happened to come across him—such an encounter would have been extremely unlikely in the forest outside Sarajevo—but his near nudity was only the tip of the iceberg. His black hair, which was not quite long enough to pull back in a ponytail, had been coiffed high atop his head, cemented in place with styling gel, so that it resembled a rooster's crest, adding a full six inches to his already considerable height—he was almost six-and-a-half feet tall. His face and chest were painted a bright red, save for a three-inch thick horizontal stripe of black that ran across his eyes like a bandit mask. In his hands he held a four-foot long club, fashioned from a mostly straight piece of deadwood recovered from the forest floor. He looked like nothing less than a gigantic Native American warrior, which not coincidentally, happened to be exactly what he was.

His name was Uriah Bonebrake, though almost everyone who knew him simply called him "Bones." He was a full-blooded Cherokee Indian, but his claim to warrior status derived, not from his ethnic heritage, but rather from more than a decade of service in the

United States Navy, most of that time spent in an elite SEAL team. His present appearance—not to mention his current location—had more to do with the latter.

He jabbed his club menacingly toward a pair of men who wore more traditional military attire—green, brown, and black woodland pattern camouflage fatigues and matching boonie hats—and big smirks on their faces. "Not a word," he growled. "Not even a freaking syllable."

One of them, a lean, wiry Caucasian named Pete Chapman—though everyone called him Professor—raised his hands in a placating gesture, but the other, a tall, powerfully built African-American named Willis Sanders, refused to be cowed by the threat. "What are you so pissed-off about? It was your idea."

"No, my idea was for you to dress up like a Zulu warrior."

"Right," Willis retorted, smoothly. "Nothing racist about that."

"Are you kidding?"

"Man, we flipped for it, you lost. Deal with it."

"How's this for a flip, Shaka?" Bones extended his right arm and gave his teammate a one-fingered salute.

Willis grinned, but before he could respond in kind, another man in camouflage emerged from the trees to join them. His name was Dane Maddock, the SEAL platoon's commanding officer. "Better get up to the road," he said. "Showtime, gentleman. We just got word that—"

He stopped in mid-sentence and reached up to tilt back the brim of his hat for a better look at Bones, revealing a two-week growth of beard that was a shade or two redder than the sandy-blond, slightly longer than regulation hair hidden beneath his boonie cap, and eyes that were the color of a stormy sea.

"Huh," he said, his tone matter of fact. "I guess I don't have to ask where you stashed your socks."

"Says the white guy!" Willis chortled.

Bones threw his club down and grabbed his loin cloth. "Oh, that's it, Maddock. Let's do this. Right here, right now. Let's see who really stuffs his tighty-whiteys."

"Sorry, but I'll have to take a rain check. The Rat just left. He'll be coming through here in about twenty minutes." Maddock paused a beat, and then added, "You can flash him if you want. After all, we are going for maximum distraction."

"Kind of like getting him to play *Where's Waldo*," supplied Willis.

"I got your *maximum* distraction right here," Bones said.

"Just make it happen," Maddock said. "If we can take the Rat without firing a shot, I'll pin a medal on your... Ummm..." He dissembled a few seconds longer, then nodded to the woods behind them. "What are you waiting for? An invitation?"

"Well, 'please' would be a nice start," Bones shot back.

"I hear that word from your mom all the time," Willis said.

"Screw you, Willis."

Maddock turned away without another word. He didn't mind keeping things light, especially when so much of this latest assignment seemed to involve long periods of mind-numbing boredom while they waited for solid intel on one of their High Value Targets, but when the go order was received, the time for grab-ass games was over.

Bones' crazy pow-wow get-up was, oddly enough, not an example of such tomfoolery. Rather, it was the key element of an elaborate interdiction plan designed to roll up one Ratko Mladic, codenamed the "Rat" by the Joint Special Operations Command.

Mladic was a former commander of the 9th Corps of the Yugoslav People's Army and in that capacity, had been the architect of the four-year-long siege of Sarajevo, and the subsequent massacre of more than 8,000 young men and boys in the UN-designated "safe area" of Srebrenica in 1995. Under the leadership of Mladic and others like him, Serbian forces, had conducted a sustained effort to wipe out their hated ancestral enemies, using mass murder and systematic rape to erase the Bosnian people from existence. The conflict had introduced a new phrase into the common vernacular: ethnic cleansing, and the rest of the world had finally taken notice. NATO troops were enforcing the peace, UN investigators were chronicling the atrocities, and he Rat was number one with a bullet on the hitlist for the CIA-led Balkan Task Force which had been given the mission of hunting down all the "butchers of Bosnia" and bringing them before the Hague to stand trial for crimes against humanity.

The Agency had been tracking Mladic's movements, mostly with aircraft—RC-135 "Rivet Joint" and U2 spy planes, and MQ-1 Predator unmanned aerial vehicles—occasionally supplemented by human intelligence assets on the ground. Despite changing his location every few days, intel analysts poring over the data usually knew Mladic's approximate location to within a twenty-mile radius. In some rare instances, such as today, they not only knew where he was, but where he was headed next, which was why Maddock's platoon—currently attached to the BTF—was waiting on the side of a remote mountain road, ready to ambush the Rat's motorcade.

Because NATO and the Bosnian government wanted to see Mladic put on trial for his crimes, Maddock's orders were to take him alive if at all possible, which meant that, instead of just triggering a couple claymores and blasting the hell out of whatever was left, his SEALs would not only need to stop the motorcade, but extricate Mladic from his vehicle without a significant exchange of gunfire.

The idea for the operation was a variant on an idea dreamed up by the Army's Delta Force a couple years earlier. Facing a similar set of circumstances, they had planned to bring the target vehicle to a stop by deploying a mat studded with razor-sharp titanium spikes capable of puncturing the car's tires, after which a shaped charge would be used to blow the doors off, stunning the occupants in the process. But because the HVT inside would be accompanied by bodyguards—seasoned veterans of the long conflict—they would immediately adopt a defensive posture, which was why, before the vehicle reached the ambush, they would pass by a man walking down the road in a gorilla costume. The idea was that seeing a gorilla walking down the road in the middle of Bosnia might just be weird enough to confuse the bodyguards for a few seconds, creating the perfect conditions to strike. The plan—props and all—had been given the go-ahead, but the target had failed to show up.

Bones had been the one to suggest a variation of the plan—albeit with an assegai-wielding African warrior instead of a gorilla—and on Willis' immediate objection, had agreed to—and lost—the coin-flip, which was why he would be the one strolling down the roadside, shaking his club—and hopefully, nothing more—at the passing cars.

Maddock quickened his pace as he neared the edge of the road, ducking down behind a thicket of brush where his comms operator, Matt James, was hunkered down with a standard-issue black plastic radio handset pressed to each ear. Each radio was keyed to a different secure frequency—one for internal communications within the SEAL platoon, the other connected to the Tactical Operations Center at the safe house in Sarajevo, where their CIA handler was waiting. James also had a SEAL sat-phone set up to provide almost instantaneous contact with JSOC back in the States. Before they could execute their plan, he would need to check in with all three.

"Give me the platoon freq," Maddock said. James passed over the handset that had been at his left ear. Maddock keyed the mic. "All Hunter elements, this is Hunter Zero-Six. Sitrep, by the numbers. Over."

One by one, his squad leaders reported in their readiness. While this was going on, Bones, Willis, and Professor joined him and James behind the copse.

James gaped, goggle-eyed, at Bones. "Holy cow," he whispered.

Bones folded his arms across his chest, flexing his impressive biceps as he did. "Don't pretend this isn't the most awesome thing you've seen on this crap deployment."

Maddock ignored their banter and when the radio check was done, switched to the second handset. "Midnight, this is Hunter Zero-Six. We're cocked, locked, and ready to rock, over."

"Midnight," short for "Captain Midnight" was a career CIA officer named Bruce Huntley. Maddock didn't much care for Huntley, or for Agency spooks at all. Spies like him stretched the reasonable limits of the Machiavellian credo "the end justifies the means" recruiting gangsters, drug traffickers and general all-around dirtbags to carry out their various schemes. But like the proverbial broken clock that was right twice a day, once in a while, that amoral unscrupulousness really did serve the greater good.

The response was immediate. "Hot damn. You guys be sure to get some Polaroids, will ya? I bet the Rat craps his pants when he sees Crazy Horse walking down the road."

Maddock was glad that only he could hear the radio message. "Roger, out." Maddock passed the handset to James, and was just reaching for the sat-phone when the commo operator called out. "Target just passed OP Alamo!"

Observation Post-Alamo was exactly one mile from their current position. While conditions on the mountain road were not conducive to highway speed, Maddock guessed they were no more than ninety seconds from contact.

He shot a glance at Bones. "Go."

Bones gave his club a vigorous shake, then jogged out into the open. Maddock grabbed the sat-phone and initiated a call to his SEAL Team commander in the Joint Operations Center in Fort Bragg, North Carolina. After contact was made, but before he could utter a word, a frantic shout issued from the handset. "Hunter, this is Goliath Zero-One. Operation is on hold, repeat. You are on hold. Confirm, over."

Maddock was momentarily dumbfounded. Hold? When he finally found his voice, he replied. "Say again, over."

There was a lag of a second or two as the transmission bounced to the other side of the planet, but the swiftness of the reply was still surprising.

"You heard me, Dane." Radio brevity protocols were not absolutely necessary when using the SEAL sat-phone, but Maddock was nevertheless a little surprised to hear his given name, especially from Goliath—a.k.a Commander Hartford "Maxie" Maxwell. Maxie only ever called him by his first name when he needed Maddock's undivided attention.

"Sir, we are sixty seconds from go. We can't just hit the 'pause' button. If we don't do this, the window closes."

"Then let it close. This isn't my decision, Dane. Pull the plug."

Maddock bit back a rare obscenity. This wasn't the first time they had gotten all dressed up only to have the party cancelled at the last minute, but this was literally the last minute. He swore again, then through gritted teeth, said, "Understood."

He threw the sat-phone down and grabbed the platoon radio. "All Hunter elements—Abort, abort, abort. Do not engage. I say again, do not engage. Over."

He handed the radio back to James before the storm of outrage began, but that didn't mute the response from Willis. "Abort? What kind of crap is that? We've freakin' got him in our hands."

"Target just passed OP-Bataan," called out James, as he dutifully monitored the commo traffic. "Half a mile out."

"We could just go for it," Professor suggested. "You can say the signal was garbled. Easier to ask forgiveness than permission."

"That's what I'm saying," agreed Willis.

But Maddock just shook his head. "Orders are orders," he said, "You don't have to like them, you just have to follow them." It was a variation on a familiar, if distasteful, saying in the Teams, but the words were especially bitter now. "Following orders" meant a mass-murderer would escape justice yet again, and God alone knew when they'd get another chance like this.

In the near distance, the whine of an approaching automobile engine was audible, and as the seconds ticked by, it grew to a near roar.

Professor cleared his throat. "You think maybe we should tell—"

Before he could finish the question, a new sound rose above the engine noise—the piercing cry of a Cherokee warrior preparing to go into battle. Through the screen of branches, Maddock could see Bones at the edge of the road, waving his club and whooping like a madman. The approaching vehicle, a dark gray sedan, slowed for a moment, swerving to the opposite side of the road. Then, as if sensing the trap that would never be sprung, the engine revved and the sedan rocketed past.

"Never mind," Professor muttered.

"He's gonna be pissed," Willis added, shaking his head.

"He's not the only one," growled Maddock.

Huntley was seated on the sofa with his feet propped on the coffee table, watching CNN on the television set in the front room when the SEALs arrived back at the safe house. A man of average height and build, with a face that could only be described as average—not handsome, but not ugly—he typically had two operating modes, varying between sarcastic surfer-dude, and hyper-manic cheerleading patriot. He was presently in the former state, and didn't look the least bit surprised by the fact that the Rat was not with them.

"Pulled the rug out from under you, didn't they?" He made a tsking sound. "That's why I let all my calls go straight to the machine, especially when I'm running an op."

"You knew," Maddock said. It wasn't a question. "You knew when I called in, and you didn't say a word."

"Let's just say I had a feeling something like this would happen. Every time we get this close—" He held up his hand, thumb and forefinger mere millimeters apart. "Somebody in D.C. gets cold feet. One of these days, we'll beat them to the punch, and then they'll turn around and pat themselves on the back for being so decisive."

Maddock just shook his head. "Why do we even bother?"

"Because we have to, man. The flag-waving, hot-dog eaters of the great U.S. of A. expect us to. We're the good guys, they're the bad guys, and the good guys always win. Unfortunately, that's not how things work in the real world."

"Why not?"

It was a rhetorical question, but Huntley, mistaking Maddock's tone, answered anyway. "It's all political crap. The Serbian government has been helping these guys. Hiding 'em out. Running interference. 'Ve know nuffink.'" This last part was almost unintelligible.

"Everyone knows it," he went on, "but nobody wants to say anything about it because it will embarrass them, and they'll throw a tizzy and threaten to pull out of the Dayton Accords. Doesn't help that they're cozy with Russia, and we're supposedly playing nice with Ivan these days. At least that's what the President and her husband seem to think. If you believe that, I've got some waterfront property in Arizona you might want to look at."

"So we really are just spinning our wheels."

"Come on, you're a smart kid. It's all about timing. Today wasn't our day, but maybe tomorrow the Russkies will do something to royally piss us off… Or maybe we'll screw the pooch and need a big win to put us back on top… Something to remind the world that we're the good guys and they're the bad guys. That's when we'll make our move. It's all about the optics."

Maddock had no response to that, but he was oddly grateful for the other man's brutal honesty. It brought some much-needed clarity.

What if we aren't the good guys?

For as long as he could remember, things had always been just that simple. Maybe he was as naïve as one of Huntley's "flag-waving, hot-dog eaters." Right and wrong, good and evil, light side or dark side… Most of the time, it was easy to tell the difference.

So why did we just let a mass murderer slip through our fingers? Optics?

He wondered if Maxie would be as forthcoming as Huntley.

He left the CIA man in the front room and headed to the TOC—a secure room inside the safe house containing, among other things, an encrypted phone line back to the JOC.

He stared at it for a good five minutes before finally picking up and making the call. He was a little surprised when Maxie himself answered. "I figured you would have already packed it in for the night," he said, consciously stalling.

"It's not even lunchtime here," Maxie replied. "Besides, I was waiting for you to call."

Maddock was close to the SEAL Team commander, close enough to dispense with military protocols, but he was venturing into uncharted territory. "You give the orders, and we follow them. You don't owe me an explanation." He let the words hang in the air like a slow-pitched softball.

He expected a gruff, "Damn right," but instead, Maxie's tone was conciliatory. "I know you're frustrated, Dane. *I'm* frustrated, and I've been taking cocked-up orders and saying 'Yes, Sir,' a lot longer than you have. The only answer I have for you is what I tell myself. We took an oath to follow the orders of our elected civilian leaders, and unless they are illegal or immoral, we are duty bound to carry them out."

"The Rat is wanted for about 8,000 counts of murder," Maddock fired back. The accusation seemed insufficient to describe the crimes that had been committed. He had visited the site of the Omarska camp, one of nearly seven hundred detention camps where thousands of Bosnians and Croats had been detained and systematically exterminated. He had seen the mass graves where hundreds of bodies had been dumped and covered over by bulldozers. "Letting him go is both illegal and immoral."

Maxie was silent for several seconds, and when he spoke again, there was a profound sadness in his voice. "We can talk about this when you get here. If you feel so inclined."

Something about the way he said "when you get here" told Maddock that Maxie wasn't talking about the end of their rotation in two weeks' time. "Maxie, are you recalling us? We can do the job. It's not a problem."

"It's not that," Maxie said, with the same grave tone. "And I'm not bringing the platoon back. Just you. Emergency leave. I've already cut your orders."

"Emergency?" A cold surge of adrenaline raced through Maddock's veins. "Maxie what's happened?"

It was the nature of military life that one's duty came ahead of crises on the home front. Emergency leave was a rare thing, reserved for only the direst circumstances, like a dead or dying spouse or child. Maddock had neither—a career in Special Operations took a toll on families, and while he deeply loved his girlfriend, Melissa Moore, they had not yet discussed taking their relationship to the next step.

"I'm sorry, Dane. There's just no easy way to say this. I should have told you yesterday when it happened, but I needed you to stay focused on the op. For all the good it did."

"Who, Maxie?" Maddock pleaded.

"It was a car accident. Your parents… I'm sorry,

Dane. They're gone."

TWO

"When I told you we were going to be searching for Nazi gold, I'll bet you thought it would be a little more exciting than this."

Lia Markova didn't need to look back to identify the person standing right behind her and probably reading over her shoulder, but she did anyway, giving the man—her boss, Professor Oleg Petrov—a patient smile. "I am an archivist, professor. This is exactly what I expected to be doing."

"Of course, but still…" The historian wagged his head in mock despair. "It's so dry. These men were the monsters of the Great Patriotic War, and yet in these documents, they seem like mere *apparatchiki.*"

Lia suppressed a smile. *Apparatchik* was an old Soviet-era term used to describe low-level Communist Party officials—political functionaries so mired in procedure and bureaucracy that life for those under them became a sort of living hell. "My *babushka* would say the apparatchiki *were* monsters."

"That is true enough." He laughed, a little too enthusiastically, Lia thought, and then changed the subject. "Well, if you've had enough excitement for one day, why not join me for a drink, or perhaps two. We can discuss the banality of evil."

And what would your wife think of that, Lia didn't say. She really couldn't fathom why Petrov had set his sights on her. In a country filled with glamorous women, all vying to be international supermodels or alternately, trophy wives for wealthy American millionaires, she was merely ordinary. She was too short and too thin; one cruel former lover had told her that she had the body of a small boy. Her nose was too prominent, her hair and eyes were an uninspiring dull brown, and her thick eyeglasses made her look like an old spinster librarian—which, if her mother was to be believed, was exactly what she was turning into. She could not think of a single reason why the professor would be hitting on her, aside from the fact that he was a man, and she was young, single, and—at least so far as he was concerned—available. She glanced at the wall clock, and was surprised to see that it was almost six in the evening. She had been at it for nearly ten hours. No wonder her brain felt like mush. But she didn't dare let Petrov know.

"Thanks for the kind offer, professor, but I feel like I'm finally hitting my stride. I think I'll keep at it a while longer."

She had actually been on the project for the better part of a week, but most of that time had been spent organizing the materials, cataloguing them geographically. This was the first day she had spent actually reading the documents.

The goal of the project was to scour all contemporary records for clues that might lead to long-lost caches of Nazi gold bullion, secret Swiss bank accounts, or other treasures to which the Russian government might have a claim. They were desperate for hard currency. The economy, already weakened after decades of Cold War spending, had suffered a nearly fatal blow with the too-rapid shift to an unfettered free-market economy. A few oligarchs had grown obscenely wealthy, while the rest of the country starved. The Kremlin wasn't even able to pay its army, and a discontented army was never a good thing. Petrov, working under a government contract, was hoping to find some previously untapped vein of wealth, and to that end had put together a team of archivists and historians to take a fresh look at the records from the Second World War, or as many Russians still referred to it, the Great Patriotic War.

Unfortunately, those records were as dry as dust, and unlikely to contain anything of real import, but feigning sincere interest seemed like the easiest way of avoiding Petrov's advances without actually insulting him and putting her career in jeopardy.

He flashed a big-toothed grin and shook his finger at her. "Are you trying to make me look like a… What do the Americans call such a man? A slacker?"

Lia managed a polite laugh. "Never, professor."

"Okay. I let it go this time, but don't stay too late. And don't ride the Metro. Take a taxi when you leave. I will reimburse you."

The offer was surprisingly chivalrous and seemed to contain no obvious ulterior motive. "I promise," she said, and this time her smile was sincere.

As he left, she returned her attention to the document displayed on the screen of the microfiche reader. Written in English, which Lia spoke fluently, it contained a report filed by a British officer who had interrogated a captured SS officer named Grothmann, one of Heinrich Himmler's top aides, captured along with the Reichsführer as they tried to disappear into the countryside.

"They succeeded in crossing the Elba to Neuhaus in a small fishing boat fitted with an auxiliary motor. GROTHMANN states that the boat was loaned to them, and that the fisherman who provided it had no idea whom they were assisting."

She jotted down "Elba to Neuhaus" in her research notebook. Later, she would have to consult maps of the region in order to retrace the men's footsteps.

"From Neuhaus they proceeded on foot to the neighborhood of Meinstadt. BRANDT, MUELLER, and KIERMEIER left the party to go into the town of Bremervorde with a view to having their 'Ausweise' stamped by the British Town Major, but unfortunately did not return. HIMMLER wanted to go after them, since MUELLER carried something of great importance, but MACHER and GROTHMANN, believing that the others had probably been captured, insisted they continue on to Meinstadt, where they were detained by three Russian soldiers."

"Something of great importance?" she murmured. The lack of specificity was not altogether surprising since this particular report was unclassified. A more specific description of the item, and perhaps even a full transcript of the interview, probably existed, buried and forgotten in a top-secret archive in London or Washington D.C.

It was probably another dead end, but Petrov had explicitly directed the project team to report anything of note, even if it seemed insignificant. If she waited until the following morning and it turned out to be something even mildly important, her failure to follow protocol would give the professor leverage with which to pressure her into joining him for extracurricular activities.

She rose from her workstation and hurried through the archives hoping to catch Petrov, but the guard at the front desk informed her that he had already departed, so she returned to her desk and called his mobile phone number.

When the call was picked up, the first thing she heard was loud music. She thought perhaps he was in his car, listening to the radio, but then she heard voices... Petrov muttering an apology... A woman urging him to stay with her.

He certainly didn't waste any time, she thought.

Petrov's voice now sounded more forcefully in her hear. "Da?"

"Professor Petrov? It's Lia."

"Lia. Did you change your mind?"

"No, professor. I mean, that's not why I called." She paused a beat, hoping that her reply had not offended him. "I found something... It's probably nothing, but you said...."

"Da, da. Just tell me what it is."

"It's from the report on the interrogation of Werner Grothmann, Himmler's aide de camp." As she read the relevant section aloud, the ambient noise changed—the music giving way to a soft roar, like the wind or road noise, suggesting that Petrov had left the previous environment to find a quieter place to continue the call. When she finished, he let out a thoughtful hum.

"This man, Mueller. Is there any additional information about him?"

"Nothing. That's the only mention."

"Hmmm. Mueller is a common German name, but assuming that he was a senior member of the SS, it might refer to Gestapo Müller."

Lia recalled the name. There had been two senior SS men with the name Heinrich Müller, so to avoid confusion, one of them—the one who was head of the secret police—was often referred to as Gestapo Müller. "I thought he died in Berlin."

"The last known sighting of him was in the Führerbunker a few hours before Hitler committed suicide. Müller wasn't the sort of man to kill himself, so I suspect he managed to slip out of Berlin ahead of the arrival of the Red Army. There were rumors that the Americans recruited him and gave him a new identity. And of course, they believed that we—or rather the old KGB—are the ones who turned him. I don't know if either is true, but if this report is talking about him, then it would at least add a footnote to his story. But what is this item of great importance he carried?"

"I have no idea. That is why I called you." Lia realized too late that it had been a rhetorical question, but Petrov seemed not to have heard.

"Something that the head of the Gestapo was unwilling to entrust to anyone else... Something important enough that Himmler himself was prepared to risk being captured to recover." He hummed again. "Keep digging. Call immediately if you discover anything else. I will make some inquiries of my own."

Lia frowned. She was beginning to regret having given the appearance of diligent interest, but before she could reply, the background noise abruptly ceased; Petrov had already rung off.

"Forget him," she muttered. "I'll do it tomorrow."

After ending the call with Lia, Oleg Petrov regarded the phone in his hand for a moment, trying to decide what to do next. He had promised Nadia, the raven-haired beauty waiting at the bar of the glitzy night club, that he would be right back as soon as he dealt with a small matter from work, and it was a promise he was eager to keep. He rarely indulged himself like this, but since Lia was proving resistant to his advances, he needed some kind of outlet for his pent-up amorous energy. He suspected the lovely Nadia was a prostitute. Ravishing women rarely took such a focused interest in him, but if she was a prostitute, then she was almost certainly a high-end prostitute, and the idea of hiring her services for a few hours had its own appeal.

But he should probably let Telesh know about Lia's discovery.

Sergei Yukovitch Telesh was one of the most powerful men in the Russian organized crime underworld—maybe the most powerful—which meant that, for all practical purposes, he was one of the most powerful men—maybe the most powerful—in all of Russia. He was said to be close friends with the new prime minister, an ambitious former-KGB officer, and whether Telesh was merely an influential advisor or the real power behind the throne, there was little question that what Telesh wanted, he got.

Even though the research project was being funded by the Ministry of Finance, Petrov was sure that it had been initiated at Telesh's urging. He couldn't fathom why—the gangster was already obscenely wealthy. All Petrov knew for certain was that, just a few hours after receiving his appointment to head up the project, he had been invited to Telesh's Moscow apartment for an informal meeting, and there, had been given an envelope stuffed full of fifty-ruble notes.

"A gift," Telesh had said, expansively, "For a dedicated public servant."

Petrov of course had understood that there would be strings attached to the "gift," but all he would have to do is report any discoveries to Telesh first, before passing the information along to the Ministry of Finance. Since Telesh already had his hooks in the project—and more to the point, since the mobster was unlikely to take "no" for an answer—there was no point to refusing the bribe, so Petrov had taken the money and enjoyed it. Up to this point, there had been nothing to report, but now he was faced with a decision. Call Telesh with this seemingly insignificant bit of trivia? Or enjoy a night of distraction with the lovely Nadia?

Telesh would demand that he drop everything and immediately begin chasing down the lead. It was probably nothing. The "something of great importance" was probably something to do with the Nazi officers' escape plan, maybe a map or a list of sympathizers who might provide safe harbor. And whatever it had been, it was almost certainly gone now, captured by the Allies or lost to the ages.

But without the largess of Sergei Yukovitch Telesh, he would not even be able to afford a woman like Nadia. And Telesh was not the kind of person he wanted to cross.

With a sigh, he dug out the card with Telesh's private number and dialed. Telesh picked up on the second ring. "Hello?"

His voice was silky smooth, almost seductive, and completely at odds with his physical appearance— Telesh was a large man, and not in a good way. His mostly balding head was round and piggish, with multiple chins, and sat atop a squat blob of a body. Yet, despite his rather ogre-like exterior, he was considered by many to be extremely virile. That probably had something to do with his money and power, and the aura of danger that seemed to cling to organized crime figures. His smooth voice and friendly manner easily won over anyone who might be of use to him, while simultaneously fooling his enemies into thinking him ignorant of their designs. Petrov had easily—and quite knowingly—allowed himself to fall under Telesh's spell; better to be with a man like Telesh than against him.

"Sergei Yukovitch," Petrov began. "It is Oleg Ivanovitch Petrov. I am head of the historical research team. We spoke—"

"Yes, of course I remember you, Oleg Ivanovitch. And I told you to call immediately if you discovered anything. I take it this means you have something to tell me?"

"Yes. I mean, I have something, but I don't know if it will be of significance."

"Why don't you just tell me and let me decide?" Telesh's tone was sublimely cheerful, almost paternalistic.

"Of course. It was in a document relating to the capture of Reichsführer Heinrich Himmler. One of his aides, when questioned, mentioned a man named Müller—I think it must be Gestapo Müller—who took something of great importance to Himmler."

He expected some kind of reaction, but instead there was only a long silence. Petrov thought perhaps the call had dropped. "Hello?"

"I am still here," Telesh said, and this time his tone was different. There was an eagerness in his voice, a hunger. "It is good that you called me. I wish to discuss this in person. I will have my driver bring you here."

Petrov swallowed down his disappointment. So much for an evening of delight with Nadia. "I am at the club on Znanenka Ulitsa and—"

"I know where you are," Telesh cut him off. "I will speak with you when you get here."

"How do you—" The call terminated before he could complete the question. Nonplussed, he stuffed the phone into his pocket and headed down the alley to the front entrance of the night club. He let his gaze rove up and down the street, wondering which of the cars was coming for him. Telesh's apartment was only a few blocks away, on Butikovsky Pereulok, in the prestigious Khamovniki neighborhood near the Moskva River. He wouldn't have to wait long, even with city traffic.

But how had Telesh known where to find him?

"Oleg?"

Petrov turned toward the sound of the familiar voice and spotted Nadia, waving as she walked toward him. Her strides were long and confident, her face utterly blank, like a model on the runway. Petrov sighed heavily and went to meet her. "Nadia, my dear. I am so very sorry, but I must leave. Something has come up at work."

Her expression did not change. "I know."

As she reached him, she sidestepped and pivoted around one-hundred-eighty degrees. She hooked his right arm with her left, and then pulled him along toward the street, just as a boxy, black Lada sedan pulled up at the curb.

Petrov felt faintly ill. "You work for him." It wasn't a question, but an answer. This was how Telesh had known where he was. How many other spies had been sent to watch him, follow him, day in and day out?

"Of course," she said, tersely. "He is very interested in your work." She opened the rear door. "Get in."

He slid into the back seat and she got in after him, scooting close. The press of her body against his felt oppressive, intimidating. He had liked the idea of Nadia being a high-priced call girl, but this... He couldn't wrap his head around it.

The car did not take him to Telesh's apartment, but instead took him back to the university. The building occupied by the Faculty of History was dark and deserted, but there was a light burning in one window. His office.

Telesh was sitting at his desk. "Petrov. Good. You're here. Show me what you found." It was a demand, not a request, spoken with none of his customary silkiness. The mobster's manner was abrupt, not quite threatening, but only a few degrees removed from it.

Petrov swallowed nervously, then nodded and motioned for Telesh to follow him. "It's in the document archives."

Lia wasn't at her workstation, and he could only surmise that she had left shortly after calling him.

Smart girl, he thought, wishing he could as easily brush off the consequences of his call to Telesh.

He switched on the microfiche reader, and was relieved to see that the film was still in it. After flipping back a couple frames, he found the portion Lia had read to him. "This is it," he said. Translating the English into Russian for Telesh's benefit. He could feel the man's bulk not hovering so much as hanging over his shoulder, poised to crush him. "It does not say specifically what Müller was carrying," he said when he was done reading.

Telesh said nothing and when Petrov looked up, he saw the man's eyes moving back and forth as he read. After a moment or two, his pudgy lips began to curl in a smile of satisfaction. "I did not dare to hope that the search would bear fruit so quickly." His eyes met Petrov's. "Who discovered this? It wasn't you."

"No. It was one of the archivists. A graduate student. Lia Markova."

"Where is she?"

"I don't know. Her flat, I would think."

"You will call her," Telesh said flatly. "Tell her that you need to see her here, right away."

Petrov swallowed again. He felt lightheaded. This was all dreadfully wrong. "I… I am certain she knows nothing more than what you see here."

"Then she knows too much."

Darkness began to close in around the edges of Petrov's vision. If he had not already been sitting, he would surely have fainted straightaway.

She knows too much.

Telesh already knew what the "something of great importance" was; he had been looking for it all along, and now that he had a solid lead, he was going to eliminate anyone outside his own inner circle who might expose his search.

What was it? A fortune in gold? Was that worth killing for?

Petrov already knew the answer to that question.

She knows too much. And so do I.

"Petrov," Telesh rumbled. "I'm waiting."

Even though he was breathing rapidly, panting like a dog, Petrov couldn't seem to catch his breath, but he nevertheless took out his mobile phone. He stared at it for a moment, trying to remember what he was supposed to do next.

Call her. Call Lia. But what is her number? "Office," he managed to gasp. "Her number. My Rolodex."

Telesh shot a glance toward Nadia. The raven-haired beauty was already moving, striding from the room like some kind of beautiful but deadly automaton, leaving the two men alone.

For a fleeting instant, Petrov contemplated fleeing. Telesh would never be able to catch him. He could run, and then he would be safe and so would Lia….

Nadia reappeared, stalking toward them, a small card clutched in her right hand. She thrust it at Petrov.

He stared at the card, seeing the letters and numbers, struggling to make sense of them.

"Do you need me to dial it for you?" Nadia asked, icily.

He shook his head and then punched in the digits for Lia's mobile phone. It rang once, then again. Three times. Four.

"She's not—" he started to say, and then stopped when the trilling sound ended and he heard Lia's voice.

"Hello?"

He swallowed again, his mouth now dry as a desert. "Lia, it is Oleg. Where are you? I thought you were working late."

There was a long silence, followed by a heavy sigh. "I was tired, professor. I need to get some sleep. It will wait one more day."

What do I say?

"Lia, this cannot wait. I need you to come back here."

Another long pause. "Look, professor. I really am flattered that you want to spend time with me, but I think right now it would be better for both of us to keep things professional." She spoke rapidly, as if it had taken all her courage to make the declaration.

She thinks I am hitting on her. The thought pained him. He was not summoning her to an assignation, but to an execution.

He glanced up at Telesh. The man's eyes shone out from his ogre-face with a warning that burrowed into Petrov's soul. *Do not cross me.*

"Lia," Petrov said, his mouth so dry that he almost coughed the word. "You must listen to me very carefully and do exactly as I say."

"Professor…"

"Run, Lia. Hide. They are going to kill—"

There was a flash of blue light and the next thing Petrov knew, he was lying flat on his back. His ear and the side of his head felt alternately hot and numb. His hand was empty. The phone had been knocked away.

Petrov felt a strange warmth at his groin. It took him a moment to realize that his bladder had just let go.

A baleful moon floated into view above Petrov— Telesh's bloated face. "That was a very foolish thing to do, professor. Most unwise."

THREE

East Hampton, New York

It was a beautiful day, which made the graveside service seem all the more surreal. Maddock moved like someone walking in a dream—shaking hands, accepting condolences from family friends with what they probably mistook for stoic reserve. In truth, he felt numb. Even though he had looked inside the polished caskets, looked upon their faces, he couldn't bring himself to believe that any of it was real.

For most of his life, he had understood that he would outlive his parents, but it was never more than an abstract intellectual concept for him. In his career as a SEAL, confronted on an almost daily basis with the fact of his own mortality, he had begun to think it pretty unlikely that he would actually survive them.

He certainly never imagined that he would bury both of them in a single day.

Hosting the wake at their house—his house, now—gave him something to do, something to keep his mind occupied, but it also meant surrounding himself with pieces of his childhood. This wasn't the house where he had grown up, of course. His father's military career meant that they never stayed in any one place long enough to put down roots. After retiring from the Navy Hunter Maddock and his wife had relocated to East Long Island because of its close proximity to Gardiner's Island—the location of the only confirmed instance where a pirate buried his loot for later retrieval. But while the house was a place the younger Maddock had only visited occasionally in his adult life, the things in it—pictures, mementos, books—were all too familiar. The dusty study where Hunter had spent endless hours researching pirate lore, searching for the lost treasure of the notorious Captain William Kidd, was like a fixed point in the universe—an unchanging room that seemed to exist in every house they had ever lived in.

But now it was missing something—missing someone—and it would never be the same.

He sat at the desk, idly brushing away the thin layer of dust that had settled on the blotter. There was a framed picture resting on one corner—a picture of the whole family together, taken shortly after his graduation from the Naval Academy.

Two of the three people in the photograph were gone. *I'm all that's left.*

He wasn't sure what to do with the house, yet. His first impulse was to sell it. What use did he have for a house?

But then he thought about all the memories he had made in a house like this one. He would never have any new memories of his parents, only regrets for missed opportunities. Maybe it was time to start making new memories. And maybe this was the place to do it.

"Dane?"

He looked up and found Melissa standing in the doorway, looking beautiful, even in mourning black. They had been together and more or less exclusive for the better part of a decade, shared an abiding passion for history and archaeology—she was currently working at the National Museum of American History, part of the Smithsonian Institution in Washington DC—and he genuinely enjoyed her company. Why hadn't he popped the question? "Hey. I was just thinking about you."

"I was wondering where you snuck off to," she said. Her tone was apologetic rather than reproving. "Do you need some time?"

"No." He shook his head, then smiled up at her and reached out his arms. "Come here."

She crossed the room and took his hands in hers, but there was something tentative in her movements, as if she wasn't sure that this was what she should be doing. She kissed him lightly, then drew back. "Coach is looking for you."

"Is he?" Marco "Coach" Cosenza had been Maddock's Little League coach, and had stayed a family friend ever since. He had eventually relocated to New England where he chartered his boat *Sea Foam*, for fishing and SCUBA diving trips. Cosenza was one of the few people in the house who knew Maddock as well as he knew his parents. They had spoken briefly at the cemetery, but there hadn't been opportunity to catch up. "Let's go see what he wants."

Cosenza was in the front room, pretending to study a framed print on the wall beside the fireplace—a flat reproduction of the Lenox Globe, a historical map from the early sixteenth century, one of the few antique maps to bear the warning of what lay beyond the unexplored frontiers.

HC SVNT DRACONES.

Here be dragons.

"Coach!"

Cosenza turned to him, a wary smile on his lips, and extended a hand. "Dane. Good to see you. Dress blues look good on you."

"I don't get to wear them very often," Maddock replied. The import of this hit him almost as soon as the words were out, but he hid his dismay behind a smile, accepting the handclasp. He felt Melissa's hand on his arm, her breath in his ear.

"I'll leave you two to talk," she whispered, and then was gone.

He returned his attention to Cosenza who, almost awkwardly, was still holding Maddock's hand. "How have you been? How's boat life?"

"More work than I expected. I tell you, I'm seriously thinking about going ashore for good."

"No. Really? Give up *Sea Foam*?"

"You know what a boat is? It's a hole in the water into which you pour money. I think I'd rather just sit on the beach. Know what I mean?"

Maddock smiled. "I don't think I'd ever get tired of being on the water, but I am..." He shook his head.

"I'm seeing things differently."

Cosenza gave Maddock's hand a knowing squeeze, then his smile fell. "Dane, listen. There's something I need to say to you." He took a deep breath, as if trying to summon the courage to deliver bad news. "Your father was a good man, but he was... Complicated."

"I don't need you to tell me that."

"I know. But sometimes, the consequences of decisions we make come back to haunt us long after we think we've paid the price. Someday, you might learn things about your father that will surprise you. Maybe even disappoint you."

Cosenza gave his hand another firm squeeze. "Just remember that he was a good man, and that he loved you and your mother very much."

"Coach, what are you trying to tell me?"

Cosenza seemed ready to elucidate, but just then, another familiar voice intruded.

"Dane." It was Maxie. Like Maddock, he was attired in a dark blue dress uniform with the distinctive eagle-trident-pistol badge that identified him as a SEAL. Maxie had been at the graveside service but had left early without offering an explanation.

Maddock nodded to the other man. "Coach, this is my CO, Commander Hartford Maxwell. Maxie this is an old friend, Marco Cosenza."

Cosenza released Maddock's grasp and exchanged a quick handshake with Maxie. "I hope you'll pardon the interruption," the latter said, "but I need a private word with Dane."

"Of course," Cosenza said. "Dane, just remember what I told you."

He stepped away quickly, as if granted an unexpected reprieve. Maddock just shook his head. People could be weird at funerals.

Maxie cleared his throat to get Maddock's attention, and then cast a glance around the room. "Is there someplace a little more private?"

"Sure. This way." Maddock led him back to the study, closing and locking the door behind them. "So, I guess it's time for that talk?"

"Dane, I'm sorry to—" Maxie paused, took a breath, and then started again. "How are you holding up?"

"I think I'm still trying to..." He stopped, remembering who he was really speaking with. "Actually, I think I'm starting to see things clearly for the first time. I've wasted the last ten years of my life. While I was busy playing Rambo, the world slipped right through my fingers. I should have been building a home, a family... A life. My parents... I should have given them grandchildren. And don't tell me about sacrifices made for the greater good. I'm not even sure what that means anymore."

Maxie stared back at him for several seconds. "Feel better now?"

Maddock uttered a short, humorless laugh. "Yeah. I do. I'm done Maxie. It's time I started actually living my life."

"Okay." Maxie nodded. "Now that you've got that off your chest, we need to talk. I've got new orders for you."

Maddock gaped at him. "Orders? Are you kidding? Did you not hear what I just said?"

"I read you loud and clear," Maxie replied. "But you don't get to just say 'take this job and shove it.' There's a procedure you'll have to follow, and until you've jumped through all those hoops, you are still under orders."

"For God's sake, Maxie. I just buried my parents."

"And I had to move heaven and earth to let you do that," Maxie shot back. Then he softened a few degrees. "Dane, this comes from way above my pay grade. SECNAV signed these orders. There's nothing I can do to block this. You've got two options: do as ordered, or jump ship. Trust me, the brig is not where you want to start living life on your own terms."

Maddock's gut was churning. He knew Maxie was right, but that didn't mean he wasn't going to submit his letter of resignation before leaving. "So where am I going?"

"Russia." Maxie gave a heavy sigh. "The NSA flagged an ECHELON intercept in Moscow two days ago. A mobile phone call between a history professor—Oleg Petrov—and a university archivist—Lia Markova. They were both working on a project to search for Nazi loot. During the course of the call, Petrov warned Markova that her life was in danger, after which the call ended. The intercept got kicked to the Naval attaché in Moscow, who tracked Markova down and debriefed her. She didn't know much, but our officer thinks the threat to Markova is real."

"What exactly is the threat?" asked Maddock.

"Uncertain. The Kremlin is sponsoring the research project, but there's a long list of agencies and people who might be interested in finding a cache of Nazi loot. We do know that Petrov is missing. Our working assumption is that he was coerced into making the call to Markova in order to lure her into a trap, and that his captors probably punished him for warning her off. You'll be providing security and logistical support for Markova's exit. Bonebrake, Chapman, and Sanders are already en route. They'll meet you on the ground in Moscow. You'll be traveling commercial using your Jim Abbott alias. Your flight leaves JFK at 1900 hours, so you should probably wrap things up here."

Maddock shook his head, resignedly. "Why me? This isn't our AO. None of us speak Russian, and Bones and Willis will stick out like a pair of sore thumbs."

"Personal request from the attaché. Evidently, she thinks very highly of you clowns."

"She?"

"An old friend of yours. Zara Leopov."

FOUR

Moscow, Russia

Owing to the time difference, it was early afternoon when Maddock's flight arrived at Sheremetyevo International Airport. He traveled by taxi to the historic Arbat—a brick paved pedestrian street popular with tourists—and wandered around for half an hour to make sure that he wasn't being followed. He wasn't, or rather, if he was, his shadow was skillful enough to avoid detection. The more likely explanation was that his cover was holding, and he was just one more American sightseer.

Although the collapse of the Soviet Union had wrought profound changes, in many ways, Moscow still resembled the Hollywood version he had experienced in countless spy thriller movies watched in his formative years. Despite showing many of the trappings of modernity and capitalism, it still felt like an old city. More Brooklyn than Manhattan, there were few glass and steel towers, and plenty of squat, graceless Constructivist concrete structures, interspersed with the occasional Byzantine onion-domed church or bizarre, logic-defying Stalinist monstrosity.

As he wandered about, he couldn't help but think how incredible it was that he was walking the streets of the Russian capital. Growing up, he had always imagined Moscow as a forbidden city, a place where few Westerners dared visit, and where KGB agents in black trench coats lurked around every corner, waiting to whisk suspected spies—and everyone was a suspected spy—off to a dank interrogation room somewhere under Lubyanka Square, never to be seen again.

Even though there was the perception of openness, he knew better than to think that he was on friendly soil. The rivalry between America and Russia went beyond the ideologies of Capitalism and Communism. The KGB agents in black trench coats hadn't simply gone away when the USSR fragmented. They had just changed their initials, and added burgeoning Twenty-first Century technology to their arsenal, which was why he was surreptitiously checking his six for any hint of surveillance.

It had taken a while, but the further Maddock got from his parents' house and all its strange familiarity, the more the events of the day began to slip from his mind like a bad dream. Somewhere over the North Atlantic, the sting of being denied time to grieve subsided, to be replaced by something almost like relief. There was nothing he could do to change what had happened, but at least this—duty, orders, a mission—was something he knew how to deal with, even if it no longer gave him the same satisfaction it once had.

He wasn't sure how he felt about working with Zara Leopov again. The two prior occasions where they had worked together had not exactly gone smoothly, but he supposed their shared history counted for something.

Born in Soviet Russia, Leopov's parents had tried to escape when she was just a young girl. The effort had only partly succeeded. Leopov's father had sacrificed himself to ensure that his wife and daughter would find freedom in the West.

Leopov had honored her father's memory by joining the US Navy, and putting her cultural and linguistic expertise to good use as an intelligence officer, working directly against the government that had taken him from her. That had been her plan, at least. By the time she had finished her training, the Cold War was winding down, the old Soviet menace collapsing from within. Now, Russia was something else—not quite an enemy, definitely not a friend—but no longer a police state with closed borders.

During both of their previous missions, Maddock had been given cause to wonder about her true loyalties. Now that the Motherland was free, would she continue to honor her obligations to the country that had offered refuge? In both instances, his suspicions had proven baseless, and evidently her superiors had complete trust in her loyalty, but he remained uneasy about the coming reunion. The fact that Leopov had specifically asked for him was unusual, to say the least.

From the Arbat, he took two more taxi rides, each to a randomly selected hotel, and after entering the latter, he slipped out a back entrance and headed to the nearest Metro station on foot. There, he purchased a thirty-day Smart Card from an automated kiosk, and consulted a map of the rail system. He could not speak more than a few phrases of Russian, and had no ability to understand it when spoken or to read its crazy backward alphabet, but he knew where he had to go. Like most subway maps in the developed world, the Moscow Metro was color-coded, and once he figured out where he was—at a station on the Orange Line—he was able to navigate to a connecting Green Line train, which brought him to Sokol Station, a short walk from his ultimate destination in the nearby residential neighborhood.

The safehouse was situated on a narrow tree-lined street, a few blocks from the urban maze of austere apartment blocks. The house, which judging by the architecture, was at least thirty years old, was nice, if a little run down. Maddock knew that under Communist rule, the average Muscovite had been obliged to live in small apartment flats assigned by the government, and that free-standing homes such as this were reserved for senior party officials. This one had probably been considered a mansion in its heyday. Now, it was just another piece of real estate, which the American government had acquired through a series of cut outs and shell companies. According to public records, it was a rental property owned by an Iranian oil company.

Bones greeted him at the door. "*Dobro pozhalovat' v Moskvu*," he said, stepping aside with a flourish to allow Maddock entrance.

"Do I want to know what you just said?"

Bones shook his head, disparagingly. "Way to encourage multi-culturalism, dude."

"He said, 'Welcome to Moscow,'" intoned a familiar female voice from just beyond the door. Zara Leopov stood there. Like Maddock and the others, she wore casual attire; her outfit consisted of blue jeans, and a leather bomber jacket over a dark red T-shirt. Her long, straight honey-brown hair was pulled back in a ponytail to fully reveal her high Slavic cheekbones and eyes that were almost black. "He really wanted to impress you. He practiced for nearly an hour." Her tone was disapproving, but there was a hint of a mocking smile on her lips. "Now you have made him sad."

"He'll get over it," Maddock replied, sounding a little more dismissive than he intended. "Sorry. That's the jet lag talking."

Leopov reached out a hand to touch his shoulder. "I heard what happened. I'm so very sorry."

Maddock sighed. He'd heard those words so often that they'd ceased to have any real meaning. He looked past her to the front room where Willis and Professor were on their feet, waiting. He saw the same sentiment, unspoken but easy to read in their eyes.

"Yeah," he muttered. "I mean, thank you." With an effort, he managed a smile. "It's good to see you again, Zara."

"Why don't I believe you," she murmured, almost too softly for him to hear—almost.

"These are pretty cool digs," Bones said quickly, as if to force a change of subject. "A lot nicer than that crap-shack in Sarajevo. In case I forget to say it, thanks for getting us out of that goat rope."

"Don't thank me," Maddock said quickly, nodding at Leopov. "It was her idea."

Bones grinned at her. "I get that you'd want to

spend some quality time with me, but why did you have to invite him? Trying to find a date for your ugly sister?"

Leopov shrugged. "I thought you two were a package deal. Isn't that a thing with you SEALs? Swim buddies, forever joined at the hip?"

Fearing what Bones might say in reply, Maddock stepped inside, closing the door behind him. "I'm here, now. Let's get down to business."

Leopov inclined her head and then turned and gestured to the front room. When they were all seated, she took a manila folder from the coffee table and handed it to Maddock. He flipped it open and saw that it contained a few candid photographs of a harried-looking young woman who bore a passing resemblance to pop singer Lisa Loeb. There was also a typed transcript of a debriefing, and a map of the city with Russian names written in both Cyrillic and Roman alphabets, but no additional markings.

"We were just discussing how to proceed," Leopov began. "I don't know how much you were told, but I'll start from the beginning so that we're all on the same page."

Maddock nodded for her to continue.

"Lia Markova is a graduate student at Moscow State University, dual major in Library Science and Twentieth Century Russian History. Three days ago, while working on a research project for the History department chair, she evidently discovered something she wasn't supposed to see. About an hour or so after she told her boss about it, he called her back. At first, he tried to get her to join him at their workplace, but then he shouted a warning for her to flee for her life. And that's exactly what she did. She's been hiding out in the sewers—there's a whole hidden city down there. Anyway, long story, short, the NSA intercepted the call and routed it to the Embassy, and I was tasked with bringing her in."

"Why you?" Maddock asked "I mean, why Naval Intelligence? Why did the CIA pass this up?"

"Two reasons. First, I'm actually Russian, which means I can move around the city with a little more freedom than anyone else. Second, it's believed that Lia might be more receptive to a female than a male. Honestly, though, I think the real reason is that the station chief doesn't think it's worth his time. He's not going to risk getting his assets blown to rescue a damsel in distress, especially if she's bringing nothing of value to the table."

"I guess saving an innocent life isn't reason enough," said Maddock.

"It's not," Leopov replied, evenly. "Espionage and chivalry are mutually exclusive. We're all playing the long game here. It takes years to cultivate an asset, and the intel they provide might save hundreds, even thousands of lives someday. You don't throw that away to save one life."

"I guess that's why I'll never be a spy. I could never make a calculation like that." He regarded her thoughtfully. "If you agree with the Agency's assessment, why are you trying to save her?"

She flashed a tight smile. "Because I'm too much like you. And… I think what Lia found might be more important than anyone realizes. Anyone but the people hunting her, that is."

"What exactly did she find?" asked Maddock.

Leopov indicated the file with the transcript of Lia's debrief. "It all seemed to be triggered by something she found relating to the capture of Heinrich Himmler at the end of the war. Specifically, there was mention of a high-ranking SS officer named Mueller, whom she took to be Heinrich Müller, head of the Gestapo."

Professor leaned forward. "Heinrich Müller was the highest-ranking SS officer whose fate remains unknown," he explained. Professor had earned his nickname by virtue of his encyclopedic knowledge of trivia and his tendency to lecture. "He was last seen in Berlin, shortly after Hitler's suicide, but he was never captured and his body was never found. Theories about what happened to him range from suicide to an escape to Argentina."

"If he is the same man mentioned in the documents Lia was researching," Leopov said, "Then he was still alive a week later, and somewhere near a place called Bremervorde."

"It's a little town in the north," said Professor. "About halfway between Hamburg and Bremen. We know that Himmler was in Flensburg, near the Danish border, a few days earlier, so he was traveling south when he was captured." He paused a beat. "If that helps."

"The document indicated that Müller was carrying something of great value but it doesn't say what," Leopov continued. "Given his seniority, it must have been pretty important. Plans for rebuilding the Reich. Bank account information. Who knows what? Himmler committed suicide before he could be interrogated. Since there's no indication that Müller was captured in Bremervorde, it's likely that he escaped with it, whatever it was."

"And took it to Argentina?" Bones suggested.

"Possibly. My working theory is that somebody— possibly someone in the Russian intelligence service— has been looking for Müller, and when Lia contacted her boss about what she'd found, it tripped an alarm and they went after her."

"Why?" Maddock countered. "It doesn't sound like she actually knows anything."

Leopov spread her hands in a gesture of helplessness. "Maybe she knows more than she realizes. Or maybe they're just tidying up loose ends. All I really know is that she's in danger, and we can help."

Bones leaned forward. "Are we sure there's really a threat?"

"Her boss seemed to think so, and now he's missing."

"There could be any number of explanations for that. Maybe he owed some money to Ivan the Loan Shark. Maybe his jealous wife was on the warpath."

"There's something else." Leopov paused a beat,

and then lowering her eyes in embarrassment, added, "I think I've been made."

Maddock, who had been idly perusing the transcript of the debrief now looked up sharply.

"Yesterday afternoon, I noticed I had picked up a tail," she went on. "I don't know how long they've been watching me, but I called Lia on the burner phone I gave her and warned her to change locations. She's still safe."

"Isn't it standard operating procedure for the FSB to keep tabs on embassy personnel?" asked Professor.

"Not everyone. Until now, they've pretty much ignored me. It's possible that this has nothing to do with Lia's situation, but then again, if they're looking for her, it would be SOP to ramp up surveillance on anyone they think she might turn to. That would include embassy staff."

"But you shook them?" Maddock pressed.

Leopov's chagrinned expression deepened. "No. I didn't want them to know I knew. I made a couple of stops to create a false trail, but nothing too crazy."

"Did they follow you here?"

She spread her hands in a helpless gesture.

Willis sat back, clapping his hands on his thighs. "Damn, girl. You couldn't have led with that?"

Maddock could barely contain his ire. "So now *we're* compromised." He was starting to remember why he hated working with Zara Leopov.

"It's not as bad as it seems," Leopov said. "They know that I came here a couple hours ago, but that's all. They don't know you guys are here."

"They just saw me walk through the door." Maddock countered. "You should have waved me off."

Leopov shook her head. "No, listen. We can turn this against them." She held his gaze, a conspiratorial gleam appearing in her eyes. "I've got a plan."

FIVE

Despite his initial misgivings, Maddock had to admit that Leopov's plan was pretty good. While not as elaborate as their aborted plan to roll up the Rat in Bosnia, it relied on the same principle of misdirection and had a low probability of escalating into violence. This would be a stealth mission, relying on tradecraft not combat prowess. Shooting their way out of a bad situation simply wasn't an option. They didn't even dare carry weapons. If things went south, their only salvation would be to go full ghost-mode—disperse, disappear, and make their way to a friendly border.

They spent forty-five minutes going over the details, troubleshooting and working out contingencies, and then Maddock and Leopov left together to carry out their part of Lia's rescue. As they reached the street, Maddock quickly identified Leopov's watcher—a man sitting in an idle taxi cab parked half a block away. Maddock had noticed the cab on his initial approach but not realizing that Leopov was already the subject of surveillance, had dismissed it. The fact that it had not moved in at least an hour was more than a little suspicious. He considered approaching it and asking the driver to give them a ride, but decided that would just invite trouble. Instead, he pretended not to notice the taxi, and they continued on foot to the nearby Metro station.

As they walked, he easily spotted two more watchers—a pair of hulking men in slovenly track suits who looked enough alike to be twin brothers. Both were hyper-focused on Maddock and Leopov, and it was a challenge to avoid accidentally making eye contact with them. Their lack of subtlety surprised Maddock. "It's like they don't care if we know they're following us," he told Leopov as they waited on the platform.

"I noticed that. Maybe they're the ones we're supposed to see."

Maddock had considered that possibility but dismissed it. "I think we're dealing with amateurs here."

"Not FSB?"

"Hard to say. Who else might have an interest in this?"

"Possibly finding a fortune in Nazi loot? Who wouldn't?"

Maddock shrugged. "Well, it doesn't change what we have to do."

"Maybe makes it easier."

"Let's hope."

The train arrived a moment later and they boarded. The men in track suits got on as well. In what appeared to be an attempt at actual tradecraft, they entered the car through different doors, but once aboard, they resumed their flagrant vigil.

Maddock and Leopov rode the Green Line train a few stops to Tverskaya where they took the connecting underground tunnels to Pushkinskaya Station, and boarded a Purple Line train one more stop to Kuznetsky Most. Another underground tunnel brought them to Lubyanka Station where they emerged from the underground into the infamous Lubyanka Square.

During the Cold War, both the square and the station had been renamed for Bolshevik hero Felix Dzerzhinsky, founder of the *Cheka*, the original Soviet secret police agency. There was still a bust of "Iron" Felix in the vestibule of the station, but the statue in the square had been destroyed by protestors following the failed coup by hardliners to oust the Soviet premier Mikhail Gorbachev. In its place, a memorial had been erected to honor the victims of the notorious Gulag prison system. But even though the fall of the USSR had brought a measure of freedom to the Russian populace, the Lubyanka Building, the imposing yellow structure that had served as the headquarters of Dzerzhinsky's police agency under all its various names, remained under the control of its latest incarnation—the FSB.

He glanced over at Leopov, curious to see her reaction to this enduring symbol of the oppressive regime that had taken her father from her, and was surprised to see that her gaze was focused in the opposite direction, specifically at an even larger brick building which featured several high arches framing enormous banners showing children at play. She noticed his attention and threw him a wistful smile. "Is Detsky Mir," she said. "Is largest toy store in all of Russia."

Maddock did not fail to notice that her accent, normally all but undetectable, had thickened considerably.

"I think my parents brought me here when I was child," she added, and then shook her head as if the memory had slipped away. "Was long time ago. We should get moving."

She gestured to the south, where a brick pedestrian lane led away from the plaza. As they walked past storefronts Maddock surreptitiously checked their six o'clock in the window reflections, and wasn't at all surprised to see the two men in track suits trailing along. He was starting to reconsider Leopov's assertion that the men might be part of a larger surveillance team, and that their blatant obviousness was intentional, but for the moment, it suited his purpose to continue ignoring them.

They strolled at a leisurely pace down the lane until emerging in the vast open square around which several of Moscow's most iconic and historic structures stood. The Grand Kremlin Palace—a magnificent yellow structure topped with ornate arabesques, rising above the massive red brick wall that bordered the southwest side of Red Square. To their left, at the southeast corner, was an even more iconic symbol of Moscow. Saint Basil's Cathedral, with its multi-colored domes, looked a little like something built out of Christmas tree ornaments.

Maddock could not help but feel awed by his proximity to the buildings, which were not only monuments in their own right but symbols of Russia—symbols that, despite their beauty, had for most of his life represented the oppressive government of the USSR—the enemy of freedom.

They headed out across the square, orienting toward the low, ziggurat-like structure positioned in front of the Kremlin wall. While not as impressive as Saint Basil's Cathedral, the step pyramid, composed of blocks of a polished red granite-like stone called porphyry, marked the exact center of Moscow, and contained the embalmed remains of the first Soviet leader, Vladimir Lenin. There was an honor guard of soldiers stationed at the door of the monument, which was open to allow visitors to view the preserved cadaver. Maddock also spotted a few uniformed policemen amidst the small crowd of people milling about the plaza—mostly tourists, bundled up against the chilly weather, busily snapping pictures with disposable cameras. When they reached the middle of the square, Maddock turned a lazy circle, as if immersing himself in the panoramic experience.

"Looks like Tweedledee and Tweedledum are still with us," he murmured.

"What a surprise," Leopov replied. "Spot anyone else?"

"No. You?"

"No, but I do see our girl. Right where we told her to be."

Maddock followed her gaze to a spot near the north corner of the mausoleum where a lone female figure stood, bundled up in a fur-lined winter coat. Her features were partially concealed behind a scarf that was wrapped around her head and lower face, and a pair of sunglasses hid her eyes, but rather than throwing doubt on her identification, these measures confirmed it. In a phone call made from the safehouse, they had warned the woman to keep her face covered.

Maddock took a deep breath. "Okay. Then let's do this."

They made a beeline for the woman, striding purposefully, all the while aware that the men wearing track suits were matching their pace. Maddock kept his eyes on the policemen and the soldiers. He hoped their mere presence would keep the pursuers from doing anything outrageous, but he also knew that if the men tailing them were government agents, the police would either keep their distance, or take the side of the enemy.

As they got within a few yards of the woman, Leopov called out, "Lia!"

Uttering the name aloud was like pulling the trigger on a starter pistol. Maddock managed to take one more full step, but even as he set his foot down, he became aware of movement all around him. The rapidity of the response confirmed Leopov's suspicion that the pair he had dubbed Tweedledee and Tweedledum were only a small part of the surveillance effort. Six men—including the men in track suits— converged on them like warrior ants responding to an attack on the hive. The others wore belted leather jackets and trench coats, almost exactly like the KGB agents in the old spy films he had watched as a kid. Two of the men had pistols drawn, held low and mostly concealed from the view of passersby. The others moved in closer to physically restrain Maddock, Leopov, and the woman they had come to meet. Before Maddock or the others could respond to being accosted, one of the men advanced on the woman and roughly snatched her scarf away, knocking her sunglasses askew in the process.

"Hey!" she shouted angrily, as the unveiling released a cascade of brown ringlets. Her dark eyes shot an accusing glance at Maddock. The goons holding them had a similar reaction as they realized what Maddock already knew.

Although there was a passing resemblance to the

woman Maddock had seen in the photographs at the safehouse, this person was, without a doubt, not Lia Markova.

After Maddock and Leopov departed, the man in the off-duty taxi continued to watch the house from which they had emerged. His confederates would continue following the Americans, hopefully to where the Markova woman was hiding, but he had other business. He waited about ten minutes before getting out and heading to the front door of the residence. As he neared the door, he slipped his right hand into the deep pocket of his leather jacket and curled his fingers around the butt of a compact Makarov pistol. He was prepared to shoot through the pocket if circumstances dictated, but hoped it would not be necessary—it was his favorite jacket.

At the door, he checked for surveillance cameras, and seeing none, let go of the pistol and reached into a different pocket to produce a ring of keys. He shuffled through them until he found one that matched the profile of the lock, and then proceeded to insert it in the keyhole. They key was a cut down blank—called a "bump key"—and while it did not match the arrangement of the wafers inside the lock mechanism, it would, with just a little extra effort, permit him to enter.

With his left hand, he exerted pressure on the bow of the key, as if trying to turn it, and then delivered several solid raps with his right fist, all aimed at a spot right next to the latch, jostling the wafers inside the lock, causing them to jump up and down. After a few failed attempts, he chose a different key with the same profile and tried again, this time with more success. On the fourth such blow, the resistance from the lock vanished and the key turned smoothly.

He quickly put away the keys and drew the pistol, keeping it at the low ready as he eased the door open, though he doubted he would need it. If there was anyone inside, they would almost certainly have come to investigate all the racket he had raised with the bump key.

Unless of course they had known that someone was trying to break in, and were waiting to ambush him once he was inside.

As he entered, he brought the gun up, holding it out with both hands, shoulders squared and ready to fire.

The entry foyer was empty. He kept moving, the gun held steady, finger on the trigger, as he moved into the front room. There were two mugs on a table, both empty, but nothing else of note. He moved briskly through the house, checking each room, always leading with the pistol, even though each opened door confirmed his suspicion that the residence was unoccupied. When he cleared the last room, he took out his phone and dialed a number. When the connection was made, he reported that he had found nothing.

"Never mind that," came the answering voice at the other end. "They are walking toward Red Square. They may be planning to rendezvous with Markova in a public place, for all the good it will do them. Come here. Now. Hurry."

"*Da*. I'm on my way." The intruder thumbed off the phone and headed for the door.

In a small room concealed behind a false wall at the end of the hallway, Bones, Willis, and Professor watched the man's exit on a closed-circuit video monitor. As he got in the taxi and sped away, they breathed a collective sigh of relief. The search of the premises had been rushed and unprofessional. Not only had the intruder overlooked the secret room, but also the state of the art miniature cameras hidden inside and out.

"That was lucky," said Professor.

"Dude looked more like a bouncer at a strip club

than a spook," Willis remarked.

Bones nodded. "Hope he kept his day job."

"I think that would probably be his night job," Professor pointed out.

"Whatever. I'm just glad we don't have to hang out in here any longer." Bones pushed on the back of the false wall, carefully swiveling it out into the hallway of the residence. He stepped out and then stretched, tipping his head back and letting out a jaw-cracking yawn. "No offense, but you guys are a little ripe."

Professor wrinkled his forehead in dismay and self-consciously sniffed the air, casually lowering his nose toward his armpit. He shrugged. Willis just rolled his eyes.

Bones moved through the house to the front room and peeked out through the window even though the cameras had confirmed the intruder's departure. "Coast is clear," he announced. "We'd better get moving."

Professor lingered in the small room, watching his friends leave on the video monitor. When he was certain that no one had been left to maintain surveillance on the building, he shut off the equipment and restored the false wall to conceal the secret room, then headed out as well.

He did not immediately see Bones and Willis, but knew the route they were taking, and followed it until he spotted them, half a block away and moving north toward the Leningradsky Prospekt. His teammates were taller than he with longer strides, so he had to quicken his step to maintain the interval, but he had no intention of catching up to them.

Bones and Willis paused at the intersection, staring at something off to the left for several seconds before swinging to the right and heading down the avenue. The apparent object of their fascination came into Professor's view a moment later—an enormous geodesic sphere, easily sixty or seventy feet high, rising out of a ring-shaped foundation like a black bubble poised to lift off and escape into the heavens. They had passed it earlier on their approach to the safe house and Professor had subsequently learned that it housed the Sokol Tunnel Control Center, part of the Moscow Metro system. Composed of triangular panels of dark glass, Professor thought it looked like the compound eye of an insect, but Bones had dubbed it "the Mother of All Disco Balls." This time however, Bones and Willis hadn't really been looking at the Tunnel Control building.

Professor reached the same spot a few moments later and followed their example, facing the elaborate structure and, to all appearances, gawking at it like a tourist. From the corner of his eye however, he could make out the figure of a woman. That she was in fact female was not immediately obvious. Bundled up inside a soiled, castoff coat, her head and face were mostly hidden by a heavy scarf and a mangy fur ushanka hat. Professor only knew that this apparent homeless derelict was a woman because he had been told to meet her here.

"Did you see my friends?" he asked, speaking slow and enunciating carefully, even though he had been told that the woman understood English.

"Yes." The reply was a hoarse, tentative whisper.

"Hold out your hand as if you're asking me for money."

When she did, he turned to look at her, seeing her clearly for the first time, but still barely recognizing her as the same woman he had seen photographs of less than an hour ago. He reached into his pocket, took out a wad of ruble notes, along with a Metro card, and placed them in her outstretched hand. "Go after my friends. Keep close, but not too close. They're going to the Metro station. Get on the same train they do. I'll be keeping watch from behind. Got it?"

"Yes." Her voice was even more fearful now.

Professor forced himself to look away. For her sake, he had to treat her like an annoying beggar, ruining his sightseeing vacation. Still, he couldn't leave her without at least a few words of assurance.

"We're going to get you to safety, Lia. Everything is going to be okay."

SIX

Maddock yanked his arm free of his captor, and snarled, "Hey, hands off."

Dumbfounded, the man—the one he'd dubbed Tweedledum—made no attempt to hold him. He, like the rest of the group that had descended upon them, appeared to be in a general state of confusion after being thrown this curve ball. They had clearly been expecting to round up Lia Markova and the Americans who were coming to her rescue, but this woman was not Markova, which meant they had seriously screwed up.

Maddock's outrage was mostly play-acting, and far more restrained than the situation might otherwise have warranted. He needed to make a scene, but not too big a scene. Just enough to convince their assailants to make a hasty retreat.

The reaction of Lia's double was neither a performance, nor understated, not surprising since she had no idea what was really going on. The woman, a high-priced escort who catered to wealthy foreign visitors, had no idea of the role Maddock and Leopov had cast her in; she had merely been told to rendezvous with an adventurous American couple in front of Lenin's tomb, and then to give them the VIP treatment. Now, seeing a small fortune about to slip away, she rounded on the man who had accosted her, and unleashed a torrent of Russian invective, shaking her finger in his face threateningly, driving him back a step with the mere force of her wrath.

The unfolding incident had already attracted the attention of a pair of nearby policemen who were regarding the scene with increasing curiosity. It was only a matter of time before they decided to intervene.

Leopov stepped forward, arms raised placatingly,

and spoke in Russian. Maddock didn't understand a word of it, but if she was sticking to the script, she was giving them a version of the same story they'd given the decoy, deferring to the men as if they were vice cops, explaining to them that it was all a misunderstanding. Prostitution was illegal in Russia, but enforcement was haphazard at best, and the police, more often than not, were more interested in receiving bribes than taking anyone into custody. Of course, these men weren't vice cops, but Leopov's explanation would give everyone a chance to simply walk away.

It almost worked.

One of the men—an oily character in a long leather jacket—barked an order, silencing both Leopov and the decoy, and then reached into a pocket and took out his mobile phone. As he looked away to begin punching in a number, Maddock gave the others a big friendly grin.

"Is this a problem?" he whispered through his teeth.

"Could be," Leopov said through her own big smile.

"Crap. Plan B?"

Leopov gave an almost imperceptible nod. "Think so."

"Crap," Maddock muttered again.

Plan B—which barely met the dictionary definition of a "plan"—was to split up, run like hell, and rendezvous at an easy-to-find public location.

The man held the phone to his ear and returned his attention to his captives. His dull black eyes radiated menace.

"Ready?" Maddock asked.

"Ready," replied Leopov.

Maddock casually repositioned his feet, sliding his right leg back. "Set?"

"Mmhmm."

As the Russian opened his mouth to speak, Maddock shouted, "Go!" and burst into motion, charging the man with the phone and slamming into him before any of their assailants knew what was happening. The Russian was knocked backward, off his feet, the phone flying from his grasp. Maddock used the impact to redirect his momentum, veering to the left, heading back toward the northwest entrance to the square. Leopov was half a step behind him, slipping through the opening he had created, but pivoting in the opposite direction, toward St. Basil's.

Maddock sprinted flat out for fifty meters, shouting for people in his way to move. He did not once look back to see if he was being pursued—he assumed he was—or to check on Leopov. There was nothing he could do to help her, except maybe draw off some of the pursuit. With her intimate knowledge of the city, she stood a far better chance of slipping the net than he did.

His own unfamiliarity prompted him to stick to what he knew. He'd reviewed a map of the area around the Kremlin, but map recon was no substitute for a walkthrough, so his part of Plan B relied on the KISS—Keep It Simple, Stupid—principle. He backtracked the narrow street they'd come down earlier. As the blocky yellow Lubyanka building came into view, it occurred to him that he was literally running toward FSB headquarters.

He rounded the corner, taking a hard right to head southeast, and risked a quick glance back, immediately spotting Tweedledee and Tweedledum. They were at least thirty yards behind him, and flagging from the exertion. Outrunning them wouldn't be a problem. There was no sign of the other men who had accosted them; he hoped they hadn't all gone after Leopov.

He set his sights on a distant but distinctive landmark, a tall building to the southeast that looked, from a distance at least, like a church spire, but instead of a cross, the structure was topped with a star and wreath, a symbol of the old Soviet era in which it had been built. Maddock had no intention of running all the way to it—it was more than a mile away—but in the unfamiliar city, it was an easily spotted reference point. After a couple hundred yards, the street took a slight bend to the south and he lost sight of the tower, but now he could make out his actual destination, a sprawling rectangular building that occupied at least two city blocks and rose to a uniform height of at least a dozen stories. Just visible from ground level, rising up from the center of the massive structure, was a smaller tower, emblazoned with enormous Cyrillic letters that identified it as the Hotel Rossiya. It looked more like a massive walled fortress with an inner castle keep than a five-star lodging, and indeed, for most of its storied history, it had held the world record for largest hotel, supplanted only by the Excalibur Hotel and Casino in Las Vegas.

The Rossiya was not Maddock's ultimate destination either, but another easily found reference point and the ideal location for him to rendezvous with Leopov. Her escape route, as earlier agreed upon, had been more circuitous owing to her familiarity with the city, but if she had not been caught by her pursuers, she would be waiting for him at the southwest corner of the hotel, near the Bolshoy Moskvoretsky Bridge which spanned the Moskva River.

If she had not been caught.

He glanced over his shoulder again. If Tweedledee and Tweedledum were still on his trail, they had fallen so far behind that he couldn't see them any longer. That was a hopeful sign and he slowed his pace to a jog as he moved down the sidewalk to the east of the hotel.

"Dane!"

It was Leopov, but her shout had come from behind him.

That wasn't a hopeful sign.

He turned and wasn't at all surprised to find her running toward him at a full sprint, with a trio of men chasing after her. As their eyes met, she made a frantic chopping gesture, and shouted, "Go! Go!"

So much for Plan B, he thought.

He quickened his step, gradually at first, then when she started to overtake him, matching her pace.

"Couldn't shake 'em," she gasped, panting for breath. He surmised she had been running without let up the whole time.

"I guess we should have come up with Plan C," he replied.

"I have. You're not gonna like it though."

Same old Zara, he thought, frowning.

She veered toward a small wooded area at the hotel's corner and ventured inside. The trees offered some concealment from the pursuers, but Leopov did not leave the path, and a few seconds later, they emerged onto the sidewalk that ran along the front of the hotel. Directly before them was a six-lane street on which cars zoomed by recklessly, and beyond that, the Moskva River. Maddock pulled a step, waiting to see which way Leopov would turn, but she didn't, nor did she slow down. Instead, she charged headlong into traffic.

"Damn it!" rasped Maddock, hurrying to catch up to her.

The air was suddenly filled with the squeal of brakes locking, tires skidding, and horns blasting out in irritation. Maddock winced at the crunch of a collision from somewhere off to his left. Directly ahead, in the innermost westbound lane, the driver of a yellow taxi stomped on the brakes, screeching to a stop, but was half a second too slow. Maddock and Leopov both veered to the right, trying to avoid being struck, but Leopov was likewise too slow. At the last instant, she threw herself onto the hood of the car to avoid having her legs cut out from under her. She hit with a thump and rolled up onto the windshield, but then promptly rolled back down to land on her feet beside the car, evidently unhurt, and kept going.

By some miracle, they made it across the eastbound lanes without getting killed, but the disruption of traffic cleared a path for their pursuers. As they reached the broad concrete sidewalk overlooking the river, Leopov cut to the right, heading west. As Maddock started to follow, he felt a sudden pressure at his throat, as if someone was trying to garotte him. One of their pursuers had gotten close enough to snare his shirt, pulling the collar tight against his Adam's apple. Reflexively, Maddock clawed at the constriction and succeeded in getting his fingers in between his neck and the fabric, but even as he tried to get some breathing room, his attacker pulled again, with enough force to nearly yank Maddock off his feet. Unable to break free or tear loose, Maddock did the only thing he could think of—he planted his feet, skidding to a stop, and then hurled himself blindly backwards. The pressure at his throat vanished immediately, but the relief was short-lived as the back of his head struck something hard and sharp. He pitched back, mentally bracing for a hard landing, but something broke his fall—or rather, someone. He crashed down on top of his assailant, who was likewise supine, with sufficient force to knock the wind out of the man.

Maddock capitalized on the momentum of the fall by throwing his legs into the air and curling into a reverse somersault that rolled him over the stunned attacker's head. He finished in a crouch, and immediately spotted Leopov, about twenty-five yards ahead, still running, one of their pursuers still hot on her tail.

It took him just a fraction of a second to do the math. There had been three men chasing them. One was writhing on the ground in front of him, blood smearing his face where the back of Maddock's head had smacked hard into his mouth and nose. Another was chasing Leopov. So where was Number Three?

Sensing his vulnerability, he ducked his head, and was just about to roll to the side when the blow fell. Something hard and heavy—a weighted sap or the butt of a pistol—swiped across the back of his head. Ducking spared him the full fury of the impact, but he nevertheless saw stars for a second or two. He managed to complete his intended evasive maneuver, and as he rolled, he saw a hulking leather-jacketed figure moving in for another attack.

Maddock rolled again, almost all the way to the waist-high concrete guard rail on the river side. Ignoring the pain, he bounded up and squared off against the Russian just as the man drew back to deliver another blow. This time, Maddock was ready for him. He easily evaded the swipe, and then seized the man's arm as it flashed past, using a simple Judo maneuver to redirect the man into the guard rail, flipping him over it and out into the river. Maddock continued turning until he was facing west again and took off after Leopov and her pursuer.

She was a good fifty yards away now, and despite the fact that he was a faster runner, he knew there was no way he would be able to reach her before her pursuer did. Still, he had to try. He dug deep and pushed as hard as he could. He could feel the burn of lactic acid in his muscles and the ache of repetitive impact vibrating up from the soles of his feet to his shins to his knees.

But it was working. He closed to within twenty yards… Fifteen….

Ten yards ahead, he saw Leopov's pursuer reaching out to snare her ponytail. Maddock tried to shout a warning, but his heaving lungs couldn't supply enough breath for more than a barely audible croak.

The man's fingers closed on her hair and he started to pull.

Leopov skidded to a dead stop, and then pirouetted in closer to her assailant, her left knee coming up fast, right into the man's crotch.

Maddock winced involuntarily as the Russian dropped to his knees, curling into a pathetic ball.

So much for rushing to save the damsel in distress, he thought.

Leopov spotted him and flashed a triumphant grin. "What are you waiting for?" she shouted, and then turned and started running again.

Maddock slowed to a more sustainable pace, catching up to her a few seconds later. "What's your hurry?" he panted. "We lost them."

She glanced over, grinning. "Plan C, remember?" The words came out in gasps; she was clearly feeling the exertion, too.

"I thought running into traffic *was* Plan C."

"Just part," was her cryptic reply as they passed under the pink granite arch of the Bolshoy Moskvoretsky Bridge, their original rally point. Before he could challenge her, she veered toward the guard rail and, slowing to a walking pace, peered over the edge as if looking for something in the water. "Here! This is the place," she called out, and then proceeded to climb onto the guard rail.

Maddock stopped beside her. "Zara, what are you doing?"

"Getting wet," she said with a laugh. "I told you you wouldn't like it."

"This was your plan? Swim across the river? You don't think you could have at least mentioned what you had in mind?"

"Why do you complain? I thought you SEALs preferred to be in the water."

"Yeah, actually I've been thinking about a career change. Besides, there's a perfectly good bridge right there."

"Well, you don't have to worry. We are not swimming across river." She swung her legs out over the water, scooting closer to the edge in preparation to lower herself down. Directly below, the concrete-reinforced river channel sloped away to disappear beneath the dark surface, but a few paces to the right, there was an opening in the embankment wall—a culvert or possibly the outflow to a storm drainage system. The opening was at least twelve feet in diameter, all but three feet of it above the water level. A steel gate secured with a padlock blocked access to it.

Leopov pushed off, sliding down the curving wall to splash into the shallows at the edge of the embankment. Then, using the gate like a ladder, she pulled herself up to grab ahold of the padlock. To Maddock's surprise, it was already unlocked. Leopov then grasped the gate and awkwardly began pulling it away from the opening.

"I could use a hand," she grunted.

Still shaking his head, Maddock clambered over the guard rail and allowed himself to slide down to join her. The chilly water instantly soaked through his jeans and filled his hiking boots. The slope of the embankment made it difficult to get a good foothold, which was probably why Leopov was having difficulty opening the gate, and as Maddock tried to move closer, his feet slipped out from under him. He barely managed to grab one of the vertical bars of the gate, preventing himself from being fully immersed. As he steadied himself, he muttered, "I don't even want to think about what's in this water."

"No, you probably don't," agreed Leopov.

Working together, they succeeded in opening the gate enough for Leopov to slip through. Once inside, she stood without difficulty in the knee-high water. As Maddock squirmed through the opening, a small flashlight blazed to life in Leopov's hand.

"I see one of us came prepared for crawling around in the sewers," he remarked. "Would have been nice if you'd given me a head's up in advance."

"You should always be prepared," she replied, grinning. "Is Boy Scout motto. You were a Boy Scout, weren't you?"

Maddock scowled but didn't answer.

She laughed. "And this is not sewer. It's the *Niglinka*… The Neglinnaya River." She pointed the flashlight deeper into the tunnel and started walking, moving slowly to avoid unnecessary splashing. "As city grew," she went on, "the river was dammed up, and diverted through these tunnels. Now is completely underground—five miles long. Is part of flood control system and even connects to Metro tunnels."

"Is this where Lia was hiding?"

"Not here precisely, but we can get there from here. There is a whole secret city down here. There is a local group of urban cave explorers—they call themselves 'the Diggers.' I have been exploring the underground with them for a few months."

Maddock gave a grunt of acknowledgement. He was still irritated with her for not explaining this part of her plan, but complaining about it wouldn't accomplish anything. "They must have seen us go in here. Do you think they'll come after us?"

"I doubt it," she replied. "But I'm sure they'll be covering the exits. They were more resourceful than we anticipated."

"Guess I was wrong about them being amateurs."

"Yes. They didn't seem to want to involve the police, though. I think maybe they are Bratva... Russian mafia."

Maddock had heard stories about the rise of organized crime gangs in Russia. Although they had always existed, they had flourished since the collapse of the rigidly authoritarian Soviet government. Their reputation for ruthlessness and brutality put the Sicilian Mafia to shame.

"Fortunately," Leopov continued, "we won't be leaving by any of those exits."

Beyond the opening, the river channel was confined to a deep trough running down the center, and to either side, raised platforms allowed them to pass through without wading. The air smelled foul—a mixture of stagnant water and mildew—but after a few minutes, Maddock grew accustomed to the stench. As they continued in silence, he saw that a variety of architectural techniques had been employed in creating the underground river channel. Some sections looked ancient, consisting of fired clay bricks, joined with mortar to form a continuous arch like the inside of an enormous pipe. In some places, the brick had decayed so badly, the passage looked more like a natural cavern than the product of human ingenuity. Other sections were constructed of concrete slabs, and eschewed the round tunnel design in favor of square angles. Several times they passed graffiti, and Leopov always stopped to examine the scrawls, as if they might contain information about what lay ahead. Then she would resume walking without offering any explanation. Once or twice, he thought he glimpsed movement in the darkness ahead. If the Moscow Underground really was like a second city, then it only stood to reason that it would be inhabited, probably by people who preferred to be left alone.

Three times they came to junctions, and each time she paused, scrutinizing the passages as if checking them against her mental map. Maddock watched her face in the diffuse glow of the flashlight, and noted that she didn't look particularly confident about her eventual choices, but thought better of second-guessing her. He was keeping his own mental map, and if they had to backtrack, he felt reasonably sure he could get them back to the entrance.

A few minutes later, they passed an iron ladder affixed to the wall, rising up to disappear into a narrow vertical shaft. Leopov shone her light up into the shaft for a moment, then gave a satisfied nod. "We are in right place."

Maddock expected her to start ascending, but instead she kept going. He quickened his step to catch up to her. "Was that one of the exits you were talking about?"

"No. Just a manhole cover. I don't think we want to pop our heads up in the middle of Kutuzovsky Prospekt. What we want is just ahead."

As promised, about fifty yards further up the passage, they came to a section of the tunnel where the wall had crumbled away, exposing a hole just big enough to crawl through. Maddock pointed at it. "That's how we're getting out of here?"

"Don't worry. We only have to crawl a little ways."

Maddock rolled his eyes. "Sure. Why not?"

Leopov just laughed and then began insinuating herself into the hole. With her body mostly filling the hole and blocking the flashlight's beam, Maddock was plunged into darkness, but after a few seconds, diffuse light glowed in the passage, silhouetted around

Leopov's crawling form. "Come on," she called out, her voice muted. "What are you waiting for?"

Resignedly, Maddock squirmed into the hole. There wasn't quite enough room for him to move on hands and knees, so instead he had to lie flat and low crawl, propelling himself forward with his feet. The passage wasn't solid stone or concrete, but compacted dirt. It was dry and appeared stable enough, but he was acutely aware of the close confines and the fact that there were literally many tons of earth suspended above him, held up by little more than inertia. He didn't want to linger in the crawlspace any longer than he had to. After about five yards of crawling toward the light, he felt the ground beneath him began sloping down. The grade continued to decline until it was all he could do to keep from sliding down the rough surface. The passage still looked dry, but he could feel dampness seeping into the fabric of his trousers. He estimated they had descended a good thirty feet, possibly more—well below the level of the river.

"You do know where we're going, right?" he shouted down the passage.

Her reply was barely audible, as if she was speaking from inside a crypt. "Yes. I have been here before."

The answer fell short of encouraging, but shortly thereafter, the passage leveled out again and then opened up into a much larger tunnel. As Maddock got to his feet, making a futile effort to brush away the accumulation of mud and grime, he spotted parallel iron rails, corroded with age and disuse, resting atop black wooden ties.

"A subway tunnel?" he wondered aloud.

"Yes," Leopov confirmed. "This was the D-6 Line, part of Metro Two. A secret underground train system that runs deeper than the Metro. It was built by KGB… Commissioned by Stalin during the Cold War. It connects government offices all over Moscow. It was to be used for emergency evacuation of government leaders in the event of a nuclear war."

"Was? As in not anymore?"

Leopov shook her head. "It was too costly to operate and maintain, especially as a secret program." She shone her light down the passage to their immediate left, revealing the track bed. The roughly excavated tunnel was braced with badly corroded iron support beams. "Come. We go this way."

She started off at a brisk walk, staying between the rails. Maddock followed, albeit a little more tentatively. The wooden crossties felt mushy underfoot, so he made a conscious effort to tread on the gravel in the space between them. He soon found his stride and increased his pace, catching up to Leopov.

They moved in silence for several minutes until the tunnel opened up into a larger area. Leopov played her light back and forth, revealing a raised loading platform. A skeletal iron stairwell ascended at the back of the platform, presumably leading up to the sub-basement of some Soviet-era government office building. Maddock was about to ask where it led when he glimpsed movement at the edge of the area illuminated by the flashlight

Leopov recoiled involuntarily, jerking the light sideways, revealing more scuttering shapes.

"Oh," she groaned. "Rats."

Maddock grimaced. Under ordinary circumstances, he liked rats about as much as the next person, which was to say, not at all, but he wasn't particularly afraid of them. Like most wild or feral animals, they preferred to run away from humans, attacking only when cornered or driven mad by hunger or disease. The biggest rodent-related threat was from diseases like plague and hanta virus. But down here, a hundred or more feet below the city streets, his apprehension grew exponentially. This was their world.

"You said you've been here before," Maddock said. "You didn't mention anything about rats."

"I didn't come this far."

"Are you actually sure you know where we're going?"

"The Metro Two tunnels all converge at Ramenki-43. It is a bunker the size of a city, modeled after the NORAD headquarters at Cheyenne Mountain. They built it to survive a direct hit by atom bomb. The walls are steel, several feet thick, and there are big doors like at Fort Knox. In the event of a nuclear attack, they could have sealed it up and survived for years. That was the plan, at least. There is only one entrance above ground, under Moscow University. If we are where I think we are, it should be just another mile or so."

"And we'll be able to get back to the surface?"

Leopov's nod was less than enthusiastic. "Some of the Diggers claim to have entered through the main entrance. I don't know exactly where it is, but it should be easy to find from inside the bunker."

Maddock uttered a weary sigh. "We should keep moving," he said.

She nodded, but he could see that the unexpected encounter had left her rattled. She turned the light back into the subway tunnel and resumed moving, but after just a second or two, she abruptly pivoted and shone it back onto the platform.

The circle of light revealed hundreds of scurrying shapes.

"Maddock…" Leopov's voice quavered with fear.

"Keep going," he urged. He placed his hand against the small of her back and gave her a gentle but firm push to keep her moving. She complied, but he could feel the tension in her body, vibrating in her muscles like an electric current.

"They'll leave us alone," he assured her, adding silently, *I hope.*

But as they moved further along the tunnel, leaving the rudimentary subway station behind, the rats were always there, just beyond the reach of the light and with each subsequent encounter, the creatures seemed to lose a little bit more of their fear of the strange intruders in their subterranean realm. A few refused to flee when the light revealed them but held their ground, staring back with their eerie pink eyes, noses twitching above long yellow incisors, moving only when Maddock aggressively stomped his foot at them.

Leopov made another abrupt turn to check behind them, and this time the light revealed a river of gray furred bodies flowing up the track bed between and to either side of the rails. They did not flee the light either, but continued with their slow, relentless advance. Leopov turned again, bringing the light forward. The swarm was moving in from all sides.

Maddock lashed out with his foot, catching the nearest rat with his toe and punting it into the darkness. The suddenness of the move startled several of the creature's brethren who scampered away, momentarily opening a gap in the squirming mass, but Maddock knew it wouldn't last long.

"Zara! Run!"

He didn't wait to see if she would take the hint, but charged down the tunnel, kicking his feet out ahead of him with every stride. Squealing rats flew through the air ahead of him. Their cries and chittering filling the tunnel with an ungodly tumult. He could feel claws scrabbling against his pants legs and teeth slashing at the leather uppers of his boots. Worse, even though they offered little resistance individually, their combined mass felt like running through ankle deep mud; with each step he had to correct his balance or risk taking a nose dive into the swarm. After about fifty yards, the mass of rats through which he was plowing thinned out a bit, allowing him to run unhindered, but judging from the noise level, the surge from behind was only growing, and reinforcements were emerging from the shadows to either side. The rats were in a frenzy now. Nothing would dissuade them. Their only hope was to stay ahead of the horde until they could reach the surface again. He took some comfort from the fact that the light level around him remained more or less constant—Leopov was keeping up—but if she was wrong about there being a way out at the end of the line, they were screwed.

She wasn't wrong about the bunker.

About five hundred yards further along, they entered a section of tunnel where the walls were sheathed in thick plates of steel, which formed a narrow collar, just big enough to allow a train car to pass through. The collar supported one of the vault doors Leopov had described.

"Crap!" Maddock rasped when he saw it.

The door was closed.

SEVEN

As he moved down the platform, Bones caught the eye of a loitering policeman. The man did a doubletake, his eyes flitting back and forth between Bones and Willis. Bones flashed a big grin and kept walking.

"That's right, assclown," he muttered. "Just keep looking at the freakshow."

"Freakshow?" Willis retorted. "Speak for yourself. My man is clearly in awe."

"Ha. He's a cop, and you're black. Think about it."

The police officer continued to scrutinize the pair, as if trying to decide whether their mere presence constituted a violation of the law. But then his gaze slid away from them both, fixing instead on something behind them.

Bones groaned, knowing without looking what had arrested the man's attention. If there was one thing in the Leningradsky train station more conspicuous than a six-foot-five Cherokee and his equally tall and broad African-American traveling companion, it was the mangy-looking ragamuffin trailing fifty steps behind them.

Bones risked a quick glance back, just as a panicked Lia executed a hasty about face and began hastening back toward the exit.

"Damn it," Bones murmured. "Nothing suspicious about that."

Professor, who had been trailing a few steps behind her, shrugged helplessly, a silent question in his eyes: *What should I do?*

Bones swung back to the policeman again, but the man's attention was now laser focused on Lia. After only a brief moment of indecision, the cop lurched into motion, striding purposefully after her. He brushed between Bones and Willis without even giving them another glance.

Bones didn't know if the man had recognized her as a wanted fugitive—was she?—or if he was merely responding to her guilty retreat. Either way, it was a serious monkey wrench in the works.

"We need to distract that guy," he said, turning to Willis. "Hit me."

Willis, who was watching the cop move away, was slow to process the odd request. "What?"

"Hit me. We'll fake a fight. He'll have to come back and break it up."

"And we'll end up in jail." Willis shook his head. "I don't think so."

"Well, we've got to do something." He made a full turn, searching the platform for something he could use to create a diversion, but every idea he came up with ended the same way—with him or Willis or both of them getting arrested for disorderly conduct. "I'd kill for a gorilla suit right now," he muttered. "What if we—"

Before he could complete the thought, a loud, booming voice filled the air.

"Oh, say can you see…"

Bones slowly turned toward the source. Willis, his head thrown back, eyes gazing up at the high canopy above the platform, drew the last note out longer than should have been humanly possible, and then, without pausing to take breath, continued in the same smooth baritone. "By the dawn's early light…"

All over the platform, heads were turning in his direction. The policeman looked too, but after a moment, appeared to lose interest.

Bones quickly added his voice and, what he lacked in perfect pitch and rhythm, he made up for in sheer volume. "What so proudly we hailed at the twilight's last gleaming?"

Nearly everyone on the platform had stopped to look and listen. A few—probably American tourists—had their hands over their hearts, evidently moved at this impromptu display of patriotism in the heart of the capital of America's longtime political rival.

The policeman stopped again, turned and took another look at the two men. His eyes narrowed with naked suspicion.

Uh. oh. Bones thought. *Looks like this might get us arrested, too.*

Willis launched into the next line, "Whose broad stripes and bright stars," but Bones skipped ahead, turning the volume up to eleven to drown his friend out.

"And the rocket's red glare…" His voice cracked on the high note, eliciting a wince from several onlookers. He stopped singing and faced Willis with an accusing look. "Dude, you totally screwed it up."

Willis gaped at him. "Man, are you kidding me? *I* screwed up?"

"It's okay. You can't be good at everything. Stick to things your people are best at. Basketball. And dancing."

"My people?" Willis' deep voice rose an octave and his massive hands curled into fists at his sides, but there was a knowing gleam in his eye.

In his peripheral vision, Bones could see both amusement and bemusement on the faces of the gathered onlookers, but more importantly, he saw that the police officer was still staring at them. Further down the platform, Lia had reached the exit and, a moment later, had disappeared from view. Professor was right behind her.

Bones threw up his hands in a gesture of surrender. "Hey, it's all good," he said. "Remember, the white man is the real enemy."

Willis grinned. "True that." He extended his right hand. "Truce?"

Bones made a big show of accepting the handclasp, and then pivoted, curled one beefy arm around Willis' shoulders, and threw his head back to resume singing. "O'er the land of the freeeeee…"

Willis joined in for the big finish. "And the home… Of the… Brave!"

The policeman frowned, shook his head, and then, evidently remembering his original purpose, turned away, but he was too late. Lia was gone.

"Play ball," Bones muttered.

A second look revealed that Maddock's first impression had been only partially right. The subway tunnel was indeed blocked by the massive vault-style door, but the door was not completely closed. Rather, it had been left slightly ajar.

Maddock kept running toward it, slowing only when he was close enough to see the gap between the inside edge of the door and the steel frame. Four or five inches. Just enough to let air flow between the tunnel and the bunker beyond.

He gripped the door in both hands, braced his left foot against the doorpost, and pulled with all his might but to no avail. The foot-thick steel door didn't budge an inch.

He tried again, straining until he thought his tendons would snap, but the heavy door refused to move. Like similar doors in bank vaults, its movement was controlled by a powerful hydraulic system—a system that had probably not been activated in decades, if it had not been removed altogether.

Behind him, the noise of the approaching rats had reached a fever pitch, filling the air with a sound like white noise.

"Try to squeeze through!"

Leopov's reply was barely audible over the din. "I won't fit."

Maddock knew he certainly wouldn't be able to scrape through the gap, but Zara was smaller and might have a chance. "Try anyway!" he ordered.

She ducked under his outstretched arms and insinuated her left arm into the narrow opening all the way to her shoulder. That was as far as she could go. Maddock tried a third time, but the door was as immovable as a mountain.

Something brushed against the back of his leg. He looked down to find half a dozen rats trying to ascend his pant leg, their little claws scrabbling for purchase on the fabric, He shook his foot, dislodging a few of them, but even as they fell away, more rushed forward to take their place. Maddock left off his futile attempt to open the bunker door, planted both feet on the ground, and began tearing the rats loose, flinging them into the darkness and kicking at any who tried to get close. Fifty yards further back, the main body of the swarm was continuing its relentless advance, rolling forward like a tsunami made of teeth.

He looked around, desperate to find a solution—a ladder that would allow them to climb above the ravenous creatures, a tool or even a piece of metal that would help him pry the door open just a few more inches, but there was only the door, the steel-clad walls, and rusty, disused subway tracks.

Maddock stared at the rails for a moment, then knelt down to get a closer look. As he had earlier noted, the crossties were rotted and spongy, compressing under the weight of the heavy steel. The tracks disappeared under the vault door but he followed them back until he found the joint connecting two sections of track. He curled his hands around the top of the rail just past the joint and tried to lift it.

Amazingly, he succeeded. It was heavy, much heavier than he had expected, the steel flexing under its own weight so that he was only able to raise one end of the long metal I-beam a few inches off the ground, but it was something.

"Zara! Give me a hand here!"

Leopov, who was busy kicking away rats, did not look back. "What?"

"I'm going to use this as a lever. Maybe pry the door open a little wider."

"Will that work?"

"Have you got a better idea?" he snapped. "Come on."

He didn't wait for her to respond, but bent his

knees and lifted the rail again, this time pulling it along as he shuffled toward the door. The rail, which was about thirty yards long, must have weighed at least a ton, but it nevertheless yielded to his efforts, sliding an inch, then another… And then Leopov was there, adding her modest strength to his. The rail slid nearly eighteen inches before Leopov lost her grip. The sudden shift caused Maddock to lose his hold as well, but the minor success had buoyed his mood.

"Good!" Maddock shouted. "It's working. Again."

Working together, they shifted the rail three feet on the next try. When it fell from Maddock's fatigued grip, it was almost touching the door.

"One more time."

This time, when he lifted the rail, Maddock pushed it sideways, lining it up with the narrow gap. "Now. Push!"

The rail slid into the gap so quickly that Maddock had to let go to avoid losing his fingers. Without his hold, Leopov couldn't hold the rail up, and it clattered noisily to the ground. She uttered an oath in Russian, cradling her hands together as if to soothe an injury, but there was no time for recriminations or apologies. The swarm was almost upon them.

"Hold them off!" Maddock shouted as he ran down the length of the rail, kicking rats away with every step. When he reached the distant end of the rail, he bent to lift it and shoved a few more inches into the gap. It was harder without Leopov's help but he did not ask for assistance; he needed her to keep the rats at bay just a few more seconds.

When he finally had the rail inserted about halfway through the gap, he changed position and began pushing sideways, pressing the rail into the vault door. He had no idea if it was even possible to move the door—it wasn't inconceivable that the hinges were frozen with rust—but this was his Hail Mary play. If it didn't work, they were toast.

But it did work. After a few seconds of pushing with all his might, he felt the door giving way, ever so slightly. The gap was now an inch wider.

He tried again and this time the door moved another two inches. But the rats were upon him, swarming up his pant legs and, seemingly in defiance of gravity, scurrying up the length of track toward his hands. He let it fall, hoping it was enough, and started kicking away as many rats as he could. "Zara. Try it now."

Leopov didn't need to be told twice. With a final kick that launched a rat into the darkness, she spun around and raced for the door, slowing only when she reached the gap. This time, she didn't just put her arm through the opening, but a leg as well, and then, with only a slight effort, she squirmed the rest of the way through, vanishing from view and leaving Maddock in near total darkness.

Maddock was right behind her. He stuck his left arm through, but then felt resistance as the hard edge of the door frame dug into his chest, stopping him cold.

He grunted in surprise and dismay, wondering how Leopov, with her additional up-front endowments, had made it through where he could not. Then he felt something stab into his calf, and after shaking his leg to dislodge the rat, he pushed harder, scraping through as he forced himself deeper into the opening.

There was a tearing sound and then the resistance vanished as his shirt tore apart. He spilled forward, bare-chested, practically landing in Leopov's arms.

He had just a moment to take in his new surroundings. The rails continued through what looked like a station or transit hub, with an elevated platform and an opening in the wall that looked remarkably like an oversized hatchway on a ship or submarine. The hatch cover—a large square with rounded corners and a wheel-operated latch mounted in the center—had come off its hinges and lay flat on the platform. The tunnel continued on into the darkness, beyond the reach of Leopov's light. In the darkness behind him, he could hear the squealing of rats as they clawed over one another in their frenzy to get through the gap and reach fresh meat.

Leopov was shouting, urging him to keep moving. Maddock recalled reading that rats could squeeze through holes the size of a quarter. With the vault door forced open about eight inches, there was plenty of room for the flood of rodents to pour through. Scores of them were getting through with each passing second, and they did not seem inclined to wait for the others.

Maddock got his feet under him and followed her, sprinting toward the raised platform.

The exit from the platform fed into a small room-sized chamber. The concrete walls were covered in peeling green-gray paint. There was another hatchway at the opposite end, and another door off its hinges, tilted up against the wall. They hurried through it and into a long, litter-strewn tunnel that led to yet another hatchway with the door removed.

"I'm sensing a theme here," Maddock observed. The hatch doors, while not as large as the one that had' blocked the subway tunnel, nevertheless looked solid and quite heavy. Maddock guessed their original purpose had been to seal off sections of the bunker from contamination, but that didn't shed any light on the mystery of who had removed them or why.

Leopov, breathless from the run, nodded but said nothing.

The tunnel ended at the foot of an ascending staircase—concrete steps with rusted metal handrails to either side. Maddock bounded up, taking two steps at a time, and as he rounded the corner onto a midway landing a few seconds ahead of Leopov, he glanced back the way they'd come. The narrow stairwell was filled with squeals and the tap-tapping of tiny claws on concrete. A hundred pairs of pink eyes gleamed up at him as the rats scrambled up the steps.

The stairs ended at another open hatchway. Beyond it was a transverse passage that presented them with their first decision. Maddock chose left, fully aware of the fact that a dead end might mean a literal dead end. The passage continued uninterrupted for several hundred feet before branching again, this time at a four-way intersection. Maddock chose left again, but after about fifty feet they began to pass regular-sized doorways to either side. Most were open for inspection, but Maddock knew they didn't have time for exploration and doubted there would be anything of value—practical or otherwise—contained within. But there was something familiar about the doors and their spacing, and as they reached a corner—another left turn—Maddock realized what it was. The bunker's floorplan reminded him of naval vessels he'd served on. This was important because it meant there would be an internal, utilitarian logic to the layout. Like a big ship, the bunker had been designed to accommodate a large population—perhaps hundreds or even thousands of people—and to facilitate their movements throughout its interior.

If he was right, the corridor would make another left turn, and then another, describing an enormous square, to bring them back to where they had started. But there would be at least one or two stairwells positioned equidistantly throughout the square to provide access to the upper level.

The turns were exactly where he thought they would be. So was the ascending stairwell, but Maddock did not allow himself to breathe easy. There was still a lot that could go wrong. The stairwell might not go anywhere, or might lead them into a hopeless maze of corridors and passages. And the rats were still coming. Worse, their ranks were growing, supplemented by members of a rodent colony that had infiltrated the bunker. Hundreds more poured out of the open doorways on each landing they came to, drawn to the tumult of the swarm and the echo of their footsteps.

They climbed three flights before running out of stairs. Maddock's heart stuttered as he saw that the doorway leading off the landing was closed off with an intact marine-style door. Mentally bracing himself for disappointment, he ran to it and gripped the wheel at the center, wrenching it hard to the left.

The wheel didn't budge.

A wave of squealing rats crested the top step and swept toward them. In seconds, the swarm was all around them, nipping at their feet, scrabbling up their legs.

"C'mon, damn it!" Maddock growled. "Turn!"

Leopov reached under his arms, gripping the wheel at the twelve and six o'clock position, and howled like a banshee as she threw everything she had into the effort.

With a rasp of friction, the wheel moved.

"Yes!" Maddock cried.

Once loosened, the metal began to turn smoothly, rotating half a turn before stopping in the fully open position. The undogged door easily swung inward, as if someone had greased the hinges. Maddock didn't question this rare bit of good luck, but shoved Leopov through the opening, leaping in after her.

Leopov, shouting curses in Russian, kicked at the rats still clinging to her clothes and tangling in her hair. Maddock however ignored their explorations, and instead focused on mitigating the threat. As soon as he was inside, he grabbed the edge of the door and swung it back into place, putting his shoulder into it to supply enough momentum to literally crush any resistance from the rodent vanguard. The sharp edges at the side and bottom of the door mercilessly sliced through furry little bodies like butcher's shears, and with a final resounding crunch, the door was once more in its frame.

Maddock continued leaning against the door as he swatted and kicked away the rats that had managed to slip past. Those he dislodged and hurled away into the darkness, perhaps sensing that they no longer held any kind of numerical advantage, did not make another attempt, and after a few seconds, even their squeals diminished, leaving Maddock and Leopov in blessed silence.

Maddock finally allowed himself a sigh of relief. He

gave himself a quick once over. His bare chest and back were scraped raw, but that seemed to be the worst of his injuries. "Are you okay?" he asked Leopov. "Did you get bit?"

"I don't think so," she replied. "They just nibble, looking for soft places."

Maddock resisted the urge to chuckle. If there was one thing Zara Leopov wasn't, it was soft. "Thank goodness that door opened."

"And closed."

"Yeah. We were lucky that whoever took all the other doors off left that one…" He trailed off as he considered the import of what he had just said. "Huh," he mused. "Why do you think somebody did that? Took all the other doors down but left that one in place?"

"I can answer that," boomed a loud, thickly accented voice from the darkness at the far end of the corridor.

Maddock started involuntarily at the sound and Leopov let out a surprised yelp. There was a laugh from the darkness, and then a figure stepped closer, into the reach of Leopov's light—a squat, piggish-looking middle-aged man. Several more men—the same men who had accosted them in Red Square—appeared from behind him, striding forward with guns drawn and aimed at Maddock and Leopov.

"I shut that door to keep out the rats," the man said with a humorless chuckle that did not reach his eyes. "I guess it didn't work."

The man had spoken in English, a clear indication that he knew who they were. Maddock shot a glance at Leopov, looking for inspiration. She returned a shrug, then raised her hands and faced the pig-man. "Hey, look. I know we probably shouldn't be here. We got lost. We promise not to tell anyone about this place."

The man made a disdainful flicking gesture. "Don't treat me as fool. I know who you are, Zara Leopov, and I know that you are American spy."

Leopov winced, but kept her composure. "I am the

American naval attaché, but that doesn't make me a spy. My friend and I weren't doing anything illegal. When your goons accosted us, we ran. What were we supposed to do? For all we knew, you were gangsters trying to kidnap us."

"Gangsters. I like this word." He laughed and then extended his thumbs and fat forefingers to make little pistol shapes. "I make an offer you can't refuse, no?" He laughed again. "I am gangster."

Leopov's nose wrinkled in disgust. "Yes, I know you are." She half-turned to look over at Maddock. "He's **Sergei Yukovitch Telesh**, a boss in the **Solntsevskaya Bratva**." She returned her gaze to Telesh. "And I guess I should have expected to find you down here surrounded by rats."

Telesh shrugged. "It was mistake for you to think you would be able to escape me. When you went into the Niglinka passage, I knew you would eventually come here. These old tunnels were like playground for me when I was growing up in Soviet Union. We used them to smuggle goods all over city."

"Look," Maddock said, "clearly there's some kind of misunderstanding—"

The gangster jerked his finger-guns toward Maddock, his smile gone. "Shut up," he snarled. "There is no misunderstanding. You are hiding Lia Markova. Tell me where she is, or else."

"Or else what?" Maddock challenged. "You'll kill us? You're going to do that anyway."

"Kill you?" Telesh put the emphasis on the second word. "I don't think so. You are much too valuable to me alive. No, I have much better idea."

He turned and nodded into the darkness behind him. There was a shuffling sound and then the two men Maddock had earlier dubbed Tweedledee and Tweedledum appeared, with a reluctant hostage suspended between them. Maddock immediately recognized her as the woman Leopov had hired from an escort service to act as a decoy for Lia Markova.

The woman glared at the men but offered no

resistance. A crust of blood on her lips suggested that she had learned the futility of fighting back the hard way.

Maddock's gut twisted with apprehension as he guessed Telesh's intention. It was one thing to face one's own death with stoic reserve, but a threat to an innocent was something else. Still, he could not sacrifice the mission, nor could he jeopardize one life—Markova's—to save another. "Sorry, Telesh, but we couldn't tell you where she is even if we—"

Telesh brought up one hand and abruptly closed it into a fist, whereupon Tweedledum let go of the woman's arm, and then with unexpected suddenness, stepped behind her, clamped her head between his massive paws, and gave it a savage twist.

The sound of snapping vertebrae was like an electric jolt to Maddock's nervous system. A metallic taste filled his mouth as Tweedledum let go of the woman, allowing her lifeless body to slump to the floor. He started forward, more a reflexive action than a move to attack, but Telesh's men were ready for him. They swarmed forward and closed in on him and Leopov, bodily restraining them both.

"Bastard!" Leopov snarled.

Telesh sneered. "That is what means gangster in Russia."

"You didn't have to do that," Maddock said. The protest sounded pathetic in his ears.

Telesh affected a look of indignation. "I did nothing. You did this. Or that is what police will believe." He nodded his head toward Leopov. "You hired this woman, no? That is what the witnesses will say. You hired her to show you and boyfriend good time, but then things got rough. He killed her, dumped body in Metro tunnel."

Leopov was incredulous. "You're framing us for murder? That's your plan?"

Telesh laughed. "No. This is plan." He opened his fist into another finger-gun and pointed it at Maddock. As his thumb came down, something heavy crashed into the back of Maddock's head and then there was only darkness.

EIGHT

With their impromptu performance, Bones and Willis had the full attention of the policeman for several minutes, but rather than escalating the situation with further shenanigans, they stood by meekly until the man finally lost interest and resumed meandering up and down the platform. Not long thereafter, the boarding call was given, and the two men filed onto a passenger car and found seats. Bones surreptitiously scanned the other passengers, but saw no sign of Professor or Lia.

"Think they're okay?"

"Sure," Willis said, confidently. "Prof knows what he's doing."

Bones did not doubt this for a second, but that didn't mean he was reassured. Unfortunately, there would be no way to know for certain until they reached their next destination, the northern port city of Saint Petersburg—a journey that would take several hours. Even if everything had gone off perfectly, Professor would not risk making contact with them while there was even the slightest chance that they might be under surveillance by police or FSB agents.

And if something had gone wrong... If Lia had been caught, or Professor, or Maddock and Leopov, there wouldn't be a thing he or Willis could do to help them out. That was the nature of their job, but it didn't make waiting any easier.

After the train left the station, he did his best to play the part of wide-eyed tourist, gawking at the landscape as it passed them by and offering boisterous commentary. After a couple hours of this, with the train now well away from the urban environs of Moscow and deep into the boreal forests of western Russia, he managed to nod off and slept sporadically during the remainder of the journey.

Upon arrival at the Moskovsky railway station they disembarked and moved to the spacious Renaissance-inspired lobby where they pretended to browse the contents of a souvenir kiosk while watching the other passengers filing off the arrival platform. Bones hid a relieved smile when he spotted Professor, walking by himself, nose evidently buried in a tourist map. He did not acknowledge Bones and Willis, nor did they give him more than a casual glance. But as the human flow dwindled to nothing with no sign of Lia, Bones grew anxious again.

"Did you see her?" he finally asked.

Willis, who was trying on sunglasses and watching the crowd in the reflection of the provided mirror, murmured, "Check the newsstand at your three o'clock."

Bones rolled his gaze slowly in the suggested direction, and caught the eye of a young woman who was standing in front of an adjacent kiosk, apparently trying to bum cigarettes from passersby. She wore a long black T-shirt, belted like a tunic dress, and with her spiky black hair, black lipstick and eye makeup, and black fingernails, she reminded Bones of Winona Ryder's character in the movie *Beetlejuice*.

"The goth girl?" he asked, smiling at her. She wrinkled her nose at him then turned on her heel and marched toward the exit. He grinned. "She's hot, but I don't mess with jailbait."

Willis stared at him over the top of a pair of mirrored aviator shades. "Seriously?"

"What? You think she's legal?"

"Man, Sherlock Holmes has nothing to worry about." Willis returned the sunglasses to the rack and then turned toward the lobby. "Come on. Let's go find Prof."

Bones shrugged and followed the other man to the exit. Once outside, they joined a line of people who appeared to be waiting for rides. A few minutes later, a black sedan pulled up near them and a familiar face appeared in the lowered passenger window. It was the goth girl.

"Hey sailors," she called out, in slightly accented English. "Need a lift?"

Bones gaped at the young woman, then flashed a sidelong glance at a laughing Willis. "Wait, is that…?"

He looked at her again, and this time, was able to recognize the face behind the exaggerated black make-up, the same face he'd seen in the photograph at the safe house—Lia Markova.

Shaking his head in disbelief, he circled around to the opposite side of the car and slid into the back seat behind the driver—Professor.

Bones cast a suspicious glance at Willis who took the seat behind Lia. "You knew it was her? How?"

"Easy. She was wearing Professor's belt."

"That's quite a transformation," Bones remarked as the car pulled into traffic. "I guess when you retire from the Navy, you can step right into a new career as a punk makeover artist."

"Best I could manage under the circumstances," Professor replied. "Amazing what you can do with shoe polish." He glanced over at Lia. "I promise, it will wash off eventually."

Lia's black-painted lips curled into a wan but grateful smile. "A small price to pay for my life," she said. "Thank you all."

"Don't thank us yet," said Professor. "We've still got a long ways to go."

They drove west along a main boulevard. Professor informed them that it was Nevsky Prospekt, named for somebody famous, but Bones willfully tuned him out. Nevsky was just a name on a map for him, nothing more.

After a few "crazy Ivan" maneuvers to make sure they weren't being followed, and several more unprompted lectures from Professor, they left the city behind and headed west on a narrow, poorly maintained two-lane highway. There was sparse traffic on the tree-lined road and even fewer residences. After a while, Professor ran out of things to talk about and they rode on in silence.

About half an hour after leaving the city, Professor pulled the rented car to the side of the road and shut off the lights. They waited in darkness for another few minutes to make sure that they had not been followed, and then got out and began hiking into the woods. A short trek brought them to a white sand beach at the edge of the Gulf of Finland. Bones could see twinkling lights out on the water—fishing boats coming and going.

"There," Willis called out, pointing to a spot further down the beach to the east. Bones' sharp eyes immediately picked out the faint red gleam of a hooded flashlight about fifty yards away. He produced his own penlight and used it to flash out a message in Morse code. A few seconds later, the red light began flashing an answering message. With the correct countersign given, they moved cautiously to the rendezvous point where two men in nondescript oilskins waited near a beached skiff.

Lia sucked in an apprehensive breath.

"Don't worry," Professor assured her. "They're friendly."

"Americans?"

"Finnish Coastal Jaegers."

"They're commandos like us," Bones supplied. "Only not quite as badass."

"We've done joint training exercises with them in the past," Professor continued. "They're good guys."

One of the pair offered a terse greeting in halting English, but that was the extent of the conversation. Like Bones and his companions, the Finnish commandos were focused strictly on accomplishing the mission, which in this case meant getting off the beach and out into the water as quickly as possible.

Bones remained on high alert as the Jaegers first rowed, then motored the flat-bottomed boat out into the Gulf, but the transition out of Russian territorial waters was completed without incident. The skiff pulled up alongside a run-down trawler where two more "fisherman" were waiting to help them aboard. Only then did Bones allow himself a small sigh of relief. They had accomplished the main objective of the mission. Lia was safely out of Russia.

"This is where we say good-bye," Professor told her.

Lia let out a dismayed yelp. "You're not coming?"

Professor shook his head. "Our covers are still intact. We might need to use them again someday, so it's better if we leave through the front door. We'll head back to St. Petersburg. Play tourist for a while. I've always wanted to visit the Hermitage."

Lia's gaze darted toward the men waiting on the fishing boat then back to Professor. Clearly, she wasn't happy about being handed off like a football.

"Don't sweat it," Bones said, making a scooting gesture. "You'll be fine. Dane and Zara are waiting to meet you in Helsinki."

But then one of the ersatz fishermen made a braying sound like the buzzer on a game show and called out, "Sorry, Squanto. Survey says: Wrong answer."

A premonition of dread seized Bones. His skin suddenly felt too tight for his body. He snapped his gaze up to the man, recognizing both the face and the voice. "Captain Midnight? What the hell are you doing here?"

"Ruining your vacation." The CIA officer paused a beat before continuing. "Maddock and Leopov are missing, which means your op, which was crap to begin with, is now completely FUBAR."

"Missing?"

"Earlier this afternoon, the Moscow police put out a BOLO for two Americans who bear a striking resemblance to your pals. They're wanted for questioning in connection with a murder investigation—dead hooker fished out of the Moskva..." He paused and snorted with laughter. "Fished hooker. Get it?"

"You're a real humanitarian," Bones said, rolling his eyes to hide his dismay.

"Simmer down, Geronimo. I'm just the messenger. Anyway, when the Moscow station chief realized that the naval intelligence attaché was implicated in a murder, he decided to bring in a professional."

"Really?" Bones dead-panned. "Who is he sending?"

Huntley ignored the dig. "Word on the street is that a Russian mobster named Telesh is behind all this. Unfortunately, he's connected—I'm talking best pals with the Russian prime minister. Maddock and Leopov are in the wind, which I guess is better than being in a Russian prison cell, but this is still a major league diplomatic balls-up. I've talked to your CO and he mostly brought me up to speed on this epic cluster, so I understand the what, but not the why." He turned his gaze on Lia, and the young woman, who already looked deathly pale in her improvised Goth get-up, went a shade whiter. "Why the hell are you so important?"

Maddock did not lose consciousness completely, or if he did, it was only for a moment or two. As his awareness returned, he felt strong hands lifting him, turning him onto his belly. His arms were pulled together behind his back, secured with several yards of heavy-duty tape. A strip of the sticky adhesive was slapped over his mouth, and then the world went dark a second time as a sack hood was dropped over his head.

Primal panic surged through him. He couldn't breathe. He was going to suffocate inside the sack.

Pull it together, Maddock, he told himself. *You will suffocate if you don't calm the hell down.*

With an effort, he brought the urge to breathe under control, held what little breath he had left. Beyond the confines of his hood, his captors were manhandling him to his feet, but he let himself go limp in their arms, as if he had indeed passed out. After a silent ten-count, he succeeded in drawing a shallow breath through his nostrils.

It was enough.

He decided this was a positive development. Telesh wanted them alive. If he had wanted to kill them, he wouldn't have bothered with tape and sack hoods; he would have simply ordered Tweedledum to snap their necks, too, and left the bodies for the rats.

Maybe the gangster planned to interrogate them to learn Lia's whereabouts. Maybe they would be held for ransom, or sold to the highest bidder. Ultimately, it didn't matter. Eventually, an opportunity would present itself for escape, and when it came, Maddock would be ready.

He could not say with certainty how much time passed. He drifted in and out of consciousness, partly as a strategy for coping with the reduced supply of fresh air, and partly because there was nothing else to do.

His captors carried him for a while, then deposited him on a flat surface—probably the bed of a truck or some other vehicle. The hood was heavy enough to muffle most sounds but he could feel vibrations rumbling through the floor beneath him and could sense changes in acceleration and turns. After a while, he was lifted and carried again, and then once more put in a prone position. Another vehicle… No, a plane. There was no mistaking the surge of power as the aircraft accelerated for take-off, the steep climb to cruising altitude, the rapid change in air pressure inside his head which he could only equalize by working his jaw to pop his ears.

The flight lasted a couple hours, which told Maddock that they were probably still in Russia. Once the plane was on the ground and not moving, he was half-dragged to another vehicle. He needed to relieve his bladder and tried to tell his captors as much, but his muffled shouts accomplished nothing. If something did not change soon, he would have no choice but to urinate in his pants.

The ride lasted another hour, and this time, he was fully awake and present for every twist, turn and pothole. The last mile or so was the worst as the vehicle crept along at a snail's pace, grinding along a gravel road that felt about as smooth as the surface of the moon. Finally, the torturous journey ended. Maddock was dragged out of the vehicle. The change in position gave him a moment of relief, but the jostling that followed pushed the limits of his self-control. After a few minutes of being carried, he was deposited in a kneeling position on a hard, cold floor. He felt something tugging at his wrists and then, miraculously, his hands were loose. His arms were stiff and partially numb, and all he could do was let them hang limp at his sides.

The hood was abruptly snatched off his head. He winced as light flooded into his eyes, and when he sniffed in a grateful breath, he nearly gagged. The air reeked of urine and excrement.

Something rattled behind him. He turned, still blinking back tears, just in time to see a chain-link gate swing shut, closing him in a narrow stall. Through the blur and the diamonds of steel mesh, he could just make out the silhouette of his tormentor. A moment later, he heard the distinctive click of a lock bolt being thrown, and then the silhouette was gone.

He was in a jail cell.

No, that wasn't quite right. It was a cell of sorts, but not one meant for human prisoners. The light that still brought tears to his eyes was streaming down from a single naked incandescent bulb mounted on the ceiling. It illuminated a narrow stall framed on three sides by chain link fencing. The remaining wall was concrete, as was the floor which was covered in mildew-spotted straw.

There was a disturbance outside the confines of the cell. Maddock moved closer, pressed his face against the chain-link and saw two of Telesh's thugs with a hooded and bound figure suspended between them.

Leopov.

He tried to shout her name, and was reminded of the tape covering his mouth. He reached up with still-tingling fingers and tore it away. "Zara!" He decided to hide his relief at seeing her behind a façade of outrage. "Let go of her you bastards."

They paid him no heed, but wrestled Leopov into the stall to his left where they cut her bonds and removed her hood.

As the men exited and locked the stall, Maddock shifted to the shared wall. On the other side, Leopov was covering her eyes with her hands as if weeping.

"Zara, I'm here."

Leopov's head came up, her tear streaked face searching him out. Her fingers tugged at the tape strip, ripped it away. She gasped in a breath, shuddered in revulsion. "Dane? Where are we?"

"I don't know," he admitted, and then added. "A dog kennel, I think. That's about all I know."

"Was dog kennel," said a voice from just outside Leopov's cell—Telesh. "Former owner of this dacha raised wolfhounds. I do not like dogs so have found other use for it, as you see."

Maddock swung his gaze in the direction of the voice. His vision was still a little blurry but his eyes had adjusted to the light level and he no longer had to squint to make out the ogre-shape of their tormentor. "What kind of sick bastard doesn't like dogs?"

Telesh uttered a harsh laugh but did not further opine on the topic.

"Dacha?" Leopov asked.

"Yes," Telesh went on. "Was built for senior party members. I got sweet deal. Is near Gelendzhik. You know Gelendzhik?"

Maddock did not recognize the name, but Leopov did. She nodded, and then, presumably for Maddock's benefit, said, "It's a resort town on the Black Sea coast. About a hundred and fifty miles from the border with Georgia." Then, with a note of chagrin, she added, "It's pretty remote."

"Yes," Telesh confirmed. "A good place to get away from it all, no?" He laughed, then his voice took on a hard edge. "I have made you…" He made a little explosion with his fingertips. "Disappear. No one will look for you here. The police think you are murderers. Your government will not come to your rescue. Your only hope is to tell me what I want to know. So, I ask you again. Where is Lia Markova?"

"And I will tell you again," Leopov replied. "We don't know. That was the whole reason we arranged a decoy. To distract you so she could slip away on her own. She didn't tell us where she was going, and we didn't ask."

"You must have some idea where she is going," Telesh pressed, softening a little, almost pleading. "Some way to contact her."

"Why on earth do you think we would ever tell you?" Maddock challenged. "You're going to kill us anyway. And if we give up Lia, you'll just kill her, too. At least this way, she lives."

"You are mistaken. I do not want to kill the Markova woman. Petrov made a mistake. Frightened her. I don't want to kill her. You…" He waved dismissively. "You, I don't care about."

"What do you want with her?"

"Is none of your business. Now, will you tell me?"

Maddock spread his hands. "Sorry, but like the lady said. We just don't know."

Telesh regarded them both for several seconds. "For your sake, I hope this is not true. I give you time to think about it." He wrapped his hands around his arms and gave a mock-shiver. "It gets very cold here at night. I'll come visit you tomorrow morning. Maybe have hot meal for you. Maybe not. We will see what the morning brings."

With that, the gangster turned and walked away.

Leopov watched him leave and continued to stare into the empty darkness beyond the cell. "Well?" she said, not turning to look at him. "Whose turn is it to come up with a plan?"

Maddock laughed despite himself, then reached out to weave his fingers into the steel mesh of the gate. He shook it experimentally, rattling the heavy-duty padlock which held the latch bolt in place. The lock was solid enough, but the same could not be said for the 12-gauge wire that comprised the chain-link web. Time and gravity had allowed the diamond-weave to sag in several places. "If Telesh thinks this can hold us, he's in for a shock. But if this place is as remote as you say, then breaking out of this cage will be the easy part. I don't suppose you've got any old friends in this neck of the woods."

She shook her head. "I've never been here, but if we can get to a phone…" She trailed off, turned to look at him. "Do you believe him? About Lia?"

"You mean that he doesn't want to kill her?" He shrugged. "Does it matter?"

"What do you think he really wants?"

Before Maddock could answer, a new voice joined their conversation. "I know."

He whirled around to see a figure rising from a nest of straw in the cell to the right of his—a haggard looking man with greasy hair and soiled clothes. His eyes were sunken, cheeks hollow from days of privation.

"I know what he wants," the man said. He sounded as miserable as he looked, but he nevertheless struggled to his feet and approached the barrier between them. "You are Lia's friends?"

"Who are you?"

Behind him, Leopov gasped. "Maddock. It's Oleg Petrov. Lia's boss."

In the trawler's galley, over cups of hot coffee, Lia told her story. Her account raised more questions than it answered.

"Müller, huh?" Huntley rubbed the stubble on his chin.

"If it was Gestapo Müller," Lia said, "Then the item

mentioned might really be something important to the Reich. Something valuable."

"If," Huntley retorted. "It's a pretty common name. Especially in Germany. Could be someone else."

"It doesn't matter who he is," said Bones, emphatically. "What matters is that the guys who are after her—" He jabbed a finger at Lia. "This Russian gangster, Telesh… He thinks that's who it is, and he wants whatever it was Müller supposedly took with him."

"And that matters why exactly?"

"Jeez, you're a real douche sometimes. Telesh is out there, looking for it. He probably has Maddock and Zara. That's probably why they haven't made contact." He did not allow himself to consider the possibility that his friend might already be dead. "We've got to go back to Moscow. Your people are obviously keeping tabs on this guy. Tell us where to find him and we'll take care of the rest."

"Slow your roll Hiawatha—"

"Give it a rest, man," Willis snapped.

"No, you give it a rest, Buckwheat. You guys don't get to run rogue ops whenever you feel like it. Maddock and Leopov knew the risks. Now, we'll keep our eyes and ears open, and if we get a lead on where they are, we'll pursue it. If we can extract them, we will. But under no circumstances are the three…" He looked over at Lia and amended. "The four of you setting foot on Russian soil. Not ever again, *capisce*?"

"You can't expect us to just sit on our asses and do nothing."

Professor raised his hands. "Look, if we can't take direct action, maybe we can work a different angle."

"Like what?" Huntley asked the question a millisecond ahead of Bones.

"Telesh is looking for Müller, and finding whatever Nazi loot he took with him. That's where he's gonna go. If we can find it first, then he'll come to us. Or we can use whatever it is for leverage to get Dane and Zara back."

Bones snapped his fingers and pointed at Huntley. "And I know just where to start.

"The CIA has a ton of classified files from the war. Stuff that nobody wants to talk about. Nazis getting get-out-of-jail-free cards after the war. Scientists and military officers. Operation Paperclip. Operation Overcast. Dustbin. Ashcan. That's just what the public knows about, but I'll bet it's the tip of the iceberg. If the Russians don't know what happened to Müller, maybe the CIA does. And just maybe, that will lead us to whatever it is Telesh is looking for." He paused a beat, daring Huntley to dismiss him. When the intelligence officer did not reply, Bones went on. "You get us access to those files. Help us find Müller and the loot, and we'll leave Russia to you."

Huntley regarded him with something that might have been skepticism or admiration. Finally, he chuckled. "What, so you're treasure hunters, now?"

"Yeah," Bones retorted. "I guess we are."

NINE

Near Gelendzhik, Russia

"Lia is safe?" There was a note of cautious optimism in Petrov's tone. "She got away?"

From the opposing cell, Leopov answered. "Thanks to your warning."

"Thank God for that," the Russian said, leaning heavily against the chain link wall. "At least I will not have that on my conscience." He sighed, then looked at Maddock again. "You are Americans."

Since there was no hiding it, Maddock nodded. "I'm..." He hesitated, wondering whether to use his alias. Since Telesh already knew their real names, there didn't seem to be much point. "Dane Maddock. She's Zara Leopov."

Petrov peered through the mesh, squinting to make out Leopov. "You are Russian?"

"Born here, but raised in America."

"Ah. That would explain why you are not Leopova."

Maddock gave her a quizzical glance.

"In Russia, the female surname is always feminized," she explained. "My father was Leopov, so my last name should be Leopova." She shrugged. "There was a mix-up when I started the naturalization process. Long story, and now's probably not the time for it."

"Agreed." Maddock said. "Right now, I think we should focus on getting out of here. My back molars are floating."

Petrov returned a blank look.

"He means he has to pee," explained Leopov. "I do too. I don't suppose Telesh lets you out for bathroom breaks."

Judging by the smell, Maddock already knew the

answer to that question, but Petrov confirmed it. "No. I thought he would, but…" He shook his head. "Whatever you do, don't go on the straw. You'll need it to keep warm. I learned that lesson the hard way."

"That's not going to be a problem," Maddock said. "We're not staying."

"I do not understand," Petrov said. "You are prisoner here, just like me." He paused a beat, then his eyes lit up. "You know how to escape? You must take me with you."

Maddock exchanged a quick glance with Leopov, a look that said, *Can we trust this guy?* Her ambivalent shrug indicated that she both understood the unspoken message, and shared his concerns, but that was something they could figure out later.

"This cage was designed to keep dogs, not people," he said, kneeling down to inspect one section of sagging chain link. He wiggled it back and forth experimentally. There was about an inch of free play. "We've got something dogs don't have."

"Our intellect?" Petrov suggested.

Maddock chuckled. "The jury's still out on that, but I was talking about opposable thumbs. And one other thing." He stripped off his belt and held it up. "Tools."

"You have a lockpick in a secret compartment?"

"Uh, not exactly. That would come in handy though." He knelt down and threaded the inch-and-a-half thick leather strap through the chain-link at the bottom of the gate, and then brought it back through, securing the loop with the buckle. He then stood and, gripping the end of the belt with both hands, gave it a hard yank.

The sagging mesh came up several inches, the deformity expanding across the neat diamond-weave pattern. The gate remained intact but without its early perfect symmetry—more like a tangle of wire than a net now—and at the bottom, the gap had grown by several inches.

Maddock waited a moment, looking and listening to see if one of Telesh's men would appear to investigate the disturbance, and then yanked on the belt again, and this time succeeded in widening the gap enough to fit through.

He immediately dropped flat and squirmed through the opening. The chain-link raked his shirtless back but he kept going until he was on the other side. He immediately bounded to his feet, gripping the belt between his hands like a garotte, and started down the aisle toward where Telesh and the others had exited. As he passed her, Leopov whispered, "Hurry back."

He didn't stop.

Passing a few more empty stalls, he came to a simple wooden door with peeling paint. There was no doorknob, but through the crack between the door and jamb, he could see that it was held shut by a thin metal bar—probably a simple cabin hook latch. He inserted the end of his belt into the narrow gap and slid it up. With hardly any resistance, the latch popped out of the eye bolt, and the door practically fell open. Maddock waited a beat then edged through the doorway.

Beyond lay a large dimly lit garage, that looked like it might have been a repurposed barn. There were no cars, but four Suzuki LT500R "Quadzilla" all-terrain vehicles stood lined up against one wall. Work tables sat against the opposite wall, along with shelves full of sundry tools, mechanical parts, and cartons of oil.

A quick search of the shelves yielded a wire cutter, which Maddock slipped into his pocket, and a tire iron, which he decided would make a better weapon than his belt, should the need arise. Even better, he found an old cloth jacket hanging on a nail. He pulled it on. It was a little tight around the biceps and across the shoulders, oil-stained and decidedly musky, but better than being shirtless.

Hefting the tire iron, he continued down the length of the garage to the far end which was closed off with a set of carriage style doors. A regular door was set against an adjacent wall and Maddock tried it first. It wasn't an exit, but something even better—a bathroom. The sink basin was streaked with an oily residue, and Maddock didn't even want to think about the stains in the bowl of the commode—he just knew this was an opportunity he couldn't afford to pass up.

After relieving himself, he returned to the carriage doors and eased them open a few inches. Night had fallen over the world, but across the darkened driveway stood an enormous, if somewhat rustic, two-story house, with light shining out through several windows. He studied the house's exterior for several minutes, watching to see if there were roaming sentries or motionless lookouts posted on the porch, but aside from an occasional roar of laughter from the house, all was still and quiet.

He pulled the door closed again and headed back to the kennel. As he cut through the links of Leopov's cell, he gave her a hasty report on what he had observed and outlined his plan.

"I think we can roll a couple of those quad-bikes outside, get them a ways from the house before we fire them up. You know how to ride one?"

She nodded.

"We can disable the ones we leave behind," he continued. "That should give us a good head start."

"Too bad we don't know which way to go," Leopov remarked. "You say there are no guards at all?"

"Nope. Either he seriously underestimated us, or…" He gave a slight nod in Petrov's direction.

Leopov nodded. "That is my concern as well. Still, it's not like we have much of a choice."

As if waiting for his cue, Petrov let out a low wail. "You're taking me with you, right?"

Maddock gave the Russian a hard stare. "It's not going to be easy. And when Telesh figures out we've escaped, he's probably not going to bother trying to take us alive."

Petrov went pale, but nodded. "I don't care. I can't spend another night in here."

"All right. You've been warned." Maddock moved down to Petrov's stall and clipped through the mesh. "The only way this is going to work is if you keep your trap shut. Do what we say, when we say. No questions. No hesitation. Got it?"

Petrov nodded.

"Okay, next question. Can you drive a quad bike?"

"Uh, I don't know. I rode motorcycles when I was younger."

Maddock considered this for a moment, then shook his head. "I don't think we can chance it. You'll ride with me." He wrinkled his nose. "But first, I think you need to make a pit stop."

Working as stealthily as they could, Maddock and Leopov rolled one of the ATVs out of the garage and down the tree-lined dirt driveway until they rounded a bend that hid the house from view. Maddock instructed Petrov to wait there with Leopov, and then headed back for a second vehicle. The house had grown quiet, and some of the upstairs windows were dark, but the downstairs lights continued to blaze. Maddock quickened his pace. If Telesh decided to send one of his goons in to check the status of the prisoners, then their escape attempt would be stillborn. They had been lucky so far, but luck was capricious.

Unless it isn't really luck, he thought.

Luck or not, he made it back to the garage without attracting any attention. He lingered there just long enough to yank the spark plugs from all but one of the remaining ATVs, after which he rolled the still functional quad bike through the carriage doors and started down the primitive driveway.

He was fifty yards from the garage, nearly to the bend, when an angry voice called out from behind him. He couldn't make out what was said, probably because it was spoken in Russian, but he didn't need a translator to know that their luck—if it was luck—had just taken a turn for the worse.

He risked a glance back and saw dark windows lighting up as the call roused the inhabitants of the house. A door opened, spilling light and shadows onto the drive as men raced out onto the porch.

Maddock pushed the quad faster until he was nearly running, then hopped onto it, swinging his leg over the saddle seat. Quickly, so as not to lose the momentum he had built up, he squeezed the clutch lever, tapped the differential into first gear, and then popped the clutch and twisted the throttle.

The Suzuki shuddered and almost stopped dead, but then the 500 cubic centimeter two-stroke engine caught and roared to life, shooting forward like a rocket off the launch pad. As it did, the road ahead lit up in the glow of an aftermarket headlight attached just forward of the steering column. Maddock considered trying to find a switch to turn off the lights, but decided that being able to see the road ahead was worth the risk of being visible from a distance in the night. He ran out first gear, shifted, and then he was at the bend. He skidded around the turn and almost ran into Petrov.

He squeezed the clutch and front brake levers simultaneously, and shouted. "Time to go, Zara! Petrov…" In the moment, he couldn't remember the man's first name. "Climb on or get left behind."

As the Russian historian clumsily mounted behind Maddock, Leopov stood on the kickstarter of her own quad, and a moment later, a second strident chainsaw buzz filled the air.

"Better hang on!" Maddock shouted. As Petrov's arms encircled his waist, Maddock eased off the clutch and the little quad bike lurched into motion.

A noise like a backfire sounded over the dual engine roar, then another and another—not explosions of uncombusted gas in the exhaust system, but pistol reports. Petrov's already frantic embrace tightened.

"Keep low!" Maddock shouted, as much for Leopov's benefit as Petrov's.

Accompanied by a near constant torrent of gunfire, the two ATVs shot down a more or less straight stretch of the drive, but after just a few seconds, and no more than a tenth of a mile, a hairpin turn put a crimp in their escape plan. Still getting a feel for the machine, Maddock geared down and crawled through the bend. As he made the about face, and just before he poured on the throttle, he glanced back down the way they'd just come, and saw headlights coming around the first bend—not a quad bike, but something bigger, probably the van that had brought them to the remote dacha.

Crap, he thought. He had been hoping for a cleaner getaway than this.

Leopov shot ahead of him, her headlights illuminating a long straight stretch, rising across the flanks of a forested hillside—a switchback.

He twisted the throttle, ran out second gear, shifted to third. The headlights were lost from view, hidden behind the trees, but the noise of gunfire continued for a few seconds more. Maddock couldn't tell where the shots were going, but it seemed unlikely that any of them were meant to find an actual living target. Telesh's men had to realize the futility of shooting blind, but that did not seem to lessen their enthusiasm for it.

Another horseshoe bend loomed ahead, forcing him to slow, but not quite as much as before. The big tires squealed a little as the machine started to drift, but maintained contact throughout the turn. Once around the bend, the road began a sweeping left curve and then headed straight up the steep grade. Unburdened by a passenger, Leopov raced ahead, while Maddock had to gear down to avoid stalling. As a result, he was only about halfway up the climb when Leopov's machine crested the rise and abruptly went dark as her machine dropped out of view.

"They're behind us!" Petrov yelled.

Maddock risked a glance back just as a pair of headlights emerged from around the bend, maybe two hundred yards behind them.

Cursing under his breath, he ran the throttle to its stops, pouring two-cycle fuel-oil mix into the carburetor. Despite the wind of their forward motion, the smell of hot oil rose up around him as the engine temperature spiked. And then, as if he didn't have enough to worry about, the shooting resumed.

"Come on," he growled. "Move it!"

As if in response to his supplication, the Fates decided to show pity. The ascent flattened out a little, which gave the reluctant machine a chance to regain some of its momentum. Maddock quickly upshifted. He could almost feel the quad breathing a sigh of relief as he let off the throttle before releasing the clutch. With considerably less effort the four-wheeler shot forward, devouring the last bit of road leading up to the summit

Maddock's exuberance at finally catching a break was short lived. In the instant that the bike surged over the crest, he realized two things. The slope on the other side was much steeper—the red taillight of Leopov's quad was still visible, which meant she was probably only about a hundred yards or so ahead of him, but he judged it to be a good fifty vertical feet below him. That wouldn't have been a problem except for the second thing—he was going way too fast.

The engine roared again as the quad's compact tires lost contact with the road surface. Maddock felt his stomach drop as the machine took flight, soaring out into the air. He had only a fraction of a second to process what was happening and devise a strategy for maintaining control, and in that brief interval he saw everything around him with astonishing clarity. Illumed in the circle of light from the headlamp, the sloped road surface slid past beneath the front wheels, falling away almost but not quite as quickly as the vehicle itself.

The wheels had been straight at the moment of liftoff, and the bike was keeping a true course—that was one point in their favor. With the added burden of a passenger, the nose of the quad was starting to rise—not necessarily a bad thing under the circumstances, but if it came up too high before the back wheels set down, the little machine would rebound and go tumbling end over end, pitching him and Petrov headlong.

His brain quickly shuffled through the list of riding techniques he had picked up over the years. Even if he stuck the landing, the impact would be rough. He had to compensate for the jolt, but how?

The answer was not only obvious, but instinctive, a trick he had picked up as a kid, jumping his Huffy off ramps cobbled together from fruit crates and 2X6 planks. He squeezed the clutch and put the gear selector in neutral, then tried to stand up on the pegs, both to correct the pitch and use his slightly bent knees to absorb some of the shock of the landing.

There was immediate resistance. Something… no, someone was holding him fast; Petrov's arms were wrapped around him like a seat belt.

There was no time to explain what he was trying to do, what he needed Petrov to do in order to save their lives. His only chance was a pure, brute force solution. He redoubled his efforts, straining to lift Petrov off the saddle like a powerlifter executing a back squat. The Russian, who had nothing to hold onto except Maddock's waist, clutched even tighter as Maddock lifted him off the seat, and then….

There was a faint screech as the rear tires met the road, and then a crunch as the front tires came down. The weight on Maddock's back seemed to multiply by a factor of ten, overwhelming him, slamming him back into the seat, even as the quad bounced back into the air.

He held on for dear life, trying to lift himself up again, but there was no time. The ATV came down a second time, bounced a little more and then, miraculously, stayed on the road, coasting down the steep hill.

Maddock's knees were throbbing and he felt like a billy goat had just head-butted his ass, but despite the discomfort, he allowed himself a whoop of joy. But as the exhilaration of the jump faded, he risked a glance back and saw the rising glow of automobile headlights shining up from beyond the crest of the hill.

He clutched, shifted into third gear. The quad jerked a little as the engine compression fought to catch up with the machine's momentum—a problem easily corrected with a twist of the throttle—and then they were charging down the hill.

Further down the road, Leopov's taillight winked out as she rounded a bend. Maddock followed her into a series of serpentine turns that swerved back and forth across the downslope. The air, which had chilled noticeably during the initial ascent, grew warmer again as the dirt track led down into a sheltered valley. Up ahead, Leopov's red light grew brighter as the distance between them shrank.

She's stopped, he thought, and then saw why. Leopov had arrived at a Y-junction. Both paths continued the descent but without knowing more about where they were, it was impossible to say which was the quickest route to freedom.

It was a coin-flip.

But then a third option occurred to him. As he rolled up beside Leopov's idling machine, he pointed into the woods off to the left. "Pull into the trees and shut down!" he shouted.

To her credit, Leopov didn't question or challenge the seemingly unorthodox decision, but quickly wheeled in the indicated direction and drove into the treeline, with Maddock right behind her.

The ground beyond the graded dirt track was irregular in the extreme, crossed with half-exposed tree roots, but the quads were called all-terrain vehicles for a reason. Leopov drove about fifty feet into the woods, then stopped and shut off her engine, instantly reducing the light level by fifty percent.

Maddock pointed his quad in her direction, then shut it down, coasting the last few yards in total darkness.

In the sudden quiet, they could hear the noise of a vehicle roaring down the hill somewhere behind them. A yellow glow briefly suffused the forest as the van rounded the last bend, and then dimmed as it passed by. Maddock held his breath as the vehicle reached the fork and paused there, its occupants evidently pondering which direction to go. Faint shouts were audible over the din. What was happening? Had they seen through the ruse?

The van's engine revved, the glow brightening as it turned toward them…

And then it passed by again, diminishing into the distance as the vehicle continued down the left-hand path.

Maddock let out his breath in a sigh of relief. "They bought it."

"Yes, they did," Leopov remarked. "Unfortunately, I think maybe they chose that direction because it's the road that leads to Gelendzhik."

Maddock grinned into the darkness. "I hope they did. Now we know which way to go."

"I do not understand," interjected Petrov. "They will be watching the town and all the roads leading into it. We will not be hard to spot, especially riding on these machines."

"You're right," agreed Maddock. "That's why we're going to walk."

"Walk?" Petrov squealed, plaintively.

"We'll stay on the road when we can," Maddock went on, "and duck back into the woods if we see someone coming." He glanced over at Leopov. "You said we're near the border with Georgia?"

"Yes. Maybe a hundred miles or so. But if we can get to Sochi, there are ferries that can take us across the Black Sea to Turkey. That's a lot closer. We should be able to borrow a car once we get to Gelendzhik."

"It must be many kilometers," Petrov protested. "We'll freeze."

"As long as we keep moving, you'll stay plenty warm."

"You are Russian, are you not?" Leopov cajoled. "What is a little cold. Or would you rather sleep in a dog's bed? In your own filth?"

"Fine," Petrov sighed in resignation. "I just hope it

is not far."

TEN

Helsinki, Finland

"This was the battleground," Bruce Huntley remarked, almost wistfully, as he stared out the passenger window of the delivery van. The streets they passed were clean and well-lit, but owing to the late hour, almost completely empty of both vehicular and pedestrian traffic, giving them a surreal post-apocalyptic vibe.

Professor leaned forward for a look. "You must be talking about the Battle of Helsinki during the Finnish Civil War of 1918. Imperial German forces supported the White faction against the Red Guard."

Huntley looked at him like there was a banana growing out of his forehead. "I'm talking about the Cold War. A neutral country sitting on the Soviets' doorstep. This was the chessboard for the spy game. I've never been here, but man, I've heard some stories."

Professor nodded slowly and leaned back in his chair. Beside him, Bones chuckled. Although he probably didn't realize it, Huntley had just rescued them all from another tedious lecture.

The van brought them to an alley and stopped at the back entrance to a restaurant. Huntley produced a key to unlock the door and then led them inside and up a narrow stairwell to a modestly decorated upper story apartment.

"You can crash here tonight," he said. "Figure out our next move in the morning." He glanced at Lia and then jerked a thumb toward a closed door off the main sitting room. "Shower's in there. You'll probably want to wash that crap out of your hair. I mean, unless you're diggin' the Morticia Addams look."

"A mixture of rubbing alcohol and cold water should do the trick," Professor assured her, and then looked to Huntley. "Do you have some? A first aid kit, maybe?"

Bones laughed. "Dude, this is vodka country. Bound to be a bottle of Finlandia around here somewhere."

Huntley snorted. "Leave it to the Indian to sniff out the booze. Might be some in the kitchen. Better let me get it, just to be on the safe side."

"If it's all the same to you," Lia said quickly, "I would like to get started searching for Gestapo Müller. The sooner we figure out what happened to him, the sooner I can go back to my life."

Bones, who was still trying to think of a retort for Huntley, almost missed the sadness in her tone. Professor evidently did not. "We'll get started while you clean up. Don't worry. We won't rest until we've figured this out."

She gave him a grateful smile, and after accepting a clear glass bottle from Huntley, headed into the little bathroom.

When the sound of running water was audible from within, Huntley shook his head. "Poor girl. She thinks this ends with everything going back to the way it was."

"Why can't it?" asked Professor. "You said this guy Telesh is a mobster. A criminal."

"You gotta update your world view, Braniac. Who do you think has all the power in Russia right now? The mobsters, the oligarchs... They're running the show. The government does what they're told." He shook his head. "Your girl is burned. Hell, she might not even be safe stateside. The Bratva has a long reach."

Bones forgot all about the earlier insults. "You're joking, right? I mean, the Agency is gonna have that covered, aren't they? A new identity? WITSEC."

Huntley shrugged. "Not my call. I suppose it will depend on how valuable she can be in the long term. My guess is that she doesn't know much, but hey, depending on how this turns out, maybe you can help her get a job at the Simon Wiesenthal Center, hunting down dead Nazis."

"God, you're such an asshole," said Willis.

Huntley grinned and seemed about to respond in kind, but Bones stepped between them, towering over the Agency man. "Shouldn't you be checking in with Langley? Maybe get someone looking through those old files for information about Müller?"

"We should also give Maxie a call," Professor added. "Maybe he's heard from Dane."

Huntley looked vaguely disappointed at having been denied his customary repartee, but nodded. "Yeah. I probably should do that. There should be a commo room behind the bedroom closet. It'll be close quarters, so you'll have to let me go first." He nodded toward the kitchen. "There's food in the pantry. Help yourselves."

After he was gone, Professor let out a weary sigh. "He *is* one of the good guys, right?"

Bones shook his head. "If he is, then maybe it's time for a career change."

"Uncle Sam may sign his paychecks," replied Willis. "But good?" He shook his head. "I don't think even he would lay claim to that." He stared at the closed bedroom door for several seconds, then went on. "What do you think's really going on here? It's gotta be more than just some old Nazi gold, right?"

"I guess it depends on how much Nazi gold we're talking about," said Professor. "We know that when the writing was finally on the wall, the Nazis hid a bunch of stuff in bunkers all over Germany and Austria. By some estimates, there could be as much as forty billion—with a 'b'—dollars' worth of treasure still hidden away. Not just gold, but works of art. Secret Nazi weapons research. The senior Nazis truly believed they were going to be able to put the pieces together again, carry on the fight. Remember the stuff we found at Lake Toplitz?"

Bones groaned. "I'm trying to forget it, actually."

"Maybe what we're really talking about... What this Russian, Telesh, is really after, is a map or maybe a ledger with the locations of all of the bunkers where the Nazis secreted their stolen wealth."

"Hitler's Little Black Book," Willis mused.

"Man, I'm so sick of Hitler," Bones sneered. "Treasure or not, if I ever got my hands on something like that, I'd wipe my ass with it and flush it down the toilet."

"That's juvenile," called out Huntley from the bedroom doorway. "Even for you."

Bones folded his arms across his chest. "In Mexico, they believe that everyone dies three deaths. The first death is when your heart stops beating. The second death is when your body is buried. The third death is when nobody remembers your name. I guess that makes Hitler immortal, right? Maybe the world would be a better place if we could just forget him forever."

"I'm not sure I agree," countered Professor. "I guess I belong to the school of thought that says, if you don't learn from history, you're doomed to repeat it."

Bones shrugged, but kept his stare fixed on Huntley. "Maybe so, but I think a lot of white folks have a secret hardon for Nazis."

"Not always secret," murmured Willis.

Huntley, surprisingly, had no comeback for that. He uttered a sound that might have been a chuckle, and then shrugged. "Well, I doubt you'll get your chance. I put in a request for information about Heinrich Müller. Turns out, the Agency and its predecessor—the OSS—conducted an extensive search for Müller at the end of the war. They never found him, but all the evidence suggests that the Soviets rolled him up. Turned him. Gave him a new identity."

"That doesn't make any sense," Professor countered. "If the Russians knew what happened to Müller, they wouldn't be pulling out all the stops looking for him."

Huntley spread his hands in mock surrender. "Hey, you asked me to look into it. I did. That's what I found. End of story."

"Professor is correct," called Lia, stepping out of

the bathroom amidst a billowing cloud of steam. She wore a white terry cloth robe—about four sizes too big—and had her hair wrapped up turban style in a towel. "Petrov had clearance to view Kremlin archives. If Müller had been turned, he would have known. It is more likely that the Americans captured him and turned him."

Huntley shook his head. "No, that was just something the Soviets put out to deflect suspicion. Red propaganda."

"Just for argument's sake," Bones said, speaking forcefully enough to silence both of them. "Let's say there's a third option. He got away clean. How? And where did he go?"

Lia and Huntley regarded each other like opponents on opposite sides of a poker table. Lia eventually broke the silence. "Thousands of the Nazis escaped to South America at the end of the war using smuggling routes called 'ratlines.' The first, organized by the Vatican, led through Rome. The other went through Spain."

"Spain was technically neutral during the war," Professor put in, "but Franco was sympathetic to the Axis cause. And there were a lot of Nazi and Fascist sympathizers in the Church before, during, and after the war. They bought into Hitler's narrative of a restored Holy Roman Empire, and they despised Communists."

Lia nodded. "However, I think that if Müller had used one of the ratlines, he would have left a trail. That is not a secret anyone can keep. Someone would have talked. Knowing that, Müller probably would have chosen an escape route that minimized contact with others."

"Like a U-boat," said Bones.

"We know for a fact that at least two U-boats made it to South America. U-977, under the command of Oberleutnant zur See Heinz Schäffer, and U-530, commanded by Oberleutnant zur See Otto Wermuth. Both vessels refused Admiral Dönitz's orders for the

German navy to stand down, and made a successful run to Argentina where they surrendered to the Argentine navy. There were no passengers, only crew, and all were thoroughly interrogated before eventually being repatriated to Germany."

"If Müller had been hiding among them," Professor said, "he almost certainly would have been identified and taken into custody. Any cargo or documents would have been seized."

Bones glanced over and saw Professor's eyes dancing excitedly. *Somebody's in love,* he thought.

Lia nodded. "There are many contradictory accounts of the voyages, and we know that both vessels made stops along the way. Schäffer allowed sixteen married crewman to leave at Bergen, and then made another brief stop in the Cape Verde Islands."

"Cape Verde," interjected Huntley. "Where's that?"

Professor was ready with an answer. "It's an archipelago, about three hundred and fifty miles off the West African coast."

"I guess they don't teach geography in the CIA," taunted Bones.

"I work the Eastern European desk. Sue me."

Professor went on. "It's an independent nation now, but back then, it was a Portuguese territory. Like Spain, they were neutral during the war, but leaned right."

"So Müller could have gotten off there, taken an extended tropical holiday."

Lia frowned. "It's possible, but just as with the ratlines, I think someone would eventually have talked. Müller left no trail at all."

"Yeah, you can never count on a Müller report," Bones said.

Professor frowned, shook his head, then returned his attention to Huntley. "The same would be true if he somehow made it to South America." "There were rumors about Mengele being down there for years, even though they never managed to track him down."

Huntley shook his head disparagingly. "If he didn't get caught, and he didn't escape, what's left?"

"Easy," Bones said. "He got killed."

"The most plausible hypothesis has always been that he never made it out of Berlin," agreed Lia. "But the evidence I found suggests otherwise."

Bones shook his head. "I mean after that. We know that two U-boats made it to South America. Were there any others? Maybe one or two that got sunk along the way?"

Lia and Professor exchanged a glance. "There were over a thousand U-boats in the Kriegsmarine during World War II," Professor said. "Even I don't know what happened to them all, but I can tell you the records do exist. Most of the boats that weren't lost in combat were scuttled as part of Operation Deadlight, but I know that several went missing. There was one—I can't remember which—"

Bones let out an exaggerated gasp of surprise. Professor rolled his eyes and kept talking. "Some divers reported finding the wreck off Cape Cod about ten years ago, but it turned out to be a mis-identification. The boat they thought they had found is still missing."

Lia nodded her affirmation. "If Müller was aboard a vessel that subsequently sank, it might explain why he never resurfaced…" She hesitated and then smiled. "That is pun, no?"

"That is pun, yes," Professor said.

Huntley clapped his hands to his thighs. "Well that settles it. The ocean is a big place and we don't have a clue where to begin looking. And even if, by some miracle, you found the wreck, anything made out of paper would have turned to mush."

"We don't know that we're looking for a book," Bones countered. "And let's not get ahead of ourselves. The first thing to do is get a list of missing U-boats. We can focus on those that went missing near the end of the war—say in the last six months."

Huntley wagged his head. "And I suppose you want me to take point on this snipe hunt."

"Actually, I have somebody else in mind. A naval historian we used to know."

"Alex Vaccaro?" asked Professor.

Huntley stiffened. "You can't bring civilians into this."

"Alex isn't a civilian," Bones said. "She's FBI... Or at least she was last time we crossed paths. She also holds the rank of Lieutenant Commander in the Navy, and I'm sure she still has her security clearance."

"FBI? That's even worse." He sighed. "I'll let you consult with him... Or her. Whatever. But limit the conversation to missing U-boats. Deal only in generalities. Under no circumstances are you to mention the name Müller, or anything else we've speculated about here." He paused a beat. "We'll set the meeting up once we get stateside."

"Stateside?"

Huntley nodded. "First thing tomorrow. We'll deadhead on an Air Force tanker plane. No paper trail that way."

"Sorry, but we're not going anywhere until we know Maddock is safe."

"Orders are orders, Big Chief."

"I'm sorry," Willis said, his deep voice dripping with sarcasm, "but since when did we start taking orders from you?"

"Since I pulled your asses out of Russia," Huntley replied, matching his tone. "And let you crash at an Agency safehouse."

"I don't remember asking for your *help*." Willis glanced at Bones and Professor. "Do you remember that?"

"All right, I tried appealing to your sense of gratitude, but now your gonna make me get out my tape measure."

"Ha. Then prepare to be embarrassed, white bread."

Professor stood up. "This macho posturing isn't helping—"

"It's working for me," countered Bones.

Huntley jumped to his feet as well, "This is my operation now, and you've been seconded to me. That means it's my way, or the highway, and the highway isn't an option."

Bones raised his hands. "Fine."

It wasn't fine, and the first chance he got, he was going to talk to Maxie about the parameters of their working relationship with Captain Midnight, but bickering about it wasn't going to get them anywhere. "We'll do it your way."

And then, in a murmur meant only for his teammates' ears, he added, "For now."

ELEVEN

Near Gelendzhik, Russia

As predicted, the temperature dropped by degrees as the night deepened. None of the three escapees from Telesh's dacha had warm weather clothes and walking briskly could only do so much to keep the chill at bay, so after about an hour of shivering and listening to Petrov complain about the cold, Maddock suggested they move deeper into the woods and warm up with a fire.

"Won't someone see?" Petrov protested.

Maddock sighed. *There's just no pleasing this guy*, he thought.

"I don't think we'll need to worry about it," he said. "This place isn't exactly hopping."

Although they had been walking along the roadside, not a single car had passed them. Telesh's men were either still searching for them further down the road, or had returned by some other route.

"It will be a small fire," he went on, "and we'll put up a lean-to to help keep the heat in. That should block lines of sight. But if you'd rather freeze…"

"No! A fire would be very nice."

There was just enough moonlight filtering through the forest canopy for them to gather deadwood and dry moss to use as tinder. While the others fashioned a crude shelter of evergreen boughs, Maddock used his borrowed tire iron to chisel a groove down the center of a more or less flat piece of bone-dry wood. He then split off a stake about eighteen inches long, and chipped a point into its end.

As he knelt over the plank, rapidly dragging the point of the stake up and down the length of the groove, Petrov whispered "Just like Tom Hanks in movie. Does really work?"

Maddock had no idea what the Russian was talking about, and didn't want to waste a breath asking. The fire-plow method was one of the most strenuous ways of starting a fire but without any other tools or means of ignition, it was all he had, and if he was going to make it work, it would require complete focus and total effort.

After only a few seconds, he could smell woodsmoke, but he did not relent until, after what felt like nearly five minutes of pistoning the fire-plow back and forth, he spied a faint red gleam at its tip. Working quickly, he dropped in some of the wood shavings and moss, and then leaned close and began blowing on the ember until it caught fire with an audible whoosh. He laid on more tinder and small pieces of wood, blowing on it to increase the amount of oxygen in the fire triangle, and in only about a minute, had stoked a modest blaze.

"I'm impressed," Leopov said, clapping softly. "I guess you really were Boy Scout."

In the firelight, her face seemed to glow, and her smile was dazzling. Maddock, who was actually feeling a little lightheaded from his exertions, managed a wan grin.

She settled down next to him, pressing her body against his. It was an oddly forward thing for her to do. Maddock could not recall her showing anything that might be interpreted as romantic interest, but then again, as Bones was fond of pointing out, he could be pretty clueless in matters of the heart. Regardless of what signals she had sent or he had missed, he was definitely receiving now.

Then an accusatory voice sounded in his head. *What are you thinking? You've got Melissa.*

Melissa.

The thought of her brought a pang of guilt, and not just at his momentary indulgence.

What the hell am I even doing here? How many times did I almost die today? How many more times will

I have to cheat death to make it home to Melissa? And what if I don't make it back? I could die, just like....

Just like Mom and Dad.

He had almost forgotten, but now the pent-up grief and guilt descended on him like an avalanche. He blinked back tears, unconsciously pulling away from Leopov.

"Don't get excited, Boy Scout," she said, misreading his intentions... Or maybe reading them a little too well. "Just trying to stay warm."

"Sure," he muttered.

Leopov regarded him silently for a moment, then looked across the fire to where Petrov was huddled. "Why is Telesh going after Lia? What does he think she knows?"

Petrov's eyes drew together in a frown. "What did she tell you?"

"Not a lot. There wasn't a lot of time. She mentioned that you had her searching through old archives looking for missing Nazi loot."

Petrov offered a thoughtful hum. "Yes, that is what we were told. I have since learned what **Sergei Yukovitch Telesh** is really looking for."

"Not Nazi loot?" Maddock asked, trying to pull himself back from the black hole of despair.

"Not exactly." Petrov hesitated as if unsure how to proceed, then asked, "Do you know story of Priam's Treasure?"

The name rang a bell, but Maddock was in no mood to fish for the memory. He shook his head.

"You mean Priam, king of Troy during the Trojan war," Leopov supplied.

Maddock could almost hear Bones' voice in his head, cracking a terrible joke... Probably something about a war fought over condoms. The thought brought a smile to his lips. "You're talking about the Iliad, right?"

"The Iliad is story. May be true story, maybe not. But Priam's Treasure is real. Was discovered in 1873 by archaeologist named Heinrich Schliemann."

Maddock nodded slowly as the memory finally surfaced. "Right. I remember this. Schliemann claimed he found the ruins of the city described in the Iliad. He excavated it and found some relics which he believed belonged to King Priam. From what I've heard, most modern scholars doubt the authenticity of that claim, not to mention the historicity of Priam and the other people mentioned in the Iliad."

"Schliemann smuggled treasure out of Ottoman Empire," Petrov said. "Most of the collection ended up in Germany, where it stayed until end of Great Patriotic War."

"When it was taken as war booty by the Red Army," Leopov finished. "They hid it away—in the Pushkin Museum, if I'm not mistaken."

Petrov scowled. "You are Russian. You know what the Nazi filth did to us. What they took from the Motherland. Is only fair that we take treasure in return."

"If the Red Army took it," interjected Maddock, "what does Telesh think he's going to find chasing down some old Nazi war criminal?"

"He seeks one specific item from the collection that was not found with the rest."

"One item?" Maddock held up a single finger to emphasize the point. "I know the Kremlin is hard up for cash, but this seems like an awful lot of trouble to go to just for one artifact. What is it?"

"Sergei Yukovitch calls it 'Helen's Charm.'"

"Helen as in Helen of Troy? The face that launched a thousand ships?"

Petrov nodded. "He believes it has… power."

"Power," Leopov repeated, incredulous. "You mean like it holds some sort of magic power? Something supernatural?"

Maddock glanced back at her, shrugged. Fireside in a gloomy Russian forest, it didn't really sound so unbelievable.

"There may be something to it," Petrov went on. "In story, Priam's son, Paris, takes Helen, wife of King

Menelaus of Sparta, for himself and refuses to surrender her, even though doing so ultimately results in destruction of his father's kingdom. I ask you. What woman is there who could possibly be worth that much trouble?"

He gave Maddock a surreptitious wink. Leopov just rolled her eyes.

"Helen was not merely beautiful," Petrov went on. "She was daughter of Zeus. A demi-god. She bewitched men. Kings. Entire armies foreswore their lives, left their homes behind to die by the thousands in a foreign land." He paused a beat. "Can you think of anyone else in history with that kind of charisma?"

Maddock immediately saw where Petrov was leading them. "You mean Hitler, right? You think he got his hands on this… this Charm. And used it to… What exactly? Bewitch the German populace into following along with his mad scheme to rule the world?" He frowned. "Okay, when I say it out loud, it doesn't actually sound completely crazy."

Petrov was silent for a moment, as if gathering his thoughts. "There is story, told by eyewitness, of what happened on night of November 8, 1923."

"The Beer Hall Putsch," Maddock supplied. "Hitler's first attempt to seize power."

"Yes. Hitler had been trying to gain the support of Gustav Ritter von Kahr, leader of Bavaria, for his plan to seize control of German government, but Kahr did not want to submit to Hitler, whom he viewed as rabble rouser. Eventually, Hitler decides he's had enough of waiting and orders six hundred of his *Sturmabteilung* paramilitaries to surround Munich beer hall where Kahr is giving speech to three thousand supporters.

"Hitler marches in, holds crowd at point of machine gun and declares formation of new government in Bavaria, and his determination to overthrow what he called 'the Berlin Jew government.' One eyewitness, a history professor, said attitude of crowd changed in seconds. 'Hitler turned them inside out as one turns a glove inside out,' he said. Like 'hocus-pocus, or magic.' His words."

A sudden shiver ran down Maddock's spine. It might have been just the chilly night air.

Petrov went on. "More than two thousand marched out of the beer hall carrying the swastika, ready to overthrow government. They failed. Sixteen Nazi stormtroopers were killed and many more arrested, including Hitler, but as you know, that was not the end." He sighed. "I do not know if Hitler possessed Helen's Charm, or if it exists at all, but I do know that Sergei Yukovitch believes it is real. That is what he seeks."

Maddock nodded. "Okay, so Hitler has this Charm, uses it to seduce the German people into following him, into fighting his war, even turning a blind eye to the Holocaust, but it's not enough to guarantee him a victory." He cocked his head to the side. "History repeats itself. The Trojans lost their war, too.

"Hitler chooses suicide. Müller takes the Charm, escapes Berlin, escapes Germany and then… What? Disappears?"

"That is what Sergei Yukovitch believes. And Lia Markova is first person to find a clue about where he might have gone."

"And now he thinks she can lead him the rest of the way," finished Leopov.

Petrov nodded, then looked thoughtful for a moment. "She is very intelligent. Maybe she *can* find him. But I also think she is… How do you say? A loose end?"

"That's how you say it."

"Da. If she helps him find it, good. But if she is out there, maybe helping someone else find it? Not so good for him."

I guess that's why he kept you alive, Maddock thought, but didn't say aloud.

"What is this Charm, exactly?" asked Leopov. "Some kind of amulet?"

Petrov shook his head. "I don't know. Among the

pieces in Priam's Treasure are two golden diadems. Schliemann called them 'Helen's Jewels.' There is picture of his wife wearing them. But those are in Pushkin museum with rest of collection. Maybe there is another diadem, or some other piece of jewelry. I think Sergei Yukovitch knows what it is, but he does not tell me."

Maddock studied Petrov's gaunt face, looking for some hint of deception. The Russian seemed sincere, but given the circumstances, Maddock wasn't inclined to trust him. He turned to Leopov.

"What do you think?" he said, speaking in a low voice.

"If Telesh really believes the Charm can do all of that, it's no wonder he is obsessed with finding it. But if you're asking if I believe in some arcane power…" She shrugged. "I suppose it's not the craziest thing I've ever heard. Even if it isn't something real, it might have enormous symbolic power, especially in the hands of a man like Telesh."

"Agreed. We can't let him get to it." He looked back to Petrov. "We need to know more about this Charm. How did Telesh learn about it in the first place?"

"Before he becomes gangster, Sergei Yukovitch works for KGB, but his father was with Red Army in Berlin. This is just speculation, but perhaps his father was one of the men who brought Priam's Treasure to Russia. Maybe there was something in the museum records, or perhaps something revealed during interrogations, that told of Helen's Charm. And how Hitler was able to use it."

Maddock nodded. "Okay, that makes a lot of sense. But whatever it was they learned, it didn't help them find the damned thing."

"So where do we start looking?" asked Leopov, a touch of eagerness in her voice.

"Let's worry about that once we've made it out of Russia alive." He hugged his arms around his chest, savoring the warmth. "Get some sleep. I'll take first watch. We'll leave before first light."

TWELVE

Washington DC

The seven-hour time difference between Helsinki and the East Coast meant that, even though the trans-Atlantic flight lasted more than ten hours, it was not quite noon when the Air Force tanker plane set down at Andrews Air Force base in Prince George's County, Maryland. Despite their collective anxiety over Maddock's uncertain fate, the three SEALs slept through most of the flight and were fully rested and alert upon arrival. A black Ford Expedition with impenetrably dark tinted windows drove out to meet them on the tarmac.

Bones regarded the vehicle with undisguised wariness. "Nothing conspicuous about that ride," he muttered.

Huntley looked over at him. "You'd rather hail a taxi? Or maybe take a city bus?" He jerked a thumb at Lia. "I thought you would appreciate a little discretion, but hey, if you want to stroll down the Mall with her on your arm, I'm cool with it."

Bones frowned but offered no further protest. He didn't like being under Huntley's thumb, and his gut told him that the spook was probably exaggerating the degree of risk to Lia, but that was no reason not to err on the side of caution.

The SUV bore them swiftly through DC traffic on the 12th Street Expressway, passing through the National Mall, turning right onto Constitution Avenue, past the multi-museum complex collectively known as the Smithsonian Institution. The driver turned left on 9th Street and headed north around the block to the Pennsylvania Avenue entrance of the National Archives building, right across the street from the US Naval Memorial Plaza. One block further west sat the utilitarian eyesore that was the J. Edgar Hoover Building, headquarters of the Federal Bureau of Investigation. The SUV pulled into the lane reserved for tour buses and, when they were directly in front of the glass door entrance, the five passengers disembarked and headed inside. Lia, despite her mental and physical exhaustion, perked up at the sight of the neo-classical monument to America's most sacred documents. Bones supposed that, for a professional archivist, this was the equivalent of a trip to Mecca. Or maybe Disney World.

They were rushed through security, receiving visitor badges which had been set aside for them, and were escorted to a small reading room on one of the upper stories, well off the tour route, where FBI Special Agent Alexandra Vaccaro sat waiting.

Alex—Bones recalled that was what she preferred to be called—appeared little changed by the years since their last encounter. Her hair was uniformly dark brown—she had evidently eschewed the blonde highlights he recalled—but her green eyes were every bit as vivid as he remembered, and her olive complexion was smooth and wrinkle free, even when she smiled upon seeing them. Yet, as attractive as she was, Bones felt strangely ill at ease in her presence. Alex was one of those brainy types, who seemed not only immune to his charm but actually to find it offensive, and who seemed inexplicably drawn to Maddock, despite the fact that the stick up his tailpipe had not loosened appreciably in all the years they had known each other.

Professor, who had known Alex the longest of any of them, greeted her. "Special Agent Vaccaro, it's good to see you again. Thanks for meeting us. I hope it was no trouble."

"Trouble? I literally had to walk a whole block and cross the street." She smiled. "But seriously, Professor, if you call me anything but Alex, I may have to arrest you."

She gave him a hug then turned to Bones and hugged him as well. Bones returned the embrace awkwardly, and then breathed a sigh of relief when she moved on to hug Willis. Professor introduced Lia and Huntley by name only, an omission which Bones felt certain Alex had taken note of.

After handshakes were exchanged, the historian-cum-FBI agent turned to Bones. "Where's your fearless leader?"

"Maddock? He's... Uh... On leave. His folks were killed in a car accident." Bones regretted uttering the half-truth as soon as it was out of his mouth.

"My God, that's terrible."

"Yeah," Bones mumbled.

An uncomfortable silence followed. Alex finally broke it. "So, why did you want to see me? I'm guessing—based on your choice of meeting places—that this is more than just a social call." Her emerald eyes flicked to Huntley, then settled on Lia. "Official business."

"More or less," Professor said, equivocally. "You know how it is. You're looking for something, turn over a rock and fall down a completely unexpected rabbit hole. We're hoping you can help us find our way back from Wonderland."

"No promises," she replied, "but I do enjoy a mad tea party now and again. What's the big mystery?"

"U-boats. Specifically, boats that went missing near the end of World War II."

She arched an eyebrow. "So, you're hunting Nazis now?"

Bones watched Huntley from the corner of his eye. The CIA man had repeatedly stressed the importance of keeping the exact nature of their search a secret, but if he was bothered by Alex's deductive insights, he didn't let it show.

"Like I said," Professor answered. "It's a rabbit hole."

Alex nodded and then moved to a nearby computer workstation and immediately began entering information into the search window. As she typed, she said, "As I'm sure you know, the Germans—and the Reich in particular—were meticulous record keepers, and we captured a lot of their naval records at the end of the war, so this shouldn't be too difficult."

She hit the 'enter' key a final time to initiate the search, and a moment later, the screen changed to display the requested data. Her eyes moved back and forth as she read silently, then she resumed speaking. "So, in 1945 only four U-boats went missing, fate unknown. They are: The U-296, which disappeared in March, while on patrol in the North Channel between Ireland and Great Britain; the U-396, reported missing in April, last known location, near the Shetland Islands; also in the same month, the U-398, lost either in the North Sea or the Arctic Ocean; and the U-1055, lost in the North Atlantic while en route to the English Channel."

As she summarized the list, Bones marked the locations on his mental map of the world. Alex clicked on the first entry and the screen changed again. "U-296 was probably damaged by an RAF torpedo, and likely went down shortly afterward."

Click.

"Ditto, the 396."

She clicked again and was silent for several seconds as she perused the next listing. "This is kind of interesting. There were rumors that the U-398 was refitted before leaving on its last patrol in April of 1945. Unknown changes may have been made to the external shell and there was some restructuring of the internal cabin bulkheads."

"May have?"

"There's nothing in the Kriegsmarine records to confirm it. The rumors probably came from the naval engineers who worked on the boat in dry dock, and were interrogated by the Allies after the end of the war. Anyway, the last reported contact was on April 17, four days after leaving Bergen. No indications that the boat encountered enemy forces."

Bones glanced over at Lia who was nodding thoughtfully.

"And last but not least," Alex went on, "The U-1055. Last contact, April 23, 1945. Now, seventeen days earlier, the boat was fired on by Royal Navy motor torpedo boats. They reported no damage, but they might have been worse off than they realized."

"U-398 seems like the best candidate," Professor said, "especially with those modifications."

Alex swung her gaze around to meet his. "Best candidate for what, exactly? You know, I could probably help you narrow this down a lot more if you told me what you're looking for." She paused a beat, just long enough to ascertain that more information would not be forthcoming, and then continued, "You've already given me more than enough to draw my own conclusions, so there's really no point in playing your cards close to the vest. You think the Nazis tried to smuggle out something, or maybe someone, aboard a U-boat at the end of the war. That's actually a pretty widely believed notion, all evidence to the contrary, so whatever you've got, it's probably not the earth-shattering revelation you think it is."

Huntley finally broke his silence. "Guilty as charged, Nancy Drew." He shifted his gaze to Bones. "I told you this was a waste of time, but now you've got it on expert authority. Case closed."

"Nancy Drew?" Alex's mouth curled in a wry grin. "If that's your idea of witty banter, you could learn a thing or two from Bones. I grew up on Nancy Drew. Why do you think I got into law enforcement?" She regarded him for a moment, and then said, "You're CIA, aren't you?"

For once, Huntley was rendered speechless.

"That's what I thought," Alex went on. "Well, that explains the Secret Squirrel routine. Okay, so as I was saying, the someone or something you're looking for must have dropped off the grid completely at the end of the war. And whomever it or whatever it was, it would have to be pretty important to warrant this level of attention." She cocked her head to the side. "You're not chasing Adolf, are you?"

"No, never found him all that attractive," Bones said. He laughed but cut himself short and became serious. They still had no idea what the "something of great importance" was, so why couldn't it be the Führer himself? "Why? Do you think he might have made it out? Faked his own death?"

Alex maintained a neutral expression. "I really doubt it, but it's not completely implausible. The official story is that Hitler and Eva Braun took cyanide capsules. She died, but evidently the poison wasn't working fast enough, so he shot himself in the head. Goebbels and several other high-ranking party officials then burned the bodies, in accordance with his final wishes. A few hours later, when the Red Army stormed the bunker, they found charred bone fragments which they took and buried in an undisclosed location.

"Now, while there isn't any evidence to contradict the official record, there isn't a whole lot to support it. In my line of work, we have a saying. No body, no crime. We only have the eyewitness accounts of loyal Nazi officers who might have been trying to cover up their Führer's escape. To the best of my knowledge, the remains were never subjected to any kind of forensic examination, but you can bet the Soviets didn't want anyone thinking that Hitler might still be alive. Even a rumor of it might have been enough to prolong the war. I would say the most compelling evidence to suggest that he didn't fake his death and escape is the simple fact that he never showed up again." She paused a beat. "But if he escaped on a U-boat that was subsequently lost in transit, that might explain why."

Bones realized that she was watching them carefully for a reaction. He decided to give her one. "Friggin' Hitler," he said, shaking his head. "He's like a cockroach that won't die."

Alex continued to regard them a few seconds longer, then shrugged. "Well, it's probably just a wild conspiracy theory, but sometimes it's fun to play them out as a thought experiment. Two U-boats actually made it to South America, so despite what I just said, it's not impossible that one or both of these other boats made the attempt and sank en route. Either 398 or 1055, though if I were a betting girl, my money would be on 398. Those modifications might have been made to add fuel tanks to extend its range and create a secret internal compartment to conceal VIP passengers or cargo from the crew."

"For argument's sake," Professor said, "Let's say that's what happened. How would we go about trying to track it down?"

Alex tapped her chin thoughtfully, then turned back to the computer screen. After a few more keystrokes, a map of the Atlantic Ocean and its coastlines appeared on the screen. A long red line traced a route that started in Norway, continued west around the British Isles, and then turned south in a steep diagonal line that passed near the west African coast, and then hugged the east coast of South America before eventually arriving in Argentina.

"This is the route taken by the U-977 which arrived in Argentina in August of 1945. As you can see, it's a direct route, but with Allied forces still patrolling those waters, it would be a long and tedious journey. Unlike modern subs, the U-boats were a lot faster on the surface—they could only make about seven knots submerged—but on the surface, they were a lot more vulnerable to enemy ships and planes. Heinz Schäffer, the skipper of the 977, claims he made a continuous sixty-six day submerged run using the boat's snorkel, which would be an impressive feat if true. Navy experts have cast doubt on his story, and I tend to agree, but if our phantom U-boat attempted something like that, then it might explain how it was lost. A lot of U-boats sank after their snorkels malfunctioned or were swamped in heavy seas.

"If the boat did go down anywhere between here and here—" She ran her finger along the diagonal line. "—then your chances of finding it are pretty much nil.

You'd be looking in anywhere from one to three miles of water. If it went down closer to the coast of South America, or maybe in the North Sea…" She waggled her hand to indicate the odds were only a little bit better. "Those would be the places to look, but you'd be looking for a needle that might not even be in the haystack."

"And if it took a different route?" Professor asked.

She shrugged. "Might as well throw darts at the map, because I wouldn't have a clue about where to tell you to start looking."

"You said there were two U-boats that made it to Argentina, right?" said Bones. "What about the other one?"

Professor and Lia answered at the same time. "U-530."

Alex grinned and typed in a new search entry. "Okay, the U-530, was a Type Nine B-forty boat—bigger than the Type Seven, which both the 977 and 398 were. Skippered by Oberleutnant zur See Otto Wermuth. Seven combat patrols, the last of which coincided with the end of the war. Wermuth refused the order to surrender and set out for Argentina, arriving on July 10." She stopped her summary but her eyes continued to move back and forth as she read, and after a few seconds of this, her forehead creased in thought. "Interesting."

"Why don't you let us be the judge of that," said Huntley, snarkily.

Unruffled, Alex elaborated. "Wermuth destroyed his log book so there's no record of his journey. He also jettisoned the boat's anti-aircraft gun."

"Why would he do that?" Bones asked.

"Hard to say. Maybe to reduce ballast or free up room inside the vessel for additional food and fuel."

"I mean the log book. Why destroy it?" He paused a beat before adding, "What did he have to hide?"

"That's a good question. A lot of conspiracy nuts have speculated that he was carrying VIP passengers, whom he might have let off before surrendering to the

Argentine navy at Mar Del Plata."

"How do we know he didn't?"

"Wermuth and his crew were all interrogated by naval investigators. They all told the same story. If they were all lying, there would have been inconsistencies. Little things, embellishments and so forth, but enough for a skilled investigator to pick up on."

"Maybe they didn't know what was going on," suggested Professor. "Maybe the 530 was escorting another U-boat—the 398—and that was the secret he was covering up. The crew might have known what was going on."

"There's something else," Alex went on. "About a week before Wermuth surrendered, a Brazilian cruiser—the Bahia—sank under mysterious circumstances. Thirty-odd survivors of a crew of about four hundred. According to them, the crew had been conducting an anti-aircraft live fire exercise when the ship exploded. It was assumed that they hit a mine, but when the 530 showed up in Argentina a week later, some of the Brazilian brass thought the Germans might have hit her with a torpedo."

"Could they have?"

"The math doesn't quite add up. The Bahia's last reported position was zero-north, thirty- west. About six hundred miles from the Brazilian coast and about 3,000 miles from Mar Del Plata. There's no way the U-boat could have traveled that far in six days."

"But it could have been another U-boat. The 977. Or the 398."

Alex inclined her head, ceding the point. "The official finding in the matter of the sinking of the Bahia is that it was an accident. In the course of the live-fire exercise, the AA-gunner inadvertently fired into the depth charges on the rear deck, triggering the explosion that broke the ship."

Bones rolled his eyes. "And the Roswell crash was a weather balloon."

"What if the Bahia encountered the 398 and they sank each other?" Professor mused.

"If," Alex echoed. "It's an unlikely if, but it would at least give you a place to start looking."

"Zero-north, thirty-west," Bones murmured. "Middle of nowhere."

"Deep water, too," Alex added. "Twelve to fourteen thousand feet."

"Assuming that the U-boat went down in close proximity to the Bahia," Professor interjected, "say, a ten-mile radius… That's probably a generous estimate. Our search area would be relatively small. If we could get our hands on an Argo rig… Like what Bob Ballard used to find the Titanic… We could map the seafloor in a matter of days. If the U-398 is down there, we'd find it."

"And if it's not?" sneered Huntley.

"Then we'd be back to square one, but at least we'd know one place the 398 isn't."

Huntley shook his head disparagingly. "Sounds like a colossal waste of time. Not to mention taxpayer money."

"If you think so," retorted Bones, "then cut us loose. Believe it or not, the Navy actually has the resources to handle maritime search operations."

That seemed to catch Huntley off guard. He eyed Bones warily as if sizing up a potential adversary. After a few seconds of this, he shrugged. "It's not my decision. Let me make a phone call."

Then, without further comment, he turned on his heel and strode from the room.

THIRTEEN

Trabzon, Turkey

The ferry pulled into the port of Trabzon, on the northern Turkish coast, about an hour before sunset, and quickly offloaded most of the passengers.

Most, but not all.

The three who remained aboard were not technically passengers at all, but stowaways. They had sneaked aboard the vessel in Sochi, blending in with the catering crew, pushing large carts full of food up the supply gangplank, and had managed to keep out of sight during the four-hour crossing of the Black sea. They lingered in hiding a while longer, waiting until the decks were nearly clear, and then, posing as janitors packing out bags of refuse, made their way down the gangplank and melted into the flow of pedestrian traffic.

Although they were in the country illegally, Turkey was a NATO ally, and as such, Maddock could easily have contacted the embassy in Ankara and obtained official approval for their presence, but doing so would have meant hours, or possibly even days, spent waiting for all the diplomatic hurdles to be cleared. It also would have meant exposing their mission to government officials who did not have a need to know, and who might very well inadvertently compromise them. He didn't know how far Telesh's reach extended, and didn't want to find out the hard way.

They meandered through the city for several blocks, avoiding contact with locals and occasionally doubling back to make sure they weren't being followed. Eventually, they came to a busy street bazaar, where Maddock risked approaching an English-speaking tourist who informed him that they were near the town square or *Meydan*. After making small talk for a few minutes, Maddock casually asked for recommendations—food, lodging, a bank. He was only interested in the latter.

After rejoining the others, Maddock found a pay phone and dialed the operator. Thankfully, the person on the other end of the line spoke enough English to make sense of his request, and in a matter of just a few seconds, he heard a ringing sound over the scratchy connection, and then a familiar if guarded voice came on the line.

"This is Maxwell."

"Collect call from Mr. Hunter," the operator explained, a little hesitantly. "International long distance. Will you accept the charges?"

Maddock felt a twinge of grief upon hearing the stranger utter the alias he had provided. He'd chosen it because it had been the unit callsign he'd used in Bosnia, and knew that Maxie would immediately recognize it, and the need for discretion, but hearing it aloud made him think of his father.

There was only the briefest hesitation as Commander Hartford Maxwell processed this information. "Of course."

"Thank you." There was a faint crackle of static as the operator disconnected from the call, and then the background noise disappeared. Maddock spoke quickly. "Uncle Maxie! You'll never guess where we are?"

There was a brief pause, which might have been transmission lag, and then Maxie replied. "I guess I won't."

"Turkey," Maddock said. "A city called Trabzon. On the north coast."

"How's your vacation going? Your aunt and I were concerned when we didn't hear from you after your flight."

Maddock would have liked nothing more than to brief his superior on all that had happened to Leopov and himself, and he was burning with curiosity regarding the outcome of the mission to rescue Lia, but now was not the time for that conversation. "We're doing great. I'm about to head out to pick up some souvenirs, but I'll have to exchange some currency first. There's a bank near the town square. I'll probably go there."

"Sounds like a plan. Pick me up something. And call again when you can."

"Will do." Maddock hung up without further comment and went back to where Leopov and Petrov were waiting. They continued idling in the bazaar for another fifteen minutes, setting aside a few items to purchase later—fresh clothes, food, and a cellular phone. Only then did Maddock circle back to the bank he had spotted earlier. Although it was past the end of the business day, he wasn't at all surprised to find a man waiting by the door to meet him.

"You are Mr. Hunter?" the man said in halting English.

"I am. I believe you have something for me from Goliath."

The man gave a satisfied nod upon hearing the prearranged codeword and admitted Maddock without delay. Five minutes later, he left with a fat roll of Turkish lira in his pocket.

He rejoined the others and, after paying for their various purchases, headed into the *Meydan*. While Leopov and Petrov voraciously tore into the repast they had purchased—none of them had eaten in well over twenty-four hours—Maddock used his newly acquired cellular phone to call Maxie.

"Took your sweet time," grumbled the SEAL Team commander.

Maddock did not bother making excuses. "Did Bones and the others get out okay?"

"As far as I know, everything went according to plan. They reached Helsinki without any problems. Unfortunately, there was a change of management at the last minute. I haven't heard a peep from him, which is strange. You know how he likes to talk."

Although not encrypted, the wireless telephones were more secure than land lines, but there was always a chance that the call could be intercepted, particularly if Maddock was reading Maxie correctly. *Change of management* meant someone had co-opted their mission—almost certainly the CIA, but why had Bones gone radio silent?

Still, maybe it was for the best. "If you hear from him, let him know that we hit a few snags on our way out, but managed to slip away without too much trouble." He paused a beat, then added, "Just like Luke and Leia escaping the Death Star."

"O-kay," Maxie replied, slowly, consternation audible in his tone. "I'll pass that along. So what's next on your itinerary?"

"We're going to hop a bus to Ankara. We'll need new travel docs so we can fly out of here." He looked over at Petrov who seemed to be closely following the one-sided conversation. "There was one little wrinkle in our getaway. We've picked up a… a stray." He gave a quick if vaguely worded summary of their capture and escape.

"I see," Maxie said when he was done. "How do you want to handle that?"

Petrov evidently grasped that he had become the subject of the conversation. "I cannot return to Russia. Telesh would kill me."

"If we can get you to the embassy," Leopov said, "you can request asylum. But there are no guarantees."

Petrov frowned. "Asylum? I had not considered anything quite so formal."

Maddock raised a hand to silence them, then spoke into the phone again. "We'll keep him with us for now. We'll need some docs for him as well."

"That may be a little trickier. The new management might have a thing or two to say about it but I'll do what I can from this end."

"Understood. I'll call again when we get to Ankara."

As Maddock hung up, Petrov asked. "What about

Lia? Is she all right?"

"She's fine," Maddock assured him. It was probably the truth.

Petrov wasn't satisfied. "Where is she? Are we going to join her?"

"Not just yet. There's something I want to check out first, and I think your expertise may come in handy."

"My expertise? I am historian."

"Exactly. The ruins of Troy, where Schliemann found Priam's Treasure. They're here, aren't they? In Turkey?"

"Da. Is on the coast, near the Dardanelles."

Maddock nodded. "Telesh wants Helen's Charm. If we're going to stop him, or get him off your back for good, we need to know what it is. Maybe we can get some answers in the place where it was discovered."

Troy, Petrov explained, was not, in fact, one city, but nine different settlements, built one atop another over the course of nearly five millennia. It was the second of these—inhabited until about 2250 BCE when it was destroyed by fire—that Heinrich Schliemann identified with the besieged city described in the Iliad, and excavated, uncovering not only a portion of the city's foundations, but also a collection of royal artifacts—many of them wrought of gold and silver. In the century-plus that followed, as the discipline of archaeology matured and the site was more thoroughly and scientifically explored, Schliemann's determination was judged to be off by about a thousand years. If there had actually been a Trojan War—and there was no consensus on its historicity—then the city described in the Homerian epic would have been the seventh incarnation of the city, which existed between about 1300-1250 BCE.

Regardless of whether or not the events of the Iliad had any basis in history, the site—officially known as the Hisarlik archaeological complex—and the nearby city of Çanakkale benefited tremendously from the legendary association. The site was more a theme park, replete with an enormous mock-up of the Trojan Horse and battle re-enactments by performers in bronze armor.

"So what are you hoping to find here?" Leopov asked as the battle recreation concluded to a smattering of applause.

Maddock shook his head uncertainly. "I'm not sure. Context, maybe?"

"How is that going?"

He managed a smile. "You know, despite all the touristy stuff, I'm still in awe of what this place represents. Five thousand years of history. Even if the Iliad is fiction, the people who inspired that story lived and fought and died here." He paused a beat, then added almost wistfully. "I think my dad would have really loved to see this." He shook his head again and turned to Petrov. "Let's see if we can find someone to tell us more about the site."

A helpful tour guide directed them to one of the resident archaeologists who introduced himself as Dr. Aslan.

"You want to know about Schliemann?" Aslan seemed a little irritated by the topic, but managed a diplomatic smile. "A controversial figure. His methods were amateurish at best. He was a treasure hunter, a looter. More interested in proving that he had found the city of Homeric legend than in advancing the cause of real knowledge." He sighed. "And yet… Without him, would any of this exist? Who can say?"

"Where did he find Priam's Treasure?" Maddock asked.

Aslan produced a map of the site which delineated each of the levels of the city in different colors, and pointed to a rectangular structure near the center of the illustration. "Here. It was in May of 1873. Schliemann wrote that he had been excavating the wall of what he believed to be the palace of King Priam, when he discovered a large copper artifact—probably a shield or cauldron. Realizing that such a find would have great value, and not trusting his own workmen, he dismissed the laborers for their afternoon meal, and continued the work on his own, removing the items in secret in order to smuggle them out of the country."

"How did he manage that?"

"He claimed that his wife hid them under her shawl."

"Must have been a pretty big shawl," remarked Leopov, dubiously.

Aslan gave her a knowing smile. "The story is almost certainly a fabrication. In fact, Schliemann himself later admitted he had made it up. His wife, Sophie, was not even present for the discovery. At the time, she was in Athens, attending her father's funeral. It is more likely that he had help from someone else. When Sophie Schliemann was photographed wearing the Jewels of Helen in Athens the following year, Amin Efendi, the official who had been tasked with monitoring Schliemann's progress, was sent to prison, whether for simple incompetence or for taking a bribe to look the other way, who knows?"

"And the treasure ended up in Berlin?"

"Most of it. Schliemann sold a few items to raise funds, and later returned some of the gold to the Sultan in exchange for permission to return to the country for further archaeological investigations. Those pieces are on display at Topkapi Palace."

"They let him come back?"

"Perhaps they believed he would eventually return the rest of the treasure. He had always claimed that his reason for removing it was to protect it from being stolen by corrupt government officials.

"You must understand, it was a very uncertain time in my country's history," Aslan went on, almost apologetically. "The Ottoman Empire, which had endured for nearly 700 years, was teetering on the edge of economic collapse. Perhaps the concession to Schliemann was an overture to the German government. The Sultan knew he would need to make alliances with European powers in order to hold the Empire together and resist Russian aggression."

"A mistake as it turns out," opined Petrov. "The alliance with the Central Powers put them on the wrong side of World War I. Things did not go so well for Ottoman Empire after that."

"Politics do not interest me," Aslan retorted with a shrug that did not entirely hide his displeasure. "My area of interest is the ancient world."

"Getting back to Priam's Treasure," Maddock prompted. "You mentioned 'the Jewels of Helen.' I assume that Schliemann came up with the name?"

"A conceit on his part. The golden diadem was indeed fit for a queen, but it almost certainly was not worn by Helen of Sparta, if she ever existed at all."

"Did he ascribe any other pieces to Helen?"

"None that I'm aware of but it would not surprise me. You might enquire at the Topkapi museum. In addition to the authentic artifacts, they have replicas of the entire collection. Of course, you…" He eyed Petrov with thinly disguised disdain, "could always visit the real collection at the Pushkin Museum in Moscow."

"You know, we just might at that," Maddock said, taking Petrov's elbow and steering him away before he could say anything else inflammatory.

When they were alone again, Leopov asked, "Well, did that give you the context you were looking for?"

Maddock did not answer the question directly, but instead posed one of his own. "Why do you think Schliemann changed his story?"

"What are you talking about?"

"First he said his wife helped him sneak the treasure out. Then he claimed she wasn't even there."

"Why does it matter?" pressed Leopov.

"I don't know. Maybe it doesn't. It just struck me as an odd detail. Why mention it at all?" He looked from Leopov to Petrov.

"Maybe someone caught him in the lie," replied Leopov. "Maybe the story about his wife was meant to deflect suspicion from his real accomplices. But then someone figured out that she wasn't there when it happened, so he had to admit the truth."

Petrov had another idea. "Schliemann was German, but his wife, Sophia, was Greek. The Greeks and Turks have never gotten along. It is an enmity that goes back... well, at least as far back as the Trojan War. Perhaps the idea of a Greek woman helping steal the treasures which rightfully were the property of the Turkish people added insult to injury."

Maddock pondered the competing explanations for a moment, then directed his attention to Petrov. "Just how many pieces are in the collection?"

"I don't know an exact number, but several dozen."

"And some of the pieces are big, right? Aslan mentioned a copper shield? And a cauldron?"

"Yes. There were also many cups and utensils of silver and copper. Some gold as well. Also blades of copper—lance heads, daggers, axes."

"That's a lot of metal to dig out of the ground during the workmen's lunch break. Probably would have taken a few trips to get it all away from the excavation."

"Which suggests the story about his wife sneaking it out under her shawl is probably the lie," said Leopov.

"Maybe."

Leopov did not miss his equivocation. "But you have another idea, don't you?"

"We're looking for Helen's Charm, right? Something that allegedly has the power to..." He shrugged. "Bewitch people, I guess."

"You think Schliemann used Helen's Charm to hide what he was doing." Leopov's tone was not so much incredulous as accusatory. "You think it is real."

"I'm just floating the idea. Let's say the charm was something like a ring or necklace, something that he might have pocketed and given to his wife as a gift. And then later..." He shook his head. "I don't know. I guess it does sound crazy."

"Sergei Yukovitch does not think so," Petrov said. "He thinks Helen used the Charm to make Paris fall in love with her, and to make Priam endure a decade of war to protect her. And he believes Hitler used it to deceive an entire nation into following his mad schemes. Using it to smuggle treasure seems like a very little thing by comparison."

"Schliemann probably thought he was being clever by claiming his wife helped him, but it backfired on him," added Leopov. "But that still doesn't tell us *what* it is."

Petrov cocked his head to the side thoughtfully. "Helen's Charm went to Berlin with the rest of the collection, and that's where Hitler got his hands on it. But it was not with the rest of the treasure that Red Army took to Moscow. If we could find a record of the treasure when it was acquired by museum in Germany, and then compare with what is in Pushkin Museum, we might be able to figure out what we are looking for." Then, as if in afterthought, he added, "You should put Lia on the job. She's very good at this sort of thing."

"I'm not sure she's available at the moment," Maddock replied, "But you're right. We need to go to Berlin."

FOURTEEN

Off the coast of Brazil

After days of nearly non-stop air travel, Bones was grateful to once again feel the deck of a ship and the roll of the waves under his feet. Unfortunately, that was about the only thing he felt grateful for.

Huntley's phone call had yielded what had seemed at the time like good news. The Agency had agreed to fully underwrite a search for the U-398. Despite his boast to the contrary, Bones wasn't at all certain that he could convince Maxie to convince the Navy brass to take on what would probably amount to a wild goose chase, so letting the CIA handle the logistical challenges sounded like a win-win situation.

One of the biggest challenges was finding a research vessel from which to conduct a search of the target area, and Huntley had come through for them. Under the auspices of a dummy corporation owned by a shell company in Delaware, he had leased the *RS Besnard*, an oceanographic vessel owned by the University of Sao Paolo, ostensibly for the purpose of conducting sea salinity surveys of the Amazon discharge zone. Huntley had also taken care of the travel arrangements, providing forged passports which would stand up to the closest scrutiny. He had, in fact, thought of everything, and was so uncharacteristically accommodating that Bones had begun to smell a rat.

Before leaving for Brazil, he had casually asked Huntley for five minutes to check in with Maxie. When the CIA man had told him that it was already taken care of, Bones had tried being a little more insistent, at which point Huntley had fallen back on his tried and true excuse.

"No can do, Sitting Bull. Loose lips sink ships, and

in case you forgot, that's exactly where we're gonna be. On a ship, I mean."

"Come on, dude. I'm not asking to call my girlfriend. Maxie's my CO. He's got a need-to-know."

"Not right now he doesn't. We are radio silent until further notice. No phone calls, emails, tom-toms or smoke signals. Not until I tell you otherwise. Copy?"

"Well can you at least find out if Maddock made it out okay?"

Huntley had only offered an indifferent shrug.

The episode had left a bitter taste in Bones' mouth that still lingered two days later as the *Besnard* cruised along the equator toward the last known position of the *Bahia*.

When they arrived at the target coordinates, Professor and Willis set to work deploying the Argo, a remotely operated camera sled designed to operate as deep as 20,000 feet, on loan to their expedition from the Woods Hole Oceanographic Institute. With the Argo's multiple cameras and high-intensity searchlights, they would be able to conduct a "flyover" survey of the benighted depths by towing the array back and forth across the search zone in overlapping lanes—a technique known to treasure hunters as "mowing the lawn." If they spotted something of interest they would be able to zoom in or even direct the Argo to move in closer, and if further attention was warranted, they could send down Jason, a remotely operated vehicle—or ROV—equipped with sonar, magnetometers, and a manipulator arm for taking samples.

Professor, in particular, was ecstatic at the chance to use the legendary deep-sea survey equipment. Argo and Jason had both been used in the successful search for the Titanic several years earlier, and the fact that Huntley had been able to procure them and have them transported half a world away told Bones that the spy's agency bosses were taking the search seriously, even if Huntley did not seem to be.

They found the wreck after just two hours of

searching. It was not a pretty sight. Following the explosion which had obliterated the stern, the naval cruiser had sunk quickly—eyewitness accounts from the handful of survivors reckoned the ship had gone down in about three minutes. The rapid descent had continued apace, and the *Bahia* had been nearly vertical when it arrowed, bow first, into the seafloor. The impact had devastated the funnels and superstructure, but by some quirk of fate, the hull remained upright, jutting up from the murk like a dark tower in a Tolkienesque fantasy tale.

In the control room of the *Besnard*, Professor zoomed in for a closer view of the wreck. Twisted beams and armor plates, encrusted with oxidation, blossomed like a flower at the upraised stern, but in the middle of that flower was a gaping wound that seemed to drive all the way to the heart of the stricken naval vessel.

"Something blew her open all right," Professor announced. "Hard to say whether it was an enemy torpedo, or one of her own depth charges though."

"Mark the location," Bones said, "And resume the search."

Eight hours of searching however yielded no further results. No wreckage, no debris field that might indicate a damaged vessel of any stripe.

With dusk settling over the world, Bones set up a duty roster to continue the search through the night. Ideally, the research ship should have been crewed by at least a dozen officers and able seamen, but the secrecy of the mission prevented that, so it fell to the three SEALs to operate both the ship and the ROV.

"We'll run round the clock," Bones said. "Prof, you hit the rack. Willis, you'll watch TV." He jerked a thumb at the console where a large video monitor displayed the surreal but unchanging landscape of the deep ocean floor. "I'll stay at the wheel. In four, we'll rotate."

"I want to help," Lia said. "What can I do?"

"How 'bout you get me a sandwich," Huntley said.

"Get your own damn sandwich," Willis shot back.

Bones gave him an approving nod, but then went on. "Actually, we're going to be living on coffee, so having someone available for galley duty will really help. We could also probably use an extra set of eyes to watch the video feed."

"Don't look at me," Huntley said, feigning a yawn. "I'm just here to ensure the security of this operation."

"Then why don't you park your ass in the radio room and leave us alone?" Bones retorted. Huntley had already set up a cot in the ship's communications room and kept the door locked when he wasn't inside.

"This isn't a pleasure cruise," Bones went on. "Saying that we're all going to have to pull our weight is sugarcoating it. This is going to be a slog, and the longer it goes on, the worse it will get."

Huntley folded his arms over his chest. "Just how long is it going to take?"

"It'll take as long as it takes."

Professor added, "Even with the right equipment, and a general idea of where to start looking, it still took weeks of searching to find the Titanic. We haven't even been at this a full day."

"Weeks?" Huntley snorted in disgust.

"It won't take us more than a few days to complete our grid," Professor clarified. "But if we don't find the U-boat there, we'll have to expand our search area."

"We're shooting in the dark as it is," Huntley retorted. "You don't even know for certain that there is a U-boat out here."

"You know, what would really help our chances is if you'd let us consult with Alex. She could keep digging into the archives."

Huntley frowned, but seemed to actually be considering Professor's request. Finally, he shook his head. "No. I'm sorry, but we have to keep a lid on this. If you can't find it, it probably means there's nothing to find. I just hope you figure that out before we're all old and gray."

With that, he turned on his heel and stalked away.

"God, I hate that guy," Willis sighed.

"It's almost like he's rooting for us to fail," Professor mused.

"You just figuring that out?"

Bones stared at the monitor. "Why do you suppose that is?" he said. "He takes over our operation, won't let go, gives us everything we ask for, even though he doesn't think we'll find anything. What's his angle?"

"Maybe someone higher up in the Agency doesn't share his low opinion of our treasure hunting game," Willis offered.

"But then why tie our hands? Why not let us consult with an expert?" Professor shook his head. "Something about this stinks."

Willis turned his gaze to Lia. "Maybe we've got it all wrong. Maybe it's about keeping us—or maybe just her—out of the way for a while."

Lia stiffened in alarm. "Me?"

Bones shrugged. "Spooks are always playing games."

"And we're the pawns," Professor added, nodding sagely.

"Homie done playin'," Willis growled. "I say we toss his ass overboard."

Bones smiled at the thought but shook his head. With Maddock still LIA, it fell to him to keep the team out of trouble, and that meant exercising impulse control.

"As much as I'd like to, we're gonna have to come up with a fix that doesn't land us in the brig." *Being in charge really bites,* he added silently. He swung his gaze to Professor. "You really think Alex could help?"

Professor shrugged. "This was always a long shot. But maybe she could point us in a different direction."

Bones sighed and rose from his chair. "I'll go talk to him... Plead our case."

"Good luck." Willis' tone was more sarcastic than hopeful, a sentiment which Bones shared.

He didn't like the idea of bowing and scraping before Huntley, submitting to the man's authority. Following orders was the reality of military life—a reality that seemed to be chaffing a lot more as the years passed—but taking orders from a skidmark like Captain Midnight was positively galling.

Maybe it's time to cash out, he mused.

Hanging it up without putting in twenty years would mean sacrificing his retirement, but if it meant never having to deal with men like Huntley again it would be worth it. He could request a transfer, serve out the rest of his enlistment on a ship or maybe even a cush desk job. And after that? Maybe he'd do security work for his uncle, Crazy Charlie, at the tribal casino. Hell, he could always get a job as a bouncer at a strip club.

Just thinking about being done with the Navy was enough to buoy his mood a little, but the feeling ended when he reached the commo room.

He rapped his knuckles on the door. "Huntley! Open up. We need to talk."

Huntley opened the door, grinning sardonically. "Hey, I didn't call for room service, but since you're here, you can take away my dirty dishes."

Bones ignored the dig, and pushed inside the small room. "How about you and me call a truce for five seconds. Talk to each other like professionals."

Huntley smirked. Bones braced himself for another wise-ass comment, but the CIA agent nodded. "Go on."

"I need to call my CO."

"Damn, Tonto. How many times do we gotta hoe this row? Radio silence means—"

Bones raised a hand. "What happens if we call it quits?"

Huntley's smirk softened into what might have been a hopeful smile. "I knew you'd eventually throw in the towel, but I figured you'd drag it out at least a couple days. Okay, short answer: You all sign non-disclosure agreements and never, ever... *ever* speak a word of this to anyone. Break the NDA, and we'll disappear you. We're very good at that. Oh, and in case you're thinking of resuming the search on your own time... Same rule applies."

Bones nodded slowly. He had expected as much. "And Lia? What happens to her?"

Huntley shrugged. "I don't know. That's above my pay grade."

"Sounds like maybe you're not the person I should be talking to."

"Ha. You know, I could probably set that up if you really wanted."

"What I want is to talk to my boss. You know, kick the decision upstairs, like you do." Before Huntley could veto the idea, Bones went on. "Let me put this in language you can understand. With or without your permission, I'm going to be calling my commander to verify what you've told me and ask for guidance. Obviously, *with* would be the preferred option, but I'm comfortable doing it over your dead body."

Huntley's smile slipped a degree or two. "You're not that reckless."

"You're right. I'd probably just knock you senseless and hog-tie you. I think the Navy brass would understand, but if not, I'm prepared to take that hit."

"Is that a fact?" Huntley barked a short, sharp laugh. "Damn, you've got some *cajones* on you." He threw his hands up in a show of surrender. "One thing though. Commander Maxwell will be able to confirm the orders seconding you to my authority, but that's it. He hasn't been read in on the rest of it. Any of it, which means you won't be able to ask for advice. You'll have to make that call all on your lonesome. Understood?"

Bones gave a reluctant nod.

"All right then." Huntley gestured to the wall of radio equipment. "Use the sat-phone. Make your call."

Bones turned and reached for the handset but before he could dial, Huntley called out. "Hey, Bonebrake!"

Bones turned and found himself staring into the

muzzle of a compact semi-automatic pistol. Huntley held his aim for a few, meaningful seconds, then lowered the weapon. "Do we need to review the list of approved topics?"

"No, dude. I got it." Bones turned back to the phone and started dialing.

"Do me a favor, and put it on speaker."

Bones nodded without looking back, and hit a button on the console. An electronic trilling sound filled the room, and then was replaced by Maxie's familiar voice. "This is Maxwell."

"Maxie, it's me."

"Bonebrake?" The SEAL team commander sounded only mildly surprised.

"Yes, sir." He threw a glance over his shoulder. Huntley was standing just out of reach, his arms folded over his chest, the little pistol still in his right hand. Bones went on. "Sorry we've been incommunicado for a while. I take it you don't need me to explain the reason for it?"

"I'd love an explanation, but I'm guessing you won't be able to tell me very much."

"No, sir." Bones felt like he already had his answer, but he had risked everything to get Maxie on the line, and he wasn't going to hang up until he heard it explicitly. "Actually, that's why I'm calling. I just wanted you to confirm what I've been told. Are these orders legit?"

"I'm afraid so, son." Maxie paused a beat, then went on. "I've got some good news, though. Maddock and Zara Leopov made it out okay."

"That is good news."

"I guess it was a little dicey for a while, but Dane said to tell you they made it out as easy as Luke and Leia escaping the Death Star. Or something to that effect."

Bones couldn't help but laugh. "Star Wars? Maddock should know better."

"Well, that's what he told me to tell you."

"Tell him message received."

Huntley cleared his throat and called out, "Commander Maxwell. Jason Huntley, here. I'm the operations officer in charge here."

"I know who you are, Mr. Huntley," Maxie replie, icily.

"I'm sure I don't need to remind you that Maddock and Leopov are also under my jurisdiction for the duration of this operation. If they're in the clear, they need to come in. ASAP."

"They aren't *in the clear* by a longshot. They barely made it out of Russia."

"Where are they now?"

"I'm not sure. They were in Ankara, but I think they've moved on."

"Tell them to go back. Immediately. Have them report to the station chief at the embassy. He'll take care of the rest."

"I'll pass it along." Bones could almost see Maxie speaking through clenched teeth at the other end of the line.

"See that you do. And remind them not to talk to anyone. This is a matter of national security."

"So you keep telling me." When Huntley didn't reply, Maxie went on. "Bonebrake, you got anything else for me?"

Bones glanced at Huntley again. The latter shook his head and made a throat-cutting gesture. "Nothing I can talk about," Bones said. "I'll be in touch when I can."

He hit the 'speaker' button again to end the call.

"There," Huntley said. "Are you happy now?"

"Not really. You're bottling this thing up like it was the true story behind the Kennedy assassination, but you're treating our search for the U-boat like it's a joke. What's going on?

"Need to know, and you don't." Huntley uncrossed his arms and tucked the pistol into a low-profile appendix-holster. "I believe you've got a phantom U-boat to chase. Unless, of course, you're ready to call it quits."

"Which option would piss you off the most?"

Huntley laughed again, then made a shooing gesture. Bones was only too happy to leave, but as he passed through the doorway, Huntley called out again. "Hey, what was that Star Wars reference about?"

"Hell if I know," Bones said with a shrug. "Maddock's a nerd. The only thing I remember about those movies is that there was a hot chick in a gold bikini."

Huntley gave an indifferent grunt, but said nothing more. Bones didn't give him a chance to think about it, but pushed through the door and headed back to the control center where the others were still waiting.

"How did that go?" Willis asked.

"About as well as you'd expect." He checked over his shoulder to make sure that Huntley hadn't followed him, and then, in a lower voice, added. "Maddock and Leopov made it out."

Willis and Professor gave a collective sigh of relief, and Professor added. "Are they coming here?"

Bones shook his head again. "Not yet. Maddock sent us a message." He relayed the cryptic message Maxie had given him.

"What the hell is that supposed to mean?" asked Willis.

Professor was ready with a detailed analysis. "I would surmise that it means they had help to escape. In the original Star Wars film, Luke, with some help from Han Solo and Chewbacca, were able to free Princess Leia from her cell in the detention center. They escaped through a garbage disposal system and, after a running gun battle, made it back to their ship. While they were doing that, Obi Wan Kenobi faced off with Darth Vader and was killed, which might also be Maddock's way of telling us that one or more of their newfound allies met an untimely demise."

Bones rolled his eyes. "How is it that I know the answer to this and you don't?"

Professor gaped at him. "Do elaborate, please."

"Vader let them escape so he could track them.

Maddock's trying to tell us that their getaway wasn't clean. This Russian gangster, Telesh, is following them, probably hoping they'll lead him straight to Lia."

Professor nodded, then looked over at Willis. "He's right."

"It's because he and Maddock share a brain," Willis said.

"Hey, that's uncalled for," Bones protested.

Lia raised her hand, sheepishly. "Excuse me, but what does this mean for me?"

Professor took her hand and patted it reassuringly. "It means Maddock and Zara are going to lead Telesh on a merry chase, while we keep following the trail to Müller."

"I think it means something else, too," Bones added, and made another surreptitious check to make sure Huntley wasn't eavesdropping. "I think Maddock is telling us not to trust anyone."

FIFTEEN

Dam Neck Annex—Virginia Beach, Virginia

Commander Hartford Maxwell regarded the phone on his desk like it was a venomous snake, poised to strike. It was an apt simile since the phone call he was about to make posed a potentially fatal risk, though not for him.

"Maddock, what have I gotten you mixed up in," he murmured.

He shook his head ruefully. Like it or not, he had his orders, and inasmuch as they were not to the best of his knowledge illegal or immoral, he was obliged to follow them.

"Let's get this over with," he said aloud, and reached for the handset, but before he could close his fingers around it, the phone began ringing. He started a little, pulling back his hand reflexively, but after a couple calming breaths, reached out again and lifted the receiver. "This is Maxwell."

He half expected it to be Maddock, or perhaps Huntley again, goading him to push through his hesitation, but the voice that sounded in his ear was female. "Commander Maxwell? This is Alex Vaccaro. We met a few years back when I was NI?"

"The Hell Ship incident. You were Lieutenant Commander Vaccaro back then, as I recall."

"That's correct, sir. I'm at Justice now. The Bureau."

"I see." Maxie vaguely recalled Maddock mentioning the young woman's career change, but decided to dispense with small talk. "Is this official business? Because if it is, you'll have to speak with someone in JAG."

"Oh, no, sir. Nothing like that. This is actually a

personal matter. I heard that…" She paused a beat, as if trying to regroup and when she spoke again, there was a faint tremor of emotion in her voice. "I heard from a… A mutual friend that Dane… Ah… Lost his… Umm. I just wanted to give him a call. Condolences, I mean."

Maxie's pulse quickened. The "mutual friend" had to be Bonebrake, and Alex's use of the vague term suggested the conversation was something she couldn't talk about in detail.

He spoke quickly, cutting her off. "Miss Vaccaro, where are you right now?"

"Uh, I'm at work. DC, if that's what you mean."

"The Hoover Building?"

"That's right."

"Perhaps we could meet somewhere? Get a cup of coffee and catch up."

There was a long silence on the line, followed by. "O-kay."

He shot his cuff and checked his watch. Almost seventeen hundred. "There's a shuttle flight leaving Norfolk in about an hour. If I can get a seat, I should be wheels down at Reagan International by nineteen hundred hours."

"I guess I could meet you there."

"No," he said hurriedly. "Actually, it would probably be better if I came to you. I'll explain everything when I get there."

Washington DC.

After a quick flight and an even quicker taxi ride, Maxie stepped out onto the sidewalk in front of the Naval Memorial—the location Alex had suggested for their rendezvous. The memorial, which Maxie had visited on numerous occasions, consisted of a small circular plaza, fronted by a pair of fountains and ringed with ships' masts from which naval signal flags fluttered. The central feature of the memorial was the Granite Sea—a map of the globe centered on

Washington, DC, but depicting all the oceans of the world. Watching over the map, from a spot roughly in the vicinity of the Bering Sea, was The Lone Sailor, a life-sized bronze sculpture of a sailor standing on a windswept pier, his sea-bag packed and ready beside him. The southern rim of the Granite Sea was bordered by twin semi-circular half walls, with stone benches on the interior, and on the exterior, a series of twenty-six bronze high relief sculptures showing various scenes and famous personages associated with the history of the United States Navy.

The sky was already darkening into twilight, but for the moment, there was still plenty of foot traffic on Pennsylvania Avenue—mostly tourists making their way from one historical monument to the next. He surreptitiously scanned both street and park, taking note of every face, from the camera-toting visitor studying the bronze plaques on the southeastern border of the Granite Sea to the homeless man sleeping on the north steps leading down into the plaza. Any one of them might be there to keep him or Alex under surveillance, or none of them. Professionals were almost impossible to pick out of a crowd, particularly without an extra set of eyes. He would have to conduct himself as if he was being watched, and choose both his words and his actions very carefully.

His slow visual sweep ended when he caught sight of Alex, rising from her seat on a bench on the southwestern wall. Her expression was tentative, but she took a step toward him, hand extended in greeting. "Commander."

He shook her hand then gestured for her to sit. "I'd like to forego the pleasantries if you don't mind."

Alex's demeanor remained wary, but she returned to her spot on the bench and folded her hands on her lap. "Let's get to it then."

He sat alongside her, not quite close enough to make physical contact, but close enough to be intimate. "From your earlier comment, I know that you've been in contact with one of my men. Bonebrake, probably.

And I also infer that you've been read in on their current operation, which remains classified."

"That's correct. I wasn't calling you to discuss that."

"I know, but as it might be difficult to talk around it, I thought a face-to-face meeting might be in order." He dropped his volume to barely above a whisper and added, "You never know who might be listening in."

"I remember how to be discreet, Commander Maxwell."

"I'm sure you do." He let that hang for a moment, then went on. "Bones wasn't being completely honest with you. Maddock did lose both his parents in a car accident last week, but he's not on bereavement leave. He's part of the same operation. Until a couple days ago, he was out of contact. Bones was covering for him."

"He should have come up with a better story," Alex remarked.

"Yes, well, it may have been serendipity since it gave you a reason to contact me." Maxie leaned closer. "What I'd like to know is how you got pulled into this?"

Alex's gaze darted left and right, perhaps in thought, perhaps checking to see if they were being surveilled. "They needed some help with a research project. Naval history. That's my area of expertise."

Maxie studied her expression carefully, wondering how much it was safe to reveal. Strictly speaking, they weren't even supposed to be having this conversation, but his gut told him that Alex was trustworthy. "I'll be straight with you. I've been mostly cut out of this operation."

She nodded. "That doesn't surprise me. That guy…"

"You don't need to say it. The point is, you probably know more about where they are and what they're doing right now than I do. I do not like being out of the loop when my boys are in harm's way."

"I read you, Commander." Her eyes darted around again—definitely checking for surveillance. "I haven't been completely forthcoming with you, sir. I was hoping to give Maddock my condolences, but I had another reason for wanting to contact him. Something that directly relates to this matter.

"That spook—Huntley—was real cagey. I got the impression Bones had to beg to get him to let me consult, and even then, he wouldn't say much about what they were really after, other than that it involved Nazi U-boats that went missing near the end of the war. But it wasn't hard to put two and two together."

"I know this has something to do with the Russians looking for Nazi loot."

"I think it might be something more. The way Secret Agent X was acting, you'd think it was something really mind-blowing. Like the answers to the SATs or something. Anyway, Bones decided to play a hunch and search the wreck of a Brazilian navy cruiser that sunk under mysterious circumstances in 1945. His working theory is that the ship was sunk by a U-boat that may have been damaged or sunk in the battle, and that it might be carrying whatever it is the Russians are trying to find. As far as I know, that's where they were headed. Zero degrees north, thirty degrees west."

"You said you had information you wanted to pass on to them?"

"Well, I got to thinking. What if the U-boat survived the battle? Where would it go next? Our assumption was that it was damaged, but if not, and if it was carrying important cargo or passengers, it would have had to offload them somewhere, right?"

Maxie nodded. "Go on."

"I did some digging and it turns out that in August 1945 the FBI intercepted a radio message from local police discussing a raid in Villa Gessell. They were responding to a tip about some Germans who supposedly arrived by U-boat. They didn't arrest anyone, but they did turn up a short-wave radio transmitter. A couple years later, though, three confessed German agents who had settled in Villa

Gessell admitted to helping unload two U-boats on the night of July 28, 1945.

"Now we already knew that two U-boats made it to Argentina, but one of them, the U-530 surrendered on July 17. Almost two weeks prior. One of them could have been the U-977. It didn't surrender until August 17. The captain might have waited a couple weeks just to give his passengers some time to assimilate into the population. But the second U-boat... That could be the one they're looking for. Those Germans claimed to have offloaded eight trucks worth of cargo, along with dozens of passengers. There might have been more than just two U-boats out there. If so, where did the others go? I'm betting they sailed out to deep water and scuttled them to cover their tracks and hide their numbers. It may be too late to figure out where they went and what that cargo was, but those boats might still be out there, just off the coast of Argentina. That's where they should be looking."

"The Russians are taking this search pretty seriously," Maxie said after considering the revelation for a moment. "I don't think we can afford to do any less."

"So you agree, Bones needs to hear about this. I would have called him myself, but I don't have any way to contact him."

"I'm not sure I do, either. Our friendly neighborhood spook is keeping them incommunicado. I can pass the information along next time he deigns to call me, but that could take a while." An idea struck him. "I might have a workaround."

He took out his cell phone and brought up the call history. He scrolled down to an eleven-digit number, and dialed it. As it started ringing, he explained. "Huntley told me to have Maddock report to an Agency handler, ASAP. I was putting it off, but I guess there's no time like the present."

There were several clicks as the connection was made, and then Maddock's voice issued from the speaker. "Maxie? What's up?"

"I'll get to that in minute, but how are you? Where are you?"

"We're fine. We're in Berlin at the moment, following up on something."

Maxie did a quick mental calculation. The time difference between DC and Berlin was six hours, which meant that it was after midnight in Germany. "Whatever it is, you're going to have to wrap it up. Captain Midnight has new orders for you. He wants you to go to the nearest embassy and report to the station chief."

There was a long silence on the line. When Maddock spoke again, his voice was low, surreptitious. "Can't you just tell him you couldn't reach me?"

"That might work for a day or two, tops, but I think you may want to consider biting the bullet. There's been a development. I'm here with an old friend of yours..." He glanced over at Alex. She nodded for him to continue. "A certain Naval historian you worked with a few years ago."

"It's turning into a regular family reunion," Maddock remarked. "How'd she get mixed up in this?"

"Your teammates consulted with her a few days ago."

"Why did they do that?"

"They're searching for a…" He frowned and looked to Alex again, wondering how much to reveal. "A U-boat that may have played a role in the matter they're investigating. Now she has some new information for them, but no way to get it to them."

"I don't understand. Can't you just call them?"

"That change of management I told you about… It's disrupted communication. I'm not even certain where they are."

Alex chimed in. "If things went according to play, they're in the Atlantic, off the Brazilian coast."

"I'm betting that Captain Midnight will bring you all together again," Maxie said. "Even if he doesn't, you'll still be able to pass on what we've learned."

"So you need me to play carrier pigeon." There was

no mistaking the note of irritation in Maddock's reply.

Maxie frowned but decided to let the rare display of pique pass without comment. "Tell them to take a look at a place called Villa Gessell."

"It's in Argentina," Alex added, "just up the coast from Mar del Plata."

"Got it. I just have to follow up on this lead first."

"Dane, you need to move this to priority one." When Maddock did not reply, Maxie moved the phone away and saw, displayed on the small screen, the words, "Call ended."

He stared at the phone for a few seconds before putting it away. He understood Maddock's frustration, even sympathized with it, but he really didn't have the time or patience to hold his platoon leader's hand. Personal tragedy notwithstanding, Maddock was still part of a team and needed to buck up and play his part. He decided to give his subordinate a few minutes before calling him back for a more pointed conversation without an audience.

He turned to Alex again. "I'm afraid that's all we can do for now. I appreciate you bringing this to me."

"Of course. I hope it helps you guys find whatever it is you're looking for."

She stood, preparing to leave. Anticipating her, Maxie bounded to his feet and offered his hand. "I'll do my best to keep you updated," he said. "Assuming of course that I'm kept in the loop, which…"

He trailed off as he glimpsed something from the corner of his eye. In the instant he had risen from the bench and turned to Alex, the man with the camera, whom he had earlier noticed studying the bronze plaques, had shot a quick but meaningful glance in their direction. He had looked away just as quickly, returning his attention to one of the bronze relief images that adorned the exterior of the low wall that encompassed the Granite Sea. It happened so fast that Maxie's natural impulse was to dismiss it as a coincidence. Despite years of driving a desk, his training as a Naval Special Warfare operator told him to ignore that impulse.

Alex sensed the shift in his demeanor. "What's wrong?"

He saw the tendons in her neck tighten, signaling that she was about to turn her head. "Don't look," he said, his voice low but calm. "Don't react. We're being watched."

She forced herself to relax, nodded and maintained eye contact with him. Her hands fell loosely to her sides, closer to where he assumed her sidearm was holstered. "Where?"

"My three o'clock," Maxie said. "Twenty meters. Caucasian male, dressed like a—"

Before he could finish the description, the subject's head snapped up and swiveled in their direction again, and this time there was no mistaking his intent. His right hand darted into the camera bag.

"Down!" Maxie shouted, reflexively tackling Alex to the ground.

His instincts did not let him down. A fraction of a second later, he heard the muted jackhammer report of a suppressed machine pistol, and the slightly louder noise of rounds striking the wall behind them, just a few feet to the left of where they had been sitting a moment before. Maxie felt something strike his back. Not a bullet, he decided, but a fragment of stone, blasted loose by one of the rounds.

Alex had dragged her pistol—a Glock 23—from its holster and now rolled away from the incoming fire, coming up in a kneeling stance. She held the small gun before her in a two-handed grip, looking for the target, but the man had disappeared from view, ducking down behind the low wall.

Probably reloading, Maxie thought. The shooter had probably burned through an entire magazine with that one burst, which suggested either poor fire discipline, or more likely, that he had plenty more in the bag.

Some part of him—the part that had been cultivated in the Naval Academy and refined through years of leadership—was coldly assessing the situation. The gunman's decision to start shooting seemed hasty—a reaction to being discovered, perhaps—and yet the very fact that he had been packing a suppressed machine-pistol bore testimony to his capacity for violence.

The shooter had preceded him to the rendezvous, which suggested he had probably been covertly watching Alex, which could have meant that Bones' decision to involve her in the search for the U-boat had unwittingly placed her in the crosshairs. But then again, Alex was a federal investigator, and almost certainly had enemies of her own.

Either way, this seemed like a fight they couldn't win. He grabbed Alex by the shoulder. "We need to get to cover."

She looked at him, her eyes flashing with anger, and he could tell that she had no intention of backing down from this fight.

"Alex!" he yelled. "Look around you!"

To her credit, she did, and almost immediately divined the meaning behind his plea. They were the gunman's target—there seemed no question about that—but there were more than a dozen people milling about the memorial plaza, only a few of whom seemed to have grasped that they were practically in the middle of a firefight. Most remained oblivious, or worse, curious. All of them were innocent civilians, and potential collateral damage from the shooter with his fully automatic weapon or from Alex's Glock.

Motion caught his eye. The gunman was back up, stabbing the extended barrel of his weapon toward them. Alex responded by aiming her weapon at him. She didn't fire a shot, but her actions succeeded in causing the man to duck his head down, though not before he squeezed the trigger, unleashing another burst that stitched an arc across the Granite Sea.

Something plucked at Maxie's right sleeve just above the elbow. The pain came a moment later. He ignored it, and grabbed Alex by the arm, dragging her toward the end of the wall. She offered almost no resistance, which struck him as odd until he took a second look and saw why.

Alex had gone rigid. She was clutching her chest with her left hand. A red stain was visible through her clawed fingers, slowly spreading across the fabric of her blouse. There was another stain, this one shaped like a handprint, on her arm. The blood was his. Under his uniform jacket, his shirt sleeve was soaked through from his own bullet wound.

Alex's head came up, her eyes meeting his. Her teeth were clenched in a rictus of agony, but she was still clinging to consciousness. And her weapon.

She thrust it toward him.

He took it, his fingers curling naturally enough around the Glock's small pistol grip. His fingers were tingling, losing feeling. He switched the weapon to his left hand. In his younger days, before he'd gotten promoted out of operational status, he'd become proficient shooting with either hand. It was a perishable skill and he was out of practice, but accuracy wasn't as important right now as being able to break the five-pound trigger. He quickly checked left and right to make sure the gunman wasn't trying to flank their position, and then, with the Glock at the ready, risked a peek above the low wall. There was no sign of the gunman. Either he was also ducking down or, more likely, he had broken contact and melted away.

Maxie pointed the gun skyward and fired three shots.

He eased back down and placed the pistol on the stone pavement next to Alex. Her normally golden skin had gone a ghastly pale. She was losing blood and probably in shock. He awkwardly tore open her blouse, exposing the wound, about an inch above the top of her bra, and pressed his left fist against the bloody hole. His right hand was numb, useless.

The discharge accomplished what the suppressed rounds from the machine-pistol could not. Even before the echoes of the reports died away, cries of alarm went up and people began fleeing the area. But clearing the plaza was only a blessed side-effect. Maxie's real intent was to alert the authorities. FBI Headquarters were only a block away. Maxie had no doubt that help would be arriving soon.

Soon enough to save Alex? God only knew.

SIXTEEN

Germany

Maxie had not been mistaken in identifying Maddock's annoyance during their phone conversation, but he had misread its underlying cause. Maddock, who had received the call well after midnight, had been speaking in front of an audience. He, Leopov and Petrov, were sharing a hotel room, and while the others could not hear Maxie's side of the conversation, Maddock had chosen his words—and his tone—deliberately to avoid revealing too much to the others, or more precisely, to Petrov.

As Bones had intuited from Maddock's cryptic Star Wars reference, Maddock did not completely trust that luck had been the deciding factor in their escape from Telesh's villa. The mere fact that the Russian gangster had left them alone and unguarded in their makeshift prison was suspicious enough to make him think that Telesh might be tracking them somehow in the hope that they would lead him to Lia Markova. That was one reason for his decision to delay a reunion with the rest of the team in order to pursue the myth of Helen's Charm across two continents.

From the ruins of Hisarlik, they had flown to Berlin to visit the Pergamon Museum, where Priam's Treasure had been displayed until World War II. A helpful docent reiterated the tale of how the artifacts had come to the museum, and subsequently been lost, but was not able to provide any deeper insights. When the Red Army had seized the treasure from a secure bunker under the Berlin Zoo in 1945, they had also taken all records pertaining to the collection's provenance. The docent then suggested that, if they wished to know more about the man who had discovered the ruins and the treasure of ancient Troy, they might want to visit the Heinrich-Schliemann Museum in Ankershagen, a small town about a hundred miles to the north.

As it was already late afternoon, Maddock had decided to spend the night in Berlin and make the two-hour drive in the morning. For added security they had booked a single hotel room, and, as they had done every night since escaping Telesh's compound, he and Leopov took turns standing watch throughout the night. Petrov had been contentedly sawing logs when Maxie's call came in; the ringing had roused him.

Maddock's distrust of Petrov and his fears for Lia's safety were not however, his only reasons for balking at Maxie's direction to come in from the cold. The truth of the matter was that Maddock's desire to find Helen's Charm, or at the very least, learn the truth about it, had grown tremendously since visiting Hisarlik.

Over the years, he and Bones had been involved in their share of crazy treasure hunts, and from time to time, he had even entertained the notion of making a second career of it when he retired from the Navy. The idea had never been more than just an idle fancy. The Navy—the Team—had been his life for so long that thinking about giving it up had always felt like contemplating the amputation of a limb.

Lately, not so much.

They got an early start and made the drive north in just a little over two hours, taking their time since the museum did not open until ten o'clock. Ankershagen was a sleepy, rural community, surrounded by farmland, with little to offer in the way of traveler amenities. That it was the birthplace of famed archaeologist Heinrich Schliemann was the town's sole claim to fame, even though the family had moved away during his second year of life.

The Heinrich-Schliemann Museum was situated in the farmhouse where Schliemann had been born in 1822, across the road from the church where his father, a Lutheran pastor, had preached. There was no designated parking area, so they pulled off on the roadside and proceeded down a paved path to the museum. The repurposed farmhouse was guarded by a towering, if crude, mock-up of the Trojan Horse. A flight of ladder-like stairs rose up into the beast's barrel-shaped interior. Its tail was a playground slide.

After paying the nominal admission fee, they moved inside to examine the museum's collection which was about as spare as Maddock expected. There were several display cases with replicas of Schliemann's most famous discoveries—Priam's Treasure, the Mask of Agamemnon—and informational placards in German, English and French describing important biographical details. The walls were hung with portraits and photographs of the museum's namesake. The earliest pictures showed a bookish man with a bold, sweeping mustache, wearing a top hat and fur coat. Later images revealed his slight build and thinning hair. No one would have mistaken Schliemann for Indiana Jones.

Maddock's attention was drawn to a photograph that did not feature Heinrich Schliemann but rather an unsmiling, though not unattractive young woman in a high-necked dress, wearing the golden diadem and necklaces that had, if Schliemann was to be believed, once belonged to Helen of Troy.

Maddock didn't need to read the card next to the picture to know who it was. "Schliemann's wife."

"His second wife, actually," intoned a heavily accented voice from behind them. It was the museum staffer who had sold them their tickets, a pleasant looking middle-aged man with ruddy features and big, weather-worn hands. He looked more like a farmer than a curator. The little plastic badge over his shirt pocket read simply: Lars.

"Forgive my intrusion," Lars went on. "We are slow today and nothing passes the time like conversation. It would please me to answer any questions you may have."

Maddock resisted the impulse to simply blurt out

the most pressing question, and instead grasped the thread Lars had offered. "What happened to his first wife?"

"First wife was Russian," supplied Petrov. "From St. Petersburg."

Lars nodded. "That's correct. Her name was Ekaterina. Henry—that's what he preferred to be called—moved to Russia in 1844 as an agent for an import/export company. He learned to speak Russian fluently in a matter of just a few weeks—he had genius for learning languages—and became a Russian citizen. He was quite successful for many years, but in 1850, his brother Ludwig died in California while prospecting for gold. Henry traveled there to pay his respects, and soon realized that there was a great business opportunity in the gold fields. He started a bank in Sacramento, and in six months, earned his first fortune."

There was no mistaking the admiration in Lars' tone. "He returned to Russia as a wealthy gentleman, and not long after met and married Ekaterina. They had three children together, but the marriage was not a happy one. He continued to have great success in business however, and was able to retire at just thirty-six years of age to pursue his true passion—archaeology. You see, even as a young boy, Henry was obsessed with the story of the Trojan war. He learned Greek so that he could read Homer in the original language."

Petrov raised an eyebrow at this assertion. "Original language was not modern Greek," he murmured.

Lars, evidently missing the aside, continued speaking. "He studied the ancient texts and from them, and with help from a friend—an Englishman named Calvert—identified Hisarlik as the site of ancient Troy. While he was waiting for permission to begin excavating, he decided that he needed a partner and companion who was as familiar with Homer as he was. Since Ekaterina would not grant him a divorce in

Russia, in 1869, he returned to America, where the law permitted him to divorce her, and then asked his friend, Theokletos Vimpos, Archbishop of Athens, to find him a Greek woman to marry. He was quite insistent that his new wife be a Greek woman, conversant in the works of the poet. Vimpos submitted pictures of three candidates, including his niece." He gestured to the photograph. "Sophia Engastromenos. Henry immediately fell in love with her, though he was concerned about the difference in age. He was thirty years her elder."

Leopov's forehead wrinkled as she made a quick calculation and then her eyebrows shot up, aghast. "She was just a teenager."

"Seventeen years old," confirmed Lars.

Maddock was similarly dismayed. "So in addition to being a grave robber, he also robbed the cradle." He winced as he spoke the words; it sounded like something Bones might say, though perhaps more colorfully.

Lars raised his hands in a placating gesture. "Do not rush to judgment. It was a different time." He fixed his gaze on Maddock. "Remember, just a few years before, your own countrymen fought a war for the right to keep human beings as property." He let the accusation hang for a moment before continuing. "In Greek culture, at the time, it was customary for parents to arrange marriage of their children, and Sophia was of age. The bride's family was expected to provide a substantial dowry. The Engastromenos family had a very successful drapery business for many years, but had fallen on hard times and Sophia's prospects for finding a husband were not good. Then along comes a wealthy foreigner who asks nothing more than a woman with whom he can discuss Greek history and mythology."

"Right," said a still-skeptical Leopov, eyeing the portrait of the woman adorned with the Jewels of Helen. "He only loved her for her mind."

"By all accounts, she grew to love him, and there is

no doubt that she did assist with the excavations in Troy and Mycenae. She was there with him when he discovered those—" He gestured to the display case containing the replica of the diadem. "And helped him move the pieces off site to prevent them from being stolen."

"I thought that story about her smuggling them in her shawl was just a myth," Leopov countered. "Wasn't she in Athens when he found the treasure?"

"Attending her father's funeral," confirmed Petrov with a nod.

The words "father's funeral" triggered a pang of grief for Maddock, but he hid it behind a stoic mask.

Lars shook his head. "That is not correct. Sophia's father died in early May of 1873. Sophia did travel to Athens, but returned to Hisarlik shortly thereafter at the urging of her husband. On May 14, he wrote to her, encouraging her to return to Hisarlik to find solace in their shared work. She left the next day. She was most definitely there on May 31, when they discovered the golden treasure outside the walls of Priam's palace."

"The treasure was outside the palace?"

"Yes. Under a bronze shield. There were the metal clasps and handles of a chest, but the wood had burned. Henry surmised that a party of soldiers may have been trying to flee the sacking of the palace with the treasures, but were forced to leave it behind." He paused a moment and then returned to the earlier subject. "May 31, 1873 was Saturday, which is why they had the site to themselves. They worked through the night to clean and remove the treasure which they packed in with Sophia's clothing. I suspect that is what Henry meant when he jokingly said that they smuggled the treasure out under Sophia's shawl."

Maddock, recalling their earlier conversation on the subject, glanced over at Leopov. While Lars' account was by no means definitive, it seemed to confirm Schliemann's original claim rather than his later recantation. "You seem very sure of the details."

Lars nodded. "We have the written account of both

Henry and Sophia to confirm it."

Maddock seized on this. "You have those written accounts here I take it?"

Lars nodded energetically. "We have an extensive collection of Sophia's correspondences with Henry and her family, as well as many of his journals." He paused a beat and then, with a little less enthusiasm, added, "Facsimiles, of course."

"Does the phrase 'Helen's Charm' appear anywhere?"

If the question caught Lars off guard, he did not let it show. "I don't recall that expression, but that doesn't mean it isn't there. I can check our reference index if you would like."

"Please do," Maddock said.

As Lars hurried off to conduct his search, Leopov turned to him. "In 1873, she would have been twenty-one years old. A beautiful young woman, she would not have needed a magic charm to distract a customs inspector."

Maddock glanced at the portrait again. "I'm not sure I'd use the word 'beautiful.'"

Leopov gave him a wry smile, and he realized she had interpreted his comment as flattery.

"I just mean she's not my type," he amended.

"Obviously she was Schliemann's type," Petrov said, laughing.

"Trust me," Leopov said. "She is very beautiful. Women know. Don't be fooled by her serious expression. Nobody ever smiled in old photographs. Besides, this was never meant to be a portrait of her. She is just a mannequin, displaying Helen's Jewels."

Leopov's comment prompted Maddock to study the portrait more closely. He compared it with the contents of the display case containing the replica of the diadems. "What's missing from this picture?"

Leopov shrugged. "Helen's Charm?"

"If it's as important as we think, it would have been the most valuable piece in the collection. Even more valuable than all the gold. So why isn't it in this picture?"

"We don't even know what Helen's Charm was," Leopov challenged. "Or if it existed at all."

Maddock shook his head. "Let's just take it as given that it did. Hitler somehow recognized it. Telesh figured it out. The answer has to be here." He studied the photograph again. "We're just not seeing…"

He trailed off as he realized there was actually one item in the photograph that had not been reproduced as a replica and which was not listed in the official catalog of Priam's Treasure.

Before he could elaborate, Lars returned. "I am sorry, my friends, but I could not find a reference to Helen's Charm in the index. That does not necessarily mean that the expression is not to be found in the primary documents, but the only way to know for sure would be to read them all." He spread his hands in a guilty gesture. "And now, I must take leave of you. There is a tour bus arriving shortly."

Maddock thanked him for his labors and the background information. When he was gone, Leopov prompted, "You saw something. What?"

He blinked and then turned to her. "I'm not sure. Maybe nothing."

"Dane, I know that look."

He shot a glance at Petrov, wondering if he dared trust the man with the revelation, and decided that having the historian's input was worth the risk. "It sounds like they really did smuggle the treasure out by hiding it in Sophia's clothes, but why did Schliemann say they hid it under her shawl?"

"Perhaps he was trying to give the story a theatrical flair."

"Maybe. Or maybe he was unconsciously revealing something that he didn't mean to share. Like a Freudian slip. And when he realized what he had done, he backtracked. Claimed that Sophia hadn't been there when obviously she had been."

Leopov nodded patiently. "Okay, so what's the big secret?"

"I'm no fashion expert, so feel free to correct me. A shawl is like a cloak… A blanket that you wear over your shoulders, right?"

Leopov nodded. "More or less."

Maddock pointed to the photograph. "Is she wearing a shawl in that picture?"

They all took another look. "Hard to say," Leopov said.

"It is very plain looking dress," agreed Petrov. "As you say, Helen's Jewels are the important thing. Not the woman."

"What color would you say it is?"

Petrov answered quickly. "Black."

Leopov's response was less certain. "I don't think it is black. Her hair is black. The dress is lighter. But it's a black and white photograph. There's no way to know for sure."

"Could it be red?"

She shrugged. "Could be."

"What if that dress *is* part of the treasure," Maddock said. "What if it's made from fabric they discovered along with the treasure. A shawl or cloak that might have once been worn by Helen."

Leopov and Petrov exchanged a dubious glance. Petrov finally spoke. "Is not so crazy," he said guardedly. "Shawl was a common accessory for Greek women in ancient times. You see in statues from the period. And garments were of great value to ancient people. They were often given as gifts along with precious metals and jewels."

"In all the paintings I've seen, Helen is usually depicted either as nude or wearing a red cloak," Maddock continued. "Let's say Schliemann finds the cloak with all the other treasure. He's a smart guy. He knows how valuable it really is, but he also knows that people won't be as excited about an old shawl as they are all the gold and silver. So, he decides to make a gift of it to his 'Helen.' Lars said that Sophia's father had a drapery business, right? Sewing was probably the simplest thing in the world for her. She could have stitched the fabric into a dress."

Leopov raised her hands. "I'm sure she could have. What difference does it make?"

"All right, just bear with me here. What do we know about Helen? Aside from the fact that she was beautiful. Face that launched a thousand ships, et cetera?"

"She was daughter of Zeus and Leda," said Petrov. "Leda was human woman. Queen of Sparta. Zeus came to her in form of a swan and seduced her. She laid eggs."

Maddock suppressed a smile. He was grateful that Bones wasn't around to hear that.

"Same night, king lays with her. Nine months later, eggs hatch and babies are borne. Two sets of twins. From eggs come Helen and Pollux. Natural borne human offspring are Castor and Clytemnestra, who became queen of Mycenae."

"Helen was a demigod," Maddock said. "And in all the myths, aren't the gods always giving special gifts to their children to protect them from other jealous gods?"

Petrov laughed. "Zeus' wife Hera delighted in tormenting the product of her husband's adulterous liaisons. She drove Herakles to madness."

Maddock nodded. "So maybe Helen's cloak... Her red cloak... Gave her an extra boost that made her irresistible."

Leopov was less enthusiastic. "Lars said the chest with the treasure had burned in the fire. How would a cloak survive?"

"If it was a divine gift, it might have been indestructible. Or at least, impervious to flame. Or maybe Schliemann was wrong about the fire."

"He was probably wrong about a lot of things. Helen... The Trojan War... It's all just mythology. Superstitious nonsense. None of it really happened."

"I'm not saying it did, but belief is a powerful thing. Schliemann was a believer. Maybe Sophia, too. And when they found that stuff, maybe their belief that it really had belonged to Helen, daughter of Zeus, gave them a boost of charisma that helped them sneak the treasure out. Maybe Schliemann directly attributed their success to the fact that his wife was wearing Helen's shawl—Helen's Charm. And maybe that story, which Schliemann let slip once or twice, grew with the telling until, fifty years later, a young Austrian political activist heard about it and decided it would be a powerful symbol for his new revolutionary movement."

"I don't think Hitler ever wore a red shawl," remarked Leopov, dryly.

"He didn't wear it." Maddock could barely contain his excitement. When he had first entertained the notion, it had seemed so farfetched, but as he had laid out his hypothesis, step by step, his certainty grew like a wildfire. "Think about it. What would Adolf Hitler do with a big piece of red fabric?"

Leopov gaped at him. "You're kidding? You think he made it into a Nazi flag?"

"Not just any flag. The flag he carried into the Munich beerhall."

Petrov was nodding eagerly. "Of course. It makes perfect sense. The *Blutfahne*."

"Blutfahne," echoed Leopov. "Blood flag?"

"The Beer Hall Putsch ended when Munich police fired on the marching Nazis. The man carrying the swastika flag of the *Sturmabteilung* was wounded and dropped the flag. Another mortally wounded stormtrooper fell on the flag, staining it with his blood. From that moment forward, it became the most sacred relic of the Nazi party. Was used in ceremonies to consecrate new flags. Party members swore loyalty before it. Last time it was seen in public was October 1944, when Himmler conducted induction ceremony for the Volkssturm—the army of old men and boys raised up as the last defense of Berlin. Many of them did not even have weapons, but they fought to bitter end against Red Army."

"The Blood Flag disappeared after that," Maddock

added. "Neo-Nazis would love to get their hands on it."

"Himmler must have taken it with him when he fled Berlin," said Petrov.

Maddock agreed. "Of all the Nazi leaders, he was the one that really bought into the occult. But there's no record of it being found when he was captured."

Petrov was nodding. "Remember what Lia found? Why Sergei Yukovitch wants her? Gestapo Müller caught up to Himmler near Bremervorde. He must have taken Blood Flag with him. That is the thing of 'great importance,' mentioned in the interrogation transcript. The Blood Flag. Helen's Charm. They are same thing."

Leopov inclined her head in a grudging acknowledgment of the deduction. "Now we know *what* it is. We still don't know *where* it is."

"It is wherever Müller took it," replied Petrov. "KGB always believed American intelligence agents captured him. Turned him."

Maddock shook his head. "Bones and the others have been working with Lia to track him down. The working theory is that he escaped Germany on a U-boat and headed for Argentina. Whether or not he made it is another question." He thought about the call from Maxie the previous night. Had the fleeing Gestapo leader made it to Villa Gessell, carrying with him the most sacred relic of the Third Reich, and with it, the means to seduce a new generation of followers?

"Hopefully," he went on, "Müller and the Blood Flag ended up in the deepest part of the ocean, beyond any hope of recovery."

"Sergei Yukovitch is very determined man," Petrov said.

Maddock sighed. "You're right. We have to make sure that he can never get his hands on it. Or anyone else."

"And how will you do that?"

"Find it first," Maddock said, decisively. "Destroy it. Even if it is nothing more than a symbol, it's a symbol that needs to be erased from existence." He nodded toward the exit. "We'll rendezvous with Bones and the others. Pool our knowledge and hopefully figure it out."

As they headed outside, he dug out his phone and dialed Maxie's number. It rang four times before going to voicemail. As the greeting played, Maddock struggled to order his swirling thoughts into a succinct message. He gazed out across the lawn where a large bus was unloading passengers. Further out, a few more cars had lined up behind their rental on the roadside, their occupants already mingling with the tour group. Several people were taking pictures in front of the Trojan Horse replica.

One face in the crowd seemed to leap out at Maddock.

That he noticed her at all might have easily enough been explained by the fact that she was gorgeous—slender, raven-haired, with high Slavic cheekbones and full lips. She looked like she belonged on the cover of a fashion magazine, or on the arm of a tycoon. Her attractiveness in fact was what had caught his eye the first time he'd noticed her the previous day.

This second convergence in as many days might have been simple coincidence, but Maddock wasn't inclined to take any chances. He put his phone away, and changed course, angling away from the group toward the lawn in front of the museum building.

"Stay calm," he said in a low voice. "I think we picked up a shadow."

Leopov laughed as if he'd just said something hilarious, then covered her mouth as she looked at him. "Where?"

Maddock feigned laughter as well. "The brunette at my ten o'clock. About fifty yards away. Saw her yesterday at the museum in Berlin. Might be nothing, but let's not take any chances. We'll duck around behind the museum and wait to see what she does."

Petrov craned his head around to look directly at the woman.

"Don't be so obvious," Maddock hissed.

Instead of heeding the advice, Petrov suddenly stepped away from them, moving at a near jog in the woman's direction. As he moved, he cupped a hand to his mouth, and shouted, "Nadia! They know!" and then added something in Russian.

The woman flinched as if in embarrassment at being outed, but then regained her composure and fixed her gaze on Maddock and Leopov. She said something he couldn't hear and made an overhand gesture. Two burly figures detached from the crowd and started toward them. Even though their faces were mostly hidden under the brims of large floppy hats, Maddock immediately recognized them as the pair of thugs that had chased him in Moscow—Tweedledee and Tweedledum.

SEVENTEEN

"Damn it," **Leopov** snarled. "I hate that you were right about him."

"Me too," Maddock admitted. "Let's go."

He started across the lawn, heading east along the front of the building at a brisk walk. For the moment, at least, none of the bystanders had any clue what was happening in their midst, and Maddock wanted to keep it that way.

After rounding the northeast corner of the building, Maddock peeked around the corner to check on the pursuit. Tweedledum was about twenty yards away, shuffling along at a slow trot, but he appeared to be alone. The others had probably gone around the long way, hoping to cut off their escape.

"Now what?" Leopov asked.

Maddock did a quick visual survey of their surroundings. The museum building was a long rectangle running more or less east-west. The grounds were mostly open, dotted with trees which would provide some cover, but offered little in the way of concealment for an escape. The road, where their rental car waited, was only about fifty yards away, but to get to it, they would have to get past the Russians.

He wondered what Nadia and her twin goons were planning to do with them. The Russian mobsters probably hadn't thought that far ahead. Clearly, this confrontation had been neither planned nor desired. Telesh's intention had been, as Maddock had surmised all along, to have them followed in hopes that they would eventually reunite with Lia Markova. No doubt, Petrov had been covertly supplying them with updates on their search for more information about Helen's Charm—information which Telesh probably already possessed. Now that the deception had been exposed,

Telesh's next move would probably be damage control. Eliminating loose ends.

"This isn't Moscow," he said. "I doubt they'll try anything in front of all these witnesses."

"Are you willing to bet your life on that?"

"Good point." He sighed. "Okay, I'll try to lead them off. Keep them distracted. Get to the car if you can. If not, find a phone and call the local police. There must be some kind of law enforcement out here."

Leopov shook her head. "No. We stay together. Splitting up didn't do us any good before."

Maddock could tell that she was not going to change her mind, and they didn't really have time to debate the merits of his plan. Besides, she was probably right; they worked well together, and she had more than proven her capability.

"Fine," said Maddock. "New plan. We rush that guy—" He jerked a thumb toward the corner where Tweedledum was approaching unseen. "And make a beeline for the car."

"Ready when you are," she said, confidently.

Maddock gave a nod and then broke from cover, right in front of the lumbering Russian. The big man registered surprise at the sudden reappearance of his prey, but immediately threw his arms out in an attempt to scoop Maddock up. Maddock ducked under the sweep, and juked to the man's left. As the Russian pivoted toward him, Leopov dashed out from behind the corner and slipped past them on the opposite side. As she did, she aimed a back kick at the man's right knee. The strike had about the same effect as it would have if she'd kicked a tree. The Russian merely grunted, and then pivoted away from her to make another grab for Maddock who had doubled back to launch an attack of his own. He struck from the Russian's blind spot. His fist connected solidly with the man's jaw, but it might as well have been a love pat for all it accomplished. Tweedledum shrugged it off and reached for Maddock again, and this time, one of his groping hands managed to snag Maddock's shirt.

Buttons flew like machine gun bullets as Maddock's chest was suddenly bared. He backpedaled away, squirming out of the ruined shirt before the brutish Russian could reel him in like a prized marlin. His wristwatch caught momentarily on a shirt sleeve, but a hard pull tore him loose. He stumbled away, losing his footing along with his shirt.

Damn, he thought as he felt the cool grass tickling his exposed back. *This is getting to be a thing.*

Tweedle tossed the ruined shirt away and began stalking toward him. The Russian's face was a study in casual indifference—it was the same dull-eyed expression he'd shown just before snapping the neck of Lia's decoy in the Moscow underground.

Rather than attempt to rise and meet the brute on his feet, Maddock pushed up to a sitting position and then scooted backward, keeping one hand and one foot raised to ward off any attacks. It was the standard defensive position taught in military combatives classes for fending off attacks from a standing foe. Hypothetically, he could have kept his foe at bay indefinitely, or at least until an attack was attempted, at which point he would have been able to easily wrap the big Russian up in a jiu jitsu hold, but it was a hypothesis Maddock did not feel like testing.

Leopov looked as if she was about to launch another attack from behind the Russian. Maddock caught her eye and shook his head, hoping that she would get the unspoken message.

Don't bother.

Leopov, correctly interpreting the look, sidled away.

Maddock scooted back several more feet, flipped over into a prone position and then pushed up into a sprint take-off. There was no longer any need for subtlety. The altercation had arrested the attention of the other visitors, though judging by the general look of bemusement, nobody quite understood what was going on.

With Leopov just a few steps ahead of him,

Maddock cut across the lawn and headed straight for their waiting rental car. As he moved, he fished out the key fob and pressed the unlock button. The car's headlights flashed twice, signaling that the command had been received. The alarm had been deactivated, the doors were unlocked.

But as he got to within ten yards of the vehicle, he saw that something was amiss. The car was canted at an odd angle, as if the road sloped away on the opposite side. A few more steps brought him close enough to see the reason for the tilt—both of the passenger side tires were flat.

Maddock briefly debated attempting to drive off anyway—driving on flats was difficult but not impossible, and they only needed to put a little distance between themselves and the Russians. Ultimately, the decision was taken out of his hands, for as he and Leopov skidded to a stop alongside the car, Nadia rose from a crouch on the far side of the vehicle, pointing a compact Makarov semi-automatic pistol at them from across the hood.

Maddock mentally kicked himself. He had underestimated their foes. Rather than chase them around the museum grounds, Nadia had chosen to set a trap at the one place they would eventually have to go.

She aimed the gun at him. "Where do you think you—"

That was all Maddock heard. As soon as the woman began speaking, he dropped flat behind the car, removing himself from her line of sight. Leopov hit the deck as well, probably recalling the same advice he had heard repeatedly in self-defense training—it was virtually impossible to pull the trigger on a gun while talking. It was like trying to rub your stomach and pat your head. The process of synchronizing mental gears required only a fraction of a second, but it was an interval which could be exploited.

Getting out of the line of fire was only a temporary solution however. Nadia was still armed and would almost certainly be moving in order to reacquire her targets. The only question was which direction she would go. He glanced back at Leopov who nodded and started low crawling toward the rear of the disabled car. Maddock headed toward the front end. Rather than try to increase the distance between himself and Nadia's pistol, they were both determined to get a lot closer.

He squirmed up to the front bumper, poked his head out for a millisecond, just long enough to register Nadia coming around on the opposite side. The business end of Nadia's pistol snapped toward him, but he had already pulled back behind cover.

He did not keep retreating however, but instead crouched there, poised to launch himself at her like a striking rattlesnake as soon as she showed her face. He would go in low, under her gun, maybe try to take her legs out from under her. It would be a risky move, but no more so than staying put or even trying to run away.

He waited there a full second, then another, and then heard the thud of an impact followed by a cry of pain. A moment later, Nadia appeared before him, but there was no need to rush her. She sprawled out on the ground, face-first, making no effort to even arrest her fall.

Leopov emerged right behind her, now holding the Makarov and grinning triumphantly. Her elation was short-lived. As she turned her head toward Maddock, her eyes went wide. "Dane! Behind you!"

Before Maddock could react, he was yanked off the ground and enfolded in a crushing bear hug. His arms were pinned against his torso, useless. He reflexively tried to squirm out of the grip, kicking out with his feet in a futile attempt to find the ground and get some leverage against his unseen foe—almost certainly Tweedledee.

The pressure increased as his assailant tightened his hold, squeezing the air from his lungs, suffocating him. Maddock fought the natural impulse to resist and instead went limp in the other man's grasp, as if succumbing to the darkness. The big Russian wasn't deceived into relaxing his hold, but he did take advantage of the apparent victory to reposition his feet to accommodate the dead weight of his seemingly vanquished opponent. The adjustment brought him a few inches closer to the car, close enough for Maddock to reach the front fender with one outstretched foot.

He immediately pushed off, driving himself into his attacker. Unbalanced, the Russian toppled backward. He managed to maintain his hold on Maddock throughout the fall, but when he finally crashed down on his back, Maddock's full weight slammed into him. The secondary impact loosened the hold enough for Maddock to maneuver. He threw his legs up, rolling into a reverse somersault that finally broke the embrace. As he came out of the roll, he hooked an arm around the big man's neck, locking the chokehold in place with the other.

The Russian clawed at Maddock's arm, and when that didn't work, he tried to shake Maddock loose. Maddock countered by wrapping his legs around the man's waist, hooking his ankles together. Like many big men, the Russian was used to relying on his size and strength to win battles, and had no clue how to get out of the hold Maddock now had him in. His thrashing grew more frantic as the disruption of oxygenated blood to his brain sent him into a primal panic, and then abruptly ceased as the man collapsed in a puddle on the ground. Maddock held on a few seconds longer, riding the unconscious man down, maintaining the chokehold to ensure that the big Russian was out of the fight.

Maddock's heart was pounding, his pulse throbbing in his ears like a waterfall, but as the adrenaline of the fight ebbed and his tunnel vision widened, he became aware of Leopov standing a few feet away, now armed with Nadia's Makarov. She was shouting something—he couldn't quite make out what—and inexplicably pointing the weapon at him….

No, not at him, but at someone behind him.

He let go of Tweedledee and threw himself sideways, narrowly avoiding Tweedledum's headlong charge. Maddock finished the combat roll in a crouch, and backpedaled away as the lumbering Russian pivoted and came at him again. There was a fire in the big man's eyes now, a fierce determination to avenge his fallen brother.

Maddock had no desire to grapple with the man. That he had defeated Tweedledee owed more to desperation and fickle luck than to his own prowess in unarmed combat. He could see Leopov tracking the big man with the business end of the Makarov.

Shoot him, damn it, he thought, even though he knew why she was holding back. A public brawl was one thing, but discharging a gun—or God forbid actually killing someone—would bring a whole new level of unwanted attention down on them. She would use the weapon only if the Russians gave her no alternative.

And maybe she wouldn't need to. With Nadia and the other Tweedle out of the fight, the odds had swung in his and Leopov's favor.

"Check for keys," he shouted to Leopov, hoping she would understand what he was asking, and then after a quick glance over his shoulder to mark the position of the path leading back to the museum, he started backing away from the big Russian. It would have been the simplest thing in the world to outrun the man, but Maddock wanted to keep him close.

A dozen quick steps and another glance back.

Almost there.

According to legend, wily King Odysseus of Ithaca ended the ten-year-long war with the Trojans with an infamous act of subterfuge. Regardless of whether or not there was any factual basis for the legend, the episode had left a permanent imprint on the collective consciousness of the Western world—the term "Trojan horse" was synonymous with the use of deception and trickery to outwit a foe. Now, three thousand years later, Dane Maddock was going to borrow a page from Odysseus' playbook.

He turned, and then immediately ducked behind one of the upright wooden legs supporting the museum's Trojan Horse mock-up. The Russian tried to follow, but Maddock easily eluded him, snaking between the legs, always just barely out of the other man's reach. With each dodge by Maddock, the rage in Tweedledum's eyes grew hotter and his attacks, while more furious, became sloppier. Maddock wove around the horse's rear legs, slid under the long playground slide that was the re-creation's tail, and then nimbly flipped up onto the sloping metal-sheathed surface. His boot soles slipped a little at first, but with both hands gripping the siderails, he got enough traction to propel himself up the slide, toward the opening to the wooden beast's hollow interior.

Suddenly the slide shook with an impact. Maddock's feet slipped out from under him and he fell flat against the sloped surface. A quick look down revealed that Tweedledum had clambered onto the slide and was attempting to snag Maddock's dangling feet. Maddock didn't bother trying to regain his footing, but instead heaved himself the rest of the way up, thrusting himself headfirst into the barrel-like belly of the wooden horse. The whole contraption shook violently as Tweedledum fought his way up the slide.

Despite the impression of roominess from without, the interior was dark, cramped and utilitarian, with a short flight of steps leading down from the top of the slide and an even shorter walkway that ended at the ladder which descended back down to the ground.

Had the big Russian stopped to think for just a second, he would have realized that the smartest course of action would be to simply step back and wait Maddock out. There were only two ways out, and both would leave Maddock momentarily vulnerable. But the cat-and-mouse game had left the Russian too frustrated for rational considerations—which was exactly what Maddock had been hoping for.

After pulling himself inside, Maddock flipped around to face the slide and brought his legs up under him. When Tweedle's head appeared in the opening at the top of the slide, Maddock was ready for him. Gripping the rails to either side, he lashed out with both feet together, driving his heels into the man's brutish face.

As his dazed foe slid away, Maddock thrust himself back out onto the slide, but instead of riding it all the way down, he rolled over the side, landing easily on the grass below.

A loud braying sound rolled across the lawn toward him—the blast of a car horn. He oriented toward it and saw Leopov, waving to him from the open window of an idling black Mercedes M-Class.

He sprinted toward the sport utility vehicle, giving the unmoving forms of Nadia and Tweedledee a wide berth, and circled around to the passenger side.

"Nice ride," he said as he collapsed into the seat.

"Thanks," replied Leopov, smiling. "I traded up."

As she pulled away, Maddock spotted Petrov. The historian ducked his head as Maddock's gaze met his, perhaps afraid of reprisal, or maybe just embarrassed. Maddock briefly considered going after him, if only to keep him from revealing what they had discovered to Telesh. He dismissed the idea. Dragging an unwilling hostage along would only hinder their subsequent movements, and besides, the Russian gangster had almost certainly known about the connection between the Blutfahne and Helen's Charm before ever enlisting Petrov's help.

"Where to now?" Leopov asked as Ankershagen shrank into the distance behind them.

Maddock leaned back and closed his eyes. "As much as I like the car, we're going to need to get rid of it ASAP. I'm sure somebody back there already called the cops."

"Well, obviously," she retorted. "I was thinking more big picture."

"Big picture?" He opened his eyes and turned to

her. "We're going to find the Blood Flag and destroy it. Or at least make sure that it stays lost forever."

"You really think it has some kind of magic power?"

He shook his head. "I don't know, but regardless, it's an abomination." He paused a beat, then added. "Oh, I guess I'm going to need to buy another shirt."

Leopov laughed. "You don't have to dress up on my account."

Maddock allowed himself a smile.

EIGHTEEN

Off the coast of South America

"I've got some good news," Huntley announced the next morning as he joined them in the control room. "And some great news."

"Good for whom?" replied Professor, not a little sarcastically. The brutal work rotation and lack of sleep had left all of them feeling a little cranky, but Bones guessed the comment had more to do with their general distrust of Captain Midnight.

Bones echoed the sentiment. "My people have a long history of getting screwed over by white guys claiming to have good news."

"Lighten up, Tonto. It's about your boy, Maddock. He checked in as ordered and he's on his way to us. That's the good news." He paused a beat to see if anyone would contest the assessment. No one did. "But you're gonna love the next part. It seems Maddock got a lead on our missing U-boat."

Bones and Professor exchanged a doubtful look. "I didn't realize he was even looking for it," the latter said.

"I know, right?" Huntley dismissed the incongruity with a wave. "I guess he was looking at this thing from a different angle and came across some information on a little place south of Buenos Aires called Villa Gessell." He pronounced the name *vil-lah jess-sul*. "He wants us to meet him there."

"I've heard of Villa Gessell," Professor said, none-too-subtly correcting the mistake. "It was a resort built by a German developer before World War II. It had quite a reputation as a German enclave and refuge for escaped Nazis."

Bones raised a hand to forestall further discussion.

"Let's bring Willis and Lia out for this." Both were catching some rack time, but he knew they would forgive being woken up prematurely. Bones also wanted to get Lia's reaction to the revelation. If Professor had heard of Villa Gessell, it seemed likely that Lia had as well.

"Sure," Huntley said with an indifferent shrug. "The more the merrier."

Bones quickly roused the others and a few minutes later, they were assembled in the control room. Professor was studying a nautical chart of the waters off the Argentine coast.

Huntley resumed talking. "Okay, so as Mr. Wizard mentioned, Villa Gessell is a resort town, originally built by a German dude named—surprise—Gessell. He was originally just trying to stabilize the sand dunes so he could grow timber, but eventually realized that people would pay good money to stay there and eventually they turned the place into a resort. Then the war happened, and a lot of Germans fleeing the old country settled there. That's the official history that everyone knows."

A bleary-eyed Lia restated what Professor had earlier said. "There have always been rumors of high-ranking Nazis hiding out in Villa Gessell. What makes you think the U-398 ended up there?"

"It's not me, babycakes. Blame Maddock. It's his idea. He thinks that U-boat made it to Argentina, off-loaded some cargo, and then was scuttled by the crew. I checked the files on this place and I gotta say, I'm starting to believe."

Bones looked to Lia. "What do you think?"

"We're not finding anything out here. This might be worth checking out."

Professor got out a grease pen and began plotting a new search grid on the chart. The map showed a narrow band of light blue that followed the contour of the coastline. Further out, the open ocean was represented by darker blue.

"The continental shelf extends out into the ocean

for about a hundred nautical miles," he explained, mostly for Lia's benefit. "In that zone, the average depth is no more than about two hundred feet, but beyond that limit, it falls off steeply for another fifty or so miles, until out here—" He tapped the dark blue area. "We're looking at depths in excess of ten thousand feet."

"That's where we should start looking," Lia said, as if in agreement.

"Why?" inquired Huntley, sounding genuinely curious.

"They had to make the U-boat disappear," Professor explained. "Cover their tracks. If they had scuttled it closer to shore, it would have been visible from the air. And if someone had spotted it, it would have confirmed what everyone suspected—that another U-boat had reached Argentina—and that would have triggered a serious manhunt."

Huntley shook his head. "I mean, why are you still talking about looking for the U-boat? Whoever or whatever it was carrying would have been offloaded, right? Seems to me like the place we should start looking is on shore. Besides, that's where your boy Maddock is supposed to meet us."

He doubtless expected the last part to resonate with the three SEALs, but for Bones, it felt like yet another reminder that Huntley had intentionally kept them out of the loop.

"Until we have some kind of concrete evidence," countered Professor, "all of this is just supposition. We don't know if any of this is true. Finding the U-boat wouldn't necessarily prove that Müller escaped with some special secret cargo, but it would at least convince the powers that be to take the investigation seriously."

"It's not like we can just walk into town and start knocking on doors," added Willis. He slumped his shoulders theatrically and softened his normally deep baritone into an almost timid squeak. "Excuse me, ma'am, we're looking for Nazis. Have you seen any? They'd be quite old, I imagine."

Huntley laughed, though the humor didn't quite reach his eyes. "Yeah, that probably wouldn't go over so well. Especially with you and Bonebrake. How about we do this, then. Me and the two whiz kids—" He gestured to Professor and Lia. "—will take the launch ashore and make the rendezvous with Maddock. Maybe ask a few discreet questions. While we're doing that, the tall boys can start looking for the U-boat. Sound good?"

Bones held Huntley's gaze. "How about you let me talk to Maddock on the satphone. I'd like to get his input."

Huntley gave an apologetic shrug. "Maddock's using disposable burner phones. He has to initiate contact, and I don't anticipate him doing that. But if he docs call in again… Sure, I got no problem with that."

The response came as no surprise and Bones didn't bother arguing. "Fair enough. But we'll hold off running the search grid until you get back."

The spook's brow furrowed. "Why?"

"Because a hundred and fifty nautical miles is a lot farther than you think and the ocean is a really, really big place. We'll anchor a few miles off shore and wait for you to come back with Maddock. Then we'll figure out our next move."

Huntley just shrugged.

The revelation buoyed their morale. They pulled in the Argo array and set course for Mar Del Plata. With the search on hold, they were able to adjust the duty roster for more rest periods, which generally improved the mood aboard ship, at least for the first couple days. But as the *Besnard's* journey stretched out for the better part of a week, Bones' discontent returned.

Part of the problem was simple boredom. The research vessel had a small collection of old movies on VHS tape and an even smaller library of paperback novels, and while most of the offerings were surprisingly in English, they only provided a day or two worth of diversion. After that, Bones felt like climbing the walls.

"If I'd wanted to spend all my time trapped on a ship," he grumbled to Willis, "I'd have stayed in the Fleet."

Willis could only offer a sympathetic shrug.

The tedium was exacerbated however by the even bigger problem of Huntley's insistence that they have no contact with the outside world. Maddock did not call again, or if he did, Huntley chose to keep that news to himself. Bones didn't buy Huntley's claim that the communications blackout was a matter of OPSEC— operational security. It was far more likely that the spook was just dicking with them.

It was early evening when they came within sight of the Querandi lighthouse, just ten miles south of Villa Gessell. It was the second tallest lighthouse on the Atlantic coast of South America and an easy navigational marker. In the days before GPS, it would have been critically important for mariners. It wasn't hard to imagine a flotilla of renegade U-boats using it as a reference point.

Huntley pointed out across the water at the lighthouse. The structure itself was indistinct against the background but the light continued to flash out its unique identifying signature—five pulses of white light, repeating every twenty-six seconds.

"Maddock will be waiting for us about six clicks south of the lighthouse," he explained.

"That's kind of vague," complained Professor.

Huntley spread his hands. "What can I say? That's where he told me to meet him."

"That doesn't sound like Maddock," Bones put in. "He gets his tighty-whiteys in a bunch about little things like precise map coordinates."

"I'm sure he has his reasons. He's going to guide us in by flashlight. You just need to put us in the ballpark."

Bones glanced over at his teammates. Though the silent exchange lasted only a second or two, it spoke volumes.

Huntley had been jerking them around for more than a week, so his uncooperativeness was hardly a surprise. Yet, this time felt different. Huntley wasn't just inconveniencing them—he was withholding information critical to the success of the mission. And Bones wasn't wrong about Maddock's tendency to be a stickler for details.

Was Huntley lying to them about being in contact with Maddock? And if so, what was really waiting for them on that remote stretch of beach, six kilometers south of the lighthouse?

Guess we're going to find out, Bones thought as he watched Professor help Lia climb into the *Besnard*'s launch.

The open motor launch afforded no protection from the wind blasting from out of the west. Conversation was all but impossible, so Professor simply pointed the prow toward the lighthouse, headlong into the teeth of the wind, and pushed the throttle as hard as he dared. Even so, it took more than an hour for them to get close enough to see the long white crest of breaking waves silhouetted against the black water. Beyond the breakers, a broad swath of golden sand was visible— not merely a beach, but an extensive dune formation that covered a seventy-mile long section of the Argentine coast. The Querandi lighthouse was situated roughly at the halfway point where the dunes were widest—nearly two miles across.

With the shore finally in sight, Professor turned the launch to the southwest, angling into the wind as they moved parallel along the coast, just beyond the breakers. The swells were gentle, no more than a foot or two, but the wind's assault intensified. The temperature had dropped significantly, and the windchill sucked away even more warmth. He judged they were only making about four knots against headwind, and so didn't start watching the shore for

Maddock's signal until nearly another hour had elapsed.

After about fifteen minutes of searching, a flash of white light shone out from just below the dunes. He pointed it out to Huntley, shouting, "There!"

Huntley nodded, and as he returned the signal with his own flashlight, Professor turned the boat toward shore and opened up the throttle. The small beacon swept back and forth across the water a few more times before finally coming to rest on the launch, and thereafter, it shone steadily on them, guiding them the rest of the way in.

It took another ten minutes of battling the wind before the little boat finally scuffed against the sandy bottom of the intertidal zone. Professor immediately jumped over the transom and dragged the craft toward the beach until it would go no further, whereupon he deployed the sand anchor—a long T-shaped metal rod tipped with a broad-bladed auger which could be screwed into the sand deep enough to keep the boat from being carried away with a change of tide. It was probably an unnecessary precaution since the tide was still going out and it would be another hour or two before incoming waves could lift the boat enough to float it again, but Professor, like most SEALs, was a believer in Murphy's Law and the simpler axiom that an ounce of prevention was worth a pound of cure.

Huntley did not offer to help, but instead disembarked and headed toward the signal light without saying a word. Once the sand anchor was set and the boat secured to it, Professor helped Lia into the water, which occasionally reached knee height as waves rolled in, and together they made their way toward the rendezvous. He was both surprised and a little disappointed that Maddock did not rush out to welcome them.

Inexplicably, as they got closer, the beam of the flashlight shifted to shine directly in his face. He blinked and raised a hand to shield his face, but the damage to his nighttime vision was already done.

"What the hell, Maddock?"

"Maddock couldn't make it," said Huntley.

Something about the spook's tone sent a chill down Professor's spine. He put a protective arm in front of Lia, guiding her back, but he knew it was too little, too late. "What's going on, Huntley?"

"I thought you were supposed to be the smart one." There was a brief pause, and when Huntley spoke again, his tone was lower, businesslike, and clearly not directed at Professor. "We'll bring the girl along. We need to find out how much she actually knows."

Professor squinted, trying to pierce the veil of darkness in order to see who Huntley was addressing.

"And the other one?"

This voice was male and heavily accented. Given their geographical location, he figured it was a safe bet that the man was a local.

"*¿Quien es?*" he asked in Spanish. *Who are you?*

"I do not speak Castellan," the man replied haughtily, as if the very notion was deeply insulting. The additional comments allowed Professor to pin down the accent—a German accent. Professor's sense of dread multiplied.

"Huntley, what the hell is going on here?" He asked again. He didn't expect an answer, nor did he exactly need one. Whatever the spook was up to, it definitely wasn't good, and it didn't bode well for him and Lia. He was only asking to stall Huntley, postpone what he now suspected was inevitable. "Who are you really working for?" he asked, changing tactics a little. "Does the Russian mob pay better than Uncle Sam?"

"Ha," snorted Huntley from out of the darkness. "Russians. Please. Just stop. You're embarrassing yourself."

Professor shrugged. "Can you blame me for not wanting to die in ignorance? Because that's what's going to happen, right? You're going to kill me?" He turned his head to the shadowy form of the other man who had spoken earlier. "Or are you going to have your Nazi pal here do the deed." He waited a beat to gauge the reaction. There was none, or at least, none that he could discern. "Looks like I got that one right. Only you don't sound old enough to be first-gen Third Reich. I'm thinking third generation. Give me a name—I bet I've heard of your grandpa."

"Ignore him," said Huntley flatly. "He's just stalling."

"You're right," Professor went on. "What you should be asking yourself is, why? You really think we didn't suspect you? Refusing to let us contact our chain of command, splitting us up like this? The way you kept throwing up roadblocks to keep us from moving the search forward, and then, after jerking us around for a week telling us to drop everything and come here? You don't think we smelled a rat? We knew you were playing for the other side, even if we weren't sure who that was. We took appropriate measures."

Huntley stepped forward, into the light. His normally sardonic expression now possessed a hard edge. "Appropriate measures, huh?" He reached into a pocket and took out an oblong object. At first, Professor thought it was going to be a gun, but it turned out to be Huntley's satellite phone. He flipped it open and started pushing the illuminated buttons. "You should have just taken the deal I offered you." For a change, his tone sounded genuinely regretful. "You could have just walked away. This didn't concern you. Too bad this is how it ends." He pushed one final button and then pointed out toward the dark water. "Take a look."

Professor turned despite himself. "What am I supposed to be—"

There was a bright flash out near the horizon. It might have been lightning, but Professor knew what it really was.

The *Besnard* had just blown up.

Huntley thumbed off the sat phone. "No answer. So much for your appropriate measures."

He shoved the phone back into his pocket and turned to the other man. "Make him disappear."

"So are you actually a Nazi?" Professor shouted after him. "Or is this just about finding the gold? I guess that flag-waving patriot thing was just schtick."

Huntley did not answer, but the other man took a step forward into the light. In his right hand, he held a semi-automatic pistol. It was, Professor noted almost absently, a Walther P38 pistol, the service weapon of the German *Wehrmacht* during World War II. The barrel of the weapon came up until it seemed to be pointing right into his eyes.

Before Professor could even think about his options, hands clamped around his biceps holding him immobile. He started involuntarily, tried to turn and look at his captors, but then the light flashed in his face, blinding him again. An unseen foot struck the back of his knee, folding his legs into a kneeling position on the sand.

A scream tore through the night, reminding Professor that he was not the only one in jeopardy.

"Lia! Run!"

Something heavy crashed into the back of his head. There was another flash of light, then only darkness.

NINETEEN

Maddock caught the flash from out of the corner of his eye. He swung around, turning his gaze out toward the dark horizon.

"You saw it, too?" Leopov asked. "Was that lightning?"

Maddock shook his head. "I don't think so."

They both continued to stare out at the ocean but the flash did not come again. Behind them, the Querandi lighthouse continued to pulse its identifying beacon, but both sky and water remained an inky black. About twenty seconds later, a sound that might have been a short thunderclap was audible over the low rush of the incoming surf.

"Not lightning," Maddock said gravely, and then clarified. "That was an explosion,"

"You mean like from a bomb?"

"No idea. But something just blew up out there." He now looked around, uneasily. There was no reason to believe that the detonation had anything at all to do with them, but experience had taught him to be wary of dismissing anything as simply a coincidence. He and Leopov had both been on heightened alert since the encounter with the Russian mobsters at the Schliemann museum, now more than a week in the past, and what he had learned earlier in the day had only made him more vigilant.

After repeated futile attempts to call Maxie, Maddock took a chance and called direct to Maxie's office. That was when he'd learned of the attack on his commanding officer, along with an unnamed female FBI agent. The very public attack was being attributed to gang violence. Both shooting victims had been transported to Bethesda Naval Hospital. Maxie had suffered only a flesh wound and would make a full recovery, but the prognosis for the FBI agent was less certain—she was still in the Intensive Care Unit.

Maddock had immediately ended the call, destroyed the phone, and then, for good measure, changed hotels. Even though he had played no part whatsoever in bringing Alexandra Vaccaro into the affair, Maddock nonetheless felt responsible for what had happened to her. The timing of the attack could not have been coincidental. Whomever had targeted Alex and Maxie had done so because of their involvement with the search for the final resting place of the *Blutfahne,* and clearly had been monitoring Maxie or Alex or both of them in hopes of learning more. If Telesh was behind it—a reasonable assumption—then he had demonstrated a surprisingly long reach, which meant there was almost nobody he and Leopov could confide in moving forward.

It also seemed, to Maddock at least, like a clear message that Villa Gessell was worth checking out.

Unburdened by Petrov, they moved swiftly through Germany and into France where they holed up for a couple days in order to regroup and make arrangements for the next phase of their journey. From there, they traveled separately and in disguise, leapfrogging across South America to Buenos Aires. They did not take the same flights or stay in the same hotels, but maintained contact with mobile phones which they switched out every time they entered a new country.

On the morning of their second day in Buenos Aires, about a week after escaping the Russians in Ankershagen, Maddock visited an Internet Café and bought an hour of computer time. He wasn't quite sure how to begin looking for the Blood Flag, but he knew better than to simply blunder into Villa Gessell. He needed more information, and since he could no longer turn to Maxie or anyone else available through official channels, there was only one person he felt he could trust with the enquiry.

It took him a while to figure out how to access an Internet Relay Chat client. He would have definitely preferred a phone call or better yet, a face to face meeting, but the person he hoped would be at the other end of the text connection did his best work in front of a computer terminal. As soon as the chat client was open, a message appeared.

Maddock. I heard about your folks. I'm so sorry.

Maddock winced. With all that had been going on, he'd lost track of the mental box where he had compartmentalized his grief. Though well-intentioned, such condolences tore open a wound that, while nowhere near healed, had at least begun to scab over.

Thanks, Jimmy, he typed.

Jimmy was Jimmy Letson, an investigative journalist employed by the Washington Post and secretly one of the most talented computer hackers in the game. He also happened to be a former SEAL candidate—one of the more than two-thirds who "rang the bell," voluntarily quitting the ordeal known as Hell Week. Washing out had not washed Jimmy out of Maddock's life however. They had remained friends through the years, and Maddock had often called upon him for help with particularly sticky research questions.

After what happened to Cmdr Maxwell, I was hoping you'd reach out to me.

You heard about that? Maddock's understanding was that the attack was officially being passed off as gang violence.

A shootout in DC, involving a senior naval officer, practically on the doorstep of the Hoover Building? You think I wouldn't know about that?

Maddock nodded to himself. Leave it to Jimmy to see through the BS.

I would have called... Or whatever this is... Sooner, but I thought I'd give your liver a break.

Jimmy usually took payment for research inquiries in cases of bourbon whiskey.

This one's on the house. Jimmy typed. *Call it me doing my patriotic duty.*

Maddock raised an eyebrow at this. Like many journalists, Jimmy was a notorious cynic, particularly in matters involving politics and the military. Before he could think of a reply, Jimmy sent another message that clarified this seeming inconsistency.

I don't buy the official story about gang violence. This was wetwork.

Wetwork—politically sanctioned assassination.

Maddock was trying to think of how to frame his affirmative reply when another message appeared in the chat box.

This was a contract job, and I'm 99.99% certain the CIA picked up the tab.

Maddock jolted in his chair as if he'd received an electric shock. And yet, even as part of his brain went into reflexive denial, another part saw the pattern all too clearly.

Telesh had been following Petrov in hopes that they would lead him to Lia—he didn't know that she was actually with Bones, nor could he have known that they had contacted Alex Vaccaro.

But Huntley knew.

Huntley, who had moved in and taken over their mission, kept the team cut off from the chain of command, demanded that Maddock and Leopov come in for debrief.

And just minutes after Alex and Maxie called Maddock to tell him about Villa Gessell, somebody— no, not somebody... *An assassin with a government contract*—tried to kill them and almost succeeded.

Huntley knew. Huntley gave the order.

But why?

Maddock took a deep, calming breath, and then carefully typed: *What makes you think the Agency is behind it?*

The way the investigation got shut down. If it was an outside player, the FBI would be digging deep. They're not, and that tells me that the person who ordered the hit is connected.

For the first time since separating from the team in Russia, he felt real anxiety for Bones, Willis, and Professor. Were they even still alive?

Several seconds passed before another message from Jimmy appeared. *So that's the who. What I want to know is "why"? You got any ideas?*

Maddock considered the question carefully. Jimmy was a friend and a crack researcher, but he was also a member of the press, with a moral and ethical responsibility to not only discover the truth but also to publish it. That was what Jimmy had meant by 'patriotic duty.' Maddock on the other hand had a responsibility to preserve the secrecy of military operations.

Is this off the record? he typed.

Dane, are you serious? There was another long interval, and then Jimmy wrote: *You contacted me. That tells me you already know something. Well this time, my help comes with a bigger price than a bottle of Wild Turkey.*

"So much for 'on the house'," Maddock murmured, but instead of pointing this out, typed in: *A bottle? You never work that cheap.*

Somebody in the government just tried to assassinate your boss, Dane. What do you think you're going to do? Go full Rambo on them? You can't beat these guys with muscle. Sunlight is the best disinfectant... Hell, it's the only thing that seems to work in this town.

Maddock stared at the chat box. He had no idea how to respond. Jimmy was absolutely right, on every count.

A minute passed, and then a new message appeared.

You still there?

"Still here," Maddock said aloud as he entered the text. *Thinking.*

Okay, look. I'm sorry if I came on kind of strong. Off the record, what can I help you with?

Maddock hesitated. No matter how vague he tried

to be, Jimmy was smart enough to connect the dots. In truth, that was exactly what he wanted his friend to do. *I need information about a place called Villa Gessell. It's in Argentina.*

Ha. I don't need to look that one up. Villa Gessell is where all the escaped Nazis went after WW II. Another message followed quickly. *I probably shouldn't say that. I'll get sued for libel. Let's just say that there were rumors. Very persuasive rumors.*

Break.

Wait, this has something to do with escaped Nazis?

Break.

You're looking for escaped Nazis in Argentina. And someone in the CIA is trying to cover it up. Is that what's happening?

Maddock gaped at the screen, not only astonished at the connection Jimmy had just made, but at the swiftness with which he had made that intuitive leap. *I'm not quite sure,* he answered, honestly.

Well, I guess I'm not surprised. This bird's been a long time coming home to roost.

What do you mean by that?

Okay, time for a quick history lesson, Jimmy went on. *Set your wayback machine for 1945. The Nazis are crushed, the horrors of the Holocaust are exposed to the world, and the engineers of that genocide are rounded up and put on trial. Do you know how many defendants there were at Nuremburg?*

Maddock shook his head as he typed. *Not off the top of my head.*

24.

Of the 1000s of high-ranking Nazi party members who were captured at the end of the war, only 24 were put on trial. Care to guess what happened to the rest?

You mean the ones that didn't commit suicide? They escaped to Villa Gessell, right?

Wrong. They came to work for us.

Maddock nodded slowly. *I know about the scientists who were rolled up in Operation Paperclip.*

Tip of the proverbial iceberg. In addition to guys like

Werner Von Braun, the OSS and later the CIA brought over hundreds, maybe even thousands of Nazi officers, and protected them. Gave them new identities, jobs, shielded them from international prosecution for war crimes. And this wasn't just in the days after the war. It's been ongoing. They also recruited a lot more former Nazis who stayed in Germany, to help them spy on the Russians. In 1949, a former Wehrmacht officer named Albert Schnez put together a clandestine group called the Schnez-Truppe. Their goal was to create a militia to fight back in the event of a Soviet-led invasion from East Germany. They claimed a membership of 40,000—all of them veterans. A supporting member of the organization, General Adolf Heusinger was Chief of Staff of the Wehrmacht in 1944. The West German government gave tacit support to the Schnez-Truppe because they were anti-Communist. Schnez remained in the Bundeswehr, eventually retiring with the rank of Lieutenant General. Heusinger served as Chairman to the NATO military committee.

The chat box was filling up with words faster than Maddock could read. Sometimes, in his interactions with Jimmy, he forgot that the man wrote for a living. Jimmy was just getting warmed up.

You might wonder how the politicians were able to just forgive and forget. The truth is, they didn't forget, and they didn't particularly see the need to forgive. They didn't actually care about the atrocities. The Nuremburg Trials almost didn't happen. There was a lot of pushback from American politicians and even some generals, who felt that the Nazis could be a powerful ally in a war against the Soviets. A war that they desperately wanted to fight. We like to believe a version of history where Uncle Sam stood up to Adolf and kicked his ass, but the truth is, a lot of Americans did not want to go to war with Hitler's Germany. They actually supported him. In 1939, 20,000 people attended a Nazi rally in Madison Square Garden. Granted, there were 100,000 people protesting it on the street outside, but just ask yourself what happened to those 20,000 American

Nazis? You think they changed their mind when America finally entered the war?

Jimmy went on. *And that's not all. I'm sure you know about certain high-profile Americans who supported Hitler. Henry Ford. William Randolph Hearst. Charles Lindbergh. But there's one other who doesn't get talked about very much. An American banker who represented the interests of a German industrialist named Fritz Thyssen. Thyssen was literally the man who bankrolled Hitler's rise to power. Oh, the American banker? His name was Prescott Bush.*

Maddock smirked. *The baked beans guy?*

Is Bones there with you? Because I know Dane Maddock did not just say that. Prescott Bush, was the father of George Herbert Walker Bush, who aside from being the 41st President of the USA was also a CIA officer in the 1960s, where he was involved with the Bay of Pigs fiasco, and served as Director of the CIA during the Ford administration. Now, I'm not ready to go out on a limb and say that Prescott Bush was a secret Nazi, but it's the kind of information the CIA might not want getting out into the public sphere.

Maddock checked the clock. His hour was ticking away rapidly and he felt he was no closer to an answer. *Jimmy, I need you to focus. Can you think of a reason why somebody at the Agency would want to keep me from looking into Villa Gessell? Or specifically, looking for someone who might have escaped there?*

If they knew about it and didn't want anyone to know they knew? Sure. Who's the someone you're talking about? What do you want to know?

A guy named Müller . He was head of the Gestapo.

Jimmy typed, *I'll have to look into that one. Gimme a sec.*

A second was about all Jimmy needed. The next few messages were blocks of text that appeared to have been lifted whole from some kind of online encyclopedia. Much of the information contained therein was already known to Maddock. The rest was too voluminous to readily distill into useful leads.

Maddock kept scrolling down until he came to Jimmy's comments.

This guy doesn't seem like your garden variety Nazi. Wasn't a true believer. Doesn't sound like he much cared for Hitler or his policies. The only thing they shared was a deep hatred of communists. Relentless. Ambitious. Driven.

"And still missing," Maddock put in.

The evidence strongly suggests that he died during the fall of Berlin, body never identified. It was a war. That kind of thing happens a lot.

"I have information that places him in northern Germany almost two weeks later."

There was a conspicuous pause.

Interesting. Is this off the record, too?

"I'm not sure, yet. I'll make sure you get the scoop."

Okay. Well, if he survived Berlin, and didn't get captured, there is a better than average chance that he managed to escape Germany. Villa Gessell would be a logical destination for him.

"So if somebody in the government, or maybe in the CIA, knew about it, covered it up, maybe so they could turn him, use him as an asset… That might be something they'd want to keep a secret. Kill to protect."

Your words not mine, Jimmy replied.

Maddock checked the clock again. Only a few minutes left now. "They tried to kill Maxie after he told me about Villa Gessell. Could Müller still be there?"

Maybe buried there. I doubt he's still alive. He'd be almost a hundred years old.

"So I should start looking in cemeteries?"

I doubt you'd find a headstone with his name on it. But there's bound to be something there… Some clue that would put you on his trail. Something they couldn't cover up or destroy.

Like a blood-stained Nazi flag, Maddock thought but didn't type. He knew that wasn't the sort of thing Jimmy was alluding to. "Maybe the U-boat that brought him to Argentina."

Or the place where it unloaded. I found some

interesting trivia. Stuff that might not be in the local tourist's guide.

"Make it quick," Maddock warned.

Okay, VG was built on sand dunes. Sand moves around a lot, covers stuff up. In the 60s, a real estate developer uncovered a railway track leading from the sea through a big shed alongside the house of Carlos Gessell—the German who... duh... created VG. The track ended at the garden of a German mechanic who specialized in diesels. They also found a bunker full of fuel drums, pieces of a radio mast, and mechanical parts that might have been used to repair submarines.

"Is that bunker still there?"

No idea. You'd probably have to check it out for yourself. A couple other places worth checking. About five miles south of the Querandi lighthouse, there's a small concrete structure that nobody can explain. Might have been used to signal U-boats off shore. Five miles further down, there are two flat areas that appear to be paved with non-native stone. Again, nobody can explain where they came from, but it's been suggested that they might have been a platform for loading or unloading cargo. Maybe there's other stuff there, hidden under the dunes. Stuff they don't want you looking for.

Maddock doubted that he would find anything remotely incriminatory at the abandoned sites, but inasmuch as Alex's mention of Villa Gessell had apparently triggered the assassination attempt, he could not afford to dismiss anything out of hand. That was why he and Leopov, after a quick shopping trip, had made the four-hour drive to Villa Gessell in a rented Toyota Land Cruiser.

After so many days of solo travel, it was a little disconcerting to have Leopov with him again, especially without Petrov as a third wheel. He couldn't help but think of the long cold night they had shared in the woods near Telesh's villa, how she had offered herself to him, and how hard it had been to refuse. The subject never came up again—in fact, Leopov seemed to avoid any discussions that might have even led them to it—but it was never completely out of Maddock's thoughts. The drive seemed to take forever.

From Villa Gessell, they continued south on Provincial Route 11 for several more miles before stopping to let some air out of the tires in order to traverse the dunes toward the Querandi lighthouse.

It was still daylight when they arrived, and despite the remote location, the area was bustling with activity, mostly in the form of young adventure-seeking visitors zipping around the dunes on quad bikes. Rather than draw attention to themselves by venturing down the beach to the sites Jimmy had suggested, they idled away the remainder of the day at the lighthouse which, in addition to functioning as a navigational marker doubled as a small maritime museum. Built in 1922, the lighthouse had been the first building constructed in what had come to be known as the Villa Gessell district, though Carlos Gessell, the German expatriate who had founded the eponymous resort town, would not appear on the scene for another decade. Unsurprisingly, the interpretive displays made no mention of German U-boats sheltering along the coast.

With dusk darkening the sky, they pitched a tent—one of the items acquired before leaving Buenos Aires—and built a small fire to complete the illusion that they were nothing more than a couple on holiday, but once the cover of darkness was absolute, they stole from their camp and returned to the lighthouse carrying another of their recent purchases: a Minelab metal detector.

Leopov kept a lookout while Maddock quickly swept the area around the lighthouse, out to a hundred yards. He found the sort of detritus common to a heavily trafficked beach—coins, empty aluminum cans—but nothing that couldn't be dated to within ten years. Maddock had not really expected to find anything, but the search did give him a chance to test his equipment and fine tune its settings After completing a survey of the area, they headed south toward the first location Jimmy had suggested. They moved on foot rather than driving, with Maddock sweeping the metal detector back and forth as they went along. If the rails were still there, reburied by the shifting sand dunes, the device would find them.

When they saw the explosion, Maddock switched off the metal detector, slung it over his shoulder, and then took out the only weapon he currently possessed—the entrenching tool he'd been using to excavate their discoveries.

On any other covert mission, acquiring weapons— real weapons—would have been a priority, and both he and Leopov had plenty of real-world experience doing just that. The situation this time was different, though. Because they could not trust anyone with ties to the American intelligence community, the usual means for procuring unregistered guns—safe house caches and black-market contacts—were out. Other less reputable means, such as taking their chances with the local criminal element, were similarly proscribed for much the same reason. Which meant that, if they were obliged to defend themselves, they would have to do so with field-expedient weapons. The collapsible military shovel was designed with such a use in mind—it could be used like a battle-axe if needed. While there was no tangible reason to assume that the offshore explosion had anything to do with their mission, or that they were now in danger, Maddock saw no downside to being ready, just in case.

They remained there for several minutes, motionless, not speaking, watching and waiting. At one point, Maddock thought he heard a shout, or the echo of a shout. A few minutes after that, the distant but familiar noise of a two-stroke engine—possibly more than one—was audible. Maddock quickly oriented himself toward the sound, which seemed to be coming from further down the beach. He turned toward it just in time to see a pair of moving lights disappearing behind the crest of a dune a few hundred yards away.

Unlike the offshore explosion, the presence of an ATV on the beach, even at such a late hour, was not particularly mysterious. Even the shout they had heard, if it was a shout, might have been easily enough explained away.

"We should check that out," Leopov whispered. "Just in case."

Maddock nodded in the darkness. "Yeah."

Hefting the entrenching tool, he started forward, moving at a brisk jog, fast enough to cover the distance to the spot where he judged the ATV had started from, but slow enough to keep his senses fully engaged. The rush of waves soon blanketed the noise of the retreating quad bike, but his nose caught the unmistakable whiff of exhaust smoke.

Several more small pinpoints of light became visible, moving across the beach toward the surf. Flashlights, Maddock guessed, and in their diffuse glow, he could make out the silhouettes of the men who held them. The flashlights had almost certainly spoiled the men's night vision capabilities, but Maddock and Leopov nevertheless stayed low to avoid silhouetting themselves against the sky as they drew closer. The men had advanced to the water's edge where they gathered around a small inflatable boat which had been intentionally grounded, where two of them heaved a large shapeless mass over the gunwale and into the boat's interior. Their burden deposited, the men began shoving the craft toward the sea.

"Was that a body?" Leopov whispered.

That was exactly what Maddock had thought it looked like. The only question was whether it was a dead body or a living one. "We need to get over there," he said.

Before he could take another step however, he sensed movement in the darkness right beside him. Leopov started to hiss a warning but was suddenly muffled by a hand that emerged from out of the night and clamped over her mouth. Maddock immediately pivoted, raising the entrenching tool above his head in preparation to strike at the barely perceived threat, but before he could swing, a second dark figure sprang up, rising to loom over him. A long arm shot out and seized the folding shovel just below the blade, completely arresting Maddock's swing.

A familiar voice hissed in his ears. "Maddock. Damn. You're the last person I expected to see here."

"Bones?"

TWENTY

It had been clear to Bones, even before Huntley left with Professor and Lia, that the spook had no plan to rendezvous with Maddock. Why Huntley was keeping them in the dark and trying to divide their forces, he couldn't begin to guess but he knew it wasn't a good one. He was only certain about one thing. Maddock was not in Argentina. He probably wasn't even in the same hemisphere.

That was the only part of it he got wrong.

As soon as the launch was lowered into the water, Bones and Willis went to work. Since Huntley clearly wanted to divide them, finding a way to surreptitiously stay together was imperative, so rather than cool their heels on the *Besnard,* they decided to leave the ship at anchor and go ashore. As the vessel had only one launch, that meant they would have to swim, but that did not pose a hardship for the two SEALs—they were more at home in the water than on it. The ship had been outfitted with wetsuits and SCUBA equipment, including diver propulsion units capable of whisking them along almost as fast as the launch's outboard, but rather than attempt to follow the boat—a nearly impossible proposition in the dark of night—they decided to head for the lighthouse.

Underwater, with no wind to slow them down, they made good time, stealing ashore just a few hundred yards south of the beacon. After caching their gear in the dunes, they continued south on foot under cover of darkness, scanning the beach in hopes of spotting Huntley and the others. They ran, covering the nearly five miles in less than half an hour. This too posed no difficulty for them; they trained for situations like this, had in fact been doing it for nearly all of their respective adult lives.

When they spotted the beam of a flashlight ahead in the darkness, they slowed to a walk and ultimately, dropped to high crawl the remaining distance. So focused were they on what was going on in front of them, they completely missed the destruction of the *Besnard.*

Their eyes had adjusted to the darkness and they could see a lot of what was going on. Professor and Lia were easily identified with the light shining in their faces. A couple seconds later, Huntley stepped into the light as well, and there was no mistaking the hostility in his demeanor.

"Well, there's Captain Midnight," he had whispered to Willis. "You think Maddock is behind one of those flashlights?"

"You really have to ask?" Willis replied, sardonically.

"This is FUBAR." Bones squinted trying to get an accurate count of the silhouettes surrounding the spot-lit figures. "I count seven."

"I got eight," Willis countered. "Either way, long odds. Especially if they're strapped."

"You think the odds are gonna get any better if we sit here on our asses?"

"Probably not. How do you want to—"

He broke off as another man stepped forward, a gun clearly visible. Professor managed to shout an accusation, but then was dropped to his knees and viciously pistol-whipped. Another of the men seized Lia and dragged her away from Professor's slumped form.

"Crap," Bones muttered. "Let's go."

They fast crawled forward, but in the time it took them to cross half the distance, Huntley had dragged Lia away from the others. A few seconds later, small-engine noise filled the air. Headlight beams shone toward the dunes and in the glow of the trailing vehicle, Bones could just make out Huntley and Lia sitting astride the lead quad-bike as it zipped away.

There was nothing Bones and Willis could do to

help Lia—not in the near term, at least—but their teammate might still be alive. Helping Professor would have to be their first priority, even if the odds were four-to-one against them.

Then the odds got a lot better.

At first, Bones didn't recognize the pair of figures that had approached from behind them, less than ten yards to their left, closer to the surf. He tapped Willis on the shoulder, pointed them out. It had been sheer luck that the newcomers hadn't stepped on them. Bones was worried that they might be sentries, working for Huntley's unidentified accomplices, returning from a patrol, but when he heard a female voice with a Russian accent speaking English, he knew their luck had changed.

There was no time for a reunion, nor even to compare notes about what was happening further down the beach. Fortunately, Maddock and his teammates had worked together for so long that verbal communication was unnecessary. After a few quick hand signals, they divided their forces and continued toward the beached boat and the group of men who were preparing to shove it out into the surf, consigning its sole, unconscious passenger to the uncertain mercy of the sea.

Bones and Willis, still clad in their wetsuits and armed with dive knives, headed out into the surf, circling wide to come up on the boat from the far side. After giving them a fifteen-second headstart, Maddock and Leopov rushed straight ahead, charging the men. They moved quietly, staying low to present as low a profile as possible, but had to sacrifice stealth for speed. They had to strike while the men were still occupied with their grim task.

As he got to within ten feet of the boat, Maddock saw—or rather sensed—that one of the men on the opposite side of the craft had spotted him. The man had been bent over the boat's gunwale, both hands gripping it, but as recognition dawned, he stood bolt upright, one hand fumbling for the pistol in his belt. Before he could draw it or cry out in alarm, his body went rigid and then pitched forward, falling over the gunwale. Maddock half-glimpsed a hulking form moving behind the man, but couldn't tell if it was Bones or Willis.

In that same instant, Maddock reached the nearest man, who was standing back a few feet from the boat, evidently overseeing the labors of the others. He had his back to Maddock and Leopov, and went down without ever realizing that he and his men were under attack.

The blade of the entrenching tool rang like a bell as it connected with the man's skull. Maddock did not linger over the fallen man, but pivoted toward the next closest, dispatching him with the backswing. Maddock turned again, looking for his next target and expecting to meet some resistance now that the element of surprise was gone, but there was no one left.

Seven figures—Bones' count had been accurate—lay unmoving on the damp sand surrounding the boat.

Willis had snatched up a flashlight and was quickly checking the fallen men to ensure that none of them would ever again pose a threat. Bones had hopped into the boat and was checking on the status of the lone unwilling passenger.

"Prof! You still with us, buddy?"

There was no response. Maddock retrieved another flashlight and moved in closer. He wasn't surprised to see Professor's face revealed in the light. Bones had his cheek pressed against the other man's chest, the fingers of his right hand were probing Professor's throat.

"Still breathing," Bones announced. "Pulse is strong. He might be concussed."

"Does he need a hospital?"

What Maddock was really asking was, *will he live?*

Hospitalization was the option of last resort for many reasons, but if it was truly a matter of saving Professor's life they would chance it. They were all competent battlefield medics, but severe brain trauma could only be remedied with surgery.

"We can treat him on the boat," Bones answered, his tone less confident than Maddock was hoping for.

"I don't think you have a boat, anymore."

Bones looked up, his expression puzzled at first, and then angry. "That son of a..."

"I've got a vehicle parked by the lighthouse," Maddock said. "We'll carry him there. Get him somewhere safe."

Bones nodded, then his face changed again, this time to a look of horror. "Lia!"

"Where is she?"

"He took her. Quad bike. Just a few minutes ago."

Maddock spun away, tossed the entrenching tool into the boat and scooped up a fallen pistol. It was a Walther P38, similar in many respects to its eventual successor—and Maddock's preferred personal sidearm—the P99. He took a second to eject the magazine, rack the slide, catch and replace the chambered round. He blew down the barrel, hoping to dislodge any sand particles that might cause the weapon to jam if fired, then reseated the magazine. With the weapon restored—hopefully—to fully functional status, he took off at a run, following the trail of footsteps that led up the beach. Behind him, Bones was shouting for Willis to take over with Professor's medical assessment. Of the two, Willis was the more capable medic. He'd long ago demonstrated an aptitude for first aid, and had once confided in Maddock that as a child he'd dreamed of being a physician, but that career path seemd well out of reach for a kid growing up in one of the poorest parts of Detroit. Of course, Maddock knew Bones' true motivation for the handoff was a desire to rescue Lia.

The beam of his flashlight revealed a row of waiting all-terrain vehicles. Two groups of distinctive depressions in the sand marked where two more had been parked. The sand was crisscrossed with parallel tracks coming in from different vectors, but the lines leading away from where the missing ATVs had been were uncrossed.

Maddock clambered onto the first quad he came to, fired up the engine using the kick-starter, and then took off, following the fresh tracks. He figured Huntley and his accomplice had about a five-minute headstart, but he also had a passenger and no clue that someone was chasing after him.

Before long, he noticed that the ground to either side of him was illuminated. A quick glance over his shoulder revealed another ATV racing to catch up with him, a hulking figure bent over the handlebars. The engine noise made conversation impossible, so Maddock simply acknowledged his friend with a nod, which Bones returned with a fierce grin.

The next several minutes would have been an exhilarating adrenaline rush if not for what was at stake. The little four-wheelers were made for dune racing and the SEALs pushed their machines to the limit, catching air off the dune crests and expertly negotiating soft landings like Olympic ski-jumpers— the sand hills were far more forgiving than the paved roads outside Telesh's dacha. Yet, Maddock and Bones weren't chasing thrills. If they didn't catch Huntley before they ran out of dunes, they might never see Lia again.

After white-knuckling up and down the golden dunes, they crested one last rise which sloped down to melt into a dark forest. A paved road, running parallel along the bottom of the hill, crossed their path like a boundary marker separating the distinctive ecosystems.

The tracks they had been following led down to the edge of the road where two ATVs sat idle alongside two larger vehicles—a pickup truck with a long flatbed transport trailer attached, and a full-sized black SUV. The quad bikes' headlights were still on, and in their glow, Maddock could see Huntley and another man attempting to transfer Lia into the SUV. Before they could finish this task, both men turned to look up at the pair of quads charging down the dune toward them.

There was no way Huntley or his accomplice could have discerned their identities, and no reason for either man to suspect that the riders were anyone but their comrades returning, but something must have given them away because Huntley continued hustling Lia toward the far side of the SUV, while the other man drew a pistol and started firing at the approaching riders.

With a few quick hand signals, Maddock communicated a change of plan to Bones, then aimed the front end of the ATV at the shooter and held steady on the throttle. From the corner of his eye, he saw Bones veer off to the left, putting his quad on course to bisect the road fifty yards to the rear of the parked vehicles. Maddock hunkered low over his handlebars to offer the smallest possible target. At the present distance, luck rather than the man's shooting skill would determine whether or not a round found its target, but that was about to change.

He halved the distance in a matter of seconds, in which time the gunman blazed through the pistol's magazine. He fumbled the reload, betraying his inexperience, allowing Maddock to get a lot closer— close enough to be within the effective range of the pistol. Fortunately for Maddock, that cut both ways.

Without letting up on the throttle, he reached down, drew his recently appropriated Walther, and began returning fire. He aimed short, knowing that Lia was only a few feet away, concealed from view but not really protected by thin metal door panels and window glass. Of course, the other man didn't know he was aiming to miss, and so when the first shot was fired, he turned and retreated behind the SUV before taking another shot. Maddock squeezed off another round, forcing the man to duck back, and giving himself enough time to reach the road.

He drew up alongside the pickup, waiting until the very last second to jam on the brakes, and then dismounted, letting the four-wheeler roll ahead of him. Sparks flew as a barrage of bullets tore into the ATV, shattering the headlight.

Maddock crouched and crept forward, staying close to the truck and keeping its engine block between him and the shooter. Without exposing himself to view, he extended a hand and fired high, once again hoping to accomplish nothing more than to keep the other man distracted long enough for Bones to get in position.

Suddenly, the taillights of the SUV blazed to life, and a second later the vehicle lurched into motion. Grimacing in frustration, Maddock eased forward, edging around the front end of the truck. Even as he spotted the motionless form of the gunman on the pavement, he heard Bones shout, "Got him."

Maddock bolted forward, sprinting after the retreating SUV. It was a futile effort. As the vehicle raced away, he turned and ran back to join Bones who was kneeling beside the dead man, rifling through the latter's pockets. Maddock didn't have to ask what he was searching for, and could see from the disgusted look on Bones face that he hadn't found them. The keys to operate the truck were probably in the pocket of one of the men they'd killed back on the beach.

"Can you hotwire it?"

Bones glanced back at the large pickup. It was a newer model, and therefore harder to boost than the cars Bones had "borrowed" for joyrides in his misspent youth, but after a moment's consideration, he shrugged. "I'll give it a shot. While I'm doing that, do us both a favor and unhitch that trailer. We'll never catch him with that thing hanging off our caboose."

"On it." Maddock was already moving. As he rounded the bed of the truck, he heard a loud crack— Bones smashing out the window glass with the butt of his pistol. The anti-theft alarm immediately began braying.

Maddock grimaced and did his best to ignore the clamor as he bent over the hitch and went to work detaching the trailer. He didn't bother raising the tongue with the built-in jack, but simply lifted it off the hitch and shoved it away, letting it crash onto the pavement.

The alarm abruptly fell silent, and in the relative quiet, Maddock could hear the rumble of the engine.

Bones leaned out the driver's window and shouted, "What are you waiting for? Get in!"

"I'll ride in back!" Maddock replied, and then vaulted up onto the tailgate, rolling over into the pickup's bed. "Go! Go!"

Bones shifted into 'drive' and stomped the gas pedal. The acceleration was sluggish at first, but the truck quickly got up to speed. Maddock crawled to the front of the bed and leaned out to look around the cab. The wind blasted him full in the face, sucking his breath away, stinging his eyes, but he could still make out the taillights of the SUV, maybe a quarter mile away. He craned forward, getting his face as close to the driver's window as he could.

"Get next to him!" he shouted. "I'll go over."

He hadn't worked out exactly how he would make that transfer, but figured it would be a lot easier to accomplish from the bed of the truck.

Instead of acknowledging, Bones shouted, "Crap!"

The truck slowed.

"What's wrong?" Maddock said, though he no longer needed to shout. Without the rush of wind in his ears, he could now hear a violent rattling sound issuing from the vehicle's front end.

"We're screwed is what's wrong," Bones growled as the truck came to a stop. He shut off the engine but it continued to tick wildly. A plume of steam billowed up from the front end of the truck. Although none of the ill-fated gunman's rounds had found a flesh-and-blood target, one or more of them had punctured the radiator, decisively ending the attempted rescue.

Bones swore again and beat his fists against the steering wheel. Maddock just hung his head. After more than a week of guiding and protecting Lia on a journey across the globe, they had failed her.

TWENTY-ONE

McLean, Virginia

The house was modest by local standards. The Cape Cod-style house, built in 1952, sat on a wooded acre, and like most of its neighbors was barely visible from Savile Lane, the narrow road which wound through the quasi-rural residential area. According to public records, the property was owned by a trust company and, like many others in the small community situated just off the Capital Beltway and only eight miles from downtown Washington DC, was rented out to diplomats and politicians. The itinerant nature of the community's inhabitants meant that few were aware—and still fewer cared—about the identities, and comings and goings of their neighbors.

If anyone had paid attention, they might have noticed that the level of activity in the house did not seem to correspond to changes in the tenant of record. In fact, very little ever seemed to change. To be sure, the house was lived in. Landscapers regularly mowed the lawn, tended the shrubs, and, in autumn, raked and removed the blanket of maple leaves. Deliveries of meals, groceries, and other goods were accepted by someone purporting to be the tenant's housekeeper, and visitors arriving by car were not uncommon, particularly after the close of the business day. But the temporary residents of the other dwellings on Savile Lane would not have been able to pick the tenant of the blue and white Cape Cod out of a line-up, much less realize that it was the same man from one year to the next, no matter the name listed in public records.

A deeper examination of those records would have hinted at an explanation for this discrepancy. The people alleged to have resided in the house over the course of nearly six decades did not exist. The trust company that held the deed was a dummy corporation, owned by another dummy corporation, owned by yet another, to form a veritable and seemingly infinite Matryoshka doll of shell companies. The complexity of the deception was, in itself, another hint at the answer to the riddle, but an even more obvious clue was the fact that the small parcel of land on which the house sat abutted the 258-acre campus officially designated the George Bush Center for Intelligence—better known simply as CIA Headquarters.

Jimmy Letson had not started out by trying to unmask the true owner of the Cape Cod. He had discovered its existence quite by accident while trying to pick up the trail of Bruce Huntley on behalf of Dane Maddock.

There had been none of the customary banter regarding Jimmy's usual fee, nor had Maddock made any demands of him with respect to secrecy. Whatever Huntley was involved in, and no matter who had given it official sanction, it was a story that needed to be brought out into the daylight. The public didn't just have a right to know... They truly needed to know.

Jimmy had started by checking all flights leaving Buenos Aires in the hours following Lia's disappearance with Huntley. He had followed other lines of inquiry as well, since they did not know what Huntley's next move would be. Would he seek refuge in the local enclave of Nazi descendants? Or would he attempt to get out of Argentina by the most expedient means available? There were many possibilities, and Jimmy followed up on all of them.

Researching flight plans had yielded the best lead, though not because it provided confirmation that Huntley and Lia had been aboard one of the departing aircraft—a chartered air-freight plane with no passengers listed on its manifest, that had taken off the morning following Lia's abduction. The critical clue had to do with the identity of the client that had chartered the plane—Black Spring Holdings. The innocuously named company was one that Jimmy had encountered before, on a Darknet discussion board purporting to list dummy corporations created by the CIA as fronts for a variety of questionable and clandestine activities.

Jimmy did not automatically accept as gospel everything he read there—most of it was paranoid conspiracy nonsense—but neither did he automatically dismiss the information out of hand. A cursory examination of the company was enough to convince him that it was a front for something nefarious even if he could not draw a definitive link to a government agency. It had been enough to convince Maddock as well.

"They're on that plane," he had told Jimmy. "Where's it going?"

It set down in Bogota about an hour ago, but just to refuel. From there, it's nonstop to Dulles.

Dulles—Washington Dulles International—was one of three major airports servicing the DC metropolitan area, and one of the busiest air travel hubs in the country. It was also located just a few miles west of CIA headquarters.

"Jimmy, you've got to get eyes on that plane."

Jimmy did not balk at the request. Although he preferred to operate in the realm of cyberspace, his career as an investigative journalist had many times obliged him to go undercover or sneak into places where he was not welcome—trespasses that, if discovered, might have resulted in his arrest or something much worse.

A simple hack into air traffic control had provided him with the plane's runway and gate assignment. The plane would be offloading at one of the cargo terminals and an expertly forged employee badge had gotten him past the security checkpoint and into the cargo terminal, where he found a place to unobtrusively watch the destination gate.

Shortly before the plane's scheduled arrival time, a white, unmarked delivery van pulled up near the gate.

Upon landing, the plane taxied to the terminal where a single piece of cargo—a large, oblong box with the right dimensions to be a casket—was transferred directly from the plane's cargo hold to the waiting van. A dark-haired man attired as a flight attendant also boarded the van. Jimmy didn't have any pictures of Bruce Huntley, but the man matched the description Maddock had given him.

Jimmy quickly returned to his car and headed out. He did not go far however. Just before the turnoff to the rental car returns, he pulled into the breakdown lane and switched on his hazard lights. He fumbled in his trunk, pretending to search for his spare tire for the next five minutes until he saw the white van again. It was moving with the flow of traffic in the far-left, eastbound lanes.

He had a pretty good idea where the van would go next, so over the course of the next few miles, he managed to catch up to and pass it. Better to keep an eye on it his rearview mirror, rather than risk being spotted trying to tail it.

As they breezed along the Dulles Toll Road for several miles, Jimmy watched the van for lane changes. When they neared the Beltway split, he dropped back and permitted the other vehicle to overtake him.

He was mildly surprised when the van did not take either option, but instead continued along the highway a little further to take the next exit in the direction of Tyson's Corner, where it immediately turned left, to head north on state route 123, also known as Dolley Madison Boulevard.

"Ha!" Jimmy pounded his hands against the steering wheel, exultant. "Knew it."

About three miles further up the road from Tyson's Corner, the highway would run right past the south entrance to CIA Headquarters. Huntley was heading home.

But the van didn't make the expected turn. Instead, it went through the intersection and continued to the next set of traffic lights, where it turned left onto a narrow country road that curved around a large white church. A tiny little blue sign identified the road as Savile Lane, and a larger yellow diamond sign proclaimed "No Outlet."

Jimmy frowned in dismay but kept going. Even though it might mean losing sight of the delivery van, he didn't dare follow it through the turn for fear of betraying his presence. Instead, he accelerated to the next intersection—it was only another tenth of a mile—hooked a U-turn, and raced back to the Savile Lane turn-off.

There was no immediate sign of the delivery van, but Jimmy decided that wasn't necessarily a bad thing. The unlined road was barely wide enough to permit two-way traffic, and the oversized van would have to proceed with extra care. Jimmy continued along at a sedate twenty-five miles per hour, scanning first the church parking lot and then each driveway he passed.

Trees enveloped the road, hiding the houses from view, and for a moment, Jimmy feared he had lost his quarry. Then, about a quarter-mile from the highway, he spied the corner of a tall white vehicle, just barely visible down one forested driveway on his left. He made a mental note of the address, and then kept driving until he found a place to turn around, whereupon he hastened back to the road and headed back home. He entertained no illusions of playing the hero, confronting the CIA officer, and rescuing the damsel in distress. Maddock would have to take care of that.

Half an hour later, he was back in his apartment, safely ensconced behind the keyboard of his computer, doing what he did best. He was not the least bit surprised to learn that one of the shell companies named on the convoluted chain of ownership for the house on Savile Lane was Black Spring Holdings.

Maddock closed his eyes, counted to ten, and then opened them again. The view had not changed.

When they had first begun their surveillance, earlier in the day, there had at least been some activity inside the residence. Nothing definitive. Nobody emerged from its interior, but they could occasionally see indistinct figures moving behind the window panes, both on the main level and occasionally in the gabled attic windows—as was the case with many Cape Cod-style homes, it appeared that the attic had been finished to supply additional living space. After dark, there were lights burning in some of the windows on the ground floor, but those had gone out at around nine o'clock, leaving only the exterior porchlight to illuminate the house.

Maddock and Bones kept watch from a concealed hide on the southeastern corner of the property, while Willis and Leopov observed from the northwest. After dusk, Maddock had continued to peer through his binoculars, which mostly limited his field of view to what was revealed in the glow of the porchlight. Bones had switched to a night-vision scope in order to monitor everything hidden in darkness, but ultimately, they both saw the same thing.

Maddock blinked again, and then pulled back from the binos just enough to check the time. Almost midnight. *Close enough,* he thought.

"Ready to do this?" he whispered.

"I was ready two hours ago," Bones replied, his voice, a low rumble, trailed off into a yawn.

"You don't sound very enthusiastic."

"Don't get me wrong," Bones replied, a note of bitterness creeping into his tone. "I want to rescue Lia and kick Huntley's ass as much as you do. Maybe more. But I don't think we're going to find either one of them in there. It's Tradecraft 101. Don't stay in one place any longer than you have to. They're long gone by now."

Maddock couldn't dispute Bones' logic. There was no question that Huntley had brought Lia to this house, but that had been three days ago. It had taken Maddock and the others that long to make their way back to the States. During that time, there had been no way to monitor the house. Maddock didn't dare confide in anyone in the SEALs' chain of command. If even half of what Jimmy had suggested about the link between upper tier CIA officials and Nazi fugitives was true, everyone was suspect. Even those not directly involved in the conspiracy might be unknowingly reporting to someone else who was. Nor could he ask Jimmy to keep watch. In following Huntley to the house, his friend had already gone above and beyond, and Maddock couldn't ask any more of him.

Bones was right. Huntley could have moved Lia almost anywhere, and if he was half the spy he claimed to be, almost certainly had. But the house on Savile Lane was their only lead. If Huntley wasn't there, maybe the person inside would—with a little gentle persuasion—tell them where he had gone.

There was one other thing—not a clue so much as a coincidence—that led Maddock to believe the house was more than just a conveniently located Agency safe house.

Professor had been the one to pick up on it.

He had regained consciousness shortly after Maddock and Bones headed out across the dunes, but as Bones had surmised, he had sustained a serious concussion. Hours later, he was still seeing double and complaining of a "skull-splitting headache," but his mind was as sharp as ever.

When Maddock had relayed the update from Jimmy regarding Huntley's flight from Buenos Aires, Professor had chuckled—or rather started to chuckle before grimacing in pain. "Somebody has a sense of humor."

"How so?"

"*Black Spring*. It's the name of a Henry Miller novel. The second in his autobiographical trilogy that starts with *Tropic of Capricorn*."

Bones made a face. "And that's funny why?"

Maddock caught it immediately. "Henry Miller is the anglicized form of Heinrich Müller."

"You're telling me the Nazi we've been chasing came to America and started writing novels?"

"Good heavens, no," Professors said, wincing again. "Two completely different people. Actually, I think Gestapo Müller would have found Henry Miller's writing deeply offensive. Him and most other straight-laced Americans of the period. *Black Spring* was actually banned in the United States until the 1960s."

"Banned?"

"It was considered pornographic. Miller wrote explicit accounts of his sexual liaisons."

Bones sat up a little straighter. "Why have I never heard of this guy?"

Despite his obvious discomfort, Professor managed a wry smile, but refrained from further comment. "It could just be a coincidence," he went on. "Like I said, about the only thing Henry Miller had in common with the Nazis was an abiding dislike for American society. But for very different reasons. I'm sure it's just a coincidence."

Three days later, reflecting on the conversation, Maddock was acutely aware of Professor's absence. He had come to rely on the other man's comprehensive knowledge and insights over the course of the last few years. But Professor's head injury meant he wasn't fit to travel—not for a few days, at least—and so, over his protests, they had left him to convalesce at a Buenos Aires hotel with orders to check in by phone every four hours. If he missed a call, they would contact emergency services and request paramedics.

Now, it was just the four of them.

He put aside the binoculars and took out his cell phone. Cupping a hand over the screen to keep the glow from revealing their position, he dialed Jimmy's number.

"Yo!"

Eschewing the customary and utterly unnecessary exchange of greetings, Maddock simply said, "Throw the switch."

There was only a slight pause and then Jimmy

answered. "It's done. You've got five minutes."

Maddock ended the call and then switched the phone out for a handheld radio—an off-the-shelf Motorola Talkabout equipped with a headset. He keyed the mic. "We're moving."

Willis' voice sounded in his ear. "Roger, out."

Together, Maddock and Bones rose from their hide and started toward the front of the house, moving quickly but without a sound. When they were just thirty feet from the front porch, a spotlight flashed on, shining out on the patch of lawn where they were standing. Both men froze in place, and despite the fact that Jimmy had hacked into the house's security system and put it in diagnostic mode—a five-minute temporary shutdown—Maddock braced himself for the shriek of an alarm, but other than the light, nothing changed.

"Motion sensor," he whispered. "Must be independent of the security system."

"Or it's a silent alarm," Bones replied.

"Well aren't you just a ray of sunshine." If there was a silent alarm, they wouldn't know until patrol cars with armed security guards showed up to investigate. "Let's go."

They quick-stepped to the porch where Bones immediately went to work picking the deadbolt lock. Maddock kept one eye on the sweep second hand of his watch.

Jimmy's search of the security company's records had indicated external sensors only, which meant that once they were inside, they would be able to move about the house without triggering an alarm, but if they weren't all inside with the doors closed before the diagnostic cycle was complete, their rescue attempt would be stillborn.

"Three minutes left," he murmured.

"You want to do this?" Bones shot back. "Don't rush me... Ah, there it is."

IIc gave the tension wrench a little tug and the lock cylinder rotated. He removed the picking tools and quickly inserted them in the keyhole above the thumb-lever on the entry handle set. This lock yielded more quickly, and before the second hand completed another circuit, the door swung open to admit them.

Only now did they unholster their pistols. Maddock carried his Walther P99, Bones had his Glock 17—both were outfitted with suppressors. Had they been accosted by guards from the security service or worse, the police, they would have either fled or surrendered without a fight but anyone inside this house was either a hostage or a hostile. Guns at the ready, they swept into the entry foyer, ready to engage any targets of opportunity—there were none. They kept going, clearing the open rooms of the main floor of the house all the way to the rear where Bones quickly unlocked the back door. Willis and Leopov were waiting there and hastened inside, after which Bones closed and locked the door.

They had made it inside—first objective complete. Now for the hard part.

Moving single file, they did another sweep of the first floor, opening every closed door. There was a single bedroom—the queen-sized bed was neatly made, the closet empty—along with a bathroom, two more closets—also empty—a laundry room, and a pantry, which surprisingly was stocked with an assortment of canned and dry goods.

The empty bedroom was a little disconcerting since they had earlier observed movement and lights through the window, but that was a mystery that would have to wait until they had found and dealt with the house's occupants who, by process of elimination, had to be upstairs.

But the attic rooms were also empty.

"What the hell?" Bones wondered aloud, no longer bothering to whisper. "Where'd they go?"

"There's no one here," Leopov said. "Never was. It's like a Potemkin house,"

Willis shook his head. "No way. We saw people moving around in here. Don't tell me that was all smoke and mirrors."

Maddock tried to recall exactly what they had seen. Backlit silhouettes behind curtains, blinds that occasionally moved as if someone was looking out. It wasn't impossible that all of that had been done remotely with automated special effects devices, but if that was the case, where were the projectors and wires necessary to pull off the illusion?

"We've missed something," he said. "Search it all again. Top to bottom."

They did and soon discovered a false wall in the back of the closet under the staircase. It opened to reveal another flight of stairs descending to a sublevel.

Maddock touched a fingertip to his lips, signaling a return to stealth mode, and then started down, his Walther leading the way.

The steps went down further than he expected, with a landing and switchback at the midpoint, and ended in an open area too large and elaborately decorated to be merely a finished basement.

"Holy crap," Bones murmured as he stepped down beside Maddock. "What is this place?"

"Beats me," Maddock admitted.

They were in what appeared to be a hallway, but with cavernous dimensions. Maddock judged it to be at least fifteen feet wide and a good fifty feet long. The floor was carpeted with a rich burgundy Berber. The walls and the high ceiling were paneled with squares of burnished mahogany, softly lit by the glow emanating from art deco brass- and frosted-glass wall sconces, spaced at eight-foot intervals to either side.

The others joined them a few seconds later. "Damn!" whispered Willis. "I don't think we're in Kansas anymore."

Maddock nodded slowly. "Let's go meet the Wizard."

At the far end, the hallway opened into a rectangular room with a wide arched opening in the middle of the wall to their immediate left, and closed French doors centered on the walls to the right and directly opposite their position.

Maddock gestured toward the arched passage and then headed toward it with the others filing behind him. There were no lights in the space beyond the arch, but there was sufficient ambient illumination to discern that the floor beyond was uncarpeted concrete. About ten feet in, there was something that looked to Maddock like a line of golf carts linked together in a train. Harder to see were the parallel lines that ran out ahead of the carts to disappear into the gloom.

"What is that?" he said. "Some kind of tram?"

Bones stared at the line for a moment, and then began tracing invisible lines in the air. "Those tracks run northwest."

Maddock consulted his own mental map and immediately saw what Bones was getting at. "Straight to CIA HQ."

"I guess now we know where everybody went," Willis remarked, sounding defeated. "They probably transferred Lia there as soon as they got her in the front door."

"So much for our big rescue," Bones said, and then with a sidelong glance at Maddock, added, "Unless you want to take on the whole CIA?"

"Honestly, I'm tempted," he said, but knew better. Going out in a blaze of glory wouldn't do Lia any good… If she was even still alive. He shook his head. "Let's go see what's behind door number two."

The French doors opposite the arch were locked, and there was no visible keyhole. While Bones began probing the seam between the doors with the tip of his knife, Maddock moved to the remaining set of doors.

Unlocked.

They opened to reveal an enormous room—big enough to be an auditorium or the nave of a church, but without any pews. "Standing room only."

Leopov suddenly gripped his arm. "Dane, look!"

She was pointing across the great hall to the back wall where a low dais rose a foot or two above the floor. On the front corners of the dais, American flags hung from upright poles, capped with bright brass eagle finials, but it was another flag that had caught Leopov's eye.

Maddock's heart quickened.

It hung center stage at an angle from a staff mounted to the rear wall. From where they stood, viewing it head on, it looked like nothing more than a large red banner, but when he tilted his head just a little, he could see the enormous white circle occupying the center of the rectangular scarlet flag, and the black swastika in the center of the circle.

The Blutfahne.

For a few seconds, all Maddock could do was stare. It was more than just a flag, more than just a piece of fabric. He had no idea whether he was looking at Helen's Charm... A piece of cloth recovered from the ruins of ancient Troy... No idea if that even mattered. There was an aura about the flag. A supernatural aura?

Maybe. But the sensation that now gripped him wasn't something he would ever associate with charisma.

It was the same feeling he felt in Bosnia, at the Omarska camp. A feeling of being in the presence of death. A feeling of evil.

"Holy crap."

Bones' voice, a low rumble, broke through the fog that seemed to have settled around Maddock. He shook off the sensation, turned to look at his friend. Willis was right beside him, and in their faces, Maddock saw a shared look of disgust, and of resolve.

Bones started forward. "I've got this."

An amplified voice boomed out, filling the room. "Can't let you do that, Cochise."

Bones stopped in his tracks, still a good twenty yards from the dais, and brought his Glock up, pivoting in every direction, searching for a target. Maddock did the same, turning to check their six o'clock, but aside from the four of them, the hall was empty.

Huntley's sardonic voice rang out again. "Took

your sweet time getting here. I swear, I thought I was going to have to paint a sign or something."

Maddock turned his head back and forth, trying to pinpoint Huntley's location, and realized the sound was issuing from an overhead flush-mounted speaker.

"Son of a bitch," Bones snarled. "Why don't you come out here so I can kick your ass."

Huntley's laughter surrounded them. "Come on, kids, you know that's not going to happen. I'm not alone and you're boxed in. Now, why don't you put those guns down. Then, we can have a little chat."

Maddock looked to his companions and saw the reality of the situation mirrored in their eyes. Huntley had beaten them. Worse, he had outwitted them. They had congratulated themselves on picking up Huntley's trail, when in reality, he had been luring them into a trap.

But Maddock wasn't ready to wave the white flag just yet. "Where's Lia?"

"Ha. Still think you can save the damsel in distress, Sir Lancelot? Well, you're in luck. She's right here."

"Lia?" Bones shouted, regaining a little of his defiance. "Let me hear her voice."

There was a brief silence, and then Lia's voice came from the speaker. "Bones? I'm—"

She was abruptly cut off, and then Huntley spoke again. "Satisfied? Now, put those weapons on the floor and move away from them."

Maddock exchanged a look with Bones. The big man shrugged. "Do we have a choice?"

Maddock shook his head. "If he wanted us dead, we'd be dead already. He wants something. Let's find out what."

He knelt, laid his pistol on the floor, and then deposited his back-up pistol and combat knife as well. If Huntley caught them with hold-out weapons, the consequences might be severe. Bones and the others gave up their weapons as well, and then all of them took a step back.

As the last pistol was surrendered, there was

movement at the back of the hall. A pair of figures clad in black tactical gear stepped through the doorway. Both men held suppressed H&K MP-5 machine pistols at the high ready.

As the two men cleared the doorway, two more filed in behind them. The second pair carried their weapons at the low ready to avoid flagging their comrades, but moved up quickly, coming abreast of the first pair to form a picket line advancing up the length of the hall until they were only about ten yards from Maddock and the others.

One of the men snarled, "Back up!"

Huntley's disembodied voice sounded again. "Just in case you're wondering, they don't have to wait for me to tell them to pull the trigger. Make the wrong move… Hell, make any move, and they're liable to poke you full of holes before you can make another."

Maddock didn't doubt that it was the truth. The gunmen were almost certainly CIA paramilitaries from the Special Activities Division. Unlike the amateur third-generation Nazis they'd encountered on the beach near Villa Gessell, these men were trained killers—experienced killers—recruited from elite military special ops teams.

With exaggerated slowness, he took another giant step back. As the others followed his lead, one of the paramilitaries moved forward and collected the weapons, depositing them in a black gym bag.

"That's better," said Huntley. The voice did not come from the overhead speaker, but instead from the back of the room. Behind the gunmen, Captain Midnight stepped through the doorway and entered the hall. He sauntered forward, passing the paramilitaries, and took a position to Maddock's right, staying well clear of their firing line. "Now we can talk like old friends."

"Screw that," Bones retorted. "Where's Lia?"

Huntley strode forward. "Oh, she's here. I'll bring her out in a minute, but first there's someone you need to talk to." With a sweeping flourish, he directed their attention to the rear of the hall. "Meet the man who made all this possible."

TWENTY-TWO

"Holy freaking crap," Bones exclaimed. "It's the dude from that horror show!" He snapped his fingers as if trying to trigger a memory.

Willis caught on first. "Dracula?"

"No, not Dracula," Bones retorted with mock outrage. He shook his head. "How old are you? A hundred? No, there's this crazy dead dude that introduces the story. Bits of stringy hair, desiccated flesh… The Crypt Keeper! Yeah, that's it."

Willis shook his head in evident bewilderment. "Bernie Sanders? No idea, man."

Maddock didn't get Bones' reference either, and knew that his friend was only belaboring the point as a way to keep paralyzing fear at arm's length.

And maybe to piss off Huntley a little bit.

He wasn't wrong about the resemblance however. The ancient, wizened old man standing at the entrance to the hall did indeed look like a cross between an undertaker and an undead creature from a horror movie.

The man was small, maybe five feet tall, though it was hard to say for sure given the pronounced hunch in his upper torso. Patches of lanky white hair sprouted from the liver-spotted, translucent skin that seemed to have been stretched over his skull. The hands that poked out of the sleeves of his black suit coat were gnarled and bony, and yet he gave no impression of frailty and his eyes—which despite looking rheumy in their sockets—were an unnerving shade of blue.

Maddock met the old man's stare. "Gestapo Müller, I presume."

Müller started forward. His steps were cautious—understandable as he had to be at least a hundred years old—but he covered the distance with surprising swiftness. "I haven't been called that for many years," he said as he drew up next to Huntley. His voice was low, but surprisingly resonant.

"So what do they call you, then?" Bones asked. He nodded his head toward the dais. "*Der Fuhrer?*"

"Watch it, Geronimo," Huntley cautioned. "Show some respect. This man is a hero."

Müller raised a hand to silence the spook. "They don't understand yet. Go get the girl. I will explain it to them."

Huntley flashed a menacing look at Bones, but turned and headed back toward the door.

"Why did he call you a hero?" Maddock asked.

Müller tilted his head to the side and gave him an appraising look. "I've heard a great deal about you, Mr. Maddock. Some people call *you* a hero."

Bones gave a derisive snort. "When a Nazi calls you a hero, it's time to retire."

Müller ignored the outburst. "You are a warrior," he went on. "Driven by duty and honor. I admire that."

He took a step forward, almost but not quite close enough for Maddock to reach out and touch him.

One more step, you bastard, Maddock thought, *and I'll end your story.*

"Your friend calls me a Nazi," Müller went on. His German accent made his pronunciation of the last word sound contemptuous. "I never was, you know. A National Socialist. Not in my heart. They were all quite mad—Hitler, Himmler, all of them. Deluded. All that Master Race nonsense. Chasing after a fairy-tale kingdom. I never believed any of it."

Maddock shrugged. "Just following orders, right?"

Müller made an abrupt dismissive gesture. "I did what had to be done. Just as you do. I would have done anything to destroy the enemies of the Fatherland." He leaned forward. "And I *did!*"

"Which enemies were those? The Jews? The gypsies?"

Müller's thin lips tightened into a sour frown. "If you think otherwise, you are naïve. But I was referring to the Russians."

"Maybe you haven't heard," Leopov said, her voice cracking a little at first, but growing more forceful with each syllable. "But the Red Army destroyed your precious Fatherland."

Müller's frown transformed into a satisfied smile, as if she had just unwittingly played into his hands. His blue eyes held hers for several seconds, then returned to Maddock. "Do you know how we won the Cold War?"

Maddock noted the conspicuous use of the pronoun *we*. "Sure. We—that is to say, the American government, goaded the Soviets into an arms race that ultimately bankrupted them. And saddled us with a five trillion-dollar national debt, but hey—that's our grandkids' problem."

Müller's head bobbed. Was he chuckling? "We beat the Russians because we had resolve." He thumped a fist against his chest with surprising force. "We did what had to be done, damn the consequences."

"You keep saying 'we,'" Bones said. "Like you had something to do with it, sitting down here in your mom's basement for the last fifty years."

"I had everything to do with it," Müller hissed.

Before he could elaborate, Huntley returned, dragging along a young woman that Maddock had never met, and only seen briefly, on a roadside in Argentina.

"Lia!" Bones cried out.

Her eyes, red-rimmed from weeping or exhaustion or both, flashed with hope. "Bones!"

He looked as if he was about to run to her, but Huntley brandished a pistol—a SIG Sauer P226—pointed it at Bones, and then pressed the muzzle under Lia's jaw. "Stay put, Big Red."

Bones' nostrils flared but he did not move.

"Ah, good," Müller said. "Come. I will show you how we... How I defeated the Soviets."

He made a come-along gesture and then continued up the length of the hall. Huntley followed, pulling Lia with him. One of the paramilitaries jabbed his MP5 meaningfully in Maddock's direction, signaling them to get moving.

Müller stepped up onto the dais and faced the Blood Flag.

It looked enormous, especially when contrasted against the shrunken old Nazi. Up close, Maddock could see rust-colored splotches on the white circle—the bloodstains that had consecrated the Blutfahne and inspired its name. Harder to see, but still visible were the seams where the two pieces of red cloth had been joined to widen the flag, and another irregular stitch where a tear had been repaired.

"You know what this is," Müller said, not looking back at them.

"Eva Braun's beach towel?" Bones suggested.

Müller ignored him. "For nearly six decades, they have wondered—how did he do it? How did Hitler seduce an entire nation into joining his madness?"

"It's not such a mystery," Bones retorted. "Most people are idiots."

Müller abruptly turned toward him, but instead of looking angry, he was smiling. "Yes, that certainly helps. But even an idiot will think twice about sacrificing his life for a pipe dream But this..." He turned to the flag again. "With this... Even the strongest will can be turned. I saw him do it, time and time again. I *felt* it happen to me."

The uneasiness Maddock had experienced upon first glimpsing the flag now returned tenfold. He now understood why Müller had kept them alive.

"How?" he prompted. "How is that possible?"

If the Nazi knew about Helen's Charm, he declined to say. "Does it matter? It simply is. When I finally grasped its potential, I knew what I had to do."

"You took it from Himmler. Used it... Its power... To help you escape to Argentina. And then, when the CIA started closing in, you managed to turn a few of them to your cause."

Müller laughed again. "You *are* naïve. You think

they were pursuing me like some war criminal. Not so. They sought me out. They begged me to help them fight the Soviets... A cause that I was only too willing to join. I did not need to *turn* anyone."

Maddock shook his head in bemusement. "Then what do you need the flag for?"

"Resolve!" Müller thrust his fist into the air like a declaration of victory. "War is not a game for the timid. You can't know how many times your elected leaders lost heart, equivocated, tried to appease, retreat... Surrender. And why not? America had become a nation of spineless cowards, too weak, too afraid to bear the cost of victory. I supplied the courage they were lacking. An entire generation of cold warriors stood where you now stand, and swore undying allegiance to me... To my cause."

"Frigging Nazis," Bones snarled, and spat on the carpeted floor.

"Nazis. Nationalists. Fascists. Those are just labels. Strength. Honor. Duty. Victory. That is what matters."

"A shadow government?" Maddock countered. "That's your idea of honorable?"

Müller inclined his head as if to cede a point. "You are correct. The time has come for the secret warriors to step out of the shadows. To seize the fruits of our victory before the cowards and intellectuals piss it away again."

"Just like in Bosnia," Huntley said, breaking his long silence. "You saw it for yourself. Politicians don't have the stomach to take down guys like the Rat."

"Speaking of time," Bones said. "I'd say you're running short on it. Who's gonna take over this freakshow when you finally kick off?" He turned to Huntley. "You angling for that job, Captain Midnight?"

"Preparations have been made," Müller said, dismissively. "It is true. I may not live to see it, but I will go to my rest knowing that I have laid the foundation for victory in the war to come.

"A storm is coming. Our enemies multiply, rising

from the corpses of the defeated like the heads of the hydra. The Soviets are gone, but the oligarchs who have feasted on the bones of the old order imagine that they will rule as the Tsars once did. We must act first. Strike without hesitation or mercy.

"You keep talking about war and strength and victory." Maddock shook his head. "I get it. When you're a hammer, every problem looks like a nail. But there's more to life than just fighting and killing and…" Emotion rose into his throat. "And dying."

Müller's blue eyes seemed to focus on him like laser beams. "Not for men like us, Mr. Maddock. We *are* hammers. And you belong with us."

And there it was—the reason why Müller had lured them in.

Not to kill them, but to recruit them.

He held Maddock in his stare for a few seconds, then turned away again, stepping closer to the hanging Blood Flag. He reached out for it, grasped it with one gnarled hand. "With this, I could compel you to join me."

Could he? Maddock wondered. Everything they had learned about the history of the Blutfahne and the connection to Helen's Charm was supposition. Müller had as much as confirmed that the American intelligence officers who recruited him—or was it the other way around—had been willing converts. Hitler's charisma did not require a supernatural explanation any more than did the willingness of the masses to rally behind populists and nationalists.

But what if there really was something to it… What if the Blood Flag really could brainwash a person into becoming a Nazi?

"Then why don't you?" he retorted.

"When the choice is not made freely, willingly, the effect can be… Shall we say, unpredictable. I am living proof of that. I swore the oath of allegiance to the Fuhrer, but in my heart, my allegiance was only ever to Germany. When he took his own life… It was as if the spell was broken." He shook his head as if trying to banish an unpleasant memory. "But when the oath is sworn without reservation, the effect is... Transcendent."

"Count me out," Bones said. His irreverent tone punctuated Müller's oration like a brick through a plate glass window. "Or was this offer only for the white people in the room?"

For just a second, Müller's expression twisted in distaste, but then he smiled. "Since you've already made up your mind, what difference does it make?"

Bones looked to Willis. "Totally knew it."

Müller regarded him for a moment, then returned his attention to Maddock. "Do not misunderstand. I am not asking you to swear allegiance to the swastika, or to become a Nazi. You've already sworn an oath to defend your country against all enemies. I ask nothing more of you than to swear that oath anew."

"And if we don't?" Maddock asked.

He already knew the answer. Or thought he did.

He was wrong.

Müller gave a disappointed shrug. "Mr. Huntley. Maybe you can convince them."

Cold dread shot down Maddock's spine, numbing his extremities. Huntley hustled Lia forward, interposing himself between the four prisoners and the dais.

Bones barked, "Leave her out of this, you son of a bitch."

Huntley bared his teeth like a snarling junkyard dog. "You want to test me, Red Man? You want to see what I am capable of?"

Maddock raised his hands in a placating gesture. "Huntley... Bruce. Don't do this. We're the good guys, remember? We're supposed to protect the innocents. *She's* innocent."

Huntley affected a distressed look. "Oh, Maddock. Did you think I was going to hurt her?" He removed the SIG from her neck, gesturing with that hand as if he'd forgotten all about the weapon. "Is that what you thought? No, man. I'm not gonna hurt her."

Then, with an air of casual indifference, he extended his gun arm out, swung the pistol toward Zara Leopov, and pulled the trigger.

TWENTY-THREE

The report rang through Maddock like a bell, vibrating, pulsating... deafening... The world, or his perception of it, slowed to a crawl. Huntley stood before him, arm outstretched, gun in hand, statue still, or so it seemed. A bright brass shell casing tumbled through the air like a flipped coin. And beside him, Leopov—

Zara! No!

—tipped backward, falling, ever so slowly, like something in a dream.

Something clicked inside him. The rational part of his brain—the thinking, feeling, human part—shifted into neutral, and something else—a machine, assembled in SEAL school, tested in combat too many times to count—took over. Without conscious intent, Maddock moved.

He lashed out at Huntley, seizing the man's wrist, twisting it as he thrust the arm up, away from the remaining prisoners. In the same, smooth motion, he pivoted into Huntley, ramming an elbow into the spook's face, and in the process knocking Lia out of his grasp.

The pistol dropped from Huntley's nerveless fingers, falling in slow motion... Falling just like Zara was still falling.

Through the emptiness where she had been, he could see the four paramilitaries. They had lowered their weapons, and only now did it occur to Maddock that Müller, in ascending the dais and putting his prisoner between them and himself, had placed himself in their line of fire. Professionals that they were, they had lowered their weapons. Now, they were starting to raise them.

Maddock plucked the falling pistol out of the air,

reflex-aimed, fired. Shifted aim. Fired. Shifted. Fired.

Two paramilitaries went down like ducks in a shooting gallery. A third managed to twist out of the way, bringing his own weapon to bear. The remaining shooter stood his ground, weapon up, the barrel shifting to track Maddock's movements.

But neither man fired. Müller was still right behind Maddock, and a stray shot might kill the man they had literally sworn a blood oath to protect. Instead, as if by mutual accord, both men began sidestepping away from each other, moving toward the perimeter of the hall.

Maddock moved too, following the man he had missed with his third shot, ignoring the other. He fired again, and this time the shot struck center mass. The gunman winced and staggered back a step, but did not go down.

Body armor, Maddock thought and elevated his aim point, trying for another headshot. In the back of his mind, he was aware of the remaining shooter, now standing almost directly behind him with a clear field of fire. He let the worry slip away. He'd already taken two of the bastards out, and if he could take a third, the others—

Just Bones and Willis, now.

—might have a chance.

The gunman bared his teeth in a grimace of pain and fury, and triggered his MP5. Puffs of smoke erupted from the end of the suppressor and brass began spewing from the ejection port. Maddock felt the heat of the rounds creasing the air all around him… Felt something pluck at his right biceps, and a hard kick to the ribs.

He pulled the trigger… No, tried to, but the strength had gone out of his right arm. The SIG, suddenly too heavy to hold, slipped from his grasp… Thumped on the floor at his feet.

A look of triumph flashed in the paramilitary's eyes. He steadied himself, straightened, and took aim.

Maddock fell to his knees. The jolt sent a wave of

heat radiating out from the wound in his side. The smoking muzzle of the machine pistol followed him down until it was once again staring into his eyes.

He wondered who would be waiting to greet him when that empty black eye finally blinked. His parents? Zara?

Sorry, Bones. I did my best. It's up to you now.

As Maddock pivoted away from Huntley, firing the SIG again and again and again, Bones leapt forward and tackled Lia to the floor. His first thought was to get her down, out of the line of fire, but as he covered her with his body, he knew that wouldn't be enough.

Huntley was stumbling backward, dazed from Maddock's elbow strike, but as Bones met his gaze, the spook regained his balance, planted his feet and dropped into a *karate* cat stance. His lips curled back in a predatory grin, and then moved as he spoke. Bones' ears were still ringing from the report of the shot that had killed Leopov, but he could read lips well enough to know that Captain Midnight was calling him out.

Happy to oblige, assclown, Bones thought. But before he rose, he gave Lia's shoulder a squeeze. "If you get a chance, run for it!"

He didn't know if she heard him, and didn't dare wait to find out. Instead, he bounded up and charged Huntley.

The CIA officer was nowhere near as physically imposing as Bones, and his martial arts pose was almost sneer-worthy. The fact that he had dared to make the challenge should have set Bones' alarm bells ringing. His rage at Huntley for the brutal execution of Zara Leopov, and his general contempt for the man, blinded him to the possibility that Huntley might be his equal in unarmed combat.

It was a mistake he almost didn't live to regret.

As he closed with Huntley, he lowered his torso until it was almost parallel with the ground and brought his right arm up in a scooping motion which ought to have allowed him to pluck the smaller man off his feet for an epic takedown. He visualized folding the spook in half, upending him and then driving him into the floor with enough force to snap his spine. But as he moved in, Huntley did something completely unexpected—he turned on his back foot and leaped high in the air, whipping his front leg around in a spinning back kick aimed straight at Bones' face. He struck so fast that Bones didn't have time to block or even dodge. All he could do was duck his head. A fraction of a second later, the impact drove him to his knees.

Huntley's heel had scored only a glancing blow to the crown of Bones' head, but the momentum of the spin gave it sledge-hammer force. If Bones had not lowered his head at the last instant, the kick would have all but taken his head off. As it was, he found himself face down on the carpet, and all too aware of the fact that Huntley was still on his feet, somewhere behind him, and probably closing in for a killing blow. With no way of knowing from where the next attack would come, he threw himself to the left in a flat roll, turning through two and a half rotations before sitting up in the classic defensive position.

Huntley had returned to his original stance, and remained statue still, seemingly content to wait for Bones to make another move. Bones was only peripherally aware of what was happening around him. From the ongoing tumult behind him, he surmised that Maddock and Willis were still alive—one of them at least—but what about Lia? Had she managed to slip away?

He needed to end this stupid dance with Huntley while there was still time to make a difference.

"Okay," Bones growled, pushing up on hands and knees. "Let's see you try that fancy Van Damme crap again."

He was pretty sure Huntley had just gotten lucky with his high, spinning kick. It was a show-off move, the kind of thing usually reserved for Hong Kong action flicks, and dangerous to attempt in a real fight—a life-or-death fight—because it left the kicker vulnerable to counter-attack. It was the last thing Bones would have expected from a trained CIA officer, and that was what had made the attack so effective.

Fool me once, he thought, panting to keep his rage in check. If he didn't fight smart... If he let Huntley score another hit like that....

He closed with Huntley again, moving in quick but not rushing, keeping himself upright even though doing so made him a much bigger target... An impossible to miss target.

Huntley didn't take the bait, but he didn't give ground either. He just stood there, hands poised, open and flat like knife blades, a contemptuous sneer on his face, waiting... Daring Bones to commit.

Bones obliged him with a straight jab that left him wide open to a counter-attack. His intention was not so much to land a hit as to draw Huntley closer, so it came as no surprise when his punch missed completely. But before he could draw his arm back, Huntley delivered a flurry of strikes to his chest. Pain exploded through him. One of the punches had struck his solar plexus, triggering a spasm of breathlessness. Bones had anticipated getting hit, expected it even, but the sheer power behind the man's strikes left him literally stunned.

He staggered back again, gasping, but the ringing in his ears had subsided just enough for him to hear Huntley jeering, "Come on, Red Man. Is this that wild Indian fighting spirit I've heard so much about? Guess now I know how your people all ended up on the Trail of Tears."

Bones let out a howl of rage and stepped in again, arm cocked, but the attack, like the cry, was just for show. Instead of pistoning his fist at Huntley's face, he pulled the punch, and as his opponent's fists rocketed toward his exposed torso, he redirected his right hand and, with the speed of a striking rattler, caught Huntley's wrist. In the same move, he wheeled, adding the momentum of Huntley's failed attack to his spin, and yanked the spook off his feet. He held on tight, and as Huntley twisted past, he yanked back hard, as if snapping a whip. There was a loud crack and then a stuttering jerk as Huntley's shoulder joint popped out of its socket.

The spook's howl of agony was truncated as Bones reeled him back with another savage pull on the disjointed arm. As Huntley lurched toward him, Bones left fist came out to greet him. He had been aiming for the man's throat, but Huntley's stumble caused him to miss the target—he smashed Huntley's nose instead. There was another loud crack as the cartilage broke under the impact. Huntley's head rocked back, blood spraying from his mouth and nose, and then he collapsed into a writhing mass on the floor. Bones gave the man's injured arm another vicious twist. Huntley went rigid, threw his head back and let loose another shriek.

"I got your Trail of Tears right here," Bones said, and then unleashed all his suppressed fury as he drove his heel down onto Huntley's exposed neck, silencing him for good.

But through the satisfying crunch of cracking vertebrae, he heard another cry.

"Bones!" It was Lia.

He looked up, momentarily disoriented by the carnage around him, and turned toward the sound of her voice, hoping to find her at the back of the room, poised to make her escape, lingering just long enough to urge him to follow.

His heart fell when he realized the shout was coming from the opposite direction. Lia stood on the dais, almost directly in front of the Blood Flag. She wasn't alone.

The ancient, diminutive Müller was almost completely hidden behind her. All Bones could see was a sliver of pale skin and two bony hands—one of them gripping Lia's arm, the other holding a Luger P08 semi-automatic pistol, pressed up under her jaw.

"Silence!" Müller hissed, and gave Lia a shake.

Bones fought the impulse to rush the dais. "Let her go, or I swear I'll—"

"Yes!" Müller shouted back, shaking her again. "You will swear. Swear allegiance before the Blutfahne. Do it, if you care about her."

Without waiting for an answer, he took a step back, pulling Lia with him, until the low corner of the flag was draped across his shoulder. He kept the gun where it was, but let go of Lia's arm, and with his freed left hand, reached up to grip the red fabric.

"Swear it!"

Bones suddenly felt weak all over, as if all his blood had been sucked out of him. His lips parted and words began to tumble forth unbidden.

Willis Sanders had been just as shocked at the brutality of Zara Leopov's death as his teammates, and like them, he also knew to compartmentalize his emotions. In order to grieve for the dead, or for that matter avenge them, it was necessary first to survive.

When Maddock turned the tables on Huntley, disarming the spook and pegging two of the paramilitaries with textbook perfect headshots, Willis had immediately reassessed the tactical situation. Two paramilitaries, in body armor and armed with machine pistols were still more than a match for a lone SEAL with a pistol, but because their attention would be focused on the guy with the firepower, there was just a chance for an unarmed SEAL to tip the odds in Maddock's favor.

He turned and dropped into a combat roll that brought him up facing the nearest shooter—the one Maddock had been forced to ignore. The gunman had his weapon trained on Maddock, but was moving to get a clear field of fire. If he saw Willis, he gave no indication.

Willis knew his only chance at making it through the next few seconds lay in throwing caution to the wind and going fully on the offensive. He rose up into a four-point stance, and launched himself at the paramilitary operator.

In mid-leap, he saw the man's gaze swing toward him, along with the extended-barrel of the suppressed MP5. Willis was already too close for the man to get off a shot, but that wasn't what the man had in mind. Instead of pulling the trigger, he swiped the weapon at Willis' head like a cudgel.

A flash of blue filled Willis' vision, but the blow came too late to deflect his rush. He crashed into the gunman, bowled him over. The pain arrived an instant later, radiating across his skull like cracks in a windshield, but Willis fought through it, wrapping his arms around the man, immobilizing him until he could figure out what to do next.

The paramilitary fought back, frantic at first, but as the struggle intensified, his counter-attack became more deliberate. Unable to break Willis' hold completely, he nonetheless managed to wriggle his right arm loose, and commenced striking at Willis' head, targeting the raw flesh where the MP5's upper receiver had earlier made contact. Willis endured the punishment and squeezed harder. His powerful arms compressed the man's chest, and while this did not completely suffocate him, it prevented him from drawing deep breaths to replenish the oxygen his struggle was burning through. The ferocity and accuracy of his punches diminished, and then stopped altogether.

For a fleeting moment, Willis dared to hope that he had won, that the gunman had succumbed to asphyxia, but then he felt something brush against his arm. The man was reaching past him, reaching for something at his waist.

Willis craned his head around and glanced down the length of the other man's arm just as the latter drew a long fixed-blade knife from a belt sheath. The dull black powder-coat finish, clip-point and long fuller groove marked it as a KA-BAR. He raised the knife, angling the blade down at Willis' back and brought it down.

"Ah, hell no," Willis rasped as he tried to twist out of the way without completely releasing his hold on the man. He didn't see exactly where the blade ended up, and didn't feel any kind of pain shooting through his body. Had the man stabbed himself?

If he had, then the wound had either been too shallow to cause injury, or more likely had been stopped by the man's Kevlar body armor. Either way, he was drawing back for another stab.

Willis was not about to let that happen, and he sure as hell wasn't going to let go of the guy. Instead, he hurled himself to the side, rolling onto his back to shield it from further assault. As he moved, he felt a faint burning sensation in his side, and knew he'd been cut.

The paramilitary was now on top of him, but Willis didn't give him a chance to seize on this apparent advantage. He rolled again, halfway over this time, trapping the knife and the hand that held it under both of their bodies. The reversal seemed to confuse the other man, which was all the time Willis needed to adjust his hold. He moved his hands to grip the man's shoulders and then pulled him down, simultaneously thrusting his head up, ramming it forehead first into the man's chin.

The impact sent a fresh wave of blinding pain through him, but as he felt the other man go limp in his arms, he decided it had been worth it.

He rolled off the unconscious man, pinning the wrist of his knife hand with one knee as he plucked the weapon from the man's limp fingers. He saw now that the front of the man's tactical vest was smeared with blood.

My blood, Willis thought. *Bastard cut me.*

He thought about returning the favor, but then remembered that his small victory had not necessarily won the battle. He looked up just in time to see Maddock go down.

"No!"

Maddock was on his knees, a red stain creeping out from under his right arm. Over his shoulder, the remaining paramilitary was leveling his MP5 at Maddock's head.

Willis looked around frantically for the gun his fallen opponent had held, spotted it and started to reach for it, but knew he'd never be able to pick it up, aim, and fire in time to save Maddock's life.

Then he realized he had an alternative in the palm of his hand.

With a slight adjustment of his grip, he drew back and hurled the KA-BAR across the room. He used a non-rotational throw, so that the blade flew straight through the air like a dart and buried itself to the hilt in the gunman's eye.

As the paramilitary went down, his weapon unfired, Maddock's head came up. He threw a glance over his shoulder, saw Willis, and nodded in gratitude, and then wobbled a little as if he was about to pass out.

"Hang on, brother," Willis muttered, and tried to rise. He wasn't in much better shape than Maddock. His head was throbbing, both from the clubbing he'd taken and the head butt that had ended the battle, but as he hadn't lost consciousness, he figured those were survivable injuries. The knife wound in his side might be another matter. The sharp blade of the KA-BAR had definitely sliced him, piercing his lower left flank, right above the hip bone. He didn't think it had hit anything vital, but blood was seeping from the wound. He needed to get a bandage on it, maybe even some stitches to hold everything together. Hopefully, Bones was still—

"Bones!"

Willis turned toward the sound of the scream—Lia's scream. He spotted Bones first, a hulking figure stalking toward the dais, and then he saw Lia. Behind her, mostly hidden from view, was Müller, and behind them both, hanging down like a curtain poised to fall at the end of a scene, was the Blood Flag.

Some trick of acoustics enabled him to hear every word spoken by the old Nazi.

"Swear allegiance before the Blutfahne. Do it, if you care about her."

Willis felt a chill shoot through him as Müller gripped the flag. It wasn't just a feeling of dread…The flag was like a black hole, sucking in the life force of everyone in the room… Everyone but Müller.

"Swear it!"

Bones swayed and looked as if he was about to pass out. Then he spoke, as if in a daze. "I… Swear…"

"Son of a bitch," Willis shouted. "Bones! Fight it."

The cry didn't exactly break the spell, but it did get Müller's attention. He turned his gaze toward Willis, and repeated his command. "Swear allegiance!"

Willis felt the life go out of him, along with all volition. He suddenly had no desire to oppose the wizened old man, who wasn't really a Nazi after all, but a patriot… A hero who had led a decades-long secret war against America's real enemies—the godless Communists of the Soviet Union. And even though that battle was won, there were other enemies waiting to fill the vacuum, ready to sweep across the world like a storm.

The only way to fight fire was with fire.

The only way to stop the storm was to become the storm.

It was all so clear to him.

He opened his mouth and—

A sharp report startled him out of the trance. Müller's head snapped back. The Blood Flag seemed to swirl around him like a living thing—the tentacles of an octopus trying to snatch the old man up into a waiting maw. Lia gave a little shriek and squirmed out of his grip. Bones steadied, shook his head as if waking from a dream, and then ran to her.

Through the lifting fog, Willis saw Maddock, still on his knees, but with his left arm raised and stretched out toward the dais. Huntley's SIG was in his left hand, smoke curling from the barrel.

"Nice shooting," Willis remarked. "And with your left hand."

Maddock managed a wan smile. "My right isn't working so good at the moment."

He had taken a big chance firing with his non-dominant hand. If he'd been off by even a degree, his round might have taken Lia instead, but given the alternative, the greater risk would have been doing nothing.

He set the gun aside and probed his injuries with the fingers of his left hand. One bullet had punched clear through his right biceps. The flesh around the wounds had swollen almost double in size. Another round had grazed his ribs, carving a groove about as wide across as his pinkie finger and twice as long. Both wounds hurt like hell, but he didn't think either would be life threatening.

"How bad?" Willis asked.

"I'll live." As he said it, he glimpsed Leopov from the corner of his eye. She lay supine, as if merely asleep, but her eyes were open. A thin trail of blood ran from the dark hole above the bridge of her nose, and down across her cheek like a tear.

He tore his gaze away, looked at Willis again. "You?"

"I could use a Band-Aid."

"Yeah. Me, too. Bones…" He looked up to the dais where Bones was holding Lia in his arms. The big man looked as exhausted as Maddock felt, but he gave a nod of acknowledgement. "If you're done up there," Maddock went on, "we could use a hand getting patched up."

Bones glanced back at the Blutfahne. "What about that thing?"

Maddock's answer was immediate and unequivocal. "Burn it"

"I'm afraid I can't let you do that."

The smooth, almost seductive baritone, which

came from the rear of the hall was familiar, but it was the accent that was most recognizable.

The Russian accent.

TWENTY-FOUR

"Telesh." Maddock wheeled around, groping for the SIG with his left hand, but before he could grasp it, the voice called out again.

"That is very bad idea, Mr. Maddock. I am not alone. I would prefer not to stain Helen's Charm with any more blood, but I will if I must."

Maddock left the pistol where it was.

"Very good," Telesh said. "Stay right where you are. I am coming out now."

It was not Sergei Yukovitch Telesh that stepped through the doorway however, but another familiar figure—a hulking figure with dull eyes and an ugly bruise that darkened his face like a mask. Tweedledum.

Tweedledee was right behind him, but they were only the vanguard. Six more men, along with one woman—the alluring Nadia—strode in behind the pair, every single one of them armed with a pistol. Maddock recognized a couple of the men from the group that had chased him and Leopov—

Zara! I'm sorry!

—through Moscow. The others were strangers to him. They spread out across the breadth of the hall, forming a picket line even more impenetrable than Müller's paramilitaries. Only then did Telesh appear, with one more man following behind him like a loyal pet.

"Petrov," Maddock said.

"Oleg?" Lia cried out in dismay. "How can you be here? I thought you were..." She trailed off as realization dawned. "You are working with this gangster? How could you?"

"I think Nadia there might have had something to do with it," Maddock muttered.

Petrov ducked his head in evident embarrassment,

all but confirming Maddock's supposition.

Bones shrugged. "Well, she's smoking hot. Can you blame him?"

"Nadia certainly provided an enticement," Telesh said, stepping forward. "But Oleg Ivanovitch was only trying to save his own skin. I almost had him killed after he tried to warn you, Lia. I am glad now that I spared him. I could not have found this place without his help."

Maddock shook his head, bewildered. "He only knew we were going to Argentina."

"True, but that was enough. Agents of the *Sluzhba Vneshney Razvedki* picked up your trail as soon as you arrived, and followed you when you left."

"The Foreign Intelligence Service," Lia said, translating almost automatically. "You are working with SVR? I thought you were Bratva? A criminal."

"Like there's a difference," Bones put in.

Telesh laughed. "Are you making joke, or are you just hypocrite. Most powerful man in your intelligence service was escaped Nazi. Oh, yes. I heard everything." He shrugged. "I am pleased he's dead. You deserve medal for killing him."

Bones wagged his head. "When a Russian gangster calls you a hero..."

Telesh's eyes narrowed into cruel slits. "There is that word again. Gangster. Why don't you ask Mr. Maddock what happened the last time someone called me 'gangster'?" He flicked a meaningful look at Lia. "Gangster is word weak men use to insult powerful men. But I do not think very many people will call me gangster now." He looked past them to the flag hanging over the dais, and started toward it. "They will worship me."

As if anticipating some act of desperate defiance, Nadia took a step toward Maddock and the others, brandishing her pistol. "Don't move. One move and you die. All of you."

Maddock clenched his fists—or tried to. His right managed only a pathetic curl. "You're just going to kill us anyway."

"Might as well go out in a blaze of glory," Bones said in a low voice.

Willis seconded the suggestion. "I'm down."

"He doesn't want to kill you," Petrov squeaked. "All he wants is Helen's Charm. Let him have it, and he'll let us go."

"Us?" Maddock retorted. "You're not part of us anymore, Petrov."

Telesh stopped, glanced back. "You don't want him?" He shrugged. "Well I don't need him anymore. Nadia."

Nadia immediately turned her gun on Petrov.

"Wait!" Maddock shouted. As pissed off at Petrov as he was, he couldn't bear to see anyone else gunned down in cold blood. Nadia shot a glance at Telesh. When the gangster merely shrugged again, she lowered her weapon and then gestured for Petrov to join Maddock and the others.

When he reached them, Petrov seemed to be on the verge of tears. "Forgive me, Lia. I had no choice. He said that if I helped him, he would let all of you live."

Bones rolled his eyes. "And if you shove essential oils up your butt, you can cure cancer."

"Man, is this really the time?" Willis mumbled.

"There's never a bad time for calling out stupidity."

Willis flashed a puzzled frown. "Do you stick the whole bottle up there?"

"Petrov is right," Telesh said loudly, resuming his trek up to the dais. "I could have you all killed, but that would be very..." He stopped abruptly, his eyes coming to rest on Leopov's unmoving form. He frowned and then stepped around her. "Very messy. One of you might survive long enough to do something desperate. What did the big Red Indian say? 'Blaze of glory,' *da*? Maybe hurt me or one of my associates. Maybe damage Helen's Charm. I don't want that. All I want is the flag."

Maddock and the others watched, impotently, as Telesh stepped up onto the dais and moved to the rear wall where he reached up and removed the flag's staff from its wall mount. The Blutfahne must have been heavier than it looked because it dipped suddenly, the wooden pole twisting out of Telesh's grip, and fell to the floor, completely covering Müller's corpse. Maddock wondered why he hadn't just asked one of the Tweedles to get it for him, but then realized that the Russian probably didn't trust anyone else with the power of Helen's Charm.

Telesh gave a disapproving grunt, but promptly knelt and began patiently sliding the flag's sewn sleeve down the length of the staff. With this task completed, he haphazardly folded the flag, then tucked it under his arm and started back down the hall. When he reached Nadia's side, he turned and faced Maddock again.

"I know what you are thinking," he said. "Now that I have Helen's Charm, I will kill you anyway."

"The thought crossed my mind," Maddock admitted, though in truth, knowing what the Blutfahne could do—what it could make others do—a quick death was not the worst possible outcome. "I know how you feel about tying up those loose ends."

Telesh smiled. "You are worth far more to me alive. Do you want to know why? I want you to tell what happened here. All of it."

"Seriously?" Bones asked, without a trace of sarcasm. "Have you got a death wish or something?"

Telesh laughed. "What do I have to fear? I did not shelter a war criminal for nearly six decades."

Now Maddock understood. "That's what you really want. For us to tell the world about Müller and his shadow army, and how the CIA colluded with former Nazis."

"And why not? It's all true. You call me gangster. America is gangster nation. And when the world finally learns truth about it, it will be end of American hegemony. The NATO alliance will fall apart, and when it does, I will lead a glorious new Russian empire into the Twenty-first Century. With this." He thrust the bundled flag at them.

"What makes you think we'll talk? Or that anyone will listen to us?"

"I know you will try. You are a white knight."

Maddock recalled Jimmy's comment about sunlight being the best disinfectant. While he agreed in principle, the thought of being responsible for exposing a scandal that might completely upset the global balance of power gave him pause. But that was tomorrow's problem. The only thing that mattered right now was destroying the Blutfahne, or at the very least, keeping Telesh from taking it out of the country.

Okay, so he doesn't want to kill us, he thought. *I can work with that.*

There were four perfectly good MP5s scattered about the room, and one of the dead paramilitaries had the bag with their personal weapons in it.

Telesh must have read his mind. "One thing. Since I can't very well have you following me, I had my men wire the house upstairs with explosives. Semtex. Wired into the house's alarm system." Almost as an afterthought, he added, "SVR is very good at getting alarm codes. If you try to follow, house will blow up." He made a little explosion with his fingers.

Maddock glanced over at Petrov.

The historian, correctly interpreting the unasked question, nodded. "I saw them wiring blocks of plastique all over house."

"Someone will come save you eventually," Telesh said. "By then, we will be far, far away from here."

And then, as if that was the final word on the subject, the gangster turned and headed for the exit. The rest of the Russians backed away, keeping their weapons leveled at the group as they, one by one, slipped through the doors. Nadia was the last to leave, and before she went, offered a final warning.

"You will stay put if you know what's good for you."

"What's your hurry, babe?" Bones said. "Why don't you hang around a bit, get to know me. I know Maddock can be kind of a stiff, but I dig Russian chicks."

She gave him a disgusted look and muttered something under her breath—it wasn't *do svidanya*—and then she too was gone.

Maddock turned to the others. "You think he really plans to let us walk out of here?"

Bones shook his head. "I wouldn't bet on it."

"I don't understand," Petrov said, looking puzzled. "You heard what he said. He wants you to tell the world about all this."

"I'm sure he does," Maddock said. "But he also knows that we're going to do everything we can to stop him, first. And we are."

"But the bombs—"

"Are probably going to detonate as soon as they get clear of the house. Even if we aren't killed in the blast, it will take days to sift through the rubble, giving Telesh all the time he needs to get out of the country. We need to find another way out of here."

"The tram?" Bones suggested.

"That's what I'm thinking," Maddock replied. "Go see if you can get it running. If not, we'll have to walk."

"You realize it probably comes out in some deep dark basement at the CIA," Bones went on. "They aren't exactly going to be pleased to see us. Especially when they find out what happened here."

"I'm hoping that not everyone in the CIA is a secret Nazi. Either way, I suspect they'll want to know about Telesh."

"Fair enough," Bones said, and started for the exit. The others followed, but Maddock turned and headed back to Leopov.

He knelt beside her and gently pulled her eyelids down. He considered trying to brush away the blood, but knew it would probably only make it look even worse. But for that and the hole between her eyes, he thought it might be possible to believe she was merely asleep.

Swallowing down the lump of emotion in his throat, he whispered, "I'm sorry."

And he was. Not just for getting her killed, but for all the times he had doubted her, questioned her loyalty... Refused what she had willingly offered.

That was the worst thing about losing someone. Not just that they were gone, but all the things forever left unsaid.

He slid his left arm under her legs, and tried to reach under her shoulders with his right, but his injured arm could not bear her weight.

"Damn it," he whispered, angrily.

He felt a hand on his shoulder. Bones.

"Let me." The big man's voice was uncharacteristically soft.

Maddock swallowed again, nodded, and moved aside to let Bones bear her in his arms.

The tram was electrically powered and proved simple enough to operate. It had just two settings—forward and reverse—and a maximum acceleration that felt about like a jogging pace. The two-way train had bright headlights to illuminate the journey through the tunnel, which was round and smooth, like the inside of a giant concrete pipe, save for the bed of gravel upon which the tracks rested. A third rail situated between the other two was intermittently marked with yellow signs displaying red lightning bolts and the words: "Danger—High Voltage." If Maddock's mental map was accurate, the CIA complex was less than half a mile away—a distance they could cover in about three or four minutes.

Ninety seconds into the journey, the lights went out and all motion abruptly ceased.

Maddock instantly knew what this signified. "Everybody down!"

A moment later, a hot wind blew up the tunnel from behind them, followed immediately by a deafening concussion and a vibration like a magnitude seven earthquake. It felt to Maddock like the detonation had completely destroyed the house and dropped the rubble entirely into the hidden sublevel.

There was no rolling wall of fire like in movies, but the tunnel conducted the resulting overpressure wave like the barrel of a cannon, and when it hit them, it was like being shot out of one. The little tram was bucked off its rails, and caromed back and forth along the tunnel walls until the force of the wave passed. By some miracle, the cars remained upright, though in the darkness, it was hard to tell which way was up. The scorching heat lasted only a moment, but the wind continued for several seconds thereafter, bearing with it a noxious dust cloud. Maddock covered his mouth and nose with a sleeve and took shallow breaths until the worst of it was past.

"Everyone okay?"

A chorus of voices answered back, and then a light flashed on—Bones' penlight—revealing air that was thick with dust. The beam swept back and forth, illuminating all five of the tram's passengers, confirming that no major injuries had been sustained. Petrov wore a chagrinned expression.

"You were right," he said, his voice a hoarse whisper.

"We usually are," Bones agreed.

"If we had stayed there…"

"Yup."

They left the useless tram behind and continued up the tunnel, Bones still bearing Leopov in his arms. After about five minutes of walking they reached an open area that was a mirror image of the loading area they had left behind. Beyond the arched entrance was a long, narrow rectangular room with a pair of silver doors—presumably leading to an elevator—in the wall opposite the arch, and another regular wooden door on the side wall to the left, a good hundred feet or so distant. The elevator doors looked as if someone had tried to kick them in—blast damage. Bypassing them, Maddock went to the wooden door and tried the lever handle. It opened, revealing a cramped, and to all appearances, seldom used skeletal metal stairway that ascended two flights to a landing. One more flight continued up from there, but the steps rose up to ceiling level and stopped. There was a sturdy looking metal box with a hand crank protruding from it, mounted to the wall to the right of this final staircase.

Maddock tried rolling the crank. It turned counter-clockwise with little effort, so he kept going in that direction several more turns. He could hear a rattling sound behind the wall, like a bicycle chain turning on a sprocket. After about ten rotations, he glimpsed movement above, and looked up to see that the ceiling had risen a few inches, swinging away on concealed hinges. Faint light was visible through the widening crack.

"I think we found our way out," he announced to the others, and then redoubled his efforts.

It took a couple minutes, but the trap door finally rose up high enough for them to continue up the stairs. As he ascended, Maddock noted that the barrier consisted of a six-inch thickness of concrete bordered by a metal frame, but it was only when he got above it that he realized that the whole affair was actually a section of sidewalk.

They emerged into a well-lit courtyard, that looked to be a little smaller than a football field, surrounded on all sides by modern-looking structures of glass and concrete. The area was dominated by a large half-circle of lawn. The rest of the courtyard, including the spot where the trap door had opened, was paved with concrete. Café tables were placed along the sidewalk and trees sprouted through here and there.

At the far corner of the concrete arc, about a hundred and fifty feet away and lit up with spotlights was a curious structure. It was a curved, green-tinted screen, about eight feet high, perforated with irregular shapes that weren't quite discernible at a distance, but which Maddock knew were letters—eight hundred and sixty-five letters, along with four question marks.

It was the Kryptos sculpture, created by artist Jim Sanborn with the help of a since-retired CIA cryptographer, and it contained a four-part encrypted message that, in the nearly ten years since its dedication, had not been completely solved, despite the best efforts of code-breakers both in the government and the civilian world. Maddock, who was a fan of puzzles and unsolved mysteries, had read about the sculpture and its seemingly uncrackable code, but had never seen it up close, mostly because, as it was situated smack in the middle of the George Bush Center for Intelligence, it was off-limits to the public.

"Well, that answers that," he murmured. "Definitely CIA headquarters."

Spotlights suddenly flashed on all around the perimeter of the courtyard, transfixing them in blinding light, to the accompaniment of shouted commands to "Freeze!" and "Put your hands up."

Bones shook his head. "Like there was ever any doubt."

TWENTY-FIVE

Over the Black Sea—Thirty-six hours later

Maddock flexed the fingers of his gloved right hand, closing them into a fist, opening them, closing them. His grip-strength felt about right, and there was only a twinge of accompanying pain in his biceps.

"How's it feel?" Bones asked from the seat across the aisle. His voice was weirdly distorted by the oxygen mask that completely covered his face. Maddock was wearing one too, pre-breathing in preparation for the high-altitude parachute jump they would be making in a few minutes.

"Almost like I didn't get shot," Maddock replied. "Steroids are awesome."

"Yeah, until you grow boobs."

Maddock had been assured that such side-effects were associated with prolonged use of anabolic steroids, not corticosteroids—which was what he had been given—but he didn't see any point in explaining this to Bones. "Small price to pay, if it means finishing this."

He didn't need to explain what he meant by that. Bones knew. Willis knew. It wasn't something he dared say aloud, even here, thirty-five thousand feet up.

After their initial detainment by CIA security forces, Maddock had succeeded in convincing his interrogator not only of his identity—easily enough verified—but also that they had been working with Bruce Huntley on a special clandestine assignment. The tale he spun had just enough basis in fact to ring true. They had been assisting Huntley with the defection of two Russian nationals— Petrov and Lia—who had been involved in a hunt for Nazi loot and had subsequently been targeted by the Russian mob after making an important discovery. Huntley had put them all up at the safe house, but the Russians had found them, killing Huntley and Leopov, along with the paramilitaries who had been providing security. Maddock and the others had escaped through the tunnel. He conveniently omitted any mention of Gestapo Müller and the Blutfahne.

It was a risky play. If Huntley's immediate superior in the Directorate of Operations was part of Müller's conspiracy, then the lie would be immediately exposed. But Maddock didn't think Huntley's activities had been carried out with official sanction. Everything he had done, from intercepting Lia's escape in Finland, to teaming up with the next-gen Nazis in Argentina, had a seat-of-the-pants feel. Rogue ops, off the books and completely deniable.

Either the operations officer in charge believed him, or chose to accept the fiction as a better alternative than digging deeper. Curiously, no one had asked for further explanation about the tunnel they had emerged from.

Once the matter of their operational status had been sorted out, Maddock had been allowed to contact Maxie. He was pleased to learn that the SEAL commander was out of the hospital, and even happier to hear that Alex Vaccaro had regained consciousness. Maxie had arranged for them all to be transferred to the Bethesda Naval Hospital, ostensibly for treatment of their injuries, but mostly to get them out of the CIA's clutches.

Telesh was of course long gone. His private jet had left from Dulles a mere ninety minutes after the destruction of the Cape Cod on Savile Lane. Maxie was in favor of asking the higher ups to scramble interceptor jets to shoot the plane down, but Maddock had talked him out of it.

"It won't happen. Even if you could convince SECNAV to authorize action against a civilian plane that poses no immediate threat, someone will get in the way. They'll call the jets off, or order them to force Telesh to land so they can take him alive."

He hadn't mentioned the Blutfahne to Maxie either, not because he didn't trust his commander, but rather to give him deniability. If Maxie knew Maddock's true intention, he would be obligated to sideline him.

The plane's flight plan showed its final destination as Gelendzhik—Telesh was returning to his dacha, though how long he intended to stay was anyone's guess.

"You've got to send us in," he had insisted. "I've been there. I've seen the place."

This was also a slight distortion of the truth—he had only seen the garage and the exterior of the main house—but it was imperative that he be the one to lead the assault.

"We can be in and out before anyone knows what happened," he went on. "But we will have to move fast."

Maxie had agreed to run the idea up the flagpole. Maddock wasn't at all surprised when word came down from on high that the operation was a go. Somebody higher up, maybe someone who had been one of Müller's sworn followers, knew what Telesh had taken and wanted it back.

It wasn't possible or even practical to keep the Agency out of the loop. They would, in essence, be invading Russia. At best, this was an illegal action, but if they were discovered, even after the fact, it was conceivably an act of war.

The mission was simply to "neutralize the threat posed by the Russian mobster Sergei Yukovitch Telesh." Their new CIA handler had not explicitly mentioned the Blutfahne, but had only stated that a secondary objective of the mission was to "secure and recover any items of strategic and/or historic value in the possession of the primary target." Maddock had simply nodded as if in full agreement. If the man even suspected Maddock's true intent, he and Bones and Willis would have been sidelined.

Late the following afternoon, Maddock and the rest of his platoon—everyone but Professor who despite reporting himself as fully mission capable would not be able to catch up to them in time—were on a plane headed for Incirlik Air Base on the southern coast of Turkey. Because they were traveling east, it was late afternoon the next day when they deplaned. After a short hop to Istanbul, they boarded a McDonnell Douglas DC-10. The jumbo jet was part of the fleet belonging to a major air freight service, and would be making its nightly run to Moscow, but with a slight, insignificant deviation in its flight path that would take it within about forty miles of the Black Sea coast.

As the plane neared the dropzone, the flight crew donned their oxygen masks and depressurized the cabin. Maddock and the other SEALs switched from the plane's O2 supply to their rebreather units, gathered up their gear, and headed to the rear of the plane. At a signal from the pilot that neutral pressure had been achieved, the jumpmaster lowered the ramp. Maddock felt the slipstream tugging at him, pulling him toward oblivion. The air was frigid, causing beads of condensation to appear on the inside of his mask, but the cold didn't reach through the thermal coveralls he wore over his neoprene wetsuit.

"Come on," he muttered. "Let's get this over with."

He didn't necessarily hate "jumping out of a perfectly good airplane." What he hated was surrendering himself completely to the unpredictable. Mr. Murphy—he of Murphy's Law fame—had a bad habit of stowing away in the parachute bag, and even though there was a lot Maddock could do to ensure that he made it down in one piece, there was a lot more that was simply out of his control. Dane Maddock hated not being in control.

The jumpmaster gave the signal. Maddock quickly

made his way down the ramp and leaped out into nothingness.

Because he was traveling at the same speed as the aircraft, the transition was smooth, with only a little buffeting from the vortices of the slipstream. He could feel his forward motion slowing as the thin air piled up in front of him while gravity drew him inexorably down. He counted to five and then pulled the ripcord handle.

He felt a twinge of pain in his ribs as the chute yanked him out of freefall. He hoped the surgical grade adhesive the doctors had used to glue the bullet wound shut had not just failed. The sensation passed quickly and he put it out of his mind. His chute had deployed correctly, that was the important thing.

He located the GPS receiver clipped to his harness and checked his position relative to the objective. Telesh's villa was fifty-six kilometers—thirty-five miles—away on a compass heading of forty-two degrees. As the first man out, it was his job to navigate in the direction of the target. The Cyalume sticks clipped to his back and helmet would show the others the way.

Their ram-air canopies could achieve a five-to-one glide ratio—more like a hang glider than a parachute—which meant that they traveled five horizontal feet for every one foot of vertical descent. Since he was roughly six and a half miles above the surface of the Black Sea, he would, if Mr. Murphy didn't put in an appearance, be able to travel about thirty-two miles closer to the objective before splashing down. Close, but still three miles short of the objective. Fortunately, the part of that distance—the final leg—would be on land, so the SEALs would only have to swim a couple miles.

As the noise of the jet receded into the distance, he craned his head around to check the status of his teammates. They were all but invisible in the darkness, but each man had a red Cyalume glowstick clipped to his tactical vest. He counted the lights and breathed his second sigh of relief—fourteen pinpoints of light trailed behind him at staggered intervals, reaching up like a stairway to heaven.

No chute failures. So far, so good.

He spent the next half hour watching his altimeter and GPS, and making gentle corrections to the chute to stay on course. Once below the cloud layer, he turned off his rebreather and pushed the mask up, enjoying a breath of fresh if still chilly air. He could discern the irregular outline of the horizon ahead. To the left and right, he could distinguish city lights but between those isolated islands of humanity, there were broad swaths of darkness. As he drew closer however, and dropped below a thousand feet above sea level, he could distinguish a small pinpoint of light almost directly ahead—Telesh's dacha.

The water came up fast. Maddock replaced his mask and switched on his rebreather, then flared his chute, slowing his descent just enough to soften the impact with the water. The next instant, he was completely immersed and sinking fast, borne down by the weight of his gear. He didn't panic, but instead calmly turned the valve on his rebreather unit to fill his buoyancy compensator. This slowed his downward plunge long enough for him to cut loose from his chute, which in turn allowed him to swim free and begin kicking for the surface.

One by one, the rest of the platoon settled into the water. Maddock took a head count to confirm that everyone had made it down safely. He was pleased to find that they had. Once all the chutes were secured in stuff sacks, they donned swim fins and began the long swim to shore.

Despite his earlier visit, Maddock had not seen Telesh's property from a distance, but he had reviewed satellite images and knew what to expect. The dacha was situated atop a forested promontory known as Cape Idokopas, which rose some two hundred feet above the sea.

They came ashore on a sandy beach, about a hundred feet from the base of the cape where they cached their swim gear.

Bones rigged the equipment with an incendiary grenade attached to a trip wire—if anyone got too close to the concealed stash—or if, God forbid, they didn't make it back—the grenade would ignite and burn white hot, turning everything into unrecognizable slag. With their load now significantly lightened, they donned night vision goggles and began the final push to the objective. They carried suppressed AK74 rifles with Czech manufactured 5.45-millimeter rounds. When Russian authorities showed up to investigate the site, they would find no evidence to directly implicate the United States. They would no doubt suspect that an American special warfare unit had carried out the raid, but they would never admit it. Publicly, they would blame Chechen separatists, who would be only too eager to take credit.

Once their mission objectives were accomplished, they would return here, suit up, and get back in the water, swimming out to rendezvous with a waiting SEAL delivery vehicle—a multi-passenger diver propulsion unit—that had been deployed from a Turkish Coast Guard vessel earlier in the day and prepositioned several miles off shore.

They moved stealthily into the woods. The incline was steep, but not enough to require climbing equipment, and despite the fact that they were moving at a snail's pace, it took less than fifteen minutes for them to reach the edge of the clearing where the buildings were situated. In the green-tinted monochrome display of the goggles, the lights of the two-story house blazed through the trees like a sunrise.

Rather than rush the house, they dispersed along the tree line until they had eyes on every side. Aside from the exterior lights, most of the house was dark. There was a faint glow coming from one window in the front, and a brighter light shining from a kitchen window on the north side. No one appeared to be moving in the house, but there were four guards, armed with Kalashnikov rifles, occupying stationary posts on the front and back porches. They were all seated. Two of them were smoking, and all had the bored expressions of men who expected their duty shift to be completely uneventful. The SEALs observed the house for several minutes, but nothing changed.

On Maddock's command, "Execute!"—whispered into the throat mic connected to his squad radio, four simultaneous shots from suppressed rifles took out the guards.

He winced a little at the muffled reports, not because they were loud enough to be heard from inside the house, but because they accompanied the deaths of four more men. He did not feel any regret at sending them on their way—they were, unquestionably, sworn enemies of everything he held dear.

No, it was the futility of it all.

What the hell am I even doing here?

When he had first dared to test himself and try out for the SEALs, he had known that it would mean plunging into a world of remorseless violence. Unlike his father and most of the naval officers he had grown up around—men who commanded warships and trained for war at a distance—SEAL missions were almost always conducted at very close range. And while the rest of the military largely spent their time preparing for conflicts that only seldom materialized, the SEALs and other special warfare operators stayed busy.

For more than a decade, he had consoled himself with the belief that he was doing a greater good. He had killed—that was his job, after all, his duty—and taken comfort in the fact that every single target deserved that fate. But because nature abhorred a vacuum, the war against evildoers could never be won.

One of his civilian combatives instructors—a crusty former SEAL who had lost an eye in the line of duty and seemed always to be weeping from around his ocular prosthetic implant—had given the class a pep talk one day, praising them all for their dedication and sacrifice, and then, oblivious to the storm gathering in the sky above their outdoor fighting pit, had launched into a soliloquy about how defending the free world was like playing Whack-a-Mole at the arcade. You couldn't ever really win, but when the mole popped his head up, someone had to be ready to whack him.

His own words to Müller haunted him. *When you're a hammer, every problem looks like a nail.* Müller had turned those words against him. *We are hammers. And you belong with us.*

What had he done? Whack, whack, whack. What difference had it made? None at all. Another mole had popped up right away, and here he was, hammer at the ready.

After his parents' funeral, he had told Maxie that he wanted out, but he had let himself get sucked back in. *One last mission.*

Would Zara still be alive if I had said no?

He'd been cruising on autopilot since her death, since Telesh had taken the Blood Flag. He had effortlessly slipped back into the comfortable groove of death-dealing.

Here was a nail to pound... A mole to whack. And really, what other solution was there? Telesh had to be stopped. The Blutfahne had to be destroyed.

And after that?

No, he told himself. *No more Whack-a-mole. No more hammer time. I'm done.*

After this.

One more last *mission.*

Once the triggers were pulled, there was no turning back. The assault had begun.

Half the platoon, divided into two elements led by Bones and Willis respectively, moved up to secure the bodies while the rest provided overwatch. Maddock watched the front door through the scope of his rifle, ready to pull the trigger if someone stepped out to investigate the disturbances, but no one did.

When the forward elements were in place,

Maddock gave the signal for half of the remaining force to move up to the house, and advanced with them. Willis stationed his element on the front porch. At the 'go' signal, they would breach and enter the house. Bones' group meanwhile had climbed up onto the roof over the porch—they would go in through one of the upstairs windows. A third element would go in through the kitchen window, while the remaining SEALs covered the rear door from the woods.

Maddock joined the four-man stack at the front door and waited for Bones to get in position. He didn't have to wait long.

Bones voice sounded in his earpiece. "Bravo is set."

Maddock keyed his mic. "Roger. We go in five... Four... Three...."

He tensed, a coiled snake ready to strike.

"One... Go! Go! Go!"

There was a loud crack as the platoon's breacher kicked in the front door, and in the same instant, the almost musical sound of glass shattering. Maddock felt the man ahead of him shift forward, and followed close behind.

They did not charge so much as flow into the house. They had rehearsed this assault countless times in live fire training exercises. Each man knew exactly what to do, and when. As Maddock was about to go through the door, he heard two dulled reports in quick succession. One of the men had identified and neutralized a target with a controlled pair of shots from his rifle. Several more silenced shots followed, and then came the almost deafening roar of an unsuppressed rifle letting off a fully automatic burst. Another burst followed a moment later.

Maddock swung left and right, searching for any targets, but saw only his own men. The first floor had already been cleared. The shooting was coming from the second floor.

"Alpha!" he shouted. "With me. Upstairs."

He wheeled in the direction of the two-level U-shaped staircase, located at the rear of the spacious front room and approached it with his rifle at the high-ready. Willis caught up to him, and as they began ascending, turned so they were almost back to back. Backing up the steps carefully, he kept his weapon aimed high to cover the open landing above.

Maddock keyed his mic. "Bones, we're coming to you. What's the situation?"

He heard someone break squelch to initiate transmission, but before a single word could be spoken, another strident burst of automatic rifle fire intruded. When it fell silent a moment later, the radio squawked again and Bones spoke.

"We cleared three rooms on the west side, but then some asshat with an AK showed up." He was practically shouting into the mic, and because he was only about twenty feet away, Maddock heard his actual voice a millisecond before it came over the radio net, which created a weird doubling effect. "He's behind the door on the—"

The transmission was cut off by another short burst.

"Damn it," Bones continued. "He's not coming out. Just sprayin' and prayin'."

"Roger," Maddock sent back. "We're coming up. Lift fire and fall back. We'll try to draw him out."

"Got it," Bones replied. "Falling back."

When they reached the middle landing and made the turn, Willis swung around to face forward, aiming high while Maddock continued to cover low. Someone had turned on the lights on the second floor, which rendered their night-vision goggles useless, so they paused just long enough to swivel them up out of the way before ascending the last few steps. Maddock paused just below the landing to get oriented. Bones and his assault element were on the west side of the second story, down a hallway to the left, which meant the bad guys were somewhere down the shorter hall to the right. Maddock pied the corner, edging around it gradually to avoid revealing himself, until he saw the edge of an open doorway at the end of the hall. He paused there, watching, and a moment later saw the barrel of an AK47 thrust out into the open. The gunman was mostly eclipsed from view by the doorjamb, but Maddock was able to estimate his position, and as fire and lead began to spew from the muzzle of the Kalashnikov, Maddock triggered a burst into the door jamb.

The AK abruptly tilted up, stitching a line of holes in the ceiling, and then fell silent as the weapon disappeared once more.

Maddock counted to ten, expecting the shooter to make a repeat performance, but the hallway remained quiet. He edged out into the hall, weapon trained on the open doorway. The Kalashnikov did not reappear, but on the floor, extending just a few inches past the doorframe, was a foot, shod in a well-worn loafer, toes pointing up.

Gotcha! Maddock thought. Yet, as quickly as he felt the satisfaction of this minor victory, he also felt the futility of it. *Another mole whacked. What difference does it make?*

He shook off the sentiment, brought his focus back to the immediate goal. Find Telesh.

Maybe that was Telesh lying there

Find the Blutfahne and destroy it. Then it will be over.

For good. No more Whack-a-Mole.

Keeping his finger on the trigger, the butt of the rifle snugged against his shoulder, he keyed his mic with his left hand. "Target down. Moving up to check it out."

He returned his hand to the forward grip and continued slowly down the short hall to the doorway. As he neared, he lowered his aimpoint down to the spot where he imagined the fallen gunman's chest would be, just in case the man was still alive, still a threat. He knew, without looking, that Willis was right behind him, providing a second set of eyes as well as additional firepower.

He pied the doorjamb, spotted the gunman's other

foot, followed the legs attached to both up until he saw the torso and the discarded AK47 lying alongside the bulky form. Judging from the massive size of the unmoving figure, he realized it had to be one of the Tweedles. As that thought went through Maddock's head, another followed, screaming at him like a police siren, but in the split-second it took him to process it, he realized it was already too late.

The man on the floor was Tweedledee, and he was most certainly dead. The burst from Maddock's weapon had torn through the wall plaster and continued through his chest, almost certainly killing him instantly. The big Russian's eyes were fixed, staring sightlessly back in Maddock's direction. The reason for this orientation was the second thing Maddock noticed as he moved through the doorway.

Tweedledee's head was tilted up a little because it was cradled in the massive hands of his brother. Tweedledum's eyes—red with grief and rage—swung up to meet Maddock's gaze. Maddock reacted fast, changing his aimpoint, squeezing the trigger as soon as the muzzle was aligned with this new threat, but Tweedledum reacted as well. The big man erupted off the floor, flinging himself at Maddock even as rounds spat from Maddock's weapon. The sudden movement turned what ought to have been an instantly lethal discharge into a mere wounding. Maddock didn't see where the shots went, because in that instant, Tweedledum was on him.

The Russian behemoth swept the gun aside as if swatting a fly, and crashed into Maddock, driving him backward, into Willis. The collision knocked Willis askew, and sent Maddock flailing, out into the short hall. He staggered back two steps, three, trying to recover his balance. Tweedledum burst out into the hallway and charged like a bull. One of Maddock's outflung arms caught the balustrade on the landing, but before he could plant his feet, the Russian plowed into him, driving him back against the rail like a horseshoe caught between hammer and anvil. Then the upright wooden spindles supporting the rail snapped like toothpicks, and Maddock fell backward into empty air.

TWENTY-SIX

Bones stepped out into the hall just as Maddock and Tweedledum smashed through the railing and disappeared from his view. Throwing caution to the wind, he hastened to the ugly rent in the balustrade and looked down.

The air was thick with dust and smoke from all the shooting, but through the haze, he could see the descending steps where the two men had crashed down. To his astonishment, both men had recovered from the impact—maybe the big Russian had recovered a little bit more than Maddock—and were now grappling furiously. Bones aimed his weapon down at them, but the frenetic movement and Maddock's close proximity to the hostile denied him a clean shot.

Maddock's a big boy, he thought. *He can handle this. Finish the mission.*

He brought his attention back to the hallway and to the door from which the unseen shooter had turned back his element's earlier advance. The SEALs had cleared most of the house and found no sign of Telesh, but the mobster's jumbo-sized bodyguards had been defending that room with their life. Not proof positive that Telesh and his recently acquired piece of Nazi memorabilia awaited inside, but reason enough for optimism.

Nobody was defending it now, but Willis was there, struggling to get back on his feet.

Bones glanced over his shoulder to the rest of his fire team, gestured to the stairs. "Get down there and give Maddock a hand. I've got this."

He didn't wait for an acknowledgment, but instead hurried down the hall, passing Willis, and passed through the doorway.

There was a small sitting room with a pair of overstuffed chairs positioned to either side of an opening that led into another room. Bones stepped carefully over the motionless body of the man Maddock had designated Tweedledee, and moved through into an enormous bedroom, his weapon ready to engage at the first hint of movement.

He spotted someone and shifted his aim, but as his brain processed what his eyes beheld, he froze.

It wasn't Telesh or one of his men. It wasn't a man at all.

"Nadia," he whispered.

It wasn't the mere fact of her sex that stayed his trigger finger, though this certainly was a contributing factor. In the instant he saw her, his gut clenched at the thought of ending her life, even though he knew she would not have shown the slightest hesitation had their roles been reversed. What stopped him however was the fact that she was, very obviously, unarmed.

She stood beside a four-poster king-sized bed, her hands half raised in what seemed like a show of surrender. Clad only in a flimsy camisole that revealed more than it hid, she clearly possessed no weapons, nor any means to disarm him. Her black hair, which had been so impeccably styled on the occasion of their last encounter, was slightly flat on one side, as if she had been roused from bed. Bones flicked his gaze to the mattress and saw the sheets and comforter in disarray. She had been sleeping, and not alone.

Her eyes seemed to focus on him like laser beams. Her full, sensual lips parted in what might have been taken for a smile.

"You?" she said, managing to sound a little impressed. "You must want date with me very badly."

Bones' wit deserted him. He had no reply, and was painfully aware that his silence was dragging on.

She shrugged, and then coyly cocked her left hip. Her hands turned in slightly, fingers pointing meaningfully toward her bosom. "If this is what you want, just ask."

Bones swallowed. *What the hell is she doing?* he thought, and then it dawned on him. *She's stalling. She's protecting someone.*

The someone who had shared her bed.

Telesh.

Bones knew what he ought to do, what the mission and their rules of engagement demanded he do. They could not leave any evidence that this clandestine action was sanctioned by the United States government or military, and that meant leaving no witnesses. And yet, faced with the reality of executing an unarmed woman—someone who had already surrendered—he could not bring himself to do it. He was not a cold-blooded killer… Not a man like Bruce Huntley.

"On your knees," he growled, forcing the words past the lump in his throat. "Hands behind your head. Interlace your fingers."

The smile became a pout. "Don't you want to have fun with Nadia? Maybe you aren't man enough for it?" Her head tilted to the side, body turning sinuously toward the bed. "Maybe you need a little help. Something to help you party all night." She lowered one hand, reached for the nightstand. "I have little blue pills—"

The rifle jumped in Bones' hands. Nadia collapsed back onto the nightstand, smashing the bedside lamp with her body, and then slid sideways onto the floor.

Bones just stood there for a moment, staring at the place where she had been. Now that she was no longer there, he could see the small, black pistol resting atop the bedside table.

"Bones?"

Willis' voice broke through his reverie but it could not calm the roiling in his gut. His cheeks flushed hot with embarrassment.

"You had to do it, man," Willis went on. "She was going for a gun."

Bones shook himself and turned away. He felt a profound humiliation at what he had just done—a shame that could not be absolved or assuaged by bland platitudes or rationalizations. "Come on," he said brusquely. "Let's end this."

His renewed sense of purpose allowed him to push the recollection of what had just transpired into the background, but he could sense it lurking there like a beast in the shadows.

Beyond the bed, on the wall opposite the sitting room, there was another short hallway. To one side, a half-open door revealed a bathroom that was almost as large as the bedroom. Bones kicked the door open and made a quick visual sweep to ensure that the room was unoccupied, then continued down the hall to a closed door.

He turned sideways, pressed himself flat against the wall to the right of the door in order to minimize his target profile, and tried the door knob. It turned without resistance, and at a push, the door swung open.

The room beyond seemed to Bones like the very definition of a *man cave.* There were a pair of bookshelves positioned to either side of a large curtained window in the back wall, but the modern décor made it feel more like a rec room than a library. A billiards table dominated the center of the room, and there was a bar in one corner and a big plasma screen television in another. Several leather-upholstered sofas were arranged around the perimeter, except for the far wall. The only piece of furniture there was a large desk, positioned right in front of the window.

Sergei Telesh stood behind the desk, hunched over it, fists resting on the desktop. He wore a silk bathrobe that barely contained his hirsute bulk, and like Nadia, appeared to be unarmed. His head remained bowed for a moment, as if praying in anticipation of his imminent passing from the mortal world, but then he looked up, fixing his black, oily eyes on the intruders in his midst.

"Did you kill Nadia?" he rumbled. "Yes, I suppose you did. Too bad. She was amazing lover. Very hard to find woman like her, even in Russia."

Bones tried to close his ears to the man's voice, but the mere mention of the woman's name summoned her ghost. He aimed his weapon, finger curling on the trigger, but her voice filled his head.

Are you going to shoot another unarmed prisoner? Murder him in cold blood?

"You would do better to join me," Telesh went on. His shoulders seemed to tense, like a lion gathering its energy to pounce on a gazelle. "I reward those who are loyal to me."

Bones dropped his gaze to the desktop, wondering if Telesh had a weapon there, within reach. There was no weapon but his hands were not empty. Protruding from each clenched fist was a twist of bright red fabric.

Telesh's voice reached out to him again. "Anything you want. Just swear—"

The loud bang of a suppressed shot ended the plea. Telesh staggered backward, dragging the scarlet cloth with him, and then slumped to the floor, momentarily disappearing from view.

"What's the reward for that?" Willis growled as he came forward, his weapon at the ready. He circled around the desk, aimed the muzzle down, and fired again.

Bones shook himself, and rounded the desk from the opposite side. Telesh lay motionless, the Blutfahne partially covering him like a shroud.

Willis stared down at the tableau. "Man, I am so sick of this Nazi voodoo bullcrap,"

"Amen, brother," Bones murmured. He lowered his rifle, letting it hang from its sling, and took an incendiary grenade from a pouch on his tactical vest. "Only one thing left to do now."

Willis gave a nod of approval, but then pointed to something on the floor, just partially covered by the flag. "What's that?"

Bones nudged the fabric aside to reveal a handheld satellite phone. The LCD display and buttons were lit up, indicating an open line. Bones knelt and picked it up. The display showed a call in progress, the time elapsed just ticking over two minutes. He held it to his ear and heard someone shouting demands in Russian. He dropped the phone to the floor and smashed it under one heel. "Son of a bitch got a call off. How long do you think we've got?"

Willis shrugged. "I guess it depends on who he called. If it was his friend in the SVR, then I guess as long as it takes for a helicopter to get here from the nearest army base. half an hour, maybe?"

Bones was thinking more like fifteen minutes. Either way, they had to get clear of the house and back to the beach, ASAP. He keyed his mic. "Maddock, you finished up down there?"

There was silence for a few seconds, then a voice that wasn't Maddock's squawked in his ear. "The boss is a little tied up at the moment."

"Well, tell him to quit screwin' around. Objective one is done, but the bad guy got a call out before we could shut him down. Clock is ticking. We need to bug out, now."

"I'll tell him."

Willis pointed to the grenade. "Once that pops, this whole place will go up in about thirty seconds."

"Your point?"

"If there are helos inbound and they see this place burning like the mother of all bonfires, they ain't gonna stop and check it out. They won't even land. They'll just start looking for us."

Bones knew his friend was right. They needed to buy as much time for their exfiltration as possible. The five or so minutes it would take for the Russians to search the house might mean the difference between a clean getaway and another FUBAR firefight.

But that left him with a more immediate problem. "Well we can't leave this thing here." He kicked the Blood Flag with his toe. "And I sure as hell am not bringing it along."

Willis gave a sympathetic nod then shrugged. "Sorry, brother. I got nothing."

"Son of a bitch," Bones snarled. He shoved the

incendiary grenade back into its pouch, and then drew his Recon One combat knife. "Next best thing."

He was loath to touch the flag—even without its possibly supernatural cachet, it was a symbol of one of the vilest ideologies that had ever existed—so instead he placed a boot heel on one corner of the flag to hold it in place. Then, he began slashing back and forth.

As sharp as the blade was, it snagged and stuttered across the fabric. The white circle and black swastika came apart easily, but the red cloth underneath resisted the edge like it had been woven from steel wool. Instead of sectioning the Blutfahne, he succeeded only in perforating it. But with each cut, he felt his revulsion slackening. Maybe the damage he was doing, limited though it was, was weakening its power. He sheathed the blade, then picked up the flag in his gloved hands and pulled at one of the frayed cuts. Once more, the fabric resisted his efforts, but he didn't relent, and after several seconds, it yielded, tearing down the middle.

He found another weak spot and began tearing again.

"Give me half," Willis said.

Bones passed one of the sections over. Working together they managed to reduce the most sacred relic of the Third Reich to eight swatches no bigger than hand towels. The process had taken a full minute, and left them both exhausted.

"That's gonna have to do it," Willis announced, letting the pieces fall to the floor. "Time to boogie."

Bones looked down at the fragments, wishing he could do more, but Willis was right. They had reached a point of diminishing returns. Any more time spent defacing the Nazi symbol would defeat the purpose of not simply setting it on fire. But did he dare leave it? For that matter, should they bring it with them? That was after all what the CIA had, in an oblique fashion, ordered them to do. What if someone stitched the pieces together again? Would the flag retain its mystical power to sway hearts and seduce the masses?

"Bones!" Willis said, almost shouting. "Gotta go."

Bones allowed the pieces he held to fall onto Telesh's body. Willis nodded, satisfied with his response and started for the exit. Bones followed, but as he was about to re-enter the bedroom, inspiration dawned.

"Hey," he called out. "Go on without me. I'll be just a sec."

Willis glanced back, flashing an irritated look. "Dude, we need to go."

"Exactly," Bones said, and nodded toward the bathroom.

Maddock had managed to twist his falling body out from under his attacker so that, when they crashed onto the stairs, he was not crushed under Tweedledum's massive bulk. The impact nevertheless felt like… Well, like falling six feet onto a flight of stairs.

Sharp pain flared in his recently patched up bullet wounds, and a duller ache throbbed up and down his body where it had met the treads of the stairwell, but aside from that everything still seemed to be functional. He had about a second to appreciate this before the massive figure lying next to him began to stir.

Oh, crap!

Tweedledum pushed up onto his elbows and turned to look at Maddock. The fury in his eyes was undiminished—if anything, the blood that dribbled from the corner of his mouth and the dust that streaked his face made him look even more unhinged. Maddock tried to scramble away, to put some distance between them, maybe give his teammates a chance to finish what he had started, but the Russian moved too fast. One of his massive paws caught Maddock and pulled him into a crushing bear hug.

Maddock twisted and shook, trying to loosen the man's grip, but his thrashing only served to jostle them both from their precarious position. Unbalanced, the big man began rolling uncontrollably down the stairs, taking Maddock with him.

Each rotation was like falling from the landing all over again. Maddock winced and grunted and then could only gasp as the breath was squeezed out of him, but then, just as black spots began to swirl at the edge of his vision, the rolling stopped. Maddock lay atop the supine man. The embrace had loosened just enough for him to wrench his left arm free, and he immediately began to rain blows on Tweedledum's unprotected head, aiming for ears and eyes. He was peripherally aware of his fellow SEALs—five or six of them— gathering around the combatants in a circle. He wanted to scream at them to just shoot the man, but knew they were holding back to avoid accidentally shooting him.

Then, after what seemed like forever—probably only a second or two—two of them set aside their rifles and moved in closer. Maddock couldn't tell who, but he saw their hands grasping the Russian's shoulders and legs in an attempt to pin him down, pry loose his deathgrip on Maddock. Tweedledum swatted them away disdainfully, and then, rolled over. For a moment, his bulk crushed against Maddock, but then the pressure eased as, with a titanic effort, the Russian heaved himself to his feet, arms thrown wide, bellowing like a bear.

A mortally wounded bear.

Maddock lay on the floor at his feet, staring up at the giant, unable to believe that he was free. He scrambled back, removing himself from the other SEALs' line of fire, but before a single shot was fired, Tweedledum's roar fell silent. His shirtfront soaked through with blood which streamed from a pair of abdominal wounds, probably sustained when he had initially charged Maddock upstairs. He remained upright, tottering slightly on his feet, but the fury had left his eyes, and after a couple more seconds, he toppled forward.

The SEALs who had earlier attempted to tag team

with Maddock now moved in to help him to his feet. He heard them asking questions—"Are you all right? Can you move?"—but he couldn't seem to find the breath to answer. He managed to raise a hand, as if to say, *Give me a second.*

Someone else called out from behind him—Matt James, the platoon comms guru. "Boss, Bones is trying to call you."

Maddock wondered why he hadn't received that transmission, and then realized that he'd lost his earpiece in the melee. He shook his head, unable to put this discovery into words.

James spoke again, but not to Maddock. "The boss is a little tied up at the moment." There was a pause, then, "I'll tell him." James moved in closer. "Bones says they nailed OBJ one, but he might have gotten a call out. We need to exfil."

Maddock drew in a ragged breath, nodded. "Okay." The word was barely a whisper. He tried again, and this time managed a decent volume. "Okay. Give the signal. We're done here."

As James relayed the message, Maddock looked around, retrieving his rifle and other bits of equipment that had been lost during the struggle with Tweedledum. It was imperative that they leave behind nothing that could be definitively linked to the United States. He found his radio earpiece amidst the rubble of the balustrade—the cord had been yanked out by the roots—and stuffed it in a pocket.

Willis appeared above him, descending the stairs with the rest of the second story assault element in tow, save for one conspicuous absence. "Where's Bones?"

Willis grinned. "Taking care of business. He'll catch up."

Business? Maddock wondered, and then understood. *The Blutfahne.*

Bones descended only a few seconds later, a grim smile on his face.

Maddock looked up at him. "Did you burn it?"

"Nah. Came up with an even better idea." For a

moment, Maddock wondered if his friend had perhaps fallen under the spell of Helen's Charm, and at the end, had chosen to selfishly keep its power for himself, but then Bones elaborated. "It's where it deserves to be. Let's just say that no one is going to call it the *Blood-Stained Flag* ever again."

Maddock stared at him quizzically for a few seconds and then understood. "You didn't."

Bones' grin widened. "I did."

Despite feeling like he'd been run over by a bus, Maddock couldn't help but laugh. "Good. Let's get out of here."

The Pentagon—Two weeks later

Maddock looked up at the sound of an opening door, prepared to jump to his feet if he spied brass. When the door to his left—the one that exited into a corridor on the B-Ring—swung open and he spied Willis, looking impressive in his immaculate dress blue uniform, Maddock relaxed, but only a little. Willis was alone.

"Where is he?" Maddock whispered. "Is he coming?"

Willis stepped inside the small waiting room, closed the door and came over to sit beside Maddock. "Couldn't find him. His place is cleaned out. I think maybe he went back home to the Res."

"Damn him." Maddock slumped in his chair. He had covered for Bones a lot in the past, mostly in the early days, before they had become friends. As the years had piled up, Bones had matured—in his own way at least—and while he had never completely lost his irreverent edge, he had always been able to tone down his puerile impulses when orders or the mission required it. But since returning from Russia, Bones had spiraled into something that a psychiatrist would probably have diagnosed as depression. He'd been drinking more and showing up less. Three days previously, he had not even bothered to call in.

They had all been in a holding pattern, uncertain of what fate awaited them professionally, to say nothing of personally. Their Agency handler had not been at all happy to learn that they had returned without the Blutfahne—Maddock had not provided a full account of Bones' unique solution for disposing of it, but had only indicated that it had been destroyed in the raid and was unrecoverable. He didn't think the CIA would take punitive action against them for this perceived failure, but no sooner had they offloaded their gear in the team room at Dam Neck when Maxie called them into his office and took them off operational status. Maddock had told Maxie the whole story, but that had not changed anything. From that point forward, they had been more or less on their own, required to report daily to the team room. No training, no special duty—just show up and sit there until day's end.

This was not exactly a punishment. Maddock had already submitted his letter of resignation prior to leaving for Moscow, and everything that had happened subsequently had only deepened his conviction that it was time to move on. Bones and Willis had both expressed similar disillusionment with their military careers. Like Maddock, they had grave doubts about who the good guys were. Unlike Maddock, they were contractually obligated to serve out their term of service—two more years for Willis, sixteen months for Bones. There were other jobs in the navy, duty stations where they could mark time until their enlistments were up, provided of course that the brass was willing to let them go.

Maddock was beginning to wonder about that however. The things they had discovered, the dark secrets they knew—like the identity of the bodies that were buried under the rubble of a Cape Cod on Savile Lane—were things that the government dared not allow them to reveal. They were of course legally prohibited from sharing classified information with anyone, even after leaving the service, but keeping them under orders, under the government's thumb, was one way to ensure their compliance. Sending them off to rot in the disciplinary barracks at Fort Leavenworth was another.

Maddock suspected this meeting they had been summoned to would resolve his doubts, one way or another. Bones' decision to ignore orders and drop off the radar all but guaranteed a bad outcome for him.

The interior door—the one on the opposite side of the room opened, and both Maddock and Willis jumped up and snapped to attention. Maxie backed through the doorway, his gaze on the unseen figures inside. He maintained this orientation until he was clear of the doorway, as if afraid to turn his back on the room's occupants, and then closed the door firmly. Only then did he turn to face his subordinates. There was a manila folder in his left hand. He stared at Maddock and Willis for a moment, his face an unreadable mask, then spoke. "Where the hell is Bonebrake?"

Maddock swallowed, then gave the only answer he could. The truth. "UA, sir."

UA—Unauthorized Absence—was the navy's equivalent of AWOL—absent without leave. It wasn't as serious as desertion, but could still result in fines, reduction in rank, or confinement.

Maxie stared back at him, gave a grunt of acknowledgement, then turned his attention to the folder. He opened it to reveal several type-written pages, collated into three packets. He passed one each to Maddock and Willis, and then, after a moment's consideration, handed the remaining packet to Maddock as well. "When you see him, give him this."

Maddock looked down at the cover sheet. It bore the Seal of the Navy, and looked very official. He skimmed it, looking for words like "ordered to report" and "Leavenworth," but if they were present, he did not see them. The formal legalistic language contained in the body of the missive defied comprehension at a glance.

"Sir, what is this?"

"Your golden ticket," Maxie said, and for the first time since their return from Russia, Maddock saw his CO smile. "Effective immediately, you three jokers are civilians again."

Maddock glanced over at Willis, unable to believe his ears, then returned his attention to Maxie. "Honorable discharges?"

Maxie chuckled and shook his head. "Even better. You're retired. Full pension and benefits."

"That's…" Maddock was momentarily speechless.

Willis was similarly dumbfounded. "But I've still

got six more years on my twenty."

"Not any more you don't." Maxie let that settle in, then went on. "Technically, the DOD reserves the right to recall, but I wouldn't worry about that too much."

Maddock's elation at the good news was dampened a little at this caveat. "And I suppose this is all contingent on us keeping our mouths shut about what really happened."

Maxie shrugged. "You'd have to do that, regardless. This whole thing is classified and compartmented. Talk about it and you lose more than just your health insurance. That said, there is another NDA in there which you will have to sign and notarize before you leave this building." When Maddock didn't respond, he sighed. "Dane, this is a win. You got what you wanted. You're out. Go live your life."

Willis grinned and gave the papers a dramatic snap. "Hells, yeah." Then, as if remembering who he was talking to, he returned to attention. "Permission to depart, sir?"

"What are you asking me for? I'm not your boss."

Willis snapped a salute, then did an about face and exited the waiting room.

Maddock continued to stare at the papers in disbelief. Finally, he met Maxie's gaze. "Doesn't it bother you? Keeping this a secret?"

Maxie seemed to think about his answer for a long time. "Yeah. It sucks."

Maddock didn't know how to respond to that, so he didn't. He just shook his head and turned for the door.

"Hey, Dane!"

He paused, looked back.

"Keep in touch, okay?"

Once the ink on the notary stamp affixed to the exhaustive non-disclosure agreement was dry, Maddock exited the Pentagon and started walking toward the bus terminal to the southwest, even though he had no idea where he was going next. He considered catching a ride across the river to the National Mall. Maybe he would drop in and surprise Melissa with his news. She would, he knew, be overjoyed to learn that he was no longer going to be risking his life on a daily basis.

Maybe that was the thing that had always kept him from putting a ring on her finger.

He decided to wait. He'd tell her over dinner. Somewhere swanky.

Then again, now that he was unemployed, he'd have to think a little more frugally, at least until he figured out what he was going to do.

What am I going to do?

He wished he could ask his father for advice, regretted that he could not, but then realized that he already knew what Hunter Maddock would have said.

Let's work together. Find Kidd's treasure.

The thought brought a smile.

Why not?

He dug out his mobile phone, and scrolled through his call history until he found a received call from almost a month earlier. The number belonged to Allan Cole, the attorney who had acted as the executor of Maddock's parents' will. He dialed the number, and when the receptionist at the other end picked up, he identified himself.

"Good afternoon, Mr. Maddock. Do you want me to put you through to Mr. Cole?"

"That won't be necessary. Can you just give him a message? Tell him I'd like to sell."

"Okay." There was a pause, presumably as the woman recorded this brief note. "Anything else?"

"Nope. I'll be up there later in the week to pack everything." He exchanged a few more pleasantries before ending the call, then immediately dialed another number.

It rang a few times and then a booming voice sounded in his ear. "Dane! How's it going, my boy?" And then, with a note of concern added. "Are you doing okay?"

Maddock smiled and answered truthfully. "Never been better, Coach. Listen, are you still thinking about selling your boat?"

Cape Idokopas, Russia

Alexander Shamalov was a carpenter and woodworker, who specialized in hand-turned spindles and antique restoration. He had been called out to the dacha at Cape Idokopas to bid on repair work for a damaged section of the balustrade on the second story landing.

Shamalov had heard rumors about the incident, rumors of how a band of armed men had attacked in the middle of the night, gunned down the house's former owner, notorious crime lord Sergei Telesh, along with his mistress and a small army of bodyguards. As he pulled up in front of the house, the only evidence he saw that anything was amiss was a piece of plywood covering one of the upper story windows.

A stout man with a florid complexion emerged from the house and came down to greet him. "Mr. Shamalov, good afternoon. I am Mr. Ponomarenko, the property manager."

Shamalov shook hands with him and followed Ponomarenko inside. He wondered if he would see bloodstains and bullet holes. There were none, though the hardwood floor and carpets looked brand new and the walls still smelled of fresh paint.

"It is up there," Ponomarenko said, gesturing to the staircase.

Shamalov grimaced when he beheld the damage. "What happened?"

"The former owner threw a party one night," Ponomarenko said with a dismissive air. "Things got out of hand."

Shamalov did not challenge the obvious fiction. Instead he climbed up to the landing and began taking measurements. "I will need to remove an undamaged section to use as a template," he said, and then added, "provided of course that we can come to an arrangement."

"Of course."

Shamalov calculated the amount of time required for the job and the cost of materials, then tacked on a reasonable amount for labor—far less than he would normally have asked.

He had heard other rumors about this place, rumors that there would soon be a magnificent mansion built on the property, a lavish private retreat for the Prime Minister, paid for by generous donations from wealthy oligarchs. And why not? Hadn't he made them all rich?

Shamalov loved the Prime Minister, and hoped he would become President someday. The man would make Russia great again.

He told Ponomarenko his price. The man seemed pleased with the quote. "Write it up, and take what you need."

Shamalov nodded. "I'll need to get some tools from my truck." He hesitated and then decided to take a chance. "I am curious about something. I have heard that there are plans for new construction soon."

Ponomarenko frowned as if disturbed by such gossip. "You should not believe everything you hear."

Shamalov raised his hands in a placating gesture. "I only ask because I am interested in more work in the future."

The other man appeared to think about this for a moment, and then, in a conspiratorial whisper, admitted, "This is just between us."

"Of course."

"There are plans. Big plans. It will be beautiful. A palace worthy of the Tsars. But that won't be for many years. That is why I am fixing up this old dacha. The architect will live here while he works on the project."

"Well, I hope you will find my work satisfactory."

The sharing of the secret seemed to have reduced

the distance between the men. "I will provide you with a key so that you may come and go as you please. One thing though. If you need to use the toilet, use the one downstairs or out in the garage. The one upstairs is backed up and I have not yet arranged for a plumber to come take a look at it."

"Plumbers," Shamalov snorted. "Who needs them. Let me take a look at it."

Ponomarenko raised an eyebrow. "Are you sure?"

"I insist. I will have it clear for you before I leave today." It was a bold boast, but Shamalov felt certain that the problem was not as serious as the property manager believed. Then, with a wink, he added, "No extra charge."

The other man inclined his head. "Very well. And I'm sure we'll be able to find more work for such a talented craftsmen in days to come."

As Ponomarenko went to find the key he had promised, Shamalov went upstairs to get a look at the blocked commode. The bathroom was an extravagant affair, larger than Shamalov's workshop, with an enormous Jacuzzi tub on a raised platform at one end, and a walk-in shower big enough to accommodate two or three people at once—just thinking about it brought a smile to Shamalov's face. But the opulence could not disguise the foul smell that hovered in the air, and there seemed little question as to its source.

He approached the toilet cautiously, holding his breath in anticipation of the stench that would be released when he lifted the lid. His precautions spared his olfactory senses, but the vile-looking brown soup that filled the bowl was revolting enough to make him gag. He closed the lid and headed back downstairs. When he found Ponomarenko again, he inquired about tools for general maintenance.

"I hadn't thought of that," admitted the other man. "There might be something in the garage. Feel free to look."

Shamalov did exactly that, and in short order, found exactly what he needed—a handheld plumber's snake with ten meters of wire in the drum. He hurried back upstairs and, after another deep breath, opened the toilet lid, pulled out a meter of the coiled wire, and stabbed it into the murk. The device had a pistol grip below the drum, and he held it firmly in his left hand as he began rotating the knob on the back of the drum, feeding out more of the wire. He could feel a little resistance as it hooked around the turns in the plumbing, but nothing to justify the clog. He kept playing out meter after meter of wire until it came to an abrupt halt.

"There you are," he muttered. He was still taking shallow breaths through his mouth, though he was getting used to the smell.

He worked the drum back and forth, trying to clear the blockage, but was unable to make any more forward progress. After a few minutes of this, he began reeling in the wire. He grimaced as the nasty liquid dribbled out of the drum and ran down his hand—maybe he should have let Ponomarenko call a plumber after all—but then felt a mild surge of elation when the end of the wire came out of the water, with something caught in the spiral at the end.

It was a piece of red cloth.

The End

ABOUT THE AUTHORS

David Wood is the USA Today bestselling author of the action-adventure series, The Dane Maddock Adventures, and many other works. He also writes fantasy under his David Debord pen name. When not writing, he hosts the Wood on Words podcast. David and his family live in Santa Fe, New Mexico. Visit him online at davidwoodweb.com.

Sean Ellis has authored and co-authored more than two dozen action-adventure novels, including the Nick Kismet adventures, the Jack Sigler/Chess Team series with Jeremy Robinson, and the Jade Ihara adventures with David Wood. He served with the Army National Guard in Afghanistan, and has a Bachelor of Science degree in Natural Resources Policy from Oregon State University. Sean is also a member of the International Thriller Writers organization. He currently resides in Arizona, where he divides his time between writing, adventure sports, and trying to figure out how to save the world. Learn more about Sean at seanellisauthor.com.

20636279R00196

Printed in Great Britain
by Amazon